# Planet Jesus Trilogy

## BOOK ONE: FLESH & BLOOD

BY

# DOUGLAS BRODE

WITH
CREATIVE COLLABORATOR

# SHAUN L. BRODE

ARS METAPHYSICA

D1572574

an imprint of Sunbury Press, Inc.
Mechanicsburg, PA USA

**ARS METAPHYSICA**

an imprint of Sunbury Press, Inc.
Mechanicsburg, PA USA

For information about special discounts for bulk purchases, please contact Sunbury Press Orders Dept. at (855) 338-8359 or orders@sunburypress.com.

To request one of our authors for speaking engagements or book signings, please contact Sunbury Press Publicity Dept. at publicity@sunburypress.com.

ISBN: 978-1-62006-845-8 (Trade paperback)

Library of Congress Control Number: 2017932610

FIRST ARS METAPHYSICA EDITION: August 2018

Product of the United States of America
0 1 1 2 3 5 8 13 21 34 55

Set in Bookman Old Style
Designed by Crystal Devine
Cover by Amber Rendon
Edited by Janice Rhayem

*Continue the Enlightenment!*

For
SHANE JOHNSON BRODE
with pride in your many accomplishments
and
appreciation for your technical wizardry

"Eliminate the impossible and whatever remains, however implausible, is the truth."

—SIR ARTHUR CONAN DOYLE (1923)

"When living to the East of Eden the children of men began to multiply and daughters were born unto them, the Fallen Angels of God, called *Naphals,* saw that they were beautiful. They took themselves wives, and these wives bore the *Naphals'* sons. These were called the *Gibborim,* or Giants: Men of great stature."

—BOOK OF JUBILEES, CHAPTER V: 1

# FOREWORD

What follows is a word-for-word translation of a long-lost manuscript discovered last year in the area of Israel known as *Kirbit Qumaran.* This ancient site, located thirteen miles east from the city of Jerusalem and adjacent to the Dead Sea, had previously been the location for several digs. Excavations began in 1946, shortly after the discovery of the Gnostic gospels in *Nag Hammadi,* Upper Egypt, the previous year. Archaeologists scoured the Near Middle East in search of scrolls offering alternatives to those canonized works by Matthew, Mark, Luke, and John. In a highly edited and oft-revised form, these served as the basis for what today is referred to as The New Testament.

Publication of many hundreds of Dead Sea Scrolls shocked the world, presenting the same essential narrative from radically different points of view. Included were gospels attributed to the disciples Thomas, Peter, and even Judas. Hidden deep in the recesses of little-known caves, protected only by fragile clay containers in which they'd been buried, such writings proved that what for nearly 2,000 years had been accepted as the be-all and end-all as to the life of Christ in fact allowed for only a limited perception.

During the first century following the Crucifixion, numerous Christian sects (some derived from Jewish disciples of Jesus, others composed of converted gentiles) adhered to diverse texts. Rome's first Christian emperor, Constantine, eventually decided on the need for one universal Bible that would thereafter serve all who considered themselves Christian. Devout believers who

v

would not give up esoteric versions were executed, their gospels destroyed. Some hid scrolls in hopes that, several millennia hence, people living in future times would rediscover their varied and unique interpretations.

Once unearthed, such relics called into question teachings of the Catholic Church and all organized Christian sects. No single scroll was perceived as more threatening to the status-quo than the Gospel of Mary, which claimed Mary Magdalene had been Jesus's primary disciple. Also, that this Phoenician woman not only married Jesus but bore him a son, likely named Judah. From this child, Europe's imperial bloodlines were derived. If true, this would explain why generations of kings laid claim to their supposed divine right to rule, as well as why these aristocrats considered themselves interrelated.

Last year, however, a fact-finding expedition financed by London's British Museum—led by controversial scientist George Edward Challenger and renown explorer Allan Quartermain, they accompanied by America's Dr. Henry Walton Jones—revealed that, in addition to the eleven previous caves, they had discovered a twelfth. Deep inside, apparently untouched for more than two thousand years, were three scrolls.

Until now, little of the latest find has been made public. This has to do with the revolutionary impact such revelations might have on Western civilization. A number of powerful, highly secretive organizations would stop at nothing to keep the contents secret. The great question, an answer yet to be determined, is whether these scrolls are what they claim to be or are only exceptionally clever forgeries.

In the past, it was believed that Jesus wrote nothing down during his thirty-one years of earthly life, allowing the disciples to do so. How remarkable then to encounter the Gospels of Jesus, a.k.a. Jess of Nazareth.

Here, then, is the first of three. The others will follow when translation is complete. Where deemed necessary, certain phrases remain in their original Hebrew, Greek, Roman, Samarian, or Aramaic forms. These are italicized. Otherwise, everything has been converted into contemporary American-style English so the author's tone and intent, surprisingly conversational (even casual) in style, will be retained for twenty-first century readers.

Anyone about to proceed is forewarned. No claim is made here that these are what they appear to be: the autobiography of the Nazarene. Possibly those nay-sayers who have examined the texts may be proven correct in their insistence that this is another annoying attempt to create controversy around an endlessly fascinating historical figure. Those who choose to read further should do so with such considerations in mind.

Douglas Brode
Shaun L. Brode
(Translators)

*DOUGLAS BRODE visits a precise reconstruction of the Well of David. The original, located near Nazareth in Galilee, is a part of the narrative in all three books of the PLANET JESUS trilogy. (Courtesy Gail Schlientz.)*

# PROLOGUE

## Once Upon A Time in Palistine

When allowed world enough and time, everything turns to shit. There are no exceptions. Nor is the cosmos itself exempt from this intractable rule. Also, time cannot be correctly considered without space entering into the equation. This owes to the continuum that, as I would eventually learn, binds them together.

*Mull that over for a moment while I make ready to tell you my strange story.*

*Or, at least for now, how it all began.*

Consider this, too: have you ever in your life questioned what the *H.* stands for in Jesus H. Christ? Or simply accepted the inclusion of that eighth letter in the English language as . . . well, *being there*, without rhyme or reason?

In fact, it refers to several things. Akin to my opening statement, here's another rule that can't be ignored: nothing is simple, no matter how much we might wish that were the case. Life can only exist in a state of complexity.

So, as to that *H*, which somewhere, somehow came to be inserted into my name, at least when spoken on the street?

To some, it signified Herakles, Greece's mighty hero. And, like myself, the result of an agent from the heavens mating with a mortal woman on Earth. What Herakles was to the Atticans and Ionians, I would more or less become to the Jews.

And in time those who would call themselves Christians. Following my crucifixion. Actual or supposed.

*Already, though, I rush ahead of myself. Sorry!*

Here is a fitting spot to insert an anecdote stretching as far back in my memory as I can recall. Our family still lived in the village of Nazareth. There, our patriarch Joseph made a living as a full-time stonemason, also running a small fix-it shop while taking on additional part-time work as a carpenter. One day, my twin brother and I (between three and four years of age then), bored, stepped inside to watch him at work.

Being children, we were curious. So we fiddled with various tools of his trade, these haphazardly arraigned throughout the room. Joses reached for a saw, trying to imitate the actions that Joseph skillfully performed. Concerned that the boy might hurt himself, Joseph hurried over and gently if firmly removed the sharp-edged tool.

While they were so occupied, I wandered off to the shop's far side. There, I happened upon a large, black nail, which being a child, I mindlessly grasped with my right hand.

Suddenly, I began to howl. Joseph rushed over in a panic. Extending my arm, I revealed to him that I'd forced the nail deep into my palm.

"*Why*, Jess?" he asked while carefully withdrawing it. Hearing one of her children weep, my mother darted in from the adjoining house. Momentarily shocked by what had occurred, Mary swiftly washed the wound, then reached to a pile of clean linens, tying one around my hand.

"Why," Joseph, confused, asked again, "did you pierce yourself?"

Though I had a strong command of speech for a three-and-a-half-year-old, I shrugged. I had no idea. Then, brightly, I announced, "Because it was there."

*But where were we?*

*Of course! Talking about that H.*

Helios: the sun to those same ancient Greeks. That fiery ball in the sky that provides the warmth and energy so necessary for life forms to flourish in the seas and on land. And, for some nations, would in time be worshipped as a daily reminder of the one true God.

Popularly known, in my land and era, as Yahweh. Jehovah, to you moderns reading this.

Helping to explain why Egypt's Eighteenth Dynasty pharaoh, Akhenaten, placed a metallic circle that he crafted atop a cross-like symbol to represent the sun. The Ankh, intended not as an ornament but an icon, embodied his theory: Egypt's myriad traditional gods aside, for him all was one and one was all. Everything existed in unity, underscored by a single God.

He sensed this 1,500 years before I walked the earth.

Perhaps Akhenaten borrowed this idea from slaves in his kingdom called Hebrews. Or maybe they were inspired by him in a way his own citizens were not. Eventually, my people returned to our homeland, Canaan. And renamed it Israel in honor of Jacob, who had earlier earned that title, to reveal that they, like him, had been born again.

More specifically, to that part of Canaan located west of the Sea of Galilee in the country's northern territories. The River Jordan starts there as a small trickle and continues southward, like all water eager to reach its lowest possible point on land. The Jordan forms the liquid spine of Israel, finally pouring into the Dead Sea 300 meters below sea level.

*But back to the Ankh, Jess . . .*

Below that high, round cap, Akhenaten drew a horizontal bar, a visual metaphor likewise borrowed from the Hebrews. For my nation? The line that separates the dark-blue water down below from the light-blue sky above. A demarcation point. For here exists the entrance to another world, a portal to the greater, other, unknown kingdom.

If only humankind could discover some means of keeping that distant point on the horizon from receding as ships sail in its direction, the crew always frustrated by what appears close enough to touch but proves impossible to reach . . .

Below such a line, the wisest if most tragic pharaoh added a vertical extension, stretching outward as it neared the bottom on either side, away from each other. These served as Akhenaten's representations of the sun's bright rays, descending to bless the water and soil. Allowing for that precious, incomprehensible force called life.

*Or might the icon have represented something else? Some strange living being with a huge head, lengthy arms, and legs interconnected by webbing like that found between the toes of a frog.*

How fascinating that, other than the uneven object on top (more egg-shaped than circular when closely observed), this sign of that ancient religion resembled the cross. Which would come to be associated with me following my thirty-one years living (or, more correctly, surviving) on this planet.

The cross: scorned as a reminder of my humiliation and horror for more than three centuries after my "passing" from this realm. Later embraced as the world recognized the lasting importance of what took place once upon a time in Palestine.

*There I go again!* Ready to conclude my narrative before I've barely begun. Since childhood, a habit that, as you will soon grasp, has been my blessing or my curse. My cross to bear, figuratively speaking, and with no pun intended.

The third if not necessarily final concept represented by the *H* is immortality. For those wise Greeks (owing to Luke their sensibility remains strong within me) known as Hades. For them, this constituted the land of the dead. All the deceased, from the cusp of man's existence to the present day, stretched across a vast cave's interior.

At the bottom were located those who had behaved badly. Along the upward tilt, the multitudes who had plodded through their lives, achieving only mediocrity. Finally, close to the top, a special high-dry place reserved for those with immaculate records as to their life journeys. Not coincidentally, H also stands for Heaven. And in the vision of Christians, its fearsome opposite, Hell.

Not though before my time walking upon Earth. I didn't only posit paradise and the pit as alternatives all humans must someday face in the retrospective light of end-game, individual or communal. In truth, it was I—not Yahweh or, before me, Abraham, Isaac, Jacob, Moses, or David—who invented them.

*Me. Jess of Nazareth. Better known to you as Jesus.*

*But that occurred much later . . .*

Back, though, to Heaven and Hell. Like so much else in my life, they appeared to me in a dream. One of many I would experience while a creature of flesh and blood, a dichotomy that would appear and reappear often during my mission.

Meanwhile, any account of what took place, or seemed to (telling the two apart is never easy) ought to begin with my first dream. At least, the first I can recall from those days when I felt like a fresh, green bud in spring, forcing itself up out of the rough ground owing to instinct, not intelligence. Naïve enough to believe all to follow would be a grand adventure.

I was eleven and a half at the time. The dream came to me on the very night before my true journey began. It would reoccur many times over the years, without alteration.

A dream as ritual. Every detail in perfect place. But if unique images would always be present, their precise meanings I would only gradually discover. While navigating the odd, twisting pathway of life that, on the very next morning, I myself would initiate.

In time, when the exact meaning of each specific image finally became clear, the dream no longer revisited me. Perhaps because it had gradually transformed into my reality.

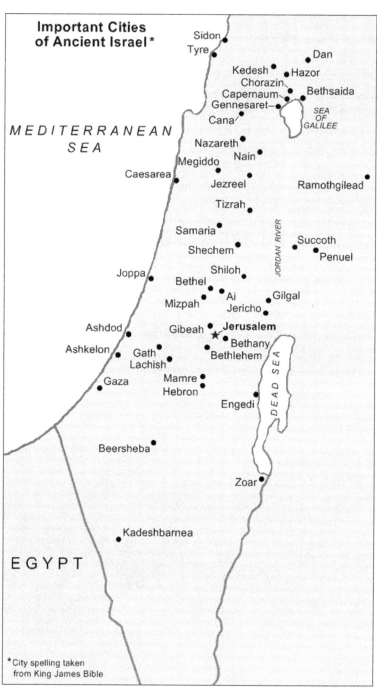

Important Cities
of Ancient Israel*

Sidon
Tyre
Dan
Kedesh
Hazor
Chorazin
Capernaum
Bethsaida
Gennesaret—
SEA OF GALILEE
Cana
MEDITERRANEAN SEA
Nazareth
Nain
Megiddo
Caesarea
Jezreel
Ramothgilead
Tizrah
Samaria
JORDAN RIVER
Succoth
Shechem
Penuel
Shiloh
Joppa
Bethel
Ai
Gilgal
Mizpah
Jericho
Ashdod
Gibeah
Jerusalem
Bethany
Ashkelon
Gath
Bethlehem
Lachish
Mamre
DEAD SEA
Gaza
Hebron
Engedi
Beersheba
Zoar
Kadeshbarnea
EGYPT
*City spelling taken
from King James Bible

*(Courtesy BibleStudy.org)*

# PART ONE

# Becoming Jesus

# 1.

Always the dream began the same way: Partly awake still, I find myself in a disorienting transition between a restless state of surrendering to sleep and pure phantasmagoria.

Ahead lies a stark terrain stretching far and wide: flat, barren, seemingly infinite. My eyes veer to the left, then to the right. On either side are vast mountains, their peaks tickling the white clouds in a clear, powder-blue sky.

All this occurs in a split second, more swiftly than I can recall it now in words, as I completely succumb to deep sleep.

Gradually, I become aware that my body is shaking back and forth as I stand on some solid object in motion. A glance downward reveals a thick slab of wood, welded by metal bolts to an open-air vehicle.

I hold leather reins tightly in my hands.

I'm aware enough of my fantastic surroundings to realize I'm riding on a chariot of the type Egyptians and Greeks favor. But this one is unique. For other than the wood upon which I balance myself, all else has been fashioned from pure gold.

Momentarily, my eyes are blinded by the sun. Blinking, I see that it hangs precariously low on the horizon, a bright, orange ball drifting down from its daily perch. Helios comes near to Earth, scorching the land below.

*What did Yahweh once promise? "The fire next time . . ."*

I know, too, though I can't grasp how or why, all that is happening around me exists for one purpose: to beckon me onward. So I slap the reins. The horses gain even more speed. There are four, all majestic. Each white, manes fluttering wildly.

I become aware of a terrible pounding on either side. With difficulty, I balance myself, sneaking brief sideways glances. Shock sets in. A quartet of beasts pursue me. Horrible things, vaguely resembling creatures that exist on Earth, though oversized, distorted, and terrifying.

To my left, a lion and a bear lunge close. The lion isn't one that might wander deep in the wilderness, for on its back enormous eagle wings spread wide. Next to this creature, the bear leans awkwardly to one side, biting down on three sharp bones held tight within its immense teeth.

They gain on me, pushing closer. Their mouths hang open; spittle pours out. They cast menacing eyes over and up at me. I can do nothing but scream 'Haaaaah!" and slap the reins again, harder, in hopes my horses will run faster.

Then, I dare peek to my right: two other monstrosities, likewise resembling worldly animals but with twisted features.

A leopard, plodding ahead on immense paws, is crowned by four identical heads, each with fangs stretching downward from wide-open mouths. Its eight eyes, red and glowing like splints of wood in a brazier, leave little doubt it plans to devour me.

Beside it races the most remarkable creature of all: a hairy thing I can't identify. The body is corpulent, its fur-covered legs seemingly too short and squat to support such immense weight. What sets this lumbering beast apart from the others are its spiraling horns. Three rise from a flat, dark forehead, four more from the top of its crown, for a total of seven.

Often I've come in contact with horned animals. But their antlers had not prepared me for these. The color? Ivory, similar to the tusks of elephants. Circling, they extend upward, as if fashioned by a craftsman to appear at once horrifying and beautiful.

All four beasts gain on us, pushing closer.

*This may be the day that I die!*

Unable to imagine how to save myself, I panic, close my eyes, and brace for whatever happens. Nothing! Do I dare look again? Rather than overwhelm me, the pursuers have inexplicably replaced the horses and now pull the chariot.

Were they dangerous only in my perception? Could these actually be allies if considered from another angle of vision? For apparently they only wish to hurry me along. Any sense of threat swiftly dissolves, though the chariot's golden surface transforms into flames that flicker outward and upward.

Finally, I spot our destination far away: a grand tower, reaching so high its cap of gold appears, from my perspective, to touch the bottom curve of the sun.

*Everything must be interconnected. But how? And why?*

That's when I realize I am no longer me. At least, not as before.

My paltry, linen tunic, identical to those that other provincial Hebrew girls wear in Israel's northern hill country, has given way to polished bronze armor. Stranger still, my body—chest encased in a breastplate, feet covered by black leather boots, a helmet atop my head—has become that of a boy.

I accept this sea change, grasping that it has occurred for some reason I do not yet understand but eventually will. All in good time.

*And place!*

*Remember: always, time and place together.*

Abruptly, we arrive at the tower's gate. As if anticipating us, the great wooden doors swing open. The beasts rush inside, pulling the chariot. And myself, frozen in place with fear. As we enter, throngs of people rush out of our way, sensing the authority of this unknown entity that invades their inner sanctum, the heart and soul of their city.

Somehow, the beasts manage to halt before crashing into a looming object just ahead. Here stands a throne, bedecked in jewels. Flowers of all colors have been strewn across its enormous seat. I know that it awaits me . . . has existed here, on this stretch of desert, in its clandestine tower, anticipating my arrival for an immeasurable period of time.

Perhaps for all eternity.

On it perches a young woman. Her face is the color of clay, her hair dark and long. The pupils of her eyes resemble a pair of black olives. She wears a white pagan gown and matching sandals to shield her small feet from sun and sand. I know that wisdom as well as beauty are here personified.

*I have no idea if she offers friendship or destruction. Nor do I believe it matters much.*

*The point is, she awaits. Me, and only me.*

5

# 2.

"Wake up. You were lost in a dream. Was it a nightmare?"

With effort, I open my eyes. My older half brother James kneels beside me on our thatched roof. We two always sleep side by side. His sensitive brow reveals concern as, leaning over my prone body, James considers his trembling half-sister.

"I'm not certain." I allow my eyelids, eager to know whether the dream might return, to close again. "Awful and wonderful, actually."

"Come on, Jess, It's time." James jostles me, gently digging a knotted elbow into my side. I manage to will myself awake.

Every evening during summer our family climbed above the stifling house to enjoy cool breezes drifting westerly from the Sea of Galilee. I twisted and turned while rising. My mat, carried up from below, offered little protection from sharp-edged sticks that, set over hardwood beams and held in place by mud and clay, constituted our roof.

I tried to shake off annoying aches and pains, resulting from my sprawling for seven hours on a bouquet of rough twigs. I glanced upward at a canopy of darkness, the sky not yet ready to begin the process of brightening for what other nations consider the dawn of a new day. For Hebrews, that precipitous moment occurs at twilight time. This has been our way for 5,000 years.

The stars sparkled giddily, set against what the pagans who preceded us in this wilderness believed to be an indigo coverlet, surrounding Earth as a shawl might the human body.

"Simon?" I shifted to my right while slipping out from under my blanket. The child beside me did not move. Firmly, I prodded my eight-year-old brother's shoulder. No dark dreams for him! Simon's ear-to-ear smile made clear that threatening thoughts did not trouble this living semblance of a cherubim. "Rise and shine, as they say."

"Who's *they*?" Simon asked, yawning like a new-born puppy.

"Everyone."

"Silly Jess. You couldn't possibly know *everyone*."

"Right you are. Then, *I* say it. Up!"

Simon rose, stretched, and offered me a mock salute. In doing so, he imitated those he had seen soldiers proffer to their officers during our era of imperial Rome's domination.

"Yes, sir. I mean, ma'am."

I cast the boy a smile, though my attention had been drawn back to the sky. Near the nebulous of Orion, at a point where three of its brightest stars align in a row, seven little lights I couldn't recall from previous study of the heavens darted away from the constellation as if aware they'd been spotted by a person down below, this disturbing their tranquility.

Initially, I believed them to be comets, meteors, or as some say falling stars. But that couldn't be, for they moved in a precise formation southeasterly. This caused me to wonder if these heavenly bodies purposefully descended toward our planet and, specifically, central Galilee, the territory that the family of Joseph calls home.

A moment later, I could no longer distinguish them. After briefly twinkling, they disappeared from sight.

"Joses," James loudly called to my twin, still sound asleep on the easterly side. "It's time."

Shivering, Joses forced open his eyes with indignation. "Just a few minutes more. Please?" He rolled over, as if by showing us his back Joses might avoid further interruption. James, more than used to this delaying tactic, rose and embarked on his ritual pre-morning trek to the roof's far side.

He jostled Joses until my twin, realizing resistance was useless, groaned in submission. Already in a miserable mood, my twin, whom I had nicknamed Jude, sat up, growling and glowering.

"It's time, girls," Mary announced.

I glanced to the roof's northernmost sector. There, my mother had already risen. Lovingly, she awakened my sisters, asleep by her side like a pair of kittens. First, Salome, recently turned five, stirred. Shortly, Miriam, two, followed suit. Then all were up and moving about as if to discard any remnants of sleep.

All in the family, that is, but Joses. He had dropped down and off to dreamland again, backside angled toward us.

"Guide the others down, Jess. I'll wake him, one way or the other."

James set about doing so while I shepherded the family to the ladder. The girls descended first, Mary watching over them with the proverbial eye of a hawk. Though no longer babies, still they remained *her* babies, and always would. Simon, his pink, fleshy fingers grasping the crude wood with which Joseph fashioned our ladder, slipped down next.

Joseph wasn't present. Three weeks earlier he had traveled the forty kilometers to Capernaum, that lofty Roman city to the northeast, located at the tip of our inland sea. Construction there demanded craftsmen, and Joseph, admired for his skills, was sought after in a way mere journeymen—*teklots*—were not.

We missed his warm personality and genial manner. Still, such a sense of loss was tempered by an appreciation of generous payments due to a true craftsmen. This allowed us to remain in better financial shape than other citizens of Nazareth, nearly a mile south, between the village outskirts and the wilderness's edge.

Despite decent harvests in the past year, and plentiful fishing to the east, ever-increasing Roman taxes, heaped upon our already considerable Temple Tax, devastated the economy.

"Cleanliness is next to godliness," Mary quaintly reminded the girls. She repeated that phrase every morning, guiding them in the darkness toward our *mikveh*. In the village, people shared a single large cavity, carved into the earth, its sides and bottom coated with limestone to hold water diverted here from nearby springs. Such a process assured that all Hebrews bathed only in "living water" rather than stagnant pools. As to my family, for the past seven years denied all such communal activity, again we were blessed to have Joseph for our patriarch. A jack of all trades, he had constructed our own small pool, with help from James, his son by a previous marriage to a woman who had died young.

"It's so cold," Salome whined as Mary steered both girls into the purifying waters, which we believed cleansed not only the flesh but our immortal souls.

"Breakfast will be ready in twenty minutes," I called out, slipping into the quiet, clammy house. There, I set the black furnace, built into the northern wall, to burning. Scraps of wood were stacked high alongside this metal oven, another of

Joseph's creations. Fresh reserves were gathered each day by Simon, collecting fuel his primary task. Mine was to prepare the morning and evening meals.

And, beginning this afternoon, to replace my twin as the one who kept an eye on our goats and sheep. This, in order to allow Joses to head north, up to Sepphoris, for his first day of Hebrew School or, as we commonly called it, Yeshiva.

As flames gingerly snapped, I kneaded together grains of wheat and barley. These Joseph acquired in trade for his talent at repairing damaged farm tools for neighbors. Knowingly, I shaped the dough that would provide our daily bread, pushing the thin, wide loaf inside our oven. Next I set to arranging vegetables and fruits, picked the previous evening from Mary's ever-expanding garden. There would be peaches and pears today, as well as figs from trees growing wild across our fertile terrain. Their presence had, on the day of our official leave-taking from the village proper, convinced Joseph and James that here was where we should make our home.

For the past seven years, we had done precisely that.

While working, I struggled to hold on to the dream, already on the verge of flying off and away. I managed to retain the memory of what, as best as I could recall, were its outstanding elements. The chariot and beasts. The lowered sun. The tower stretching upward. The throne. And the beautiful girl!

Her skin like brown velvet and deep, dark eyes with black pupils that resembled olives: the source of healthy oil, several of which I currently chopped in a wooden dish. Eyes that had locked upon me, or that male variation of me, which sprang into being within the dream.

Still, my masculine dream-counterpart did not now confuse me as did the other symbols. For here, however unlikely, was a notion I'd been pondering. Which perhaps explains why, uninvited, such a thought had entered into my freewheeling night-vision.

*But back to the girl, waiting patiently on the throne. She, the conclusion of the dream. Its epicenter as well.*

A key, perhaps, that might unlock the meaning of everything else contained therein.

Slicing oranges, I arranged them neatly on a rough, carved tray, then placing this alongside a larger platter of olives on our home's only table. And wondered how long it would be before my experiences in the world would allow me to decode the identity of each elusive element, as my ancestor Joseph had the dreams of an Egyptian pharaoh, whom the young Hebrew long ago served.

More important still, my dream's personal relevance to me and my future.

I could not have known, or guessed, as I set a ceramic jar full of honey down beside the other foodstuffs and returned to our oven to withdraw the bread, that this process would commence before the day was done. Fittingly, if in an odd way, it would start precisely where the dream ended: with the girl.

# 3.

"Hey, Jude?"

"Over here, Jess. On the high hillock."

I made my way there from memory. In the sky above, darkness had receded, the moon's creamy glow with it. Sunrise had not yet occurred. The world, or one's little corner of it, appears grey at this haunting hour.

Still, the path proved familiar. A moment later, I bounded up to where Joses sat, beside a tall oak, playing his flute. His beloved goats and sheep wandered about, braying and mewing, for no purpose other than the enjoyment of making noise. On his favorite hillock, I kneeled beside my twin. If by chance a stranger happened by, that person would likely believe he saw double, so closely did we resemble each other.

"So? What have you decided?"

I tried to conceal my enthusiasm, well aware that the easiest way to lose Joses's cooperation would be to let him know how vulnerable this awkward situation left me.

As to his nickname? I'd come up with that owing to Joses's devotion to herding. This always made me think of Judah, fourth son of Jacob and Leah. As Hebrew children, we knew their story, one of many that Joseph told at dinner on those evenings when he was not too exhausted from work. Scripture recorded that Judah had long ago lived a docile life until rising in status over his older brothers by taking on responsibility for his aged parents. Always, I hoped my lazy, lovable twin would in time similarly mature.

As to my pet name for Joses? The Greek language had become commonplace in Israel following the great invasion of seventy-five years ago. Roman leaders considered Greek more classic, as such more respectable, than their own tongue. So Judah was circumscribed as Judas. For a casual nickname, I'd shortened this to Jude.

"I'm up to it if you are."

"I don't know, Jess. Did you see the look in Mom's eyes when she asked, during evening meal, if I'd tell her about—"

"You won't disappoint her. I promise. I'll be back in plenty of time to join you here and fill you in on what I learn before we're expected back at the house."

"That's only part of it. I don't really believe you can pass yourself off as a boy. You're so feminine—"

"I can do anything I set my mind to! You know that. Besides, I dreamed a dream last night . . ." I didn't tell Joses all of it, so personal had the experience been. Besides, I didn't want to bore this shallow boy. Meanwhile, time was wasting. So I only related the part about my gender transformation. As I did, Joses's eyes widened. Like everyone in central Galilee, my twin well knew that anything that appears in a dream must be taken seriously.

"Well, I sure don't want to spend the day in dreary classes."

"Alright! It's settled?"

He shrugged, then nodded. We exchanged clothing. Jude slipped into my simple, linen tunic, fit for boy or girl; me, into his rougher, more tightly woven outerwear, complete with a hanging hood I could pull up as a shawl, hiding much of my head. Most particularly, my mid-length, girlish hair.

Mary had spent the last several weeks knitting this outfit. So proud was she that, if at considerable cost, Joses would be educated. Few provincial boys could do so these days, owing to their fathers' sorry financial states. Our brother James had been educated in Scythopolis, a further distance away in the southeast. That was before the synagogues in Sepphoris were built.

Poor little Nazareth, with its population of 333, did boast its own synagogue. Sadly, this rough construction had become so forlorn, due to the lack of funds for improvement, that no rabbi from Jerusalem would agree to live and teach here.

*You're getting off-track again, Jess. Now, where were we . . .?*

If James was cast in the role of diligent older brother, juggling a half dozen jobs to help support our family, with Joses filling the role of lovable loafer, then Jess—*me!*—was the flighty one. Many times, when Mary and I worked side by side, planting seeds in spring or harvesting produce in autumn, my mother would grasp that mentally I had drifted a million miles away.

"Go off into the meadow," she offered. "Gather wildflowers and bring them back to brighten the table. But be home in time to fix the evening meal!"

I knew that in part she said this owing to an understanding I was . . . well, as numerous Nazarenes had long since noted . . . *different* . . . from other children. In truth, though, it hurt her deeply that, when she attempted small talk, I barely bothered to reply. Mary pretended not to notice my indifference, secretly fearing that her daughter did not love her.

*"Momsa! Momsa!"*

Children had screamed that at me and Joses in the streets of Nazareth when we were little. Perhaps, Joseph and Mary had whispered to one another, these people in time will if not forget then at least forgive.

The citizens of Nazareth did neither.

Instead, they passed the rumor down to their offspring, who taunted us with the insult at every opportunity: "Bastards! Bastards!" Many parents shut their doors when we approached, we two naïve children eager to mix with other boys and girls.

Those of our own age, should we dare come close on stone-covered village streets, reached for loose rocks, pelting us until we ran away, crying.

"What did we do?" I begged of Mary as she cradled us, one under each arm, on any such afternoon.

"It's not what either of you did," she replied, weeping for our anguish, and her own. "It's what happened . . . oh, but you're still too young to understand."

"Tell us!"

"I will, Jess. In time . . ."

She kept that promise. But only after the family had been driven out entirely, to live a mile north of Nazareth.

*What had someone once confided to me that our village's name signified? Oh, of course: "The Branch." Like the limb of a tree.*

*Well, then, we were a branch of that branch.*

Our expulsion had not been Mary's fault, but mine. Villagers agreed to allow us to remain, if barely tolerated, out of concern that bandits or wild beasts might destroy us if we strayed too far. Besides, Joseph's gifts at crafting furniture and stone-masonry made him too valuable to cast out entirely.

One day, I had surrendered to my great flaw, a temperament that, when sparked, led to uncontrollable rage.

After our move, people had to make the mile-long hike to his shop with requests, still paying Joseph handsomely for his labor. For he was the best at his craft.

"Thank you, Jude," I now giggled in excitement, grabbing hold of my twin, kissing him on the forehead, to his disdain. "I'll live up to my part of the bargain. Promise!"

I scurried off on the northward path, leading to the road from Nazareth to Sepphoris. Forty-five minutes of walking awaited me. Even as I reached the Roman road, the sun rose, allowing me to see clearly and move swiftly.

# 4.

"So you're actually going through with it!"

Levi patiently waited at a spot where the barely visible path met the wider dirt road leading north, eventually joining with the great Roman road. Even before Pompey's arrival, our people had sensed a need for interconnectedness. The walkway between the path my family had scratched out of the high grass and stone construction of our conquerors was cleared by officials in central Galilee. They insisted every village inhabited by Hebrews must be accessible to all others throughout Israel.

Such an undertaking began 550 years ago, immediately following the return of our nation from bondage in Babylon.

Some scholars ascribed the idea to the prophet Jeremiah. He announced that if the tribes maintained contact with one another, physically as well as religiously, we might not be over-taken again. Invasion by Romans doused cold water on that theory. Seventy years ago Pompey employed existing trails to navigate his troops across Israel, making Rome's domination easier than in less civilized nations he and Caesar invaded.

Still, how fascinating to imagine what this terrain must look like from on-high: a vast spider web stretching out in all directions, line after line connecting dot to dot, the highways modernized by a remarkable Roman innovation: cement. Mary always loved to say that if you search for the good in anything, you will find it. Perhaps improved travel conditions made up for the continual harassment by arrogant soldiers and ever-escalating taxes. Surely, though, not all in Israel would agree.

"Did you doubt, for a moment, I would be here?"

I joined Levi. He nervously stood, with those slumped shoulders so characteristic of my best friend, at the appointed place.

Levi! How I adored him; the only true friend I had from the village. The single boy who, despite his fearful nature, dared to play with Joses and myself during our time there. Shy, sensitive Levi, always confused as to what he ought to do in comparison to what he wanted to.

*I loved him like another brother.*

*Which was not, I knew, how he wished to be loved by me.*

"No. But part of me hoped you might change your mind."

We set out on our trek. Both of us had made this trip several times before. On occasion, when either of our sets of parents experienced a rare day with no pressing work, we would travel to this city more than triple the size of our own village. Nazareth boasted less than 250 crude limestone homes, similar to other hamlets in this sprawl of green valleys, full of the natural water necessary to sustain life. These included nearby Bethlehem, where Joseph had been born, and in time Joses and myself. Here was where Mary's widowed sister Elizabeth and her son John eked out a living.

Sepphoris, nicknamed the Gem of Galilee by admirers of its copious marketplace and elegant buildings, had more than 750 houses embedded in its limestone hills, many elaborate in

design. However impressive, more recently its onetime reputa-
tion for majesty had been eclipsed by Capernaum, 40 kilometers to the northeast. Here, arraigned across a broad horizon,
a great cosmopolitan city stood. Its citizenry of 6,000 included
more Greeks and Romans than Hebrews. Though integrated,
Sepphoris remained more a Jewish settlement. At least for the
time being.

*Getting ahead of myself again. Got to avoid that!*

Merging with the road, we passed by landscapes typical of
our self-contained world in Israel's northern territories: rolling
hills, the rich soil beige and brown, dotted with small, black
rocks. Also, large chunks of clay that, from a distance, caused
the terrain to appear speckled with salt and pepper. Low-lying
valleys were lush in late summer owing to the locust-green
grass. High-rising weeds lined the ridges while a variety of trees
ranged from mighty oaks to humble acacias. Finally, colorful
wildflowers flourished everywhere.

Before us stretched one of the most productive valleys in the
country, *Beth-Netopha*. An area so fertile that even the least-
gifted farmers could reap a substantial crop here: wheat and
barley grains, onions, and olives most prevalent.

"The idea of learning how to read and write!," I marveled.
"What a thrill. And to speak with an actual rabbi, as well as
people our own age as to the meaning of ancient stories. I can't
wait."

Of Sepphoris's seven synagogues, Zion provided our destination, located where the first wayfarers happened upon while
migrating from the south. Surrounded by a large orchard, Zion
sat on the base of a ridge ascending to this mighty city, high on
a hill, filled with wonders both natural and manmade.

"If I were you, I'd be real careful as to any talking."

Levi glanced at me with concern. I'd promised to remain silent out of fear I might not successfully modulate my voice to
sound like a boy. But Levi knew me well enough to guess such
a pledge would not hold water once discourse began.

Not being a fool, I'd spent hours alone, attempting to master
an approximation of Joses's tone. I'd decided that, when called
upon to offer up my name, I'd cough and mutter something
halfway between Joses and Jesus (the latter that name I would

have been blessed with had I been born a boy) in hopes of covering my little game.

"I will, Levi. And if I appear about to lose control, I'll count on you to—"

# 5.

"Look," Levi exclaimed, pointing across the way to a field.

Lost in giddy thoughts, I snapped back to reality owing to an insistent tone of deep concern in his voice. We paused as three Roman soldiers, coming from Sepphoris, turned a bend, hidden by a line of pine trees. Most likely, these stern fellows were on patrol for highwaymen.

"Remain calm, Levi. We've done nothing wrong."

Each Roman's head was capped with a copper helmet topped by a plume, his chest covered with a formidable breastplate that had been adorned with the emperor's eagle. Their black leather boots glistened from the required morning brushing. Crimson capes slung over their shoulders protected soldiers' backs from the sun's merciless rays. Approaching, their eyes considered us with mild suspicion.

"I will," Levi whispered, his slack body now shivering with trepidation. Meanwhile, I pulled my shawl up over my head to cover my longish girl's hair.

Though we were innocent, such men could prove testy, particularly when drunk—which, as all Hebrews knew, was most of the time. Low-ranking Romans despised being assigned here, beer and wine their main means of coping.

"Where are you boys headed?" the tallest demanded as the others swiftly positioned themselves to block our way.

"Synagogue Zion, in southern Sepphoris," I said, knowing Levi would be too intimidated to speak.

"Tell me why," the leader replied, his eyes suspicious. I explained that we were Yeshiva students, this to be our first day of schooling.

"Alright, get on with you."

The leader spoke pompously, in what struck me as a surly, dismissive manner. One of his companions, a squat fellow with cruel eyes, pushed forward, forcing Levi out of his way. In doing so, the soldier's right hand slapped against Levi's face. Hurt and humiliated, my friend could not suppress a whimper.

"Sorry," the soldier sneered.

"There's no need for that," the leader snarled at his inferior.

"Alright, Cornelius," the squat one responded. He turned toward Levi and myself and spoke in what remained a considerably unpleasant tone of voice: "You may continue on."

They continued on their way without glancing back. We watched as they disappeared around another bend, this one rich with green bushes. Once we were satisfied that they were gone, Levi and I proceeded on our journey, past a stretch of farmland. The ground here was far richer than in our own rock-strewn village, which lent itself more to herding.

"I hate them so, Jess. If only I could, I'd kill—"

"Don't *think* that, much less say it. You know what happens to Hebrews who—" .

"What am I supposed to do then," he wailed, "when one slaps me for no reason?"

"Turn the other cheek. Or, likely, die."

"And you? My hot-headed friend? You would accept abuse—"

"Unlike others who have conquered Canaan, the Romans allow us religious freedom."

"Yes. As long as we pay our taxes. Which are driving my father deep into debt. In addition to the Temple Tax. Should we suffer so, paying twice?"

"Render unto Caesar that which is Caesar's. And to God, that which rightly belongs to God."

"Maybe. Still, the Zealots claim it's time to fight."

Yet another bend. As if to answer Levi more forcefully than with words, we happened upon a stretch of plain on our westerly side. The spot had recently been cleared for crucifixion, this apparently where those Romans had just been.

Three Hebrew men, stripped naked except for brief cloths wrapped about the middle sections of their bodies, hung on crosses. Their hands were tightly tied to the crossbars; immense nails had been pounded through their wrists, into the dark hardwood. Their feet were crossed, a single nail driven through both lower legs and deep into the pole. Each victim moaned in excruciating pain.

Such punishment had been designed to hold off death for as long as possible so the suffering would continue for many hours. Rome never inflicted such horror on ordinary criminals, not even murderers. If condemned to die, they would be put to the sword. Or if locals wished to handle the situation themselves, the Hebrew system of stoning was employed. Crucifixion they reserved for one crime and one crime only: treason to Caesar.

Also known as sedition. Any act, or even some casual statement, uttered by a fellow who had perhaps imbibed too much wine, if his words contained so much as a hint of resentment, much less rebellion, against Rome's absolute political authority.

# 6.

"Water. Have pity. Wet my lips?" the man in the middle called out.

Without hesitation, we dashed in their direction. Standing directly before and below these doomed souls, Levi searched for branches that might be used to carry succor up to their parched mouths. While he collected the longest ones, I set to pulling up weeds, which we wrapped around one end of each makeshift pole.

Levi opened the goat-skin water sack, dousing our crude poultices. We hurried back to the victims only to find ourselves frustrated. Standing on our toes, we barely managed to bring a touch of liquid to their heat-scabbed lips.

"Bless you," one after another said.

Levi and I whispered about what we ought to do next. There was no possible way to climb up to free them. Besides, even if we did manage that, immense nails that had been hammered deep into the wood could not be removed without pliers.

"What did you to do deserve this?" Levi wanted to know. Though I wondered about that as well, I would never have asked such a thing of these dying men.

"Blue," the victim furthest to our right managed to gasp as we, crouching below, gazed up pitifully. He attempted to tell us more, but could not. Still, we nodded our understanding. For even those as young as us were aware of a new law. However small an additional burden it placed on our nation, this had been the straw that broke the proverbial camel's back, setting a sizable portion of our citizenry to open fury in the public streets.

"The *Tallit*," the man in the middle added.

The third man concluded: "The *tekhelet.*"

The Book of Numbers commanded all Jewish males to wear a white shawl while performing morning prayers. On such a linen garment, Hebrew lettering was imprinted in blue. Never before had the Romans challenged any part of this ritual or, for that matter, any practice essential to our faith.

But as I was in the process of discovering, a problem exists not in reality but in the mind of an observer. From each of a *Tallit*'s four corners hung twisted and knotted fringes. These we called the *tzitzit*. Though not specifically commanded in our Bible, over the centuries a tradition had taken hold. Most *tzitzit* were white, like the garment itself. Several, though, were colored blue. The dye derived from crushed shells of spiny sea snails. Such a blue strand we called a *tekhelet.*

One year earlier, the latest Roman governor arrived to take up residence at Caesarea Maritima, an immense port city four days walk west of Nazareth. These political appointees came and went in rapid succession, none able to stamp out the rebellion as Augustus had commanded. More foolish than most, the latest self-important fool noticed that a *tekhelet*'s hue appeared all but identical to Roman purple, worn only by Emperors and their families, several high-ranking senators, and military officers of aristocratic birth.

The new governor, or proctor as we referred to him, had in his infinite stupidity decided that *tekhelets* appropriated the symbolic color of Rome's elite. While the *Tallit* was not challenged, nor the white *tzitzit,* the blue strands, we were informed, must be removed.

19

# 7.

Apparently, this oaf thought that, unlike the meaning of Roman purple (also derived from sea shells, of a closely related species of mussel), our blue merely served some ornamental purpose and had been chosen for its decorative beauty. He could not have been more wrong. For a Hebrew, the two most wondrous places in our world are the sky above and the sea below. A sense of divine mystery pervaded the precise spot where the heavens melted into the ocean.

At this meeting point, we believed, existed an entrance to another dimension. So to signify the power of the color blue, a dyed strand had been woven into our *Tallits*.

Rabbis, wise men, and our political leaders all begged that this restriction not become law. Astounded that such a small issue might be met with an extreme outpouring of anger, the governor insisted that not only would this indeed become an official rule but that transgressors would face punishment reserved for the Zealots: crucifixion. Messengers had carried word from the west coast to central Galilee, then turned north toward Mount Hermon or south to the city of Jerusalem.

There the palace of Herod, the Arab chosen by Rome to reign as our king, stood adjacent to our temple. Like his late father Herod the Great, the second King Herod (whose reign began the year I was born) knew all too well that we Hebrews loathed him. Some had gone so far as to nickname him Antipas: the one who stands against us. His Arabic bloodline descended from Ishmael, outcast son of Abraham.

We were the children of the children of Isaac, who five millennia earlier was anointed in the eyes of Yahweh as the original Hebrew. Both nations revered the patriarch Abraham. The acceptance of his second son Isaac, with his now-Hebrew wife, and simultaneous rejection of firstborn Ishmael, conceived with Hagar the gentile, constituted an insult that Arabic people could never forgive.

Now, Antipas would do anything to placate the high-ranking Roman officials who had placed him in his father's position of power. He stamped the governor's edict with his insignia. The bloodshed swiftly commenced. Crucifixions, which had become rare in recent years owing to Rome's appreciated tolerance of all other aspects of our faith, were now the order of the day.

*All this, over the color of a single thread.*

"Go now, boys," the writhing man in the middle commanded. "You are too young to watch us die."

We protested; he insisted. Hesitantly, Levi and I stepped away, back on to the cement highway. I wanted to see them one last time, to make certain I'd never forget.

Sensing this, Levi warned, "Don't look back."

"I must."

Thankfully, I did. Otherwise, I would not have noted the strange occurrence that followed our leave-taking. Seven small lights grew ever brighter and more distinct in the sky, steadily moving downward in the direction of the dying Hebrews. My guess? These were the same objects I'd witnessed earlier that morning from my roof.

They had not, then, been an illusion. Nor were they random. They appeared for a reason, then and now. At this point, I couldn't guess what it might be.

*Such knowledge came slowly. But when it did . . .*

*There I go again! Back, now, to where we were.*

"You look ill, Jess."

"Yes, and I'll tell you why. I learned something, here and now. No matter what storms blow over Israel, soon or in years to come, I will do anything—Levi, *anything!*—to avoid meeting my own death by crucifixion."

I turned toward the south so as to face in the direction of our faraway Temple Mount, offering a silent prayer, promising Yahweh that I could handle whatever He had in store for me.

Please, though, our one and only God. Spare me this?

# 8.

We were the last of twenty-one boys (counting Levi and, if falsely, myself) to arrive. At least we weren't late. While waiting for the rabbi to appear, earlier arrivals—mostly city youths—mulled about, meeting and greeting. They glanced at Levi and I, a pair of outsiders, two hicks from some crude village, with a vague sort of contempt. So this is how it would be!

The synagogue itself resembled Nazareth's as to its simple construction style, though more than twice the size and well-kempt. Big money dominated in Sepphoris; here was where many wealthy citizens of central Galilee chose to live among Romans.

Still, seeing the structure filled me with joy. Joseph had played a role in its design and masonry. Always I felt a deep sense of pride observing any example of his work.

Levi and I awkwardly shuffled about, uncertain as to where we might find our place. The group, we realized, had already broken down into sub-sectors based on financial status. Hoping for at least a pleasant greeting, we drew close to the crowd. Most turned away, engaging in discussions with others who like themselves were finely dressed. The tightest clique contained a dozen elegantly attired boys, likely sons of successful landowners or merchants. Ornate, expensive garments set them apart, particularly from rustics.

Everything, I was swiftly learning, exists according to contrasts. My family ate meat once a week. In poverty stricken Nazareth, we were considered rich by those who thought themselves lucky to have enough vegetables to go around. In Sepphoris, where well-to-do families enjoyed chicken every day, the family of Joseph of Nazareth would be considered poor.

Many inhabitants here were involved in the lucrative olive oil trade. They owned ships, in some cases fleets, that transported this Israeli specialty to distant ports. Others had accumulated vast farmlands. Day workers from poor villages like ours earned low payments by harvesting figs or gathering grapes. A small number of citizens controlled and profited handsomely from the wine industry, particularly owners of those elaborate presses able to transform raw produce into a divine beverage. Several of Sepphoris's upper-class residents accumulated wealth from tenant farmers who turned over most of the fruits and vegetables they sowed to these patriarchs.

*I cringe at the uneven distribution of wealth among the Hebrew people, knowing in my heart, thinking with my mind that this is essentially wrong.*

*But what to do about it? Now, there's a question!*

"The rabbi's still inside," I heard one of the well-to-do boys tell a companion, "offering his good-byes to the wayfarers."

"This rabbi," his friend replied, "is most learned."

"Of course. He's from Jerusalem!"

Even wealthy boys who looked down on us were themselves intimidated by anyone from Judea, Israel's southern sector. Our nation's lower tier, geographically speaking, counted the highest number of our elite among its citizenry. While any man among us could pronounce himself a rabbi and speak when and where he chose, those considered to be the greatest of this profession had all studied at the Temple Mount. And hoped, after proving their worth by bringing the word to isolated areas in the north, that eventually they would return home and win appointments to the lofty priesthood.

Counting heads, I guessed four boys to be sons of fishermen from the Sea of Galilee. Their non-fashionable but new tunics were what members of the emergent middle-class could afford. While not accepted by those who considered themselves the A group, neither did they draw frowns. Two other youths, dressed like Levi and myself in the rough garb of provincials, stood off to one side, in the shade of several lemon trees.

Noting the similarity of their clothing and our own, they eyed Levi and myself with interest. The taller of the two, more rugged, coarse, and outgoing, signaled us to join them. "Shalom," he called out with a voice that struck me as masculine and easygoing, an endearing combination.

"Shalom!" Levi and I replied simultaneously, warily approaching.

"You're the boys from Nazareth?" the large youth asked with a smile that suggested sincerity. Rippling muscles ran up and down his exposed arms and legs. He might have passed for one of those Greek athletes who paraded by my home on their way to competitions, each recognizable by his massive frame and uncombed head of hair as a member of this profession.

This boy's huge chin, cleft with a gash-sized dimple in its center, further enhanced his muscular appeal. An aura of excitement surrounded him; a sense that, though of our class, this unique lad must have been born for an exceptional life.

"I'm Jesus," I announced, breaking the ice.

I'd determined that this would be my name while here: near to that of my twin if not identical, also a variation on my own, the feminine equivalent of Jesus.

"You're kidding me?" The jaunty youth grinned broadly.

"Uh, no. Why ask that?"

"Because it's mine, too." His merry eyes glimmered, as if he believed this, and the whole world, to be a huge joke, existing mainly to provoke his good humor.

# 9.

"Jesus, meet Jesus," my friend joined in. "I'm Levi." Then shyness overcame him, causing Levi to lower his eyes.

"This could be confusing," I sighed.

"Why don't you call me by my family name?"

"Which is . . ."

"Barabbas."

I turned my attention to his diminutive companion. Less self-confident even than Levi, he barely made eye-contact. This boy appeared less slender than skinny. His flesh was not tan from exposure to the sun but pink and white.

"You are—"

"Judas."

"Now it's my turn to ask," I said. "Are you kidding me?"

"No." With a sudden jerking movement, Judas involuntarily pulled his head back. Self-consciously, he raised an eyebrow, thin shoulders twitching. "Why?"

"Nothing bad. It's only that Judas is my twin brother's name. Actually, my nickname for him."

"Wow," Levi dared intrude. "Talk about coincidence!"

"Your eyes are so blue," Judas sighed, glancing upward at my face. Not that I stood tall, rather that Judas was so little. He appeared smitten with me. Barabbas laughed heartily while Levi blushed. Levi had expressed such a sentiment often, though always in the context of his being a boy, me a girl.

Rare as gold was a Hebrew with the blue eyes so highly prized among my nation. King David was rumored to have had the most intense. Here was another reason why blue became our nation's symbolic color. The now-forbidden *tzitzit* on every traditional *Tallit* paid homage to our second and greatest king as well as the sky and the sea.

"All the better to see you with," I joked. Barabbas and Levi appeared vaguely uncomfortable with Judas's admiring words. As to the diminutive youth, he now appeared tearful, clearly wishing he'd remained silent. Any awkwardness dissipated owing to what happened next.

"There's the rabbi," Barabbas exclaimed as the door to the synagogue opened wide. A tall, angular man, likely ten years older than we students, stepped out of the building and into the bright sunlight. He wore the flowing robes of a religious leader. A multi-colored *kippah* topped his head like a crown, announcing that this was not some itinerant teacher but a representative of our faraway temple.

All the same, something about this man reminded me of a scarecrow come to life, even though a thick beard and matching eyebrows established his humanity.

The rabbi barely glanced at the young arrivals. Instead, he spoke briefly with two Hebrew males who followed him out. Carrying backpacks, they appeared ready to head off on their personal journeys.

Zion, or any synagogue (including our near-ruined one in Nazareth) existed primarily as a temporary stop-over, an always open "in" for traveling Jews. Members of all the tribes that composed our far-flung nation knew they were welcome any place in the world where fellow Hebrews lived. Journeyers, female as well as male, could stay for three nights, no longer. This was our law, if unwritten, as to hospitality.

Otherwise, the only function of a synagogue during my youth was for meetings between the rabbi and local political leaders. Under no circumstances could one pray here. That had to be done outside, facing south in the direction of our distant temple.

"I am your rabbi," he self-importantly stated, turning in our direction after the two travelers reached the road below. "My name is Annas. Welcome to Yeshiva."

Here was a case of hate at first sight. Something about the rabbi filled me with trepidation and contempt. Perhaps it had to do with the cruel way he had then, and always afterwards, of pulling his mouth into a wide smirk after speaking. No trace of compassion could be found in his face, though I did sense an abiding cynicism as he looked us over, mentally separating the wheat from the chaff.

There could be no doubt, from the glint in his eyes, that we four standing together constituted the latter.

# 10.

Among the well-to-do, the tallest wore an elegant coat of many hues. Such an ornate garment hinted at considerable wealth. Most likely, more money than any of his cohorts' families. At the sight of this presumptuous costume, our rabbi's eyes lit up with the glow of admiration and the possibility of self-advancement.

Clothes make the man, an old saying insisted. Passed down from generation to generation. Accepted as worldly wisdom.

*It should not be that way. The* man *should make the man.*

*Then again, there's the way life ought to be and how it is. To replace the latter with the former would be to create paradise here on Earth.*

"I," our teacher announced, holding his head high, "am Rabbi Annas of Jerusalem. I am a Pharisee!"

As he considered us, one boy at a time, I could tell that our rabbi noted my uncomfortableness with the way he went about presenting himself. I sensed the distaste I felt to be mutual.

We were instructed to form a semicircle. This began at one corner of the synagogue and curved southward. At the midpoint it arced back toward the building's far side. In the center stood that tallest student. From there, diminishing status as well as stature continued. Sons of fishermen stood at the westernmost point, the four provincials on the opposite eastern end. All faced south.

Behind us, Annas stood, speaking in ominous tones. Perhaps that was intended to suggest an aura of profundity. To me, he merely sounded pretentious.

Before the prayer session began, the rabbi walked among us, handing each boy a *kippah*. These skull caps were tinted so dark a blue that they resembled the night sky. I had to be careful while manipulating mine, swiftly curling my hair up and into the *yarmulka* as I slipped the hood down to my slender shoulders.

The time had come to pray. Annas returned to the synagogue's front door. Our backs remained to him as we cast our eyes toward distant Jerusalem.

"Thank you, Yahweh, for being so kind and generous as to not curse me by having this loyal follower be born a woman."

I came close to retching, though I knew this to be the agreed-upon manner in which such gatherings commenced.

"Easy, Jess," Levi whispered.

"Hebrew school may not be the joy I anticipated."

Next, we recited the traditional afternoon prayer:

"God is the Lord and most worthy of praise;

His greatness no one can fathom . . ."

We all knew the words by heart. The *Minchah* was repeated daily by everyone in Israel. Hebrews paused in whatever work they might be engaged in to humbly recite it.

"One generation commends You to another;

They celebrate Your abundant goodness

And joyfully sing of Your righteousness."

Some ten minutes later the ceremony concluded. Rabbi Annas instructed us to turn about, facing him again, then kneel or sit in place. Annas opened an ancient scroll containing the sacred texts in Hebrew, the ancient language we had come to study and master. Hebrew men took great pride in achieving such an education.

*And, if I ruled the world, so would Hebrew women.*

By our age, most Israelites had long since picked up the necessary skills to write as well as speak in Aramaic, the common language among all in the Near Middle East. Now we were ready to embrace a more traditional form of literacy.

First, though, came instruction in the Torah itself. This, I awaited fervently owing to my love of stories.

"We will begin at the beginning."

In an exalted voice, Annas read from his old parchment a story familiar enough: Yahweh's creation of the universe, our world, and the miracle of life. Genesis, which each boy's father had introduced him to at home, continued until Annas reached the stopping point for today: Yahweh's inspiration to add the race of man to His already copious accomplishments.

"Well?" Annas asked, considering us as he rewound the scroll. "Do any of you yet grasp that here is more than a simple story?"

A hush fell over the group. Every boy longed to raise his hand and if called on say something to hopefully please the rabbi. Such a youth would qualify as a favorite on day one. The opposite possibility gave all reason to pause: What if a response did not go over well? A blundering student might well become on this very first day the subject of a scorn that would continue throughout the semester.

# 11.

"Does it have anything to do with the different ways in which Yahweh creates each of Adam's wives?" the tall boy asked after raising a hand high and being recognized.

The rest of us waited with baited breath for the rabbi's reaction. If his eyes lit up, each would wish he'd been the one to offer this answer, and enthusiastically nod as if to imply "Yes, of course—that was on the tip of my own tongue." Should a frown appear on Annas's thick forehead, everyone would breathe a sigh of relief that he had kept quiet.

Our teacher responded with a crooked smile of approval. "Yes, indeed. It has *everything* to do with that. Remind me. What is your name?"

"Saul, Rabbi."

"Your father is a merchant from Tarsus?"

Saul nodded proudly. "The most successful tent maker in the world. He traveled to Capernaum for the summer to complete business arrangements for overland trade routes, as well as our fleet of cargo ships. These deliver merchandise from port cities on the Mediterranean to customers across the map: Alexandria, Antioch, even Rome."

"Why then do we find you here in Sepphoris?"

Beaming with self-satisfaction drawn from his illustrious father, Saul continued: "As I am eleven, he brought me with him this year to assist. Learn the trade I will someday inherit. Presently, he is headquartered in Sepphoris."

"Very good. Now, be more specific." Saul set about to speak again, but Rabbi Annas interrupted. "And stand when you speak."

Basking in glory, Saul did as commanded.

"When Yahweh created Lilith, he molded her from the earth, as he had Adam. This caused her to mistakenly believe she would be his equal. When God and Adam grasped her true monstrousness, hoping to dominate every aspect of the coupling, including those we cannot speak of owing to modesty, Yahweh banished her from Eden to live as a night creature."

Saul paused to catch his breath.

*Modesty? Try living for a while, young Saul, in a one-room limestone home near Nazareth, on the edge of a massive wilderness.*

*You lay awake at night, listening to your parents groaning in one another's arms. We know nothing of this "modesty" you sophisticated city-dwellers speak of.*

"A royal answer from one with a kingly name. Continue!"

"Then our Lord God created Eve, from one of Adam's ribs. In so doing, Yahweh corrected his earlier mistake. With a wife drawn from his flesh, she would be subservient to Adam."

"She would know her place," Annas concluded for Saul as the boy once more sat down. His immediate circle of friends huddled close, congratulating Saul while envying his success. I did remain in control, however, secretly furious, until Annas felt the need to sum everything up: "As must all women, always."

To this day I'm not certain what happened next. No way had I forgotten my promise to Levi. Yet, as I glanced to my right, I could only watch helplessly as my arm rose, like that of a wooden puppet, its master pulling on a string. I hadn't willed it to do so. All the same, up went my hand.

"Yes, boy? You, there. Do you wish to speak?"

Though the rabbi had not indicated for me to stand, I felt myself rise. I looked to Levi, already trembling with anxiety. I might ruin everything for us both on the first day. Judas's neck began twitching, doing so every several seconds.

*Note to self: If I survive whatever comes next, someday I must try to help Judas conquer that.*

"It's only . . . isn't it true that Eve also had a mind of her own? Later she's the one who listens to the serpent, then convinces Adam to bite into the pomegranate, even though Yahweh had commanded her not to go anywhere near that forbidden tree."

Momentarily, Annas appeared speechless. "That's the whole point!" Saul shouted, eager to seize the rabbi's awkward pause for a means to further toadying up. "Can't you see? The moment Adam isn't there to watch over her, Eve angers Yahweh. She, just by being a woman, caused man to be cursed."

"Let me say," Rabbi Annas, having found his voice again, mumbled, "that Lilith, created as Adam's equal, is evil, pure and simple. What the Torah teaches us here is that women can never exist on the same level as men. Seeing His own mistake, Yahweh creates Eve. An extension of man, thus inferior. Whatever sin she commits in allowing herself to be seduced by the serpent was not evil. Unlike Lilith, Eve was too stupid to know right from wrong. She sobs in repentance. Ever since, all women are likewise weak and stupid. Other than those who, like Jezebel, duplicate Lilith. In that case, they are strong and smart but wicked. Do you understand *now*?"

The rabbi raised his eyebrows high, glancing across the obedient faces of cowed students. All heartily agreed, each of the boys attempting to outdo the next in enthusiasm.

Except for only myself.

# 12.

On our way home following the three-hour study session, Levi and I stopped at the place of crucifixion. If the Hebrews proved to be alive still, we would again provide what little comfort we could. But they had passed, taking with them the knowledge that each had remained true to his essential values.

If only I could decide for myself if the color of a single thread is worth dying for. Particularly when we are free to worship Yahweh as we please in all other ways.

There is the Covenant, which must be obeyed always. Ten laws set in stone by God. Then there are the laws of men. Passed down from generation to generation until they seem inseparable from Yahweh's original edicts.

But they are not. There is the eternal and then there is the temporal.

What to do? Simply put, I don't know.

*All I knew was I didn't want to die in such a horrific manner. Anything short of that, Yahweh, and I will obey.*

*Do you accept that? Have we forged our own compact?*

The midafternoon sun beat down as Levi and I continued south toward Nazareth. With the tips of my leather sandals, I kicked at clumps of dirt along the cement and stone road.

"Jess? Why didn't you keep your big mouth shut?"

"I couldn't help myself, Levi."

"That will land you in trouble someday."

"It already has. You saw—"

"That's not what I meant. I'm talking *big* trouble!"

We turned a bend, knowing that a well awaited. Along our highways, the people of Israel had, following our return from Babylon and under the leadership of Zerubbabael, constructed wells to insure that no Hebrew would ever again go thirsty in our homeland.

Levi and I hardly expected what we heard further down the road. Angry voices shouted "Whore! *Worthless,* damnable whore!"

Hurrying along, we happened on an ugly confrontation. By the well, a girl—about the same age as us—cowered in fear. Those Romans Levi and I encountered earlier, all three now further intoxicated, menacingly closed in on her.

"Not a whore!" she insisted. "Respectable—"

I couldn't make out the girl's face as she whimpered and waved her hands in protest. She wore a beige robe with green designs on its back and front, identifying her as a Phoenician. Presumably, she had traveled here from the east, on her way to the Mediterranean. There, her entire nation had once been located, before breaking up and spreading eastward across Israel.

"We have searched the provinces since our arrival," the squat Roman laughed, "and have not yet found a single female who can honestly say—"

"Get away," she screamed, swinging her fists in a desperate attempt to fend them off. Struggling, she leaned so far backwards I feared the girl might drop down into the well.

"Come on!" I rushed forward, not knowing what to do. Yet sensing that I must do *something!*

"You said you wouldn't risk crucifixion," Levi called out, hesitating.

"I said I wouldn't for a thread of blue string. This is a person's life, a girl's honor—"

Besides, we both knew Hebrew citizens and Roman occupiers regularly engaged in scuffles. The penalty amounted to spending a day or two behind bars and a fine. Crucifixion was reserved for political radicals, not personal arguments.

I bounded up alongside them. Possessed by a combination of foolishness and reckless courage, I heard myself unequivocally state, "Leave her alone."

"Look! It's the little Jew-boy again," the second Roman laughed. "On your way home from school? Shut up and—"

Levi, huffing and puffing, arrived by my side. "You have no right to touch her," he boldly said. "Roman authority doesn't allow you to molest—"

"She's a whore," the tallest, their leader, answered. "And not even a Hebrew whore. Why would you two risk—"

I'll never know what might have happened next if it were up to us. We were as intimidated as we were outraged. My guess? They'd have beaten us to a pulp, then had their way with her. That can never be known. Suddenly, the girl froze, her frantic words and gestures ceasing. Without warning, she arched forward, her body coiling like a cobra preparing to strike.

"What the . . . ?" the squat soldier gasped.

Her arms whipped high up in the air, her mouth opening to reveal surprisingly sharp teeth. Her eyes sunk deep back into her head, as if a daemon wandering the earth had at this moment possessed her.

"She's . . . a *monster*," their leader, Cornelius, exclaimed.

Levi gasped at her transformation. I was stunned, having moments earlier caught sight of her eyes. Almond shaped with pupils black as a pair of olive pits.

Identical to those belonging to the girl in my dream.

# 13.

"*Slrinwicnosum!*" may have been what she shrieked, lunging at the Romans. The girl spoke in tongues. Words that made no sense in Aramaic or, so far as I knew, any other language.

The soldiers, hardly intimidated by Levi and myself, were clearly terrified of this girl-thing. Perhaps she recalled the wicked female spirits from old tales, related by centurions over many generations while sitting near midnight campfires.

"She's possessed!"

"Run," Cornelius ordered his followers. They did, even as she continued to screech. Touches of spittle running down from either side of her mouth, the girl ferociously pursued until the Romans rounded a bend, disappearing behind a natural wall of dark-green forest. She dropped down to the ground then, alternately howling and weeping.

"What are we to do now?" Levi whispered.

"I'm not sure. Let's . . . try to help?"

With trepidation, we cautiously stepped to where her body lay, sprawled in the dirt a distance beyond the road. She rolled back and forth, bounced up and down, sobbing. To our amazement, she gulped down chunks of earth, gnashing her teeth, howling at the sky.

"Jess? I'm scared."

"You think I'm *not*?"

Finally, she rolled over onto her back, kicking her legs and waving her arms, these movements striking me as totally out of control. Here, I feared, is abject madness.

"Let's go home. There's nothing we can—"

"I have to *try*! Think back to the streets of Nazareth, many years ago."

We exchanged glances. He knew what I referred to. I kneeled beside her, grasping her arms firmly, attempting to hold the girl down without further panicking her.

"Listen to me," I begged. "You are going to be alright. I'm here now. I'm with you. Can you understand?"

Gradually, her struggling ceased. The girl's frame, which had swelled up mightily during her fit, returned to normal. In time, she breathed naturally. Her mouth moved, though she could not yet form words. Then she opened her eyes. Beautiful eyes. Almond-shaped eyes with mesmerizing pupils that recalled black olives.

*Eyes I had seen before, though not on this Earth.*

"Whatever you did, Jess, it sure worked!"

"I'm not sure. At least she seems a bit calmer now."

The sun threatened to burn my skin, but I would not leave her side to seek shade. In time, her body relaxed, and I knew that the girl had recovered. I loosened my hold, as the bizarre truth made itself known: from her black pupils to her luxuriously long hair, the perfect chin and slender legs, here was my dream girl in the flesh.

# 14.

The girl who had sat on a throne, potentially the key to unlocking my dream's full meaning. The female that, I had assumed earlier that very day, I'd likely spend my lifetime searching for. The only thing missing was her pagan garb. Doubtless, I'd come to understand why that did not yet appear.

All in God's good time . . .

"I'm alright now, I think," she muttered, gazing up into my own eyes. "Thank you."

"I did nothing but calm you with words and—"

"I feel as if you wrestled a daemon that had overtaken me, exorcising that evil force from my breast."

"The only wickedness within was your surrender to wrath."

"Well, that's a habit of mine, when provoked."

"Mine, too," I admitted.

She sat up, if with difficulty, rubbing those beautiful eyes with her palms, trying to regain composure. "My name is Mary." I rose, offering her my hand. She accepted it, momentarily hesitating as she noticed the deep scar. "Oh! What happened?"

"It's a long story. Maybe someday I'll—"

"Another coincidence?" Levi gasped.

"I don't understand," she said. As her legs gained firm ground, Mary clenched her fists at either side of her waist.

"Throughout this day," I explained, "people I've met share a name with one of my relatives. Mary is my mother's."

She considered this, managing a smile. "If you like, call me Maggie. To avoid confusion. So! You're Hebrews?" We nodded in agreement, brushing loose grass from her tunic. She spoke calmly, as if nothing untoward had happened. "I'm Phoenician."

"We guessed that from your clothes. I'm Levi."

"Jesus."

"I know *he*'s a boy," she said, pointing at Levi and then turning to me. "You?"

"Well . . ." I answered, realizing that my shawl had slipped down from my head. I hastened to reset it. For years, I had cut my locks shorter than most provincial girls, though it did hang longer than a boy's. "Jesus is, after all, a masculine name."

*Did she buy that? I hope so.*

*The last thing I need now is another person who knows my secret.*

"We're from Nazareth," Levi ventured.

"That's where I'm headed. May I walk with you?"

"Of course."

We turned, proceeding down the road as the sun reached its high point. "I'm from Magdala, up along the coast?"

"I know of it," I replied, "but I don't believe I've ever been there. At least not since I was an infant."

"If you had, you'd remember. It's the only city in this part of Canaan with a tower."

Again, I recalled my dream. Of course! Magdalene was Aramaic for tower. Only the Phoenicians had built them previous to the coming of the Romans. We Hebrews? Never. The experience of our ancient forefathers at Babel had cured us of that.

So! Two elements of the dream had already fallen into place. First the girl, then the structure she had existed within.

When, I wondered, would I encounter a third?

# 15.

"I'm not what that Roman called me," Maggie explained after we'd continued on for several minutes in silence. She paused to kick at a cactus growing wild against the edge of the road, then yelped like a wounded puppy when its spines pierced through her paltry sandals.

We laughed. So did Maggie, once the pain diminished.

"We never thought you were," I assured her. Levi nodded in agreement. We walked on either side of Maggie as if to imply protection should the need arise. Not many criminal acts were carried out along Israel's roads these days. The wild ways of the wilderness had been subdued by Rome's presence.

*Thank Yahweh, as Mary would say, for small favors.*

"I have run away from home," she announced, as if talking to a pair of long-time friends. A stressful situation like the one we'd undergone allows strangers to quickly bond. Magadan, Maggie informed us, was the name by which Greek traders, who negotiated business deals, referred to her home town. Like other nations, hers had created colonies decades earlier on Galilee's west coast, in time fanning out across Israel.

As Levi and I knew, Magadan—Magdala to us—was what locals called an open city. Home to some Samaritans who had wandered in from the southwest. A few Greeks, Romans, even a number of Hebrews. For the time being, most members of my nation preferred towns exclusively inhabited by our own kind. That, too, though, was gradually changing along with most everything else, as Nazareth proved. Only ten years earlier, it had been all Hebrew. Now, others dwelled there as well.

Their presence, at the door of my father's shop, fascinated me. As did those thirsty camel drivers who paused to ask for a drink from our well. What were their own lands like? I'd have to wait and learn. First, though, I must discover a means by which I might travel far and wide. This had become a growing desire that I kept secret from family and my few friends.

So many customs and cultures to savor! And, best of all, diverse people to meet, each people with its own unique way of understanding the world around them.

*Let's not forget the wonderful foods I had never tasted but wished to.*

*Meals were never far from the mind of Jess of Nazareth.*

Thinking of my home raised another question. "Would you care to tell us: why Nazareth?"

Maggie bit her lip, thinking through what she should or should not say. Finally, she shrugged and related her difficult situation. "My parents wanted me to become what those Romans referred to me as. I refused."

We Galileans well knew that Phoenicians had long engaged in a lifestyle that, like their religion, derived from radically different values than our own. All the same, I wasn't completely prepared for what Maggie told us now. Rome's ever-higher taxes hit their town hard. Even the once-lucrative fishing trade suffered when boatmen were forced to mortgage their wooden crafts to pay what they owed. Beloved sons were sold into slavery, always the youngest first.

Daughters, preparing for respectable marriages, were ordered to walk the streets, bringing any profits home so that the family could eat and pay rent, along with their increasing levies. To Hebrews, such a notion was reprehensible. Our tradition insisted that we honor the next generation even to the expense of ourselves. Clearly, that was not the case everywhere.

Always, though, there are those who rebel against authority. Maggie was, among her nation, such a person. "I could never do that. No matter what anyone said about my duty to family."

"There's also an individual's duty to oneself."

"Thank you, Jess. That's what I was trying to say. Which is why I became so outraged when the Romans called me . . ."

"Still, you haven't answered," Levi reminded her. "Why Nazareth?"

"I have relatives who recently moved there. An uncle, not fond of my father."

"We hope that you find a place," I said as encouragingly as possible. Even at this early age, I'd come to believe attitude is among the most important elements in life. Already, though, I'd been through enough unexpected reversals to know that things don't always go as planned. Hebrews, of course, could not turn away a blood relative in need, no matter how awkward the situation. I knew little about the Phoenician view on this issue.

"I live in Nazareth. Perhaps I can be of help?" Levi offered.

"And if for any reason things don't work out," I added as we reached the point where my family's path veered off westerly, "my home sits just beyond that hill."

"Thank you, both of you, *so* much."

Maggie smiled openly for the first time since her ordeal. I split from them and watched while they continued south on the main road with only a few kilometers left to the village.

I'd been sincere. All the same, my words were to a degree self-serving. This was, after all, the girl I'd likely depend on to help me understand unknown symbols in my dream.

"Watch that temper," I called to her, waving.

"You should talk!" Levi reprimanded me with a laugh.

They slipped around a bend and out of sight. I found myself thinking back to that ugly day in Nazareth, seven years ago, which I'd eluded to while speaking with Levi.

# 16.

"*Momsa! Momsa!*"

I can't recall which child shouted that first. The cataclysmic event, I do remember, took place atop one of Nazareth's limestone houses at midafternoon. Kicking a ball we'd fashioned from discarded scraps of leather, the village children, boys and girls, had divided into teams. Initially, everybody appeared in a good mood, which momentarily allowed me to believe this might be the beginning of a new era. Perhaps Joses and I would now be accepted by our peer group of fellow five-year-olds?

"Be quiet!"

The reason I was allowed to join in had to do with the presence of my cousin John. Nine months older than me, he and his mother Elizabeth (my mother's sister) had traveled the four miles easterly from their home in upper Bethlehem. Their visits always raised Mary's spirits, as well as my own. On those special occasions when we were together, John assumed the role of substitute older brother if James happened to be working some job on one of the nearby farms.

Lanky, angular, and with penetrating eyes that locked onto a person and refused to let go, John spoke in a hoarse voice. Owing to its uniqueness, this always piqued the interest of strangers. Nazareth's children, having little contact with the outside world, were intrigued by anything that broke the daily humdrum. Today? John.

Playing on the street by the community well, the other kids noticed us, then waved for John and myself to join them. Joses might also have come along, but, characteristically, he opted for a nap.

"You're a *momsa*," Zenon, the group's leader, shrieked after we'd climbed to the rooftop. "*Everyone* says so."

"That doesn't make it true."

Until that day, I didn't actually know what the term meant. Only that it indicated something unpleasant. One of the boys had suggested we play kickball. The group voted to leave the street or likely be cuffed on the ears by passersby should we get in their way. So a dozen and a half youngsters hurried to a ladder leaning against an adjacent house's northernmost wall.

One by one, we climbed up. This roof was known to be stronger than most and able to sustain our weight. All had gone well enough until, at the game's height, I rushed forward, beyond my teammates, and kicked the ball hard and fast. It breezed past a heavy boy guarding his team's goal. Furious that I scored, he called out in anger that word I already despised.

"Your father isn't your father, *momsa*."

"Yes he is," I tearfully responded. "I'm Joe's girl."

I turned away, ignoring him, as my mother had insisted I do whenever a situation turned ugly, trusting that the moment would pass. But all at once the game stopped. Zenon stepped forward, spoiling for trouble. His teammates moved ahead to back him up. Nothing broke a dull day's monotony like a knock-down, drag-out fight.

"Leave her alone," John warned, stepping between me and them. He was tall enough, if irregular in build, that his presence gave them pause. "She's only a girl," he added.

However much John may have meant well, his words set me off. What did that matter?

"I can take care of myself," I announced, stepping forward and egging them on.

"It wasn't even a Hebrew, one of our own," another boy shouted. Levi stood among them. Up until this day, he'd been the only child in the village always willing to play with me. Now, he held back, not knowing what to do. I could sense that he wished to support me, though as it turned out peer pressure proved too much.

"A Roman," the heavy boy added.

"We even know his name," another—this one a girl—piped in. "Tiberon! Your mother used to meet him every day in the far pasture while Joseph worked out of town."

"How do you know?"

"My parents said so."

"They lie," I replied, breaking down and sobbing. This bit of information, I had not heard before. The words devastated me.

*It wasn't true. It couldn't be true.*

*My mother, Mary? How could anyone believe such a thing about that wonderful woman?*

The crowd surged forward, closing in. Once more, John waved them away. Anything might happen next. At that moment, Levi pulled away from the others, hurrying over to the roof's southernmost side. Perhaps his sudden action meant that if he were not brave enough to join my cousin and myself, at least he'd distanced himself from the mob.

Without knowing precisely why, I rushed to him, even as the full meaning of the term *momsa* finally hit home. "Levi," I sighed, embracing him. "My friend."

The others turned their eyes on him now. Levi understood he might be designated as one of the village's lonely outcasts should he support me. "*Momsa!*" he said, turning to face me with panic, anguish, and also concern in his eyes.

That's when I felt wrath overtake me completely. Barely aware of what I was doing, I surrendered to my inner fury and pushed hard against his chest, sending Levi flying head over heels from the roof, down to the stone street below.

# 17.

Initially, everyone was too shocked to react. Then John rushed to my side. "Jess! *What did you do?*"

"She killed Levi!" Zenon shouted.

"How'd you like me to kill you next, you smug little—"

"Murderer. *Momsa and* murderer."

"I didn't mean to do it, John," I wept. My cousin appeared as panic stricken as I felt. Desperate, I rushed to the ladder, descending as swiftly as possible. Several adults on the street had seen Levi fall and cried out for help.

"What happened here?" a sweaty, middle-aged man demanded.

"Joses murdered Levi," the heavy boy, first of the group to scale the ladder behind me, informed him. This was not the first time others had confused my name with my twin's.

"The *momsa* murdered Levi," a heavyset woman screamed as everyone ran off in different directions. No one in a village as small as ours knew for certain what to do during such an emergency. There were no doctors here as there were in larger cities like Capernaum. Indeed, most people didn't even know what the term "doctor" meant.

Eventually, the growing crowd navigated like a wave toward the mayor's house, pounding on his door.

"He's not dead," John sighed with relief after leaning down close to Levi. "Look, Jess. See his breathing?"

"Don't die, Levi," I sobbed. "*Please* don't die." I held Levi in my arms as if comforting a broken bird. His eyes remained misty. I cradled him close, weeping, and rubbed my hands against his body, responding to an instinct that made me want to provide warmth in any way I could. Help Levi, as well as anyone in need and pain.

"Jess," Levi mumbled, slowly returning to consciousness. "Oh, Jess. I'm so sorry I said—"

"*I'm* the one who's sorry. How dare I touch you in anger, under any—"

With the mayor sternly leading them, the crowd of adults and children, numbering more than fifty now, solemnly marched in our direction. "Truly," some self-appointed sage announced, "the devil is in that boy."

"Girl," John corrected them. "And Levi's alright. Look and see." He pointed to where even then I was helping Levi to his feet.

"I thought I was dead, but Jess has brought me back."

That was the first time I can remember Levi's eyes meeting mine with something beyond friendship. It would always be so after.

*Unless Maggie's appearance today changed that. And he has found another girl to dote on. Which, I must admit, causes me to wax jealous.*

*To my own surprise, not only of him. Her, too. Huh! That, I couldn't comprehend. At least, not at the moment.*

"Miracle child!" someone shouted. The mob went wild. Some Nazarenes continued to shriek that I was a murderer. Others danced in joy, insisting this strange child was the Chosen One.

"Let's get *out* of here. Fast!"

"Good idea, John."

We ran back to my house. As we entered, out of breath, Mary and Elizabeth were seated on stools, sharing the job of creating new clothes for their children. My mother, at the wheel, spun, transforming rough, sheared wool into yarn. Her sister, at a nearby loom, wove a tunic for James. They were engaged in small talk, lost in conversation about everyday things that intrigue women, until we burst in.

"What happened?" Mary gasped. The looks on our faces and rumbling on the street left little doubt. Insane with anger, fear, and motiveless guilt, I turned my wrath on her.

"I know what you are," I shrieked. "I know what you did! And I know what *I am*."

"Oh, Jess," she attempted to take me in her arms. I would have none of it, pulling away, inching over to John. He slipped a crooked arm around me. Then Joseph entered through the side door connecting our house to his shop. Sad-eyed, trembling, he deduced what had occurred. "This day has been a long time coming," he sighed.

Mary and Elizabeth bolted the door while Joseph and John reached for tools from their appointed place, readying to use these to defend us. The noise woke Joses. Yawning, he rose from his floor mat, drowsily inquiring as to what might be going on.

Outside, people stormed about. Some shouted nasty epithets. Others fell down on their hands and knees, praying. As darkness set in, they lit torches and paraded back and forth, chanting. Once they'd had enough, one by one the exhausted Nazarenes headed to their homes.

"Start packing," Joseph commanded. "We'll be out of here long before dawn, when they'll likely return."

"Where are we going?" Mary fearfully asked.

"Off to live in the wilderness," the man I had, up until that moment, believed to be my father answered. Where we would remain for the following seven years.

*So beware, Mary of Magdala, the sin of wrath. It solves nothing and only leads to self-destruction.*

*Now, so many years after my moment of madness, I vowed to try and hold myself to that self-same standard . . .*

# 18.

"Hey, Jess."

"Hello, Jude."

Awaiting my return, Joses lounged under a shady pine, atop a hillock rich with green grass and brown earth. I hurried up the rise, kneeling beside him.

"Well, Sister? This better be good!"

"It will be."

For the next half hour, I related all that had occurred, emphasizing any details that Mary would likely question him about. Eventually, I sensed Joseph's growing boredom and condensed as best as I could. At one point, I nudged my twin's arm as he gazed off to where his beloved animals wandered in a nearby pasture.

"Sorry, Jess. Continue, please . . ."

This being the last week in August, we'd soon return to sleeping inside the house that, upon our arrival at the edge of Galilee's wilderness, Joseph and James fashioned from the plentiful limestone. In addition to the one-room house, typical of most Hebraic dwellings, Joseph had added a small shop in back, attached to our dwelling, similar to our situation while still living in the nearby town. Joseph's workplace had two doors, a rarity in Israel, particularly for so small a building. One, on the northern side, allowed him access to the great outdoors that surrounded us. The other, located where our house met his shop, sharing a wall, had been added so that our patriarch could move freely between the workplace and the living area.

So here was my home, and my family. When customers could not pay for stone masonry, repair work, or carpentry with Roman *dinar,* they offered Joseph vegetables and sometimes animals. This helps to explain why we owned so many goats and sheep. The former provided milk and, with processing, cheese. The latter, warm wool for our winter garments. Also, on special occasions, meat.

*Food, glorious food! How I loved indulging myself. Despite recent claims that gluttony constituted one of the deadly sins.*

*Perhaps overeating might be unhealthy. But how could the enjoyment of every last morsel on one's plate cause moral harm?*

When strapped for cash, those who owned orchards paid Joseph with saplings. These included oleander, terebinth, and monk's pepper. Better still were fruit-bearing trees, providing fresh servings daily of lemon, orange, apple, pomegranate, and mulberry. Recently, several olive and date trees had been added.

In Mary's garden, out of sight from Joses and myself here on the hillock, chick peas, garlic, onions, horse beans, and lentils, as well as an array of spices, grew in the rich soil. Several rows of flowers added a dainty touch of beauty that finished off our little corner of the world with abundant color: iris, hyacinth, crocus, and rose of Sharon, this the favorite blossom of most Israelis.

*But back to the food!*

Fishermen living in Capernaum, as well as Bethsaida on the Jordan's eastern side, hired Joseph to repair wooden boats. They paid him with a portion of their catch. Though in-landers, we enjoyed the bounty of the great river's tributaries.

Fish, that is. Though deep inside I secretly desired to know how those succulent Mediterranean shellfish tasted.

"Will you be able to remember all that?"

"I think so. I *hope* so!"

"Me, too. For *both* our sakes."

We rose even as the sun began its downward trek. Now, the distant plain took on a purple hue, adding to the enchantment of the seemingly endless quietude. Joses rounded up his flock while I headed for the house to prepare our evening meal. As I skipped along, I noticed Mary, bent over in the center of her garden, hard at work. My fleeting movement caught her attention.

She paused, glancing over to where I hurried by. "Where were you all day, Jess?"

"Oh, here and there."

*I do not like to lie, so I told a half truth.*

*And felt suitably half guilty for having done so.*

"Oh. That's nice."

I didn't make eye contact, though that had nothing to do with recent events. Since the day of that ball game and Levi's fall from the roof, I tacitly avoided my mother. Never was I openly rude or hostile or disobedient. Should she tender me an order, some task to perform around the house to ease her work load, I nodded and set to it.

"Excuse me. I must get dinner going."

Still, I avoided eye contact for fear of what I might discover there.

*Could what those children have shouted at me on the eve of our departure be true? Had Mary indeed been unfaithful to that wonderful, wise, diligent man who cared so for us? And with one of the conquering Romans?*

*If so, instead of Joseph's blood, which ran directly from King David's, might that of a centurion rush through my veins? The very possibility made my stomach churn.*

So I avoided Mary, despite our proximity. Still hoping that time does heal all wounds, she occasionally tried to strike up a conversation. Then as now, I offered her only my profile and answered pointedly if politely.

From the corner of my eye, I noticed her shoulders sag. How it must have hurt that, after all this time, her daughter could not show her own mother even a modicum of warmth.

# 19.

"This is delicious, Jess," Salome said an hour later.

Each of us had assumed a horizontal position on the earthen floor alongside our wooden table. When not employed in this capacity, it—yet another of Joseph's creations—served, thanks to a flat surface that opened on hinges, as a storage place for clothes and other possessions.

"Glad you like."

There was in this house no space for a cabinet. Each inch of the inner walls served some capacity: the high wood pile, our current evening's food supply, a cistern filled with goat's milk for the little ones' nourishment.

"Remember how you made it so we can have this again."

I smiled at my little sister. Her cheeks were like a pair of ripe apples; her face could melt the snow on one of those high mountains far to the north, which, in my fantasies, I would someday climb, touching the distant snows on Mount Hermon.

"What flavor did you add tonight?" Simon asked.

"Cumin."

We had plenty of spices and herbs in the garden. I could season our stew with a different one for each weekday: nutmeg, pepper, ginger, saffron, thyme, mint, and dill. Each added its own unique taste to our daily bowls of lentils and onions.

"Joses?" Mary asked. "Tell me all about . . ."

Without looking up from his plate, my brother mumbled as much as he could recall of what I'd related. As it was in his self-interest to do so, he gave this little recitation his best shot. "The most important idea that is taught . . .," he began, like me not wishing to lie outright by actually saying that these were words he had personally heard, and so settling on a half-truth. Which is probably worse. While he spoke, I snuck an occasional peek at Mary, to see if our plan had worked. I felt relieved, watching as she hung on his every word.

"I have news," Mary announced once Joses finished. "Several pieces of news, all good."

In those days, there were people who made their living by carrying messages up and down Galilee, running back and forth so that distant friends could exchange information. Mary, taught to read by Joseph, shared his note that he had written two days earlier. Joseph would complete his stonemasonry four days hence. And we were invited to travel northwest and join him in Capernaum.

"I can't wait!" Salome shrieked with joy.

"You're going to have to," James gently informed her. "You aren't old enough for such a trip." She pouted a while, as did Miriam, though both eventually got over it.

"Me?" Simon wanted to know.

"Yes," Mary decided. "You're a big boy now. It's time you traveled on the roads." He roared with delight, then stuck his tongue out at the girls, setting them to bawling.

How wonderful it would be to get away for a while. So few in the working class were able to. Then again, our trip would be humble compared to those of wealthy Hebrews. Such people could afford journeys as far as Egypt, Greece, even the Orient.

"More, more," Miriam called out. "Tell us more."

"Yes, Mary," added James, exhausted from a long day's work on a neighboring farm. "Do!"

"Joseph writes here that the past three weeks have been bountiful beyond expectations. This means we will be able to visit Jerusalem at Passover to attend Temple services."

Everyone shouted with glee. *Jerusalem!* Mary assured the thrilled girls that by springtime, they would be old enough to go along, too.

For me, the thought of seeing the Holy City again, after three long years, exceeded any expectations for future happiness. To visit the mount that David had cleared as a resting place for the Ark of the Covenant? That very spot on which his son Solomon built our first temple. Almost a thousand years ago. Just think of it . . .

I would, in eight months, hear the great priests pray, the rabbi's lecture, perhaps even join them to discuss the law. If, of course, a girl was allowed to offer her opinions.

With dinner done and dishes scrubbed clean, we all climbed up to the roof again, spread out our sleeping mats, and drew the blankets tight. Long after the others had one by one dropped off to sleep, I stared up at the stars, wondering how I would get through the many days between now and *Pesech.*

The answer was not difficult to determine: by diligently studying, absorbing all I could. That way, when the great moment arrived, I would not appear to be another wide-eyed provincial but someone who could speak knowledgably.

More fascinating still, this year the Passover ceremony, according to our Hebrew calendar, would fall on Nissan 13: the precise date of my twelfth birthday.

*Considering recent coincidences in my life, this struck me as one too many for me to believe that things happened owing to mere chance.*

*What was the Arabic term? Oh, of course. Kismet!*

# 20.

"I'm in love with Maggie," Levi announced. "That's the good news."

"I can't say I'm surprised. Now tell me the bad."

"She's crazy for you. Or at least the boy 'Jesus.'"

"How do you know? Did she say so?"

"She didn't have to."

"What *did* she say?"

"Oh, Levi." He mimicked as best he could the voice of a woman in love. "What beautiful blue eyes your friend has."

"I'm hardly a threat to you—"

"She doesn't know your secret."

Panic swept through me. "You wouldn't tell, would you?"

Levi's eyes glimmered with potential mischief. "It certainly would eliminate the competition." Then he laughed and assumed a serious turn. "No! You saved my life, Jess. Seven years ago. Remember—"

"The wind got knocked out of you, nothing more. All I did was help you back up. Lest we forget, I'm the one—"

"*I* betrayed *you*. I'll never do so again."

We exchanged smiles of friendship. Turning the final bend, we approached Zion Synagogue several minutes early this second day of Yeshiva. I spotted Judas and Barabbas waiting for us on the road. We hurried to catch up.

"I must say," Barbabbas announced with a good-natured smile, "what you did yesterday was incredible."

"I would've done the same, but I was too afraid."

"That's okay, Judas. I'll try to refrain from such stuff. After all, I'm here to learn."

Shortly we joined the main group. Everyone stood in the precise places where they'd been the day before, reminding me of what creatures of habit we humans are. The rabbi exited the synagogue and led us in a repetition of our afternoon prayer ritual. Ready for the slur to women, I braced myself for his (and, more terribly, my nation's) harsh judgment.

When prayers were done, we turned and waited for the day's lesson to begin. "We will pick up where we left off yesterday," Annas announced, haughty as I recalled.

Today, he recounted the tale of Cain and Abel, the death of the latter and the former's banishment from the home Adam had fashioned east of Eden, after the fall. Saul sat, central among his cronies. He glanced back at me over his shoulder, waiting to see what this brash "boy" might say today.

Got to keep quiet. Got to!

No matter what, I mustn't get tossed out of school.

"Every tale in the Torah serves a purpose. Not only to recall our history but teach. So! The point here?"

Hands flew up everywhere. As if not to play favorites, the rabbi ignored Saul, calling on another moneyed-class boy.

"Thou shalt not kill, as would later be written in the Covenant."

"Of course," Annas replied, nodding with satisfaction. The youth's words reinforced the rabbi's high opinion of himself as a most effective teacher.

"Rabbi," Saul asked, eager to turn Annas's attention in his direction. "A question, please?" The rabbi signaled for Saul to continue. "This has always confused me. Did David, our king, not kill when he fought Goliath and the Philistines?"

"*Good* question! Happily, I can answer that. But I'd rather see if any of you can do so?" There went my hand again, into the air. A bit disconcerted that mine was the first to be raised, Annas reluctantly signaled to me.

"The Ten Commandments do not tell us thou shalt not kill. Only that we must not murder. Cain murdered his own brother, a kinsman, out of jealousy. Whereas the killing of enemies is righteous, ordained, and sometimes necessary."

Annas appeared taken aback by my articulateness. "That's correct," he admitted.

"Another question, please?" This time it was Barabbas who interrupted, his mighty hand rising like a boxer's clenched fist. "Does this justify the Zealots' actions?"

Barabbas referred to those Hebrews who challenged Rome, some refusing to pay taxes, others employing long, thin, curved blades, modeled on the preferred weapon of Saracen assassins, to murder Caesar's soldiers.

"I would have to say no, Barabbas. How many times has Israel been forced under the yoke of a conquering nation? In the past, some took sport in throwing Hebrews into oil fires if we did not renounce Yahweh and worship their idols. We should be thankful the Romans don't interfere with our religion."

To my surprise, I found myself agreeing with him, at least on this one issue.

"Maybe you're right," Barabbas admitted. "All the same, if they don't back off on the *Tallit,* maybe I'll leave home, join the Zealots, and help to kill our conquerors!"

Saul now turned his angry eyes on Barabbas. Most likely, he would do so with any among us who dared challenge whatever position the rabbi expressed.

"May I ask a question?" Judas timidly waved a hand while involuntarily twitching his neck. This sparked a round of cruel laughter from Saul's clique. Still, Annas signaled permission. "After Abel is dead, and Cain banished to the land of Nod, we are told he meets people, lives with them, and marries?" Annas nodded. "But . . . where did they come from? If Adam was the first man, how could there be others, with a town of their own?"

Annas's face turned white. This was his first teaching assignment. He'd been caught off guard. Without a viable answer, he stumbled to cover himself. "We're out of time. I'll address that at some time in the future."

He turned, brushed past several boys, and disappeared into the synagogue. Everyone, even those aristocrats loyal to Saul, sensed the rabbi's failure. Perhaps I was not the only one to learn something here. Experts who studied in Jerusalem were not necessarily as knowledgeable as we had been led to believe.

# 21.

"Levi said I'd find you here."

I'd been dozing in the wilderness near my home, waiting for Joses to join me and change outfits before I returned to the house to prepare dinner. Startled by the unexpected sound of a female voice, I rose, still half asleep. Maggie had made the short trip north from Nazareth. Earlier in the day, Levi explained she'd found lodging there with her uncle's family.

"Oh! I didn't expect—"

Maggie stood proudly, hands on hips, wearing a fine-spun linen sheath. The cloth had been patterned with varied shades of green, a color that Phoenicians held as sacred as we Hebrews did blue. Over her shoulders hung the *saddin*, a dark, wool shawl designed to suggest discreteness, yet also a touch of mystery on the part of any female who chose to wear one.

"Of course you didn't."

Everything else remained the same: the graceful lines of her form, the penetrating black pupils of the eyes. Now I also became aware of a subtle smile hinting that, young as she was, this girl somehow knew more about life than most adults.

"Well, it's great to see you again."

Levi, I realized, must have told her of my thinking place: a glen deep in those pines that lined the pasturelands. Here, sheep and goats, sensing safety, wandered and grazed. All around me, wildflowers formed a natural bed. God and nature had, so far as I was concerned, created an enchanting recluse where a girl (me) could be alone with her personal thoughts.

After returning from school I'd come directly here, still wearing male attire, my hair covered by the hood.

"Levi told me you were feeling down?"

"It's been a difficult day," I admitted. Together, we strolled through a cluster of pine trees, their robust scent presaging the approach of autumn. Maggie pressed the issue. I confided to her about the rabbi's inability to provide Judas with a suitable answer to his question.

"I felt so disappointed. He's supposed to be a wise man."

Often I'd pondered Judas's controversial inquiry myself during Joseph's telling of the story around our dinner table. Intrigued, Maggie admitted there were details in her nation's origination tale, handed down from a seafaring tribe, that did not strike her as logical. "Still, I've always loved the story . . . as a story."

"I should also accept the tale as just that," I shrugged. "Maybe Adam wasn't the first man ever. Merely first in a line that would lead to my own people."

"That makes sense. In our version, the first man and woman were Phoenicians."

"Perhaps every nation believes itself to be the be-all and end-all. And that the history of humankind begins with them."

Maggie gently took my hand, holding it warmly. We wandered aimlessly about in the soft breeze. Soon, I knew, I must join Joses and switch clothes.

"You still look concerned. Anything else on your mind?"

"Actually, yes."

I rambled on about the rabbi's daily prayer. And how, in addition to giving our thanks to Yahweh, Annas repeated that odious refrain about the female. "He thanked God that he was a man. What a terrible slight to women everywhere."

"Interesting," Maggie noted, raising an eyebrow.

"How could my nation, so wise in so many ways, accept such a notion?"

"How fascinating that you, a boy, would be upset by it."

*Careful, Jess! You're going to give yourself away . . .*

"Any person who believes in fairness would react as I did. Male or female."

"That's the way it should be, certainly. But how humans react, Jess, and how they ought to, are two different things." Maggie's eyes confronted me as she added: "Anyway, *I* agree."

"Well? That's something."

"If I understand correctly, this caused you to doubt that your Hebrew way is right?"

"Yes. Or, at least, if it's right for *me*. Maggie, I know so little about your people. Do Phoenicians think similarly?"

Maggie laughed loudly. "No, no, no. Our faith has always been organized around Astarte, the great goddess. We worship many other women as well, including her sister Anath. There are male gods, too. But our wisest deities are female."

How strange it made me feel to realize another nation's religion, which we Hebrews considered to be pagan, was to my way of thinking more correct. At least on this particular issue.

# 22.

Maggie reached into her purse and drew out a medallion. An engraved image portrayed an unclothed woman leaning back against a tree. Unashamed to go naked in the world, the female's hair blew wild and free with the wind. A snake coiled about her, binding this girl to the sturdy oak.

"This is the symbol of our faith. We believe in the goodness of nature. For Phoenicians, God is nature, and nature is a woman. A great Mother. Our men believe this as deeply as do our women."

*This figure resembles Lilith, our image of evil. Also Eve, encountering the tree and the snake.*

*Might my nation have formed our vision of evil from earlier people's concept of good by reversing their values?*

"You find salvation in the forests?" She nodded affirmatively. "Mine do so by walling out nature, particularly from our holy places."

"What do you Jews fear to encounter there?" she asked, returning the medallion to her bag.

"The Beast. A horned thing that exists at the center of darkness, somewhere in the wilderness. The worst daemon of all, tempting mankind to leave civilization and return to the old ways."

"By 'old ways,' do you mean my people's ways?" I nodded that this was so. "Huh! Our gods and goddesses all live in the woods, mainly in the branches of trees."

"Our one God, Yahweh, is a male. He lives in the sky, high above all wickedness below."

"Like Jupiter to the Romans?"

"Yes. And Zeus to the Greeks. Sun gods."

"Nations like my own believe in the moon goddess. Some call her Hecate—"

"But, Maggie. Which way do *you* think gets it right?"

"Jess! How would I know? You're the student. Me? A cleaning maid for my uncle. Not much, I admit. Still, better than being out on the streets." An invisible cloud passed over her pretty face. "At least, when he isn't drunk."

Panic engulfed me. "Maggie, you must hurry out of there—"

"Where would I go?"

"I don't know. Levi and I will figure something out."

"Let's give it some time. Maybe I'm overreacting."

I attempted to dissuade her from returning to her uncle's home, but Maggie remained firm on the subject. Following a long, awkward pause, our discussion turned back to what many young people think about: the meaning of life and where one might start the search to hopefully discover it.

"Being a Hebrew, and believing as your people do, why do I find you out here, surrounded by nature?" She had me there. I gazed around, seeing only beauty and goodness. "Don't think you must answer," she continued. "I was just wondering."

"I'm wondering about that, too."

I told Maggie that I must leave her now, to complete chores at the house. I didn't say that my job was to cook, such work assigned solely to our women.

"Jess," she asked, her voice mellow. "May I see you, talk to you again? Soon?"

This time, she held both my hands. While part of me feared that being so close might allow her to see through my masquerade, I had determined to learn from Maggie. Already, I cared deeply for her, sensing that like Levi she would be a close friend forever.

So I said yes.

"Wonderful!"

Maggie rose up on her toes and brushed her lips against mine, offering a kiss so appealingly innocent I had no idea how to respond. The experience, brief and unexpected, struck me as charmingly, if surprisingly, pleasing.

Maggie winked. She turned and headed back down the path leading to the village, without glancing back. When she was gone from sight, I likewise turned and headed toward the spot where I was to daily meet with Joses.

# 23.

"I can't tell you, John, how terrific it is to see you."

"I feel the same way. We may only be cousins, but I've always felt closer to you than my own brothers and sisters."

Elizabeth, Mary's older sister, resembled my mother but thinner and taller. She and her son John, nine months my senior, had the night before completed the forty-minute walk from their home in northern Bethlehem. Excited at having some company, Mary instructed James to kill a chicken for dinner, much to everyone's delight. This was a special occasion meal.

"It's the same for me," I admitted as we continued our conversation and cleaned up after dinner. "I can't explain it."

"Some things are better left unexplained."

*I felt what those in the Far East would call a magical connection to John. So, too, did he with me.*

*Always, we had considered each other siblings of the soul.*

The next morning we rose earlier than usual to begin our trek to Capernaum, this city two full days travel in a northeasterly direction. Joses had planned on coming but, at the last moment, rolled over and went back to sleep. Before dozing again, he offered to watch over the home fires. James planned to remain behind and care for the girls, also completing a farming job he'd already begun. Mary, Elizabeth, Simon, John, and myself bid them farewell and stumbled along our footpath to the Roman road, leading from our remote hamlet to the wide world.

As my little brother clung close to his mom, John and I walked several yards ahead. We spoke excitedly about everything that had happened since we'd last been together, the exception being my secret identity. Still, I couldn't resist raising issues that had come to fascinate me.

"John, I love living in the natural world. Might I be possessed by a daemon, though unaware of it?"

"If so, Jess, I must be, too. Like you, I love to slip away from Bethlehem and lose myself in the forest."

My cousin was the only person in my family who had always seemed as concerned with concepts larger than ordinary, everyday issues as I myself had always been. So I was comfortable telling him: "I know this may sound blasphemous, but I feel closest to God when I'm lying in the grass, surrounded by wildflowers."

"Me, too. I wouldn't mind living in the wilderness, sleeping beneath a knotty old tree."

"Not here," I teased, considering the ruggedness of the terrain we currently crossed. "You'd dry up and blow away."

"Alright, then. Maybe I'll live along the River Jordan someday. And who needs a house? Why not sleep under the stars?"

"As to that? I know our wise men claim the night is wicked. Then, pagans dance wildly around trees in the eerie lunar light, their bodies naked. Yet I *love* those hours. Staring up, wondering what the stars are, and how we are connected to them."

John hesitated before speaking again. "I've never admitted this to anyone, but sometimes I notice the stars leaving their courses, moving about in different directions."

I experienced a slight shock. "I thought it was just me! Either I imagined it or perhaps I'm crazy. Do you recall how many?"

"Seven. They swerve from Orion, past the brightness of Sirius, down to our planet. The three largest lead the way."

"So I'm *not* mad."

"Mmmmmmm . . . maybe you are, and I am, too."

"Or perhaps we notice things others miss."

"Let's keep this our secret for now."

"Agreed!"

"Jess," John continued, changing the direction of our talk, "you do know who established our most basic values?"

"Of course. Abraham."

"The founder of our religion. But that wasn't always his name."

"No. He was born Abram."

John nodded. "A member of the Harran tribe, far to the north. Pagans. Then, one day, he rose up and left, walking south to Canaan. He married, had children, and in time founded our nation. Everything we have faith in derives from his teachings. It was he who announced that the things he'd grown up believing were good—nature, trees, snakes, women—are actually evil."

"How long ago, John, do you believe that was?"

"Five thousand years, some say. Maybe longer still."

"To think that here we are now, wondering if perhaps he was wrong about everything, even as he once questioned if the people he was descended from were misguided."

"The inspiration came to him from Yahweh. Our God whispered in Abram's ear while he slept. 'Go forth and found a new nation.'"

"The Chosen People."

"Us. Hebrews."

"Would you consider me self-important if I admitted that sometimes I believe Yahweh whispers to me, informing this small girl from Galilee that she, like others who have come and gone before, must in time embark on just such a mission?"

"How can I find you self-important," John replied, "when I myself have experienced such thoughts since childhood?"

# 24.

Our little party reached a pasture at once wide and deep, its fresh grass smelling sweet. In contrast to this setting's natural charm, we observed evidence of man's intrusive presence here. Three Hebrews had recently been hoisted high on towering wood crosses. There was no need to provide succor; all were dead. Crows and ravens hovered, cawing and picking at the rotting corpses. The most we could do was pay respect to fellow Jews who, we knew, remained true to their principles.

We stopped and humbly prayed for the dead, hoping Yahweh would provide them with a considerably better existence in the next life than they had under Roman rule.

*If there is an afterlife. Admit it to yourself, Jess. There are times when you wonder.*

*Not that our Bible is specific about it. Still, we trust that there is greater force above, beyond, and all around we mere mortals. Out there, somewhere.*

We gathered together to recite, in Aramaic, the *Kaddish*: "Have mercy on them, pardon all their transgressions. Shelter their souls in the shadow of Thy wings."

*How did the one who long ago composed those lines know that Yahweh has wings?*

*Did he see God, perhaps on a descent, and note this down so generations later we would have an image of our Lord?*

*But some say that to see God is to die.*

*Others that He has no physical form. Is everywhere and nowhere at the same time.*

*Sometimes, I grow so confused . . .*

John also solemnly spoke *El Maleh Rachamim*: "God, filled with mercy, bring proper rest . . . illuminate the brilliance of your skies with the souls of our beloved who went to their eternal rest."

*Is this then the nature of the stars, what they are, why they shimmer, how they come into being?*

*Is each star the shining soul of a Hebrew who has passed?*

Privately, I renewed my request to God that I would not die in this horrible manner. How guilty it made me feel, though, to be in the presence of those so altruistic in their beliefs, while John and I had recently expressed concern, even doubt, about several of our nation's fundamental precepts.

Not as to Yahweh! The existence of a single force that shaped the cosmos? I could never question this. Only whether some of the ways in which we worshipped Him were valid.

*And, following my secret talk with Maggie, whether He might, as the Phoenicians claimed, possibly be a She.*

*Or, as I wondered after she left, an It, combining both sexes. Or, on the other hand, existing beyond earthly notions of gender?*

John and I fell silent after that, each trusting that we'd talk more in the following days. Meanwhile, we continued to maintain a distance beyond Simon and the women, boldly leading the way.

"There is so much to think upon, John."

"Yes. And to talk of, together."

Some hours later, the roadway passed through a thick forest. A stag, wandering about aimlessly, froze in his tracks when he sensed the presence of people. His head turned in our direction, doubtless wondering if we were friend or foe. The horned creature, so noble in his silence, returned my thoughts to the apparent goodness of nature. How could anyone possibly believe this beautiful beast to be evil? Its horns notwithstanding.

On the other hand, even in the presence of such a seductive world, a dark side existed. Here we must always remain vigilant for snakes. While most weren't dangerous, some poisonous vipers made their nests in the fallow earth.

I wondered again about the snake on that medallion Maggie had revealed to me. Were these legless creatures truly wicked? If so, then the Phoenicians who worshipped them must be evil.

Yet for me, Maggie, so positive and good, refuted that. Perhaps they were evil only in my people's way of seeing snakes and the world around us. If that were the case, then the evil existed not in snakes, but in our perceptions of them.

As evening set in, we reached the town of Magdala. Larger than Nazareth or Bethlehem, and once considered an important center of trade, this Phoenician community had been dwarfed into oblivion with the completion of Capernaum.

From a distance, the first building visible to us was its famed tower: such a structure to be expected in other kingdoms, rare on Hebraic land. And nothing less than startling to me personally. For I now approached the very tower I had seen in my dream.

# 25.

As to Magdala's Hebrew synagogue, the building stood two kilometers south of the city proper. This allowed comfortable distance from gentiles who mostly occupied the area. Hebrews passing by could spend the night in this solid building, then move on without needing to come into contact with Phoenicians. Owing to my family's progressive attitudes, this didn't trouble us at it might more conservative Jews.

Like other members of our nation, my family received an enthusiastic welcome by the keepers. Though we arrived too late for dinner, they generously fixed a cold meal according to the code of hospitality: No Hebrew must ever allow a kinsman to go to bed hungry so long as he has something to share.

Early the following morning we were fed melons, figs, dates fresh-baked bread, and goat's milk. With the arrival of a rabbi, all in attendance stepped outside, faced southerly, and recited the morning prayers. Owing to a decision I'd made following my classes, I hung my head low during rote repetition of lines expressing women's inferiority, written not by Yahweh but by men.

My sincere interest returned when the prayer once again expressed what I did believe: the greatness and glory of God, and our everlasting ten-rule Covenant with Him/Her/It.

We bid farewell to other families with whom we'd joined in camaraderie. Everyone assured everyone else that we would somehow, someday see each other again. All the while knowing this likely wouldn't occur. Sailors from the Mediterranean had an expression for such moments that touched me: like ships that pass in the night.

As a child, I'd vowed to hold the faces of people who stopped at our home, sipping water at the well, so firmly in mind I would never forget them. Joses laughed and called me sentimental. At night, after slipping onto my mat and curling in my blanket, I allowed memories of those ever accumulating faces to pass, one by one, silently repeating their names.

As the years went by, images of individuals faded into one another, no matter how hard I tried to keep each separate and vivid. Eventually, most dissolved into a mélange. That, I was gradually learning, is the way of the world.

"I can't stop thinking about what we spoke of yesterday," I said to John after we'd set off again, with but a few hours remaining until we reached Capernaum and Joseph.

"Me, too, Jess. Our Torah states that Earth and all else was created in six days, then Yahweh rested. But back in Bethlehem, a family of Canaanites bought a house near ours. I learned much from them. In their version of the Creation Story, their greatest god, Baal, is assisted by a female. A goddess, Balaat. If I understood correctly, these deities gave birth to the cosmos, as a man and woman might a child."

I mulled this over. "Perhaps that explains why such people hold women in a higher regard than we Hebrews do."

"Exactly! If in our history's first tale Yaweh gives birth alone, then what is the worth of a woman? All stories to follow, beginning with Lilith and Eve, on through to Jezebel, derive from that—*our*—explanation of creation."

"Want to know something? I wish ours were more like theirs on this point. Then women, myself included, would be respected. All the same, I was born a Hebrew."

"You will not, then, wander away from the faith, as a small number of kinsman have, and embrace another?"

"Never."

"How then will you deal with this difficulty?"

"I'd like to change things. Our religion has altered so since its birth with Abraham 5,000 years ago, then again with Moses 1,500 years before our contemporary life. I don't see why such a sea change can't occur once more, particularly at a time when the world around us is rapidly changing."

"For the sake of argument, what would you alter?"

"Truthfully? Just about everything would be up for consideration, excluding the Ten Commandments."

"They really are our essence. What makes us Yahweh's Chosen. The only nation with a God-given code of conduct."

"I've begun to wonder if perhaps Yahweh's idea was not, as some believe, to separate ourselves from others and, in isolation, abide by those values."

"What then?"

"Perhaps we are chosen in another way: To go out into the world and convince nation after nation that, their varied religions, languages, and temporal laws aside, our Covenant ought to also be central to their lives."

"Much like the Samarians. Or what are they called now?"

"Samaritans. I've never been able to accept our nation's rejection of them owing to their mixed bloodlines. Didn't Moses marry a woman of African descent?"

"True. And Samarians do devotedly accept our Covenant."

"They should be embraced fully as brothers and sisters."

"You'd have a hard time convincing most Hebrews of that."

"The difficult things in life are the most worthy."

# 26.

"Joses was right, Coz. You are a sentimentalist."

"Perhaps. When I was only three, and we still lived in the village, I watched in horror as Nazarenes slaughtered a lamb.

The most innocent creature imaginable. For Yahweh, they said. As its blood ran, I became ill. I couldn't fathom why, if our Lord is as kind and fair as we are told, he would want to see such a gentle thing butchered? Robbed of the life that Yahweh granted it? Incredibly, this done in Yahweh's name."

"Do you then suggest eliminating animal offerings as our ancestors did with human sacrifice?"

"Well? Isn't such a change long overdue?"

Briefly, John waxed silent. "Jess, do you ever wonder if you might have been born for a higher purpose than merely trudging through life from one day to the next?"

"I'd imagine every human wonders about that. Perhaps it's only false pride. Some delusion of grandeur?"

"Vanity."

"I so do not want to give into such shallowness. Still, in answer to your question, yes. I do."

"I'm relieved to hear that. You see, so do I."

We turned a bend and spotted Capernaum a short distance ahead. How incredibly high the buildings, many constructed in the Roman style, stretched far up into the air. I found myself walking faster, eager to partake of this city's riches.

But John wasn't yet ready to drop our discussion. "Things have gone terribly for our people since the return from Babylon. Instead of enjoying the joys of freedom in those years before the Romans arrived, our nation lapsed into a deep collective depression that remains with us still."

"We ought to move on and relish life again. Many priests claim that sinking into such sadness is a form of sin."

"How could it be avoided? The Bible, finally written down while in Babylon, is closed. No more stories to come. The great days? Behind us. We exist in a state of constant melancholy."

"Not truly living, only surviving?"

"Those are the very words I was searching for."

"It doesn't have to be that way."

"No, not if someone decides it's time we all stopped moping around and *do* something."

"The other day, I told my friend Levi that God helps those who help themselves. I don't know where that came from—"

"Well, it's what I've been thinking about lately."

"But, John! Where do we look for a leader to bring us out of our mental desert?"

"Jess, think! What were we just talking about? Why not you or me?"

"No matter what dreams we have for ourselves, we must remember: we're a pair of peasants, living in what the Jews of Jerusalem call 'the middle of nowhere.'"

"The Torah says that, in time, our Savior will enter the Holy City mounted on an ass, the most humble of animals. And that the rider will be a simple man. A peasant."

"That leaves me out! I mean, the 'man' part. So perhaps it is you? Yes, I could believe that."

"I live in northern Bethlehem. According to prophecies, the next messiah must be a resident of Nazareth. Born in Bethlehem, but raised in your village."

"Even as Joses and I were? Well, I'll keep an eye out for his arrival, not that I visit my village often."

"Perhaps you need merely look into a mirror."

John's words touched me. And flattered me. Still, I feared that, considering my dubious bloodline, it might be best to consider such thoughts mere vanity, as John had put it, and instead set out on a search for our savior.

For now, though, the time for thinking on any such subjects would be set aside. We had reached our journey's end.

# 27.

The Roman road curved to meet with Capernaum's main street. A gem of a city, the Hellenistic triumph had been constructed atop the northern end of our sea. This metropolis, three times the size of Magdala, featured architecture in the Greco-Roman fashion. Solid columns lined every important building. The exteriors, embellished with open-air pavilions, made our own thick-walled residences appear primitive.

"Oh, John," I sighed. "It's spectacular."

He nodded solemnly. "Sometimes, living where we do, it's easy to forget what wonders the world offers."

We stepped through the great gates, into the city proper. Capernaum's streets, wider than any I'd seen, were filled with a variety of people from many lands and differing classes, all rapidly moving in every direction. I experienced a pleasurable chill at the sight of seemingly endless shops crowded together. Some were housed in small buildings, painted in garish colors so as to attract the eyes of passersby. Others were located in tents of the type belonging to the Bedouins, mysterious nomads of the vast Arabian land of sand, sand, more sand, and little else.

Everywhere I looked, some flash of movement caught my eye. Men in orange robes sold food and wine. Elderly women stood behind table after table of clothing and jewelry, baskets of vegetables, and small scrolls, hawking their wares. Momentarily, I became so intoxicated with my splendid surroundings that I all but forgot our purpose: head directly for the synagogue where Joseph awaited us.

"Jess? John?" Mary called out, approaching from behind. "Can you spot the building? We must find—"

"Not to worry. I've been here before. Up this street and around, following a corner. After that, two more blocks—"

"You lead the way then, John," Elizabeth said. Simon, starry-eyed at the array of people, as well as animals and goods for sale, plus so many byways to explore, hurried close and seized my hand. The child's eyes opened wide with that unique wonder displayed by the very young. And, in rare cases, the very old.

I held back as John stepped forward. We followed him single file, winding our way through thick crowds. Individuals walked, ran, and jogged, everyone in some tremendous hurry. How different from Nazareth, where nobody appeared to have any important place to go.

*How wonderful it would be to see Joseph again! He had only been away for a few weeks.*

*Sometimes, his absence lasted three months. However long, I dearly missed him.*

"Oh!"

I halted as something unexpected caught my eye. In a plaza, one of many on either side of the street, a great white statue rose up out of a fountain. Spouts sent water flying outward, much of the liquid collecting in a pool within the structure's marble rim. Several nozzles sprayed droplets further, into the crowd, briefly refreshing some of the sun-smoldering passersby.

"Isn't that *incredible*?" John called back over his shoulder.

More than the fountain, with its ability to spread delightfully cool wetness thanks to modern machinery, the statue riveted me: an elevated marble replica of a young man, his features perfect, curly hair blown all about by a wind that had been imagined by the artist. This figure stood with great dignity on a chariot, pulled by four stallions. He wore a dazzling breastplate fit for a king and a helmet to match. Frozen in the time and space of art, the heroic male held tight to the reins as his steeds pushed on to their destination.

However aesthetically pleasing this might be to the eye of any onlooker, that was not what gave me pause. For here was my recent dream of myself as a male, captured in stone for the visual enlightenment of all.

# 28.

"Helios."

"Excuse me?"

I turned at the sound of a melodious voice and found myself face to face with the most beautiful boy I'd ever seen. I say beautiful because that term most accurately described him: facial features too strikingly chiseled from flesh and blood by God or nature to be referred to merely as handsome. He truly was gorgeous, though that hardly detracted from an overall sense of easygoing masculinity. I guessed him to be a year or two older than me. Likely, he was Greek or Roman. The oily, black hair, strong nose, and powerful yet graceful build recalled strapping athletes who often passed by our house, pausing at the well for liquid refreshment.

None, though, struck me quite as he did. Particularly, this boy's brown eyes, apparently full of amusement at some grand joke to which he alone knew the punchline. In that, he might have been a gentile version of Barabbas.

"I said, 'Helios.'"

Mary and Elizabeth hurried up to my side, fearing this big city boy might mistake me for a rube, easily taken advantage of moments after arriving here. Instantly aware of their mutual concern, he chuckled good-naturedly.

"What does Helios mean?" Simon asked as John, realizing we were no longer tagging along behind, hurriedly backtracked.

"The sun," said the youth, looking smart and stylish in a tight, white peplum of the type favored by Greeks for casual wear. He leaned down, meeting my little brother's open face with a broad smile. "That marvelous fellow up there riding the chariot? He's our sun god. More correctly, I should say, a Titan."

"What's a Titan?"

"Mmmmmmm . . . similar to the gods, only older."

"There's only one God," Simon bluntly stated, "and his name is Yahweh."

"Oh," the youth replied. "You are Hebrews then?"

Simon nodded, then glanced up again at the elegant, marble statue shining in the bright sunlight. "If he were a god, and not just a . . ."

"Titan."

"Uh-huh. What would his name be then?"

"Apollo."

"Come on," John interrupted, in no mood to let such a waste of time continue. "We've got to be going."

"Where are you headed to?" the youth asked.

"The synagogue," I boldly ventured. A girl . . . a *mere* girl, as some might say . . . would be expected in a situation such as this to remain demurely silent. The Hebrew way was to allow the oldest male present to do the talking for all.

"Oh, it's right up the road a bit," the beautiful Greek said. Nodding for us to follow, he set off at once, making his way through the crowd like Moses clearing a path for his people through the Sea of Reeds. "What's your name?" he turned and asked of me, following along behind him, thoroughly entranced.

"My daughter's name, young man, is none of your business," Mary piped in, protectively stepping between myself and the boy.

"Jess," I dared announce, not knowing what caused me to be so forward.

"I'm Luke. My family lives in Caesarea Maritima, on the western coast. We've traveled here on business—"

"Thanks for your help," John coldly told him. "I will lead my family from here."

"It's no bother," Luke laughingly responded.

Sincere so far as I could tell, his manner relaxed us. We'd been warned to be wary of strangers in a town populated mostly by non-Jews. Thugs lurked near the city gates, full of mischief for naïve and unwary visitors. But I noticed an aura of quality about Luke as to his bearing, clothing, and tone of voice, which seemed to silently whisper, "Trust me!"

"Really, you needn't worry," he continued. "I only hope to be of help to strangers in a strange land."

"And why," Mary asked suspiciously, "of all the many strangers entering Capernaum today did you decide to bless *us*?"

Luke's head angled toward me. I could tell that he, like other males, found himself mesmerized by my presence. Though not yet twelve, I wasn't so oblivious that I failed to grasp how men of all ages took notice when I passed by.

*I don't say that out of self-pride.*

*Only honesty.*

I was slender in a way people found attractive. Perhaps, when not attempting to pass myself off as my brother, I did purposefully move to emphasize what I knew to be my strongest features. I didn't plan to. It just happened.

*Remember, Jess: beware always what John calls vanity.*

"No reason," Luke fibbed to Mary. Now, it was my turn to smirk. He noticed and grinned. "Anyway, I'm harmless. Why, I'm a student, on my way home from school."

"What do you study?" I asked, not anxious to allow the conversation to end.

"Medicine." He slapped the large goatskin bag hanging from a shoulder strap by his side. "Here are the tools of my trade."

"What's 'medicine?'" Simon asked, his hand clutching mine.

"The skill of a doctor," Luke explained. "One who cares for the sick and lame."

"You mean like a rabbi?" Simon asked.

"Our people have God, prayers, and faith," I told my little brother. "The Greeks rely on highly skilled and trained people."

"Why don't we have them, too?"

"It's not our way," John added.

"Their way sounds good," Simon said. "Don't you think so, Jess?"

*From the mouths of babes, someone once claimed, we hear the voice of wisdom.*

"Perhaps the two ways might be combined into one," Luke suggested.

Before I could respond, such intriguing talk came to an abrupt conclusion as we turned a bend and found ourselves facing the synagogue.

# 29.

"Hello, my beloved family."

Releasing my hand, Simon ran to his father. Joseph scooped the boy up in his arms, lavishing kisses on the child's forehead. Simon squealed with delight. I held back until Elizabeth and Mary circled around me to stand by Joseph on either side. Mary embraced her husband, kissing him gently on either cheek. A moment later, Elizabeth repeated the gesture. Elizabeth's restraint was proper for a sister-in-law, as that role had been defined within our culture. On the other hand, many Hebrew wives would have demonstrated more delight than Mary.

Her embrace, to my mind, resembled that of a sibling.

"And my beautiful daughter. How you've matured in the past weeks! I almost didn't recognize you."

As always, Joseph's voice deeply touched me. I hurried to his side and hugged him, hoping the sincerity of my love would be felt through his wool tunic. Despite the heat, such a garment was necessary to protect his skin while chiseling and cutting ragged limestone.

"How wonderful it is to see you again!"

*I so wanted to call him father. Yet I couldn't bring myself to.*

*Not since the day when, as a child, I came to understand what people meant by the term* Momsa.

Yet how impressive and unique a man this was! Though he had heard all the rumors, Joseph always treated Joses and myself as he did his other children. Not that anyone in our household had ever openly addressed the issue. Always, though, it remained the elephant in the room.

How rare for a man to have stood by his accused wife as Joseph had for a dozen years. Most Hebrews, upon learning that their intended was 'of child' and almost certainly not by him would have ordered her to be stoned to death.

*That was another of my people's "ways" that never struck me as fair. Didn't the Seventh Commandment say "Thou shalt not covet thy neighbor's wife?"*

*If so, shouldn't it be the male responsible for such a pregnancy who ought to be stoned?*

"Thank you for inviting us to join you here," John said, at last stepping forward.

"I've eagerly anticipated this vacation for so long. You gave me something to look forward to while pounding rocks."

Pulling away while holding back tears, I noticed again what I always saw when I looked upon the face of Joseph: perennially sad eyes, blue like mine, if not so bright. Also, as Joseph had said of me, he looked older. His shoulders sagged low, likely from exhausting labor. His hair rippled with silver beyond what I recalled. The flesh of his face and arms had grown splotchy, white and red patches scattered up and down his brown legs.

Always, I promised myself, I must be thankful for the time I have left with this fine man. We don't like to think about such things. Still, nobody lives forever.

*More on that later, believe me . . .*

John shook Joseph's hand as a growing boy was expected to greet his uncle. Still holding Simon high, now hoisting his son up over his shoulders as Simon held tight to Joseph's hair, our patriarch turned to step inside, each of us following. At last, Joseph noticed the presence of a stranger hovering nearby.

"Hello, sir. My name is Luke." My beautiful Greek stepped forward and politely took Joseph's hand. Bewildered, the aging Hebrew considered each of our faces, hoping someone might care to explain.

"He took it upon himself," I volunteered when no one else did, "to make certain we located the synagogue. And you."

Joseph cast a smile of appreciation in Luke's direction, then glanced over at Mary. She rolled her eyes, casting them at me, then over to Luke. Joseph's own eyes made clear he understood what his wife had wordlessly communicated. "Well, young man," he announced, "thank you for that. Now we must enter into our home away from home. With a little luck, perhaps we'll see you again."

Joseph stepped through the stone-laced entranceway, a welcoming Hebrew letter carved into either side, and into the structure, bowing low as he did owing to this man's considerable height. John followed, and then Mary and Elizabeth, as was proper for women. I lagged behind for as long as I dared. If anything else were to pass between Luke and myself, it must be now. And he had to speak first.

"I'd hate to have to rely on luck to see you again."

"Remarkable men," I answered, twirling about so that my devastating eyes would confront him, "make their own luck."

My boldness must have threatened Luke, as now he appeared uncertain as to what he ought to say next.

Come on . . . you can do it . . . don't be intimidated by me . . . my eyes . . . my shape . . . as other men are.

"If I may ask," Luke whispered, this tallish boy leaning down a little closer to my face than was proper, "do you have any idea what your family might be doing tomorrow?"

"If the weather holds, we're planning a picnic on the beach south of the fishing wharves."

"When?"

"Late afternoon."

Luke was about to say something more. Abruptly, I turned and entered. I could sense him continuing to observe my every move until the synagogue door slammed closed.

# 30.

Thank you, Yahweh, I silently prayed first thing after rising the next morning, for seeing to it that the good weather held.

Waking early, I peered through the latticework covering a window and knew the day would be just right for our picnic. The question now was whether or not Luke would show. Deep down, I trusted that he would. Yet my mind set to work manufacturing wild fabrications as to how my beautiful Greek could be waylaid. Bad men might beat him while attempting to steal his medical supplies as Luke hurried to meet me. A gorgeous Samarian could enchant him with her perfumes and veils, dragging Luke off to her lair. What if his parents announced that their plans had changed and the entire family must leave Capernaum at once?

*I convinced myself that we were never to meet again. Oh, how this female enjoyed wallowing in the misery of such romantic drivel!*

*Future reader, please note: Though I may have been a messiah in the making, at age eleven I remained a girly-girl at heart. And, to a degree, always would.*

All through the night, I'd barely slept what with worrying keeping me awake. Naturally, then, I dozed off even as the others yawned at the first hint of light. I'd spend my morning continuing to fret over something that hadn't happened while the family set out on a tour of Capernaum, Joseph gleefully serving as our guide.

How eagerly he anticipated sharing with us this wondrous place, with its great marketplace. Mighty caravans deposited merchandise carried by ships from India and China, Italy and Greece to our port cities, continuing to Capernaum by camel. Shortly, their humped backs would be loaded to capacity with Israeli produce: olives, grains, salted fish, pickled figs, and fresh oranges, all stored in immense vats for the return journey, its first stretch overland and then continuing on by sea.

How sophisticated it all seemed, so long before I embarked on treks to the most fabled cities in the world. Perhaps more than anything, what I would take away from my life's experiences was that everything is relative. People and places, cultures and religions, can only be understood in relationship to and contrast with others.

*But away from my mind's eye, back to the present moment.*

First, we picked our way over a trail of uneven rocks, crushed hay, and worn chunks of cobblestone while entering the vast area known as the marketplace. There a horde of grazing animals lifted their heads at the sound of arriving tourists. Beasts of burden and luxurious pets stood on display in long rows of makeshift stables and crude pens. The creatures on view here included asses, cattle, goats, and sheep, all native to Galilee. Also, rare beasts I'd never seen before, only heard of: majestic Persian horses trotting around in an exclusive corral as their stern trainer slapped his whip; several lean Assyrian dogs barking at exotic Egyptian cats.

I was taken aback by the virtual zoo. Here, a caged African leopard, as rare as it was beautiful. There, a mountain goat, wandering about loose, ignored owing to its ordinariness. Each has a life, endowed by Yahweh. And each, like every human, believes his or her life to be the most valuable in existence. Whether men slap a price tag on its rump for one dinar or one thousand.

*Remember that always! In the privacy of its own mind, every living thing believes itself to be the center of the universe.*

*This will become ever more important as my tale unfolds.*

The mixture of the common and the unknown fascinated me. For someone who has never seen a simple goat, this would, like the leopard to me, appear extraordinary.

So much for the spectacular sights. A foul scent rose from the ever-increasing dung piles, overpowering Simon. As his face turned crimson, the child begged us to quickly move on.

"Can we go back to the synagogue, Jess? It smells so—"

I held Simon's hand tight as we hurried along. "In just a moment, we'll pass through this section, and that terrible smell will be gone."

"Here!" Joseph, noticing Simon's state of nausea, called out. "Follow me."

Our patriarch pushed his way through the crowd toward a gate leading into an adjoining area. The rest of us struggled among the sweat-drenched throng, trying not to lose the member of our company most familiar with this city. We wove our way through multi-colored mobs, finding ourselves in front of an open-air pavilion reserved for expensive furniture and other household items, all intended for wealthy clients. The family paused at each booth, dazzled by the bountiful treasures piled high. Fine lounges with matching chairs, these fashioned from wood as hard as iron and stained dark to enrich their smooth surfaces. These items had been transported here from Mesopotamia. Their sides were lined with intricately carved symbols, identifiable in that faraway land where they had been created. While the meanings of such signs were lost on me, I admired the craftsmanship.

We spotted Joseph and inched over to the next booth. There we observed an assortment of stools and tables carved from citrus trees. The uniquely twirled grain endowed these with a homey appearance. Unlike so much on display, they might actually be brought back to our humble residence.

Nearby, another stand offered mattresses. On its far side were spectacular oak beds, so huge that we would never have been able to fit one through our doorway. Not that we would have considered them if smaller; when indoors, Hebrew peasants slept on floors of earth, with only a woven mat between us and the ground.

"Luke," I sighed, unaware I had done so.

"What, Jess?" Mary asked, suddenly by my side.

"Oh, nothing."

"It must have been *some*thing."

"Just talking to myself."

"You do that a great deal lately."

I shrugged. "Maybe I'm crazy."

"Jess!" Elizabeth scolded, joining us. "Don't say such a thing!"

"I didn't mean it in a bad way, Aunt Elizabeth."

"Well . . . *what* then?"

"Jess is . . . a little bit . . . *different* from other girls her own age," Mary explained.

"So? The same could be said of my son John, from other boys."

*Thank you, Aunt Elizabeth.*

*You always did stand up for me, even at my most eccentric.*

Once the long line of shops reached an end, we turned a corner and found ourselves in the Milliner's Avenue. Each table here had been completely covered with fine wool from carefully selected sheep. Hawkers insisted that, when woven into pillows, the results would provide the most relaxing sleep in all the world. The wool could also serve as the basis for jackets to keep Galileans warm when the winter winds reappeared. I thought how crude our own blankets and clothing, crafted from whatever rough wool we were lucky enough to shear from our own rustic flock, likely felt in comparison.

Then again, some of our neighbors in Nazareth had fallen into such poverty that our hoary materials seemed a luxury.

*For the final time (at least for now): everything in life is relative; context determines everything.*

*Be certain never to forget this basic truth. For it would in short order come back to haunt me.*

# 31.

Turning another corner, we decided to avoid the pungent alley of cheesemakers. Moving on we shortly were dazzled by an array of gem stones: emeralds, diamonds, rubies, and many more, all rare and expensive. Here, the shopkeepers, fearful of theft, trained keen eyes on all passersby. Menacing dogs were tied close to each booth, teeth bared. A little further along the line we came upon elegantly designed, brightly polished boxes, constructed from wood bearing strange names like teak. Their surfaces were glazed with a rich substance that caused them to sparkle, and ornamented with small specks of chipped diamonds.

"Oh, Jess! Have you ever seen anything so *wonderful?*"

I glanced down at Simon, his eyes open so wide that they appeared twice the normal size.

"If I had all the money in the world," I giggled, hugging him tight, "I'd buy you any one you wanted."

A sudden sadness passed over his face. "They're not for people like us, are they?"

"Just you wait and see. Someday, you'll have one of your own."

"Really, Jess? Really?"

"Promise!" I hugged him again and his exuberant mood returned.

"You can have a present, Simon," Joseph offered, "if it's one I can afford. I set money aside to buy a gift for each of you."

That thrilled the boy. For the next hour, he considered everything on display, though none of the trade goods caught the interest of this boy. Finally, Simon's eyes lit up as he pointed to a circular tent shading a table filled with brightly painted staffs. These had been carved in a screw-like manner, appearing to be two inter-twined wooden snakes, embracing each other in a constant twist from top to bottom.

"May I?" the child asked.

"You may," Joseph said. Thrilled as only a child can be by such a simple thing, Simon rushed forward and spent a great deal of time choosing his favorite. Joseph then purchased it for him. Always, my favorite memory of Simon, locked in my mind forever: my little brother pretending to be a miniature Moses. He waved his magical wand at an imaginary Sea of Reeds. Invisible waters receded at his command.

Thanks to Joseph's success, we were able to afford to stop and rest at open-air tables in the Carousel of Foods. Here, we were treated to a midmorning breakfast notably different from anything we might consume at home.

One vendor of sweetmeats sat high on a stool, playing a juice-harp. Customers flocked to his offerings' irresistible aromas and, perhaps, his attempts at music. Other salesmen of varied foodstuffs shouted, picking out individuals in the crowd, trying to lure them their way. Several offered free samples, assuring visitors that one little taste would make it impossible to pick any other item for their repast.

"It all smells so delicious," I blurted out. "I'd like to eat everything."

I hadn't meant anything by that, though everyone laughed. The moment reminded me of how gluttonous I could be. I vowed to control myself during our present meal.

Nearby, a curvaceous Persian woman, wearing less than any female would dare back in Nazareth, perched upon a weather-worn barrel. Though she strummed a *kinnor*, men were more attracted by her beauty than the music. Her eyes were darker even than her close-cropped hair. Her radiant skin appeared as rich a hue as aged canvas. If the notes she produced may not have been precisely right, no one would ever complain about her slender thighs and lush exposed navel.

All in the crowd were enchanted, myself included.

The lady remained mysterious, avoiding eye contact with anyone. She seemed to exist in an alternative reality all her own. We mere mortals could step close, observe her, hear her. Male and female alike wished to gaze and listen. Still, she remained apart, untouchable. A man with a vulture's nose and silver beard shuffled from one mesmerized observer to the next, extending a pot. Several people dropped in *dinars* and *shekels* in appreciation of the woman's considerable beauty and modest talent.

All the while, Simon waved his staff in the air, as much in a world of his own as the stunning Persian. When he lowered his staff, I guessed it to be Moses's sign to Yahweh that the time had come to drown Pharaoh's hordes of charioteers.

*Could such a thing be real? The events of our Exodus had been told and retold from one generation of Hebrews to the next before some scribe finally set the legend down permanently 600 years ago.*

*But what did happen that day? Something, certainly. Was it as mystical as we had been led to believe? Or might there be a perfectly rational explanation . . .*

Stop, Jess! There are times for solitary thought, others for public enjoyment. Snap back to reality, which on this rare day feels more like a glorious fantasy.

After all, who knows if you will ever be in such a thrilling place again?

# 32.

John, Simon, and I sat at a crude, wood table while Joseph, Mary, and Elizabeth circled the food court. With eyes like a hawk searching for some interesting prey on the ground below, they carefully picked and chose among affordable delicacies that we all might share. Apparently, a melancholy look must have passed over my face, for John asked with concern, "What is it, Jess?"

"Some have *so* much, and others so *little*. I mean, we all *know* that. But here, seeing how plentiful life is for some, I see the problem in a more vivid manner than ever before."

I nodded toward an adjacent alley. Beggars of all nations, including our own, squatted in the thick dust. Each lost soul gathered there extended a hand, hoping for charity. Several attempted to make eye-contact with passersby, silently pleading for a coin. Others gazed downward, too hungry and forlorn to even care anymore. By local law, they were not permitted to wail, as beggars could in other cities. In Capernaum, a recent ordinance forbade any disturbance of those tourists who arrived for a good time and to spend money.

Soliciting was allowed only if the sad-faced horde remained silent.

*Always in Galilee, each farmer leaves a portion of his crop along the road for others. Among Yahweh's Chosen People, no Hebrew lets another go hungry.*

*This has been our way for five millennia now.*

"In Nazareth or northern Bethlehem, we become so used to the circumstances of our lives that we falsely believe our way is the way. Visiting such a city, we learn how much less the poorest can hope for in towns where others, unlike we Hebrews, don't provide for less fortunate kinsmen."

*The world, as I was quickly learning, is a very large place. Including many nations that did not adhere to values similar to ours.*

I considered people of means buying and selling here, there, everywhere in nearby plazas. Everyday items; rare treasures.

"But, Cousin. Nature is *so* bountiful—"

"How wrong it is that so few among the races of man own so much of that bounty?" John laughed bitterly. "And they call this 'contemporary civilization' at its most advanced."

"In the lands beyond Judea, this is, I imagine, the way things have always been."

"Now, with the advent of Hellenism, they come to live in our land and bring their pagan ways with them."

"Perhaps they'll learn a better way, observing us."

"My deepest prayer? A more even-handed redistribution of wealth, among all people, including our nation."

"In a perfect world? Yes. But is that possible in the real world we inhabit?"

My cousin considered that carefully. "Only if some bold face steps from out of the crowd and demands: 'Such inequality must end.'"

"The downtrodden would welcome such a one as their savior."

"While the rich would order such a person stoned."

My mind, as always, rushed ahead. "It might take the death of just such a one to make people realize the time has come for change."

"So who would dare speak out, knowing the consequences?"

*Who, indeed? There but for the grace of God, John, go you or I.*

*Or, perhaps, that grace may yet command one of us to . . .*

The others returned. Mary carried a brimming platter of ox meat from a kosher stand, this beast's killing properly blessed. Hebraic lettering, stamped in blue on the booth as well as the rumps of animals before they were butchered, allowed Jews to know that here they could purchase such products. The beef had been scorched black on its edges while the insides remained a golden brown. Elizabeth brought dry wheat bread. We broke the loaves into small pieces, using them to scoop up rich juices in which the delicacy had simmered for hours.

Lastly, Joseph (with an oblivious Simon marching along behind) arrived with a bowl full of berries unlike any I'd seen. Neither blue nor purple, these were bright red. Also he carried a large goblet of wine mixed with water. If there is one thing that can always stop my mouth from droning on and on, it's food.

All conversation halted; I ate voraciously while observing with amusement the ongoing carnival atmosphere. Acrobats leaped about, providing constant entertainment. Magicians summoned visitors to come see their shows. Fortune tellers drifted over to this table or that, attempting to persuade the gullible to pay for palm readings. Others hawked elixirs, guaranteed to cure all ills.

"How can people be so naive as to believe these tricks?" John wondered.

"Just watch," Joseph scornfully replied. Sure enough, there were those who parted with hard-earned coins for a corked bottle filled with mountain herbs and boiled tree roots.

"How could they believe such come-ons?" Mary wondered.

"People believe," I heard myself reply, "what they want to believe."

"And they want to believe . . .?" Elizabeth inquired.

"They *need* to believe that there is always an easy answer for everything."

"You don't think there is, Sister?" Simon asked.

"All truly great answers are complicated."

"My, my," Joseph clucked. "And where does my daughter get such profound notions?"

*Without realizing it, I'd come close to revealing my secret studies.*

*I must be more attentive as to what I say.*

"But, *look* at them," John observed. People wrapped in richly colored silks mingled with working-class peasants, like ourselves simply if respectably attired. "All off and running on his own business, blind to others. They don't have the time or interest, or perhaps the intellect, to deal with the kind of complexity you speak of, Jess."

"I know. That's why they fall for such cheap ruses."

"Will they—*people*—ever change, do you think?"

I shook my head. "No, John, I don't. Things change. The clothes we choose to wear. The manner in which different nations construct buildings. The foods we eat or decide to no longer consume. But people? I fear human nature never changes."

"Jess," Joseph marveled. "You sound like a rabbi!"

"A radical rabbi," John added.

# 33.

Along the smooth harbor wall, fishing boats, their sails slack, bobbed gently. A quarter mile to the south, a pleasant stretch of beach had been reserved for those wishing to temporarily escape the great city's distractions. However brief a period of time Galileans might have for relaxation, here was an opportunity to do so by bathing in the soothing waters. Free of charge, people could enjoy the crisp air, ever-shifting winds, and soft sand and swell of the gentle waves. For Hebrews, this offered an opportunity to contemplate the distant horizon where the soft turquoise above meets that darker hue below.

How glorious it would be to penetrate that thin, blue line. I can picture James, John, and myself on a raft. Joseph would fashion it for us from bits and pieces of driftwood.

*We paddle fast and hard. Knowing our unwavering faith in reaching that far point would allow us to slip in-between the ocean and the heavens into some other world.*

*There, we might discover the true meaning of life.*

"Here's a nice spot," Elizabeth decided. We all dropped down under a trio of palms, their enormous leaves swaying in the afternoon breeze. A short distance away, a group of local fishermen likewise sought shelter from the sun under a line of seven similar trees. Veterans of the trade, having spent their long morning and early afternoon casting nets upon the sea, they were not willing to exert themselves again until that orange-red ball began its descent in the west.

Their faces were ruddy from daily exposure to the elements, their hair wild and woolly. An aura of romance surrounded them, at least to an impressionable, rural girl. Likely, their working hours were no more exciting than our own, at least to them.

*As this glorious vision—the sun, the sky, the sea, all in harmony—occurs every day, we take it for granted.*

*If this natural beauty were to appear once, we'd perceive it as a miracle. People from the Far East? As magic.*

Two ways, perhaps, for two different nations to perceive the same phenomenon, each according to their own "way." Two names employed to describe one thing, or at least an attempt to understand this unique part of the great unknown.

*Can't you ever stop thinking, Jess?*

*Won't you ever lose consciousness and seize the day?*

When the coolness of early evening descended, the rested fishermen would rise and return to work. At that hour, the sky offers a rainbow of colors, blue supplanted by yellows, oranges, reds, and finally darkness. Now we experienced that enchanted moment when curious gulls sweep down to observe those foolish things below called humans. And the fish, energetic as they never are at midday, dance along the surface of the sea. But . . . why?

*Here, too, was a mystery. Like magic or miracles, mystery does not exist in what we see. Rather how we perceive things.*

*Children see magic, miracles, and mysteries everywhere. People too often lose that ability as we grow up, inured to the wonders around us by drab existence.*

"Jess, what are you lost in thought about *now?*"

"Nothing, Aunt Elizabeth. You know me."

"We *all* know you," Mary insisted.

*Could the wealthy, up in their mansions on the adjoining overlook, enjoy their abundant free time as much as simple souls like these fishermen did their rare minutes of reprieve from labor?*

Our own conversation diminished as each of us strained to hear an intriguing tale being recalled nearby.

"Do you remember the time," one fisherman asked his fellows, "when a wind arose without warning and blew Philip overboard?"

"Do I? Why, Simon almost drowned trying to save him."

A big fisherman sat in front of their fire. There a timeworn black kettle hung over the flames, suspended from an iron rod. Nimbly and with a skill that evidenced years of living off the water, he scaled several fish, tossing them into the boiling liquid. Here was what those in cities referred to as a pot-luck stew. Wild onions and a bit of powdered spice—thyme, most likely— were tossed in to enhance the flavor.

His three companions sat cross-legged around their cooking device. Each man licked his lips in anticipation of the humble feast to come.

# 34.

The aroma couldn't have been more enticing, particularly to anyone who looked forward to meals as enthusiastically as me. Simon, marching about with his head held high and staff in hand, heard his name mentioned and boldly wandered over.

"Hello, small one," the big fisherman called out jovially. "By your cane, I'd take it you are Abraham or Moses—"

"I'm pretending to be Moses," he said shyly, "but my name is Simon."

"How's *that* for a coincidence? So is mine."

This strapping fellow leaped up, shook my brother's tiny hand, and invited him to join them on a large, leafy mat. Filled with the impetuousness of youth, Simon—my younger brother, that is—sat himself down as if about to join their company and perhaps become a fisherman himself.

*Yet another stranger who shared a name with me or a kinsmen?*

*There must be a point where coincidence ends and something more meaningful begins . . .*

True, in Galilee many people shared several names. Every second or third girl was likely named Mary. Simon had always been one of the most popular for boys. Still, this had occurred too frequently for me not to perceive in it a pattern.

"Hebrews?" Joseph, clearly hoping the response would be affirmative, inquired.

"Hebrews!" the big fisherman replied heartily, nodding and smiling. In our world, this signaled that we were kinsmen: all in our nation were related, however distantly, by blood.

*Moses saw to that, during those forty years he insisted the people wait before entering the Promised Land.*

*Silly stories, told by those who failed to understand what actually happened, spread the falsity that, having escaped Egypt, the former slaves became lost and wandered aimlessly.*

Nothing of the sort! Moses knew precisely what he was doing. Hebrews, Africans, and members of other tribes who left along with us lived under the great mountain's shadow. They worked, they intermarried, and in time they died.

Their children formed the new Israel, our nation reborn. Each and every member now blood of the other's blood, no matter who their ancestors had been.

After the previous generation passed away, these youths were allowed to cross the Jordan. Moses, even he considered impure in the eyes of an unsparing God, had to remain on the far side.

A revitalized nation waded over the waters. Fresh and clean, virgins all in a social if not sexual sense, they stepped onto the land that bore their name.

"We have food aplenty, and wine," Joseph offered. "You can share ours if we might do the same, countrymen."

"Come over then," this Simon responded, waving.

Enthusiastically, we packed up our belongings and joined them. The large group now sat in a circle, each fisherman locating himself between two of my family members. Shortly, we were sharing the food and enjoying it all the more for such unexpected good company.

Like the tribes of Israel, we may have lived apart, but sooner or later circumstances invariably drew the people together again.

# 35.

"This is my younger brother, Andrew," Simon continued. "Our friends and fellow fishermen, Philip and Nathaniel."

We introduced ourselves as well. "May I address you by some other name than Simon?" I asked. While I hoped that my words would not be misconstrued as rude, I did want to avoid confusion. "That way you'll know I'm talking to you and not my baby brother."

"Jess! Don't call me a baby!"

"Sorry, Simon. This strapping, young *man*, bursting with desire to work miracles with his cane, seated beside me."

"I don't see why not. But what?"

"If I may say so," John interjected, "you look amazingly strong. Like a rock that has sprouted arms, legs, a huge head, and now walks about in the guise of a man."

Everyone laughed good-naturedly, Simon (*not* my brother) most of all. "Very well then," he said. "Call me Peter, the Rock. So long as I may call your kinswoman here Little Blue Eyes."

During the next quarter of an hour, we learned about their enterprise. This quartet of relatives employed nets, crafted by their mothers and wives, to gather up fish each day, then carry them to the marketplace. There, the sea's bounty was sold to fishmongers. Customers could purchase items from the catch to take home and prepare for dinner. Others were directed to a nearby booth, where workers cut away the heads, tails, and fish skins. Cooks roasted the meat or used it as the basic ingredient for a rich stew.

Still more fish were salted and stored for export, though everyone along the Mediterranean knew the best catch hailed from Bethsaida, over on the inland sea's eastern side. Nathaniel explained that each of them had been born there. Once the four fishermen had related their shared story, we did the same, describing our village in the heart of farming country, as well as Joseph's stonemasonry and carpentry.

"Hello!" I recognized a friendly voice from behind. "Are the ancient laws of hospitality observed among the Jews even as they are in faraway lands?"

It was Luke!

*I knew he'd arrive before the time came for our party to pack and leave.*

*Knew it as well as I'd ever known anything in my brief lifetime.*

"The boy from yesterday!" Joseph said, signaling for him to join us. Mary turned away, less than pleased, then cast me a sideways glance. Her critical eyes suggested she guessed that somehow I had arranged this "chance" meeting.

"You are, I trust, Greek?" Simon-Peter asked warily.

"To the core of my bones!"

Like most Hebrews, Peter had little quarrel with Greeks. Any conflict between our nation and theirs had been settled long ago. The Romans? Another matter entirely. Caesar ruled over us by force. Luke's homeland, too. No matter how decent a Roman might be, it was unwise for any Galilean to befriend an arrival from Caesar's great city for fear of angering fellow Jews. As the Romans and Greeks physically resembled one another, it was necessary for Peter to ask that question.

"Sit, then. And help yourself to whatever is left."

My turn now to cast eyes at Mary. While my mother seemingly sensed my gaze, she refused to acknowledge it. Or peer directly into the eyes of others. Could this have to do with Peter's implied distaste for Romans? Her reaction might be guilt. A name rang in my ears: *Tiberon!*

The Roman who, according to rumor . . .

Then again, I might be reading too much into Mary's silence. *No matter. For Luke was here. Oh! But this might well be the final minutes we would ever share.*

*I will myself not to think now. Only feel. And enjoy.*

As Joseph once told me long ago when I asked him the secret for a full, rich, happy life: seize the day! A lesson I hoped to learn, beginning here and now.

# 36.

"That boy!" Elizabeth screamed. "He's *drowning*."

I'd been wiping remnants of fish, bread, and cheese from little Simon's chin when my aunt's shriek caused me to bolt upright. She pointed easterly, toward the water. It was Luke! He'd jogged off to swim shortly after we packed up the plates and spoons. Peter had warned my beautiful Greek that cramps might overcome him if he entered the water, exerting himself too soon after eating.

Luke scoffed at this advice, as if he alone were free of such concerns.

For a few minutes, Luke had displayed considerable skills, knowing I'd be watching. I observed closely (while pretending to only glance over casually) as he bobbed up and down like a dolphin. Though I hated to admit it, Luke's fine form did impress me. Then Simon's messiness proved a distraction. That was when, without warning, Luke suddenly went under.

"Quick," I shouted. "Somebody *do* something!"

As for myself and my family, there was no way we might help. Living far to the west, none of us ever learned to swim. We watched, leaping up and down with concern. Panic set in: the horror that possesses those who witness a disaster in progress but can do nothing.

"I'll go," Peter called to his mates.

With that, the tall man bounded across the sand and into the surf. I expected him, now knee deep, to plunge in and swim to the spot where Luke had disappeared. Instead, Peter opted for something else, which appeared magical. Or miraculous.

As if large, invisible wings attached to Peter's shoulders lifted him, abetted by smaller ones on his heels, Peter leapt high and skipped over the water's surface. Rather than move in a straight line, he angled this way and that, turning left and then right, even back and forth in a dizzying roundelay.

Seconds later, he reached the spot where Luke, face now a bizarre green-blue and eyes set back in his head, came tearing up from underwater.

"Hurry, Peter," I frantically urged. "Hurry!"

Before Luke could submerge again, Peter grabbed hold of him from behind. This was difficult to manage, what with Luke's arms flailing wildly in all directions. In his panic, Luke slapped Peter's face hard, briefly halting the rescue attempt. After staggering about for a moment, Peter recovered and swirled Luke up, balancing the youth across his broad shoulders. Slowly, Peter proceeded back, retracing the steps precisely as he had chosen them while rushing to help.

"Brother, let us carry him the rest of the way," Andrew pleaded.

He, Philip, and Nathaniel had rushed to meet Peter and the limp boy halfway to the shore. Cautiously, they lifted Luke off of the now retching Peter, bringing the Greek to their little encampment. Other concerned beach-goers congregated nearby.

"He'll be alright," Philip insisted, as if trying to assure himself as well as the crowd. "Just you wait and see."

All four fishermen eased Luke stomach-down on the mat. Strategically, they bent Luke's arms and legs while massaging his back and sides. Finally, Peter waved the others away. Once alone, he wrapped his mighty arms around Luke's torso. Peter squeezed hard. A croaking sound emitted from Luke's mouth, followed by water.

Gradually, evidence of life returned. Luke coughed, continuing to do so for several minutes. In time, he managed to sit up. I knew then that, however close he'd come to death, Luke would survive.

"Thank you," Luke whimpered once he was up and around. To everyone's surprise he broke into a little dance of joy.

*Beware the false pride of youth, when our bodies feel so full of the life force that we believe death will never come.*

*Yet how swiftly it strikes the unwary and foolish.*

"Maybe next time you'll listen to good advice," I reprimanded Luke, glaring. Clearly embarrassed by the panicky scene he'd caused, knowing that he'd failed miserably in his plan to overwhelm me, Luke said nothing, staring down at the sand.

"Let's celebrate our new friend's return," Nathaniel suggested, he the jolliest member of their company.

"Certainly, I do feel born again," Luke whispered.

Out of a small, wooden box Nathaniel lifted a hookah, or hubble-bubble as Nazarenes called this valued item from Persia. They set this device down by the fire. First Nathaniel, then everyone else, even little Simon, inserted the pipe into his or her mouth, sucking in through the serpentine tube. Smoke filled the water bowl and, through the attached hose, we took turns drawing the contents deep into our lungs.

Its soothing qualities relaxed everyone. Soon we were mellow enough that the near-tragic incident seemed amusing in retrospect.

"Peter, I don't understand," Luke dared to ask. "How did you . . . walk on water?"

"I didn't," he chuckled. "You see, many large rocks are scattered under the surface. Spots where layers of limestone and basalt, which congealed over the centuries, rise higher than elsewhere."

"But how did you know precisely where to . . ."

"From years of fishing here, Little Blue Eyes, I memorized where each rock is, so as not to stub my toes."

*Yes, indeed. Miracles exist, and so does magic. Not in events themselves.*

*Rather, in our perception of things that, when rationally understood, become part of our everyday existence. And then seem miraculous or magical no more.*

# 37.

A lengthy silence followed. Everyone noticed the sun had begun to sink behind distant hills, now shaded purple in the dimming light. That could mean only one thing: a new day, according to our Hebrew calendar, had begun.

And, fittingly, the time had come for all of us to call it a day.

*So what now ought I to do about my beautiful Greek? I would not want to contemplate living if I knew for certain I'd never see him again.*

*Please remember, future reader, these were my thoughts as a girl who had not yet reached the age of twelve. Affairs of the heart were then entirely new to me.*

*Such feminine emotions embarrass me as I write them down. As they may well you, too, while encountering this manuscript with the knowledge of what or who I would in time become.*

Luke pointed to an ugly boil on Andrew's left knee. "Is that painful?"

"Terribly!"

Luke leaned in close, examining it. "There's a danger of infection. My I pierce and clean it for you?"

Luke explained that he currently attended medical academy in Capernaum and ranked as a top student. Back in Caesarea, his family's home, Luke studied with that city's top physicians.

Andrew turned to Peter for advice. Most Hebrews weren't comfortable consorting with doctors, fearing such practices might be ungodly. (Indeed, many in remote areas had never even heard of the term at this point in time). The cleansing of body and spirit were left to blessings by priests and rabbis.

Peter shrugged, nodding in reluctant acceptance. Luke, delighted, set to work. He opened his ever-present sack, drawing out a pincer. This he seared over the glowing coals, afterwards bringing his tool close to Andrew's leg.

"Will this hurt?" Andrew asked nervously.

"Yes," Luke informed him. "Terribly!"

With that, Luke burst the boil, allowing puss and blood to spill. Andrew yelped like a kicked cat. Having impressed us with his precision, Luke reached back into his sack. Now, he drew out a tube of ointment, applying some on the open wound. Finally, Luke tied a fresh, white linen bandage tightly around Andrew's leg.

"It will pain you for the rest of the day," he explained while tightening the knot. "By tomorrow, there will be little trace that it was ever there. In three days, your leg will be as good as new."

Everyone expressed delight. I tried to conceal my awe for fear that Luke would realize my initial attraction had escalated into considerably deeper feelings, as of course it had. We rose, shook off the sand from our bodies, and looked around at one another, all experiencing the awkward sensation that newfound friends were about to become strangers once more.

My family members shook hands with the fishermen, offering to host them whenever they might have cause to travel westward, visiting Galilee's great forests and sweet pastures.

*What about Luke? I prepared to say good-bye . . .*

"A question. May I have the pleasure of showing Jess our city's magnificent Temple of Apollo tomorrow?"

Hearing that, Joseph, Mary, and Aunt Elizabeth exchanged concerned glances. Like most Hebrews, they had mixed emotions about exposure to Hellenistic culture, even if my family had always been more progressive about such matters than many of our stringently traditionalist neighbors. Moreover, it was not permitted for a virginal Hebrew girl to spend an entire day alone with a young man not of our nation.

"Well," Joseph mused, "what do you think, Wife?"

I looked to Mary, hoping some positive resolution might now be possible. She met my eyes with a coolness born of the seven years during which I consistently denied any attempt on her part to express a mother's love.

Here was her chance to punish me, if she chooses, for the invisible wall I long ago erected between us.

"I'd be glad to chaperone," John offered. "How I would love to experience such a place firsthand!"

"As would I," I added.

Again, Joseph glanced to Mary, implying by his gesture that he was willing, though she ought to make the final decision. Briefly, Mary remained silent.

Then, "If John is to go? Then I will allow it."

Luke and I turned to one another, beaming at our victory. We would at least share another precious day together. After that? I couldn't even entertain the thought of parting forever at such a glorious moment as I now existed within.

Also, I knew I'd never again be so cruelly remote to my mother. She had come through for me in a way I wouldn't have expected after all I'd put her through.

# 38.

"Prepare to be astonished."

In the morning sun, I spotted Luke waiting patiently at our designated meeting place by the fountain where we'd first come face to face. John and I were thrilled at this opportunity to experience what most Hebrews never see: the inside of a Greek temple. We would visit those antechambers where Attican culture and religion comingled for the Greek masses, wherever in the world they might live.

"You're certain this will be alright?" I asked as John and I followed Luke through the marketplace. The daily throng made movement difficult until we veered off the main street, turning down a considerably narrower one. Luke explained that this led to a largely domestic quarter where the majority of Capernaum's Greek working-class residents dwelled. As for Luke's own well-to-do family, they resided in one of those palatial mansions high up on the ridge.

"My friends who maintain the building," Luke assured us, "said they would be delighted to welcome you for a tour."

We approached the white, rectangular building, a lengthy colonnade stretching across each side, proceeding to the main front entrance. In front of us, several Greeks of modest means, this obvious from their simple clothing, approached the heavy metal doors.

We lined up behind them, me assuming that someone would knock and we would be met by priests. Instead, something wondrous occurred. On their own, the doors swept open. Nobody awaited us inside. This, apparently normal enough to Luke, amazed us Hebrews. A door that opens all by itself, without human intervention?

Hesitantly, for we were shaken by this fantastic greeting, we followed along behind the previous arrivals. All stepped into a narrow chamber that gave me the impression it might run on forever. I glanced back, half expecting to spot someone hiding in the shadows, secretly attending to the doors. No one was there, so we moved on.

"The first of many surprises," Luke whispered over his shoulder, amused at our sheer astonishment. We felt our way along in the darkness, no candles or lamps to mark the way. Finally, we found ourselves exiting that intimidating chamber and entered a larger circular room.

Here, the sun shone in through a glass dome. On a raised platform in the room's center stood an enchantingly crafted statue of a nude woman.

"Aphrodite," Luke whispered, "goddess of love and beauty."

John, I knew, would be embarrassed. He shared the current attitude of many Galileans: unabashed sexuality, particularly in regards to the female, represented sin. Being a woman, this was an attitude I rejected.

"Perhaps we'd better leave," John suggested.

"Not on your life, Cousin."

The statue's right hand held a wine goblet alongside her head. Her left hand extended forward, palm flat. "Take a cup,"

Luke said, pointing to a supply on a nearby table. I did. Luke motioned for me to place it on her open hand. Again, I followed his instruction. Nothing happened.

"Aphrodite," he explained in a hushed voice, "expects to be paid for her wine."

Abruptly, he stepped forward, produced a *dinar* from his purse, and slipped it into a coin slot between her parted lips. Wonder of wonders, the statue came to life. Her right hand guided the goblet down, filling the cup with wine. The hand holding the goblet moved back to its original position as soon as this action was completed.

"Taste it," Luke encouraged me.

Trembling, I reached forward, removing the cup, bringing it to my mouth. Sipping, I found it sweet, fruity, refreshing. I handed the cup to John. He partook, eyes delighted at the taste.

"Thank you, gracious goddess," Luke said, bowing humbly before this ideal of female loveliness.

John and I exchanged concerned glances. Must we repeat such a gesture of deference, or as Hebrews would we be excused from paying respects to a pagan deity? Sensing our discomfort, Luke informed us that only those who shared his faith were required to do so. I sighed in relief, as did my cousin.

We next followed Luke in a counterclockwise direction. At the room's far side, I spotted something I hadn't noticed before: a triangular door, embossed with crimson and sea-green jewels. The passageway had been so perfectly cut into the wall that, from afar, it appeared to be only another detailed mosaic.

"Oh!"

As with the main entrance, this door opened on its own. The building seemed to feel our presence and, owing to some life force of its own, responded every time we made a move. The three of us hung back momentarily while the earlier arrivals continued on.

"Luke," John stammered, "This is all so . . ."

"Miraculous?"

"Yes!"

"Friend," Luke chuckled, "you haven't seen *anything* yet."

# 39.

The second room, bigger and square in shape, was dimly lit compared to the previous one's eerie brightness. Here, a purple mist hung above an ovular-shaped pool. Ornamented with small marble statues, this source of water dominated the mysterious chamber's epicenter. Warm air rose from sea-green liquid. Thin wisps of clouds circled us, adding a sense of otherworldliness.

Across this reservoir I could make out a formidable statue. A Greek warrior sporting full battle armor held his spear high, apparently sensing danger. Some gifted artisan had rendered the copper icon realistic enough that, from where we stood, I half expected it to spring to life.

I could not, as in the previous room, grasp where the light originated. There was no dome, no mirrors, no lamps or torches to maintain the grey hue that barely illuminated several areas, leaving the four corners in shadow. Without warning, a beam of white light snapped on from somewhere above, darting over and across the ill-lit area, directing our eyes from one specific detail to the next.

*This was long before I learned that light possesses a personality all its own, though that knowledge would in time come.*

A crack of thunder sounded so abruptly that John and I gasped. The white light ceased slashing about, focusing now on the far side, across from the warrior. Another statue occupied a great space there, owing to its identity. For here stood a dragon, wings outspread, mouth wide open, eyes bright crimson. The scaled body of the beast appeared silver once the cold, merciless beam of light shone down on its intricate surface covered with odious scales.

"Ooooooooh!"

Not only did I jump up, but screamed aloud as the dragon's wide-spread jaws let loose a tremendous roar. The wings flapped, slowly at first, then harder and faster. Its head methodically turned until those bright, cruel eyes stared directly at us, and fire bellowed from its parted jaws.

"Stay with me, Yahweh!" I cried, cringing in fear.

*Again, reader; I was eleven years old. And not yet schooled in the ways of the world.*

John, on my left, slipped a protective arm around my waist, to buoy me while calming himself. John's teeth chattered. His lanky body shook. "Oh, Coz! We have entered a house of horrors. Not even our Lord can save us now."

Luke, positioned to my right, likewise slipped an arm around my waist, seizing the situation to draw a frightened female close.

"Don't worry. That warrior? It's Herakles. He always saves the day. Watch, now!"

The silver and green beast screeched, beat its wings, spit out fire, and waved its head about wildly. I guessed this mythical creature would stomp in our direction and devour its observers. That was when the statue of the warrior creaked into movement, the hero's right arm slowly pulling back.

When the spear reached a position behind Herakles's right ear, he hurled it. The weapon flew across the room at tremendous speed, piercing the dragon's breast. Howling in pain, wrenching its neck, spitting out flames everywhere, the dragon entered into a succession of grotesque death throes. In time, all movement ceased. The enormous snout pointed downward in silence.

"See now why Greeks trust in our mighty men of valor?"

"I . . . I . . ."

Before I could form words, the light diminished. We could no longer perceive either warrior or dragon. After several long seconds, that bright beam of light reappeared, this time focused on an alcove that, until now, remained so shrouded in mist I hadn't guessed its presence.

"What in the name of . . .?" John gasped.

Relinquishing our free will to the light's power, we turned in unison to gaze on whatever was now highlighted. Up from the floor, as if lifted by invisible hands, a great, white chariot, pulled by four mighty stallions, rose and paused in midair, no strings visible to hold it in place.

*The chariot from my dream, in which I'd been the hero!*

A handsome, young male, holding tight to his reins, gazed at us. Before me, I realized, stood a similar if smaller version of that marble rendering of Helios I'd viewed while entering

Capernaum. Or perhaps this might be Apollo? The horses' legs moved as if hurrying across an invisible plane. Yet these beasts and the chariot they pulled remained in place, removed from any ordinary concepts of time and space.

# 40.

With this final spectacle done, we three exited the temple. Once in the sunlight, I tried to align what I'd witnessed with my previous experiences. Nothing came close. I could not be certain if I had or had not seen statues move, a dragon die, and the chariot rise up and fly now that I once again stood in the street's bright actuality.

It had all looked so real. But how could this be?

John, too shocked to say anything, staggered around in the aftermath of visiting what may have been another world. Luke guided us to a pleasantly shaded food stand where we sat on wood stools under a multi-colored canopy. Once John and I recovered our wits, we lunched on grapes, cheese, bread, and wine.

"So? Is faith in your Yahweh as the one and only God diminished by what you witnessed?"

That charming sense of naughtiness I'd come to associate with Luke appeared in my beautiful Greek's eyes. Where I might have seen pride for his Temple, I instead noticed mischief.

"We are Hebrews," John asserted after regaining his voice. "Yahweh has leveled mountains, burned great cities, flooded the world. Our faith in the One God is not so easily challenged."

"Yet I have to admit, I'm reeling."

"Seeing is believing, Jess?"

"So some claim."

"Yet you Hebrews cannot see your invisible God."

"We don't need to," John stated flatly. "We have faith."

"For Jews," I added, "it's the reverse of other nations: believing is seeing."

"Good for you. Anyway, when we finish here, I'll soon have you marveling again."

"Where will we go?" I asked.

"Back inside. Only this time," Luke added with a wink, "we will use the back door. Where the public is forbidden entrance."

Intriguing as that sounded, I had no desire to rush away from the food. Relaxing during the noon hour, Luke asked us about our recent sojourn to the marketplace. We shared with him our deep concern at the sight of such abundance in contrast to the poor who could not partake.

"Everything exists in contrast to everything else."

*Yes, Luke. Precisely what I was about to say.*

*Despite differences in national identity, and economic class, is it possible we two view the world in a similar way?*

I mentioned that Simon had been fascinated by expensive bejeweled boxes we hadn't been able to afford. Luke's eyes made clear how touched he felt by the depth of my feelings for this little boy.

"Alright," Luke announced once we'd finished our meal. "Let's take a look at everything again from another angle of perception."

In stark comparison to the crowded street in front of the temple, not a soul stood near the building's rear end. Anyone who passed by would never guess a secret entrance had been constructed here. A thick grove of lemon trees camouflaged the building's backside. What appeared to be randomly discarded garbage—broken crates, copper cans, torn fishnets, and other junk (some of it smelled nasty)—would deter even the most curious.

In the forlorn-looking alley leading from the main street to this unpleasant area, irregular chunks of limestone jutted up from the ground. Untended weeds stretched high. Any intrigued tourist who briefly considered taking a peek around the area would likely turn back at once. Only a fool would not sense that danger lurked here.

A fool, or someone who knew precisely what awaited. Someone like Luke.

# 41.

"Before we enter," he said, his tone suddenly more serious than previously, "you must swear that you will never reveal to anyone what I allow you to witness now."

Luke insisted that our oath be directed to our god Yahweh. Clearly, this was not one of his little jokes. Fascinated by the aura of mystery, we swore. That completed, he turned and led us through thick bushes and piles of trash to a precise spot at the building's rear, revealing a hidden door.

"This," he said, rapping, "is where team members enter and exit."

The door creaked open. An owl-faced man with small, hard eyes, his beard as bushy as the surrounding growth, peered out. "Oh! Luke. Hello."

"Cento, these are the friends I mentioned. They are sworn to silence."

The two shook hands. This diminutive fellow rolled his eyes with a sense of irascible humor. His tunic was filthy. When he caught me gazing at its slovenliness, Cento apologized for his appearance. He had, he explained, lost track of the time while working on something he referred to as a new "special effect."

I had absolutely no idea what he was talking about. Still, any opportunity to experience something new, and perhaps learn from it, intrigued me.

With Luke leading the way we entered a dim, clammy chamber. Its walls had been fashioned out of Roman cement, the floor composed of hard-pounded dirt. A variety of technical equipment had haphazardly been piled in each corner: chains, pulleys, gyros, thick ropes, and oddly shaped machines.

"Follow me," Cento whispered. He ushered us across the sizable room to an inner wall. At once, I guessed this separated where we now stood from the backside of the Temple's large room in which the warrior battled the dragon. I was about to ask Luke if this was so when he raised a finger to his lips, hushing me. John and I nodded our understanding. As quietly as possible, we shifted to a spot where a youth, his flesh an odious shade of yellow, stood beside a complex series of mirrors. These were fitted together in a distinct pattern, each connected to the next by wires. Nearby, oil lamps mounted on metallic poles lined the wall. Assorted color filters lay to either side.

"Meet our lighting expert, Calvin," Luke whispered.

The fellow smiled, revealing top and bottom rows of rotten teeth. As we stepped closer, I smelled the worst breath I could recall. Embarrassed to have gagged me, Calvin sullenly turned away. Ignoring us, he adjusted his equipment, fiddling with a series of odd gadgets. Watching him skillfully manipulate the levers, wheels, and pulleys, I realized that any peculiarities aside, here stood a true professional.

*Yet I had no clue as to what he might do next.*

Luke motioned for me to push closer to the wall. I spotted several peek holes, barely larger than pinpricks. Choosing one, I focused my vision. By peering through it, I could observe the adjoining Temple room. From this new perspective, I watched as a family of working-class Greeks, similar to the ones we had entered with, stepped up to the enchanted pool. They appeared astonished by the atmosphere of ancient legend surrounding them, as if an old fantasy had all at once become real.

Riveted, I watched as the warrior again hurled his spear at the monster. Beside me, Cal directed a beam of light first toward Herakles, then the dragon. The precise action we had witnessed was repeated.

Peering down into a deep cavity below the floor, I spotted the chariot, initially motionless. Fascinated, I watched as, in response to a workman's yanking on chains and deft manipulation of several levers, it gradually lifted upward.

The performance continued. This current audience appeared to be as convinced by what they were witnessing as John and I earlier were.

*Seeing, or so the old proverb insists, is believing.*

*Yet is what we see and believe necessarily the truth?*

# 42.

"Come," Luke whispered. John and I cautiously followed.

We approached a hidden trap door, built to appear like the top of a wooden crate that someone had temporarily deposited here. Luke yanked it open. A succession of stairs, dug deep into the earth, led to a secret cellar. Oil lamps were mounted on the lower walls for the benefit of those working below, crouched over machinery. Here the constricted area for laborers left no room to stand. Several men crawled about, attending to ever-more elaborate contraptions.

In semi-darkness I could make out an arrangement of complex devices just beneath the chariot, even then in the process of rising for the spectators' amazement. A huge copper kettle hung above a roaring flame. As the water reached a boiling point, workers manipulated hand pumps to direct the blazing-hot liquid through a thick tube. Water flowed out and down, finally trickling into another, smaller kettle.

"This," Luke confided, "is an invention of our Heron, the greatest scientific and mathematical genius in the world. Our temple here in Caesarea imported this particular model at great expense. Shipped all the way from Alexandria in Egypt. And in pieces! Our team reassembled it in this place several months ago."

Luke signaled to the technicians. They returned his wave, pleased that such a prestigious youth appreciated their skills.

"This isn't the only one in existence?" John asked.

"Every Greek temple that could afford one purchased this item to cap off their show." Luke then explained the mechanics of this device in such a clear way that even provincials like John and myself could grasp its workings.

What at first seemed to be magical, when understood rationally, operated on a logical system derived from a concept new to me, which Luke referred to as basic scientific principles. Water, when heated, was able to create vast energy. And, with that, enormous reserves of power. Once a person understood water's remarkable properties, Luke continued, it made sense that such technology could force air through a succession of pumps. This process employed heat and water to transform the air around us into something Luke referred to as compressed air, with the potential to manufacture previously unknown amounts of power.

"Energy," Luke insisted, "can move mountains, much less the items on view above us. These provide onlookers with statues that appear to walk on their own accord. And cause front doors to open with no attendants nearby. In situations far more significant, such energy can decide the outcome of a war."

Luke then explained that more than 200 years earlier an inventor, Archimedes, had created such machines with immense mirrors attached. He placed them on the walls of the city of Syracuse, then under siege by a Roman fleet attempting to conquer Sicily. Sunlight had been redirected and focused so that one by one the warships' sails caught fire. Syracuse's people hailed Archimedes as a great magician. Those few in the know understand him to be the world's first scientific genius.

"Amazing. Where we live, only a few days travel from here, such things are unknown."

"I'm glad for the opportunity to widen your vision, Jess. Yours, too, John."

"Are most Greeks aware of—"

"No, no, no! These are carefully guarded secrets. If the masses had any idea what occurs behind the scenes, none of these illusions would inspire them. So do remember your pledge!"

"If this is so hush-hush, how were you able to enter?"

"And with us tailing behind?"

"Because my own family manufactures this 'machinery of the gods,' as they are called, in Alexandria, then delivers them across the world."

The water pressure increased, forcing filtered air through a bellows. This was pointed up toward the chariot, which had been carefully angled so that the sudden onslaught of energy impacted evenly across its bottom. With that, the chariot rose ever further upward, from out of its hiding place into full view of the amazed spectators above.

# 43.

Again, Luke beckoned us to follow. We felt our way along, in time reaching a series of tunnels that ran directly below the building. These allowed technicians full access to multiple areas beneath the temple's unwary visitors. Here, syphons were attached by strings to numerous heating devices, each of these linked by a complex network of tubes. Workers, with the turn of a handle, could create what those above liked to call "special effects." A large, rectangular box, located below the stage where Herakles conquered the beast two dozen times during any day, tilted back and forth owing to the impact of strategically positioned water filters. Heavy metal balls, Luke explained, had been placed inside the box. When this tilted in reaction to the applied energy, they rolled back and forth.

"The sound of thunder that we heard!"

"Yes, Jess. Produced not by a lightning spear hurled down by Zeus but our machinery here below."

"How do you control the volume?" John wanted to know.

"The noise is amplified through several speakers before it reverberates around the building."

"What are speakers?" I asked, confused.

"Another of Heron's remarkable inventions."

Next, we observed an enormous pot filled with oil. Team members poured what Luke explained were 'chemicals' into the mix. A vapor, its hue somewhere between green and gray, rose. Workers employed a bellows to force this gaseous compound up through a succession of cracks and into the room above. There it filled the air, creating a convincing semblance of menacing clouds. Another technician, located a few feet further along the tunnel, controlled a metallic device by manipulating pulleys. These, I noted, screwed into the showroom's dragon statue. And so the beast's wings flapped up and down on command.

Yet another employed a steam engine to release Herakles's spear, synchronized to enter a small pre-existing hole in the dragon's breast each time the weapon was released. One more pulley forced a slender string to return the spear to the warrior's hand after any group of visitors moved on to the next chamber.

"And the statue that moves?"

"Oh, but that's the best of all, Jess," Luke said, savoring the process of what he referred to as demystification. He led us to the opposite side of the cellar. Another set of steps allowed us access back up to ground level.

We then entered a cubicle, hidden by a curtain from any visitors in the chamber.

"Good. No one's here," Luke said. He led us into the room, indicating for me to closely inspect the goddess statue. "Look," he continued. "Notice that loadstone in the goblet?"

We nodded. Luke drew another *dinar* from his purse and dropped it in. The coin sank to the bottom, landing on a miniature piston. This caused a valve to open, allowing water to dribble down. The process forced compressed air up through a tube and into the statue's inner and, as I now grasped, hollow right arm. That arm moved, again pouring wine into a cup that John, understanding fully now, quickly set in place so that the rich drink would not be wasted.

The three of us exited through the great front doors and back onto the street. Another Greek working-class family entered, ready to drop in their coin and marvel at the power of their gods.

"Well, Jess? John? What do you think?"

Before I could attempt to form words, a terrible chill overcame me without warning. My stomach churned. I felt warm sweat beads forming on my forehead. Panicky, I turned, running I knew not where, aware only of oncoming nausea.

"Oooooooooh!"

I managed to take two steps before falling to my knees and vomiting on the street. John stood beside me, not certain as to what he ought to do, while several minutes passed. Luke, the physician, kneeled down to watch me closely.

"Maybe I'm going to be alright now," I eventually said.

Together, they helped me to unsteadily rise up. Still, weak knees threatened to send me back down the moment they loosened their grips.

"Any idea what happened to her?" John asked, concerned. Doubtless my much admired blue eyes now appeared a sickly sea green.

"I'm not certain," Luke answered. "Perhaps the food was tainted, or Jess drank too much wine too quickly. Also, the heat is worse than yesterday . . ."

The boys navigated me to a large rock, helping me to ease down on its rough surface. A dreary money changer's booth hid me from the crowd on one side while a colorful magician's tent, hailing from the vast territories we call Arabia, provided a modicum of privacy on the other.

*For John to see me this way is one thing. We are, after all, family.*

But a boy I had fallen in love with? Ooooooh!

We sat quietly for a while. Gradually, I recovered. John draped a protective arm around my shoulder as he gazed off into the sky, attempting to take in all he had seen.

# 44.

"I don't have the words to express my appreciation for what you've shown us today, Luke," John sighed.

"What you experienced on your initial tour is what avatars of these machines call construction."

"I don't have a clue what that means."

"A fantasy, Jess, which appears absolutely real."

"This explains why your family is so well to do?"

Luke smiled. "We finance Heron's experiments at creating ever more elaborate shows. Once his genius has designed the latest models, we oversee the manufacturing of them for Grecian temples everywhere in the known world."

"How then would you describe our second and secretive tour?" John, more intrigued than ever, asked.

"Deconstruction. Once you've observed Heron's machines at work from a behind-the-scenes perspective, seeing becomes—"

"—*disbelieving.*"

Luke nodded. "Well! You two have been afforded a rare treat. Other than myself, my parents, and our sworn-to-secrecy workers, no one in Capernaum has any idea what really occurs inside that building."

"Is there a name for those few in the know?"

"We are called the cognoscenti. The privileged few who determine how the majority of our people comprehend the world around them. So! Questions?"

"Yes," John said. "Now I understand how it all works, but not . . . at least not fully . . . *why?*"

"First, because people need to be terrified and delighted. Most humans are shallow. The lowest of the low? Stupid and ignorant. Also, their lives are deadly dull. If priests drone on, the masses fall asleep. So we dazzle them to assure they keep coming back to witness ever-grander spectacles. But the shows are never spectacular for its own sake. Here, visitors are exposed to values that underline our religion and politics, essentially one and the same. This unites us as a nation, however scattered we may be over the face of the earth today."

"I wonder if that would work for my nation as well." In the excitement of such scintillating conversation, I'd all but forgotten how wretched I felt.

"My guess? People are the same all over, deep down."

"It's all about control of the common folk, then?"

"Not 'all,' John. Also important is that when they come here, our true believers bring money. Coins to drop into the maiden's goblet. Tickets are necessary to enter the realm of Herakles and the dragon. My family, however loyal to the state, receives a notable percentage of all incoming funds. People without coins can leave animals or vegetables as offerings. The priests of Greece eat well."

*As do my nation's priests, I recall from my previous trip to Jerusalem's temple three years ago. For there, the practice of animal sacrifice remains the order of the day.*

*Again, I am Jess, so my mind takes flight. If we Hebrews did away with human sacrifice ages ago, why do we still murder innocent beasts in the name of God?*

"So your religion," John observed, summing it all up, "is, when you come right down to it, a business?"

"All religion," Luke stated flatly, "is business. To put it more specifically, show business."

"Not ours," John objected. "We are people of true faith."

Luke couldn't help but snicker at John's radical innocence. I knew better. I had learned something here today. What I understood now far exceeded any technical knowledge about machines that I had come to comprehend.

Jess of Nazareth now possessed a greater understanding of the way of the world.

"The sad truth?" Luke added. "Religion is *big* business. Even yours, my friend."

"And," I surmised, "the bigger the religion, the bigger the business."

"Amen to that," Luke concluded, chuckling.

# 45.

While I wiped traces of vomit from my mouth, someone passing by from behind bumped into my right shoulder. Turning, I stared into the face of Saul of Tarsus, here today in Capernaum.

*Was this destiny, as Hebrews who subscribed to the vision of the Sadducees insist? Part of Yahweh's master plan, written down in a great invisible book eons ago?*

*Or were the Essenes correct, insisting that Yahweh created us, watching down with interest as we exerted free will?*

*The Pharisees argued that life existed as a combination of the two: "All is in the hands of God," as Annas liked to say, "except the fear of God."*

*Likely, I would spend my life trying to decide where I stood on this divisive issue.*

"Sorry," he muttered before recognizing my face. Then Saul's body stiffened. "You? But . . ." He glanced up and down, from sandaled feet to messy face, amazed to realize that he spoke to . . . a girl.

"You have mistaken me for my twin brother."

"I could swear you were one and the same."

"Everyone who meets them says that," John interrupted.

"No one can look *that* much alike. Even twins. As brother and sister, you couldn't be identical—"

"Of course we're not." Thinking fast, desperate to bluff him, I blurted out, "Look! My eyes. Everyone says my brother's are considerably brighter."

Scrunching his brows, Saul leaned in for a closer look. "Yes, I see that now."

*Of course, it was the other way around. But this sudden inspiration struck me as my only chance to escape detection.*

*Fortunately, the power of suggestion had the effect I'd hoped for. And confirmed my faith in the notion that believing is seeing.*

"Would you like me to say hello to him for you?" I asked, having a little fun with this curious situation.

"No. But you can tell him I said he's an ass. I'm Saul of Tarsus. He'll know that name. Tell him I said that!"

Nodding, I feigned agreement. Saul huffily marched away in the company of three friends, each of whom I recognized from Yeshiva. Once more, I'd come perilously close to being unmasked. Yet somehow, or for some reason, Yahweh had been with me.

"You didn't tell me you had a twin brother."

"You didn't ask."

Wishing as I did to put the inevitable parting of the ways off, Luke offered to accompany us back to the sector containing the city's synagogue. From our current elevation halfway up the incline, I could see down through the city gates, over to the harbor. Boats, some raw wood and others colorfully painted, bounced at the breakwater with each mild wave. Gulls swept down in search of discarded guts and tails, left behind by the fishermen, for their supper. The red-orange sun began its descent in the western horizon, transforming the sky into a glorious pink.

All too soon, we reached our destination. "I guess this is where I must leave you two," Luke grimly sighed. He reached out and shook John's hand. Sensing we wished to be alone, my cousin said he'd see me in a few minutes and continued on alone.

"Well, Luke . . ."

"Well, Jess . . ."

Without planning to do so, I extended my right arm. Luke did the same. We shook hands, as men might.

"Oh," he said, noticing the scar on my right hand.

"That's nothing. Only the reminder of an accident from when I was very young."

"Well then! Perhaps we will meet again—"

"Not perhaps. *Definitely.*"

"You can see into the future, as seers claim to do?"

"Perhaps." I raised my left eyebrow provocatively. "We Hebrews possess many powers."

"I can see nothing but your blue eyes." I knew now, and for certain, that this had not been some passing flirtation. "And no matter what you said to that wealthy oaf back there, I cannot believe your brother's eyes are even half as intense a shade of blue as yours."

*He had fallen in love with me, as I had with him.*

*We didn't employ those precise words. We didn't need to.*

"My beautiful Greek," I said abruptly. "How will—"

"I'll come to see you in Nazareth. When—"

"*Never*! It wouldn't be proper."

"I'll be there three weeks from today."

"Oh! Why so *long*?"

He laughed, turned, and set out on his way. I stood alone, silently watching, until Luke disappeared into a crowd, wondering if he might glance back over his shoulder.

He didn't.

Part of me wanted to kill him for that. Mostly, though, I longed to kiss him.

# PART TWO

# A Sea Change

# 46.

"'So the Lord rained down fire and brimstone on the cities of evil, and Sodom and Gomorrah were destroyed.' Genesis 19."

A look of satisfaction crossed Annas's face. He had, in his mind, done a great service by sharing wisdom of the ages with young, impressionable boys. The Rabbi rolled up his Torah, as he did following each reading, then set it down on a nearby table.

As we in imitation did with our own. For several weeks into study, we had each been awarded a smaller, less elaborate scroll. Hebraic letters were embossed on fresh papyrus rather than dried, yellow goat skin.

When Annas read, we now were able to follow along, if spottily, owing to our progress in reading and writing. Boys from wealthy families had an advantage. Their fathers had hired tutors to augment these lessons at home. As for the rest of us, with each study session, sons (and in one case the daughter) of working-class parents came to understand our ancient language more fully.

Ours may not have been the first nation to create an alphabet and set down words so that generations yet to come would know about us. We were, though, as each Hebrew proudly knew, the only people in history to worship the Book almost as devoutly as we did our deity. Money, land, and business aside, once a Jew achieved literacy, he emerged as a revered person in his community. In our society alone, education had become as great a sign of status as money and power.

How I admired my nation for that! And yet . . .

*He, not she. Except for me. But why men and not women? The pagans, worshippers of the Great Goddess, which Maggie told me about, would not take such an approach.*

*Is my nation as wrong about this as I believe? And, if so, might it be misguided about other things as well?*

"Now, we discuss."

How excited I had been to hear those words early on in my schooling. I'd assumed (naively, it turned out) that each of us would be free to answer as we pleased. That's the way it was supposed to be among a people renowned for love of spirited argument. From Jerusalem's educated elite to illiterates in small villages, and all of the immense working class in-between, we enjoyed thinking individually and openly discussing.

I loved that about our way, even as I despised the idea that women were excluded from such debate. Females were also barred from entering Jerusalem's Holiest of Holies. One day, I asked (in my guise as a boy) Annas what he thought about that.

"What could a woman possibly have to say to God?" he snapped back impatiently.

While many rabbis may have encouraged open discussion, Annas desired, and would allow, nothing of the sort. There was one way of interpreting a tale: his way.

Annas bragged about his status as a Pharisee. Hailing from Judea in lower Israel, he considered himself more sophisticated than the smartest man to be found in the north. At some point in each session, he would find an excuse to rant about the Galileans' laxness as to dietary laws.

"A kosher home! You *must* maintain one at all costs. No excuses, do you hear?"

*Annas! Reality is reality. There is no temple official living in our Nazareth to bless the lamb at its killing so the meat can be considered kosher, Levi dared suggest.*

Annas's answer? "Then don't eat meat, even from breeds of animals deemed acceptable."

*That's easy for you to say! You live, after all, here in Sepphoris, where kosher food is readily available.*

*The best we provincials can do is refrain from eating of the pig or shellfish. On rare occasions, when we are lucky enough to have it, should we deny ourselves a morsel of chicken or lamb?*

"Saul?" Annas asked as the boy from Tarsus raised a hand, returning to our discussion of Sodom and Gomorrah.

"Once again, the message: the wages of sin are death."

Saul's coterie of friends, sitting cross-legged as close to their unofficial student-leader as possible, applauded him. I didn't necessarily disagree with Saul's words. To me the wages of sin absolutely were, and should be, death and destruction.

*If only our discussion had stopped there. However . . .*

"And, Saul, the sin of Sodom and Gomorrah was . . .?"

"They indulged in every sort of sexual behavior without concern for marriage. All races of women and men together, with prostitutes joining in. Even men coupling with other men was tolerated in this doomed city of sinners."

*Judas, I notice how you avert your eyes when Saul condemns the love of men for others of their gender. And live in fear that this may be true.*

*It isn't! I'll explain someday. I promise*

For sin, at least as I understood it, refers to performing an act forbidden by our Covenant, which must always be the very essence of Judaism.

"And God, in his wrath, smote all there save Lot and his family," one of Saul's sycophants added, hoping to score a few secondary points. "Only the good Hebrews living in this wicked city of pagans were personally escorted out in the nick of time."

"By an angel of the Lord," Saul concluded, getting in the last word.

"Precisely." Annas beamed with pride. "Now . . ."

As if by habit, my hand thrust up, waving for attention, as my mind attempted to force it down. Against his better judgment, Annas tolerantly nodded his permission for me to speak. The rabbi looked to be in a particularly grumpy mood today. Why didn't I remain quiet?

*Oh, but the answer to that one is easy. Because I'm me.*

"Excuse me, but . . . I listened to every word and read along closely. I don't see where it states that freedom of sexuality angered Yahweh. It simply isn't *there,* on the page."

# 47.

Saul's cronies groaned in unison, as they were wont to do whenever I made a point. The central figure in their moneyed clique cast exasperated eyes in my direction. "What *else* could it possibly have been?" Saul roared.

Refusing to let his emotionally brutal attitude intimidate me, I breathed in deeply before allowing my thoughts full-flow. "In the chapter's opening, the words clearly state that the people there were not kind to one another. In this dreadful place, it was considered a crime to show warmth, affection, or respect of any sort toward one's neighbors, much less newcomers."

"And . . .?" Annas, stepping closer, demanded. The rabbi's eyes all but spat fire toward me. As always, his intent was to isolate me as the outsider who somehow had managed to worm his way in to this select company of young scholars.

"I see where Jesus is going with this," Barabbas joined in, much to my relief. At long last, a brother in verbal arms! "My family does business with Greeks, Turks, Egyptians. I know the ancient laws of hospitality, which precede our own inception as a people. They require that humans treat each other always with respect and dignity."

To my happy amazement Levi, so often hesitant, dared speak up. "Doesn't our heritage tell us to love our neighbors? Our choice to do so is what qualifies us as God's Chosen. What doomed the citizens of Sodom and Gomorrah was their lack of such values."

Encouraged, I rose from my kneeling position. Twirling my hands about in the air as if visual passion might further emphasize the point, I continued: "They were raw individualists with no sense of community. *This* is what Yahweh despised."

By this point, Saul appeared ready to rise, rush over, and tear my head off.

"As Saul says," Rabbi Annas announced, hoping to end all discussion through his words and an assumed tone of finality, "sex, and particularly homosexual sex, was the reason for their mass death in the flames of righteousness."

"I'm not so sure." Once more, Barabbas made his thoughts known. "I think Yahweh would have destroyed those cities even if sex had not been an issue. Say, perhaps, that the Sodomites had wanted to rob and kill the visitors? Wouldn't that have been as bad in God's eyes?"

"Or worse?" Levi affirmed.

*I've been waiting for you to stand up and be counted since we were children.*

*Please, Levi, never falter again.*

Of our group, only Judas kept a silent council. Yet I could see in his sad, threatened eyes and repeated twitches of his neck that he *so* wanted to join in.

"Rape, robbery, murder," Barabbas insisted. "Any of those, perpetrated on innocent strangers, would have outraged Yahweh."

"If sex is in and of itself evil, then why did Lot, as a righteous man, offer to send his virginal daughters out to the crowd in the visitors' stead? Doesn't that prove the greatest concern of Yahweh was not sexuality per se, but *any* breach as to the laws of hospitality?"

"You're getting it all wrong," Saul shouted, waving a clenched fist in my direction. Annas, meanwhile, broke into a dance of anger. As if the earth below had turned to fire, he hopped up and down, furious at having his authority challenged. As his face turned bright crimson, our rabbi appeared on the verge of a seizure.

"The only thing the Ten Commandments forbids is the act of adultery," Barabbas insisted. "If other sexual acts are sinful, wouldn't they be as prominently stated?"

"Are you suggesting," Annas asked, pronouncing each word emphatically, "that lust is *not* a sin?"

*Yes, Annas. I do happen to believe that.*

*What, though, is the proper definition of lust?*

Now, Judas could no longer hold in his passion to join in. "Rabbi, my father read that story to me many times. Didn't you leave out the final paragraph? Lot and his daughters go off to Zoar's cave, believing the entire world is destroyed. The girls desire to have babies. They believe Lot to be the last man on Earth. So they render him drunk, then all lay together. Yet Yahweh does not punish them. Wouldn't that suggest—"

*Judas! Do you realize that the entire time you spoke, not once did you allow the twitch to overtake you?*

*Free your mind of fear, and you liberate your body as well.*

A profound stillness descended on our gathered company. Neither Annas nor Saul could verbally assault the four of us. For we had made our point well, citing evidence existing within the original text.

*Not that we were necessarily right or Annas wrong.*

*Only that there is more than one way of looking at things, even that remarkable source we call the Bible.*

"Class . . . is . . . *dismissed*." Annas desperately waved his hands in the air, then spun around and hurriedly entered the synagogue, slamming the door behind him.

"Well," Saul hissed, baiting us for a fight, "the four of you have really gone and done it this time."

Other boys rose and made ready to head off in all directions on their ways home. Saul stepped close, readying his fists as a challenge to me. Before sparks could fly, Barabbas stepped between us. His pugilistic stance made clear that if there were to be a scuffle, Saul would not be matched against one of the slender students. Rather, a budding Hebraic Herakles.

"Someday . . ." Saul addressed me in a voice that left no room for doubt: we were enemies for life.

# 48.

We four walked southerly until reaching our parting of the ways. There Judas and Barabbas would head west along an unpaved trail leading to their village. As yet unnamed, the circle of thirty buildings was one of many settlements that sprouted near Sepphoris during and following the city's reconstruction.

Ten years earlier, Antipas's troops demolished the area. Rebels hiding there were captured by General Varian's legion. With their wives and children, all were crucified along a 100-mile stretch of highway as a warning to others: Do not resist Rome!

Ironically, Antipas—like his late father Herod the Great— hoped to convince the more than two million Jews living in or near Israel to accept his dream of establishing in our region the great *Pax Romana*: Peace, harmony, and safety in any territory occupied by the legions. Never had peace been so widespread since Caesar vowed to do so by force if necessary.

Like Emperor Tiberius, who had two years earlier succeeded the now deceased Augustus, Antipas would slaughter as many dissidents as necessary to achieve that. The point, simply stated: oppose Caesar's domination and perish. Accept it, and you may never know war or violence in your lifetimes.

*Initially, the choice seemed simple enough.*

*It had proven to be anything but.*

Our quartet completed the first mile and a half together, passing goat-skin sacks of water and wine back and forth. "I was so proud of you, Levi. And you, too, Judas!"

"I don't know what came over me, Jess." Apparently, Levi was amazed by his own reserves of strength and conviction. "I never thought much about any of this before. But what you said? And what Barabbas added were so clearly *right*—"

Our rugged friend, unusually quiet until this moment, announced, "I'm thinking about dropping out of school."

"What?"

We three stopped in our tracks, watching as a melancholy Barabbas slowed down and turned back to face us. "Why continue? I learn more discussing things with the three of you than from that old buzzard."

"But where would you go?"

"As I've mentioned before, Judas, I've given considerable thought to joining the Zealots."

With a powerful body, a keen mind, and a hot temper more quicksilver even than my own, as well as his growing hatred of the occupying Romans, Barabbas was the sort of boy the guerilla force hoped to recruit.

"I felt that way once," Levi said, "but Jess talked me out of it. With religious freedom—"

"Not since the ruling on the *Tallit!*" Barabbas reminded him. He had a point. How absurd that the kind of armed rebellion, which a decade earlier led to the Sepphoris massacre, could occur again, this time owing to the color of a single hanging thread.

*Why doesn't one among my nation dare approach Antipas and explain to him this could create the very sort of violence he sincerely hopes to avoid?*

*Though I guess the answer is simple: who would dare try and do so? And even if some commoner had the nerve, how would that person ever gain access to the king?*

"Jesus—and I know that I address you now by my own name, as well as yours—please don't do anything rash. Remain here. At least for the time being?"

"If only for our sake?" Levi added.

"But I *have* remained here. And for some time. Tending fields, learning to read, write, and study scripture. Only to discover the man I expected to be wise is nothing more than a foolish pedagogue."

"Well, stay then, until you learn enough from *us* to become a rabbi yourself. Then challenge Annas's views."

"Me?" Barabbas laughed out loud. "I'm a born warrior. A fighter, not a preacher."

"It's you, Jess," Judas said, joining the conversation. "If any one of us is to become a rabbi, surely it is you."

It struck me that Judas was correct. Though I'd never framed it so in my mind, I now knew what I wished to do with the rest of my life.

*Be a rabbi.*

*But was Israel ready for its first female teacher?*

"Please reconsider, Barabbas?"

"Alright then. For now, at least."

"I'm so glad," Judas shyly asserted, "that it was not the Sodomites' desire to 'know' the male visitors that brought on their fate."

"To me, the crime was in the attempt to *force* themselves on strangers. The potential for rape, not the sex act itself, infuriated Yahweh against Sodom."

"The Book of Leviticus," Levi reminded me, "does condemn homosexuality as a crime."

"Recall what its title actually means: 'The Law of Men.' Written by fallible people. Not dictated by Yahweh, as were the Ten Commandments."

"You make a good point," Barabbas observed. "It also insists there that if a man were to work on the Sabbath, he ought to be executed. Is there one among us who can honestly say he has never done so?"

"Let he who is without guilt cast the first stone."

"Very good, Jess. I like that!" Levi said.

"I wish I could claim authorship," I blushed. "In truth, I once heard my mother say it."

"All the Torah commands is that we ought to 'remember' the seventh day and 'keep it holy,'" Judas asserted, sounding ever more confident. "God says nothing as how we ought to go about doing that."

"For me, work is a holy thing," Barabbas added. "I feel closest to God when tending my field. If so, then wouldn't such labor be my way to 'keep the Sabbath holy?'"

"Yes," I agreed, "for anyone who believes in the sanctity of individual perception."

"What do you even mean by that?" Levi asked.

"The right for each of us to interpret the law for ourselves, rather than have our notions of what each rule actually means dictated to us by others."

# 49.

After departing from our friends, Levi and I continued along the main road. Built by our conquerors, this highway was comprised of well-paved slabs of stone set into place by cement. Gutters lined each side, allowing rainwater to siphon off. Here was yet another clever Roman innovation. In less than a month, the rainy winter season would commence. Then, even we Hebrews had to admit how smart and simple a solution this was to our earlier problems with flooded routes. This afternoon, though, the skies were powder blue, punctuated with white clouds.

Invariably, on our way home Levi and I briefly paused at an old stone well, shaded by oak trees and circled by acacias. This rest area, two miles southeast of Zion Synagogue, marked the halfway point of our return journey. Arriving, we leaned over the circular rim and considered our distorted reflections in the water below.

Then something unexpected occurred. Gazing down, I noticed a third reflected head, bobbing in the ripples set into motion by our lowering of the bucket.

"Oh!" Levi and I gasped in unison, turning.

Before us stood a tall, handsome man. He wore a robe that stretched from his neck to his ankles. Its soft-beige coloring was crossed by line after vertical line of color: green, yellow, purple, brown, among many others. I couldn't begin to guess what his shimmering garment might be fashioned from. The material did not resemble wool, linen, or any source for clothing in Galilee. The same held true for his sandals, apparently some sort of metal rather than leather and wood. I could not identify it as iron, gold, copper, bronze, or any other I knew of.

"So sorry. Didn't mean to disturb you. Just stopping by for a drink myself, when you are both finished."

We sipped from the barrel, then handed it to him. As the stranger partook, I was able to take in the measure of this man. My guess: he stood tall at 5' 7", perhaps even more than that. I doubted he was a Jew, as our average height in those days was 5' 4". Yet what I observed was not a Roman or Greek face. His skin lacked the tawniness, luster, and elasticity of people from our western coast. Phoenicians tended toward darkness; he was light. Blondish hair, long and uncombed if scrupulously clean, caused me to recall tales I had heard of a strange race that lived far to the north, in places with odd names like Aengland and Germanium.

More fascinating than my inability to guess his origin was the difficulty of determining his age. He might have been only a few years older than us or perhaps over thirty. I couldn't tell. He appeared ageless.

Slung around his shoulder, hanging from a thick cord, a ram's horn resembled my nation's cherished shofar, blown by our priests on holy occasions.

"You startled us. But welcome. Our system of wells was not created for we Hebrews alone, but also strangers in a strange land."

Warmly, he took our hands in friendship. "I should have announced myself. But I was intrigued by your discussion, as well as your intensity in speaking."

"About Sodom and Gomorrah? A story from our book."

Instinctively, we all sat down in the shade of the largest tree, understanding without anyone actually saying so that we'd talk for a while.

"Oh yes. I'm aware of the Bible. Know it well. But refresh my memory, please. You said . . . Sodom and Gomorrah?"

I allowed Levi to do the honors. He told the stranger that Yahweh sent two angels down from Heaven to learn if these places were as sinful as had been reported. Lot, kinsman to Abraham, had been living in Sodom with his family. He welcomed the angels, disguised as wayfarers, as was the custom of our people. But non-Hebraic citizens of the twin cities wished to harm these agents of God.

Thanks to Lot, the angels escaped, ascended, and informed Yahweh of their experiences. God knew then these were indeed wicked places. He sent the angels back to escort Lot and his kin to safety before raining down fire and brimstone.

Lot's wife, who disobeyed Yahweh and turned back for one last look, was transformed into a pillar of salt, rumored to still be standing there.

# 50.

"Yes, yes. Now I recall it clearly. But do you know that this story is not confined to your nation?"

We shook our heads no. "I come from Canaan, east of the Dead Sea rift, where this incident supposedly happened. The tribes inhabiting that area know of the occurrence, included in their own great book, the *Quran*. Lot, though, is not the man's name. He is an Arab, descended from Ishmael. They call the cities Bab Edh-Dra and Numeria."

"Then the story," Levi said, "is not only Hebraic but—"

"Universal?" I suggested.

"Ah! Now, young friends, we are onto something! I know that the tale is true. For I have seen the ruins with my own eyes."

An aura of excitement, the sort we had once hoped for from our rabbi, emanated from this stranger: his laughing eyes, an animated body, and most of all his passionate tone.

"Of course, there are many other tellings."

"Really?" Levi's interest piqued now. "Do you know any of them?" I nodded enthusiastically, hoping to learn more.

"Well, let me see . . . yes, I do remember one, and it is the strangest of all."

"Might we hear it?"

"Alright then. But don't think me mad! Once upon a time, in a star system long, long ago and far, far away, there existed Travelers. They journeyed through the skies, unconcerned as to the limitations of time and space as earthlings know them. These celestial voyagers flew in marvelous ships, powered by energy sources yet unknown on this planet. Sometimes, they would land on distant worlds, study the inhabitants, and decide if such beings might evolve into more advanced lifeforms. In hopes of achieving that, some of these Star Men mated with the females, then left on their ships. Eventually, they returned to discover whether their experiment had succeeded. The earthlings called these aliens by many names. One popular term was The Watchers. Another? The Visitors."

*So he is mad. I ought to leap up, take Levi by the arm, and run home.*

*Why then do I remain in place, grinning from ear to ear, my head bobbing up and down like a village idiot?*

"Well, in time, they visited Earth. In Canaan their relations with Arabic women led to the great founder whom you know as Abraham, explaining his vast wisdom. One day, a voice whispered from a source that he for want of a better term called God, commanded him to leave home and found a new nation. When the Star People returned, two descended from their mother ship. They—"

"Yes, well! That's marvelous. *Really.* But Levi and I must be getting home—"

"Oh, but please let me finish?"

"I do so want to hear the rest, Jess." Levi's eyes pleaded. So I ignored the voice deep inside that silently screamed: "Run!"

"I'll finish quickly. They soon discovered that while most of mankind had regressed to an animal state, Lot, like his kinsmen Abraham, proved to be the happy exception. These spies beamed up to their mother ship, explaining everything to their supreme commander. It was determined that the beastly men and women must be wiped off the face of the earth, as well as from the history of mankind, for that experiment had gone badly."

"As to Lot?"

"Oh, well. Lot! He measured up to expectations. And so was kept alive to pass his excellent blood on to others. Before the mother ship decimated the twin cities, he and his family were escorted out by angels . . . aliens . . . whatever you choose to call them. Sadly, his wife lingered behind and was reduced to atomic ash."

"Atomic . . . *what?*" Levi asked, fascinated.

I smiled sweetly at this lunatic while Levi and I rose and stepped back toward the well as if our thirst had returned.

"Listen, Levi," I whispered. "We are going to politely thank him for his company, then quickly depart."

"You think he may be possessed by some daemon?"

"That, or his mind is warped from too much sun."

"If he attempts to stop us, you run around him on his right side, and I'll do the same on his left."

I nodded in agreement and drew a deep breath. In unison, we spun about only to realize the stranger had disappeared as mysteriously as he earlier arrived.

Later, though, as we continued south toward Nazareth, I could swear I heard a shofar blowing somewhere in the woods.

# 51.

"Hello, stranger."

Looking up, I saw Mary of Magdala standing beside me, as she had several weeks earlier. Once more, I'd slipped off to that natural garden of flowers and trees I considered my private domain: a silent, shady refuge from the real world.

"Maggie! I was just thinking of you."

I'd arrived here directly after class before seeking out Joses, explaining why I still wore male attire. Maggie knew, from her previous visit, where I could be found during late afternoons: that mellow time when the day's work is done but dinner remains several hours away for a Hebrew family.

"I grew tired of waiting for you to come see me," she said with a hint of disappointment.

*I rose and embraced her, warmly though less than wholeheartedly.*

*Recall, please, future reader of this manuscript: I was not yet twelve years of age when all of this transpired.*

Maggie confused me. I sensed her strong attraction to the boy she believed me to be. And I could imagine the consequences if she were allowed to continue her romantic pursuit. Still, I wished to keep her in my life. And, however disturbing, if in a pleasant way that left me distraught, the unique experience of the kiss she'd bestowed on my lips still lingered in my memory.

"Apologies. It's been a difficult week."

We stood face to face. "I thought about coming up the trail. Several times, actually," Maggie said.

"Even as I considered hiking down to Nazareth."

"Sure you did," she answered with a touch of sarcasm. Maggie turned and stepped away, heading deep into the lush green world surrounding us, me following.

"Well, I'm not exactly welcome there."

We drifted aimlessly through the pines and, coming upon a fallen oak, sat down on its soft, rotted surface, turned white by years of exposure to sun and rain. Other than the chirping of a bird and the sound of miniature feet, field mice perhaps, scampering through the knee-high grass, a profound sense of quietude prevailed.

"I know, Jess. I heard rumors around town."

"Don't believe everything you hear."

"How about what I see?" she continued, half-teasingly.

"Only half of that," I replied, thinking of the Greek temple John and I visited, "at *most!*" We laughed, then remained silent for a while. Each of us awkwardly waited for the other to restart the conversation. Then, finally, I asked, "Maggie, how are things at that house, with your uncle?"

A dark cloud passed over her face, so open until then. "Let's not speak of it. I came here in part to get away."

"Tell me! If things are difficult, I want to—"

"Is it true," she interrupted, eager to change the subject, "that when you were very young, you killed a boy in anger, then restored him to life?"

A telling pause as I gathered my thoughts. "Let me put it this way: yes and no."

"That makes no sense. It's yes *or* no."

"Not necessarily. If there's one thing I've learned from life, it's that nothing is as simple as people wish to believe."

"Someday, Jess, will you tell me what happened?"

"Certainly."

"And, of course, I also heard about the issue of your questionable birth. You and your twin . . . sister?"

How had I managed to work myself into such a preposterous situation? "That I can answer simply enough. Yes, my sister and I are, some claim, illegitimate."

Maggie took my right hand, holding it reassuringly in her own. "That's the main reason I came here today. I want you to know that, true or not, I don't care."

"Thank you for being such a good friend."

"Oooooooh!" She stood up suddenly and, like a stern Roman soldier, marched about, furrowing her brow, upset. "Will you *stop* speaking to me that way?"

"What way? I don't know—"

"Yes, you do."

That left me speechless. In part because she was right. I did.


# 52.


As swiftly as Maggie had risen, she sat down beside me again, this time wrapping her arms around my shoulders, kissing me on my lips, forehead, and cheeks. This, much to my surprise and, however much I tried to deny it, delight as well.

Her lips tasted as if they'd been coated with honey: sweet and natural. Maggie's hair, falling across my face, smelled as fresh as wisps of new-mown hay. Her firm tongue gently forced its way into my mouth.

"Maggie," I gasped, recovering and holding the precocious girl at arm's length, "this situation is more difficult than you could possibly imagine."

"Why? Because we're of different faiths? Hebrews allow women of many nations to marry their sons, provided we accept your Creator God. I know the story of Ruth."

I tried to speak, but Maggie wouldn't let me get a word in. "Here," she said, lifting something from out of her pocket. An amulet dangled from a chain. Maggie brought it up and over my head, draping it around my neck. For a moment I assumed this to be the Phoenician image she had shared with me previously. At first glance I knew it to be something else entirely.

The odd icon, unlike anything I'd ever seen, featured at its top a black, metal nail. This had been heated, then twisted into an egg-shaped loop. Directly below it, a horizontal bar served as the base. And from that line, one more sliver of metal extended downward, pushing out at the right and left toward the bottom.

"What is it?"

"An Egyptian who stopped by my uncle's booth in the marketplace traded it for some pears and grapes. He claimed that in his homeland, this is called an Ankh. Many centuries ago a great pharaoh designed it to illustrate his own belief that the world existed in unity, each aspect in harmony with every other. The top represented the One True God, which to them is synonymous with the sun."

"Helios."

"Huh?"

"The Greek term for a sun god."

The bar beneath this reminded me of two things: first, that ever receding line between the water and the sky, a demarcation for Hebrews of the entranceway to eternity, if such a place even exists. Also, the crossbar recalled the brutal wooden cross employed by Romans to slowly kill rebellious Hebrews.

"The bottom extensions are symbolic of the sun's rays, allowing for life on the land and sea below."

"Essentially, that's what my nation believes."

"See? I wanted you to know that the idea of a single deity makes sense to me. And not just because I've fallen in love."

Nervously, I cleared my throat, buying a few seconds while trying to think of something appropriate to say. "Levi, you know, feels much the same about *you.*"

"Of course, I know. A girl *always* knows. Even if, for her own purposes, she pretends not to. But I don't feel that way about him. Levi, I want for a friend. You—"

She lunged forward, making ready to kiss me again. This time I held her off, with much difficulty and some reluctance.

"Maggie, please. It's almost dinner time. I must return—"

"Promise you'll come see me soon in Nazareth? *Please?*"

"I will."

"I'll hold you to that."

She kissed me good-bye, directly on the lips. Pulling away, Maggie offered a wide-open smile, which I found enchanting. Moments later she took the trail south, waving over her shoulder before slipping out of sight.

My mind went to wondering: if Luke were to kiss me when he arrived in a week and a half, would his lips meet mine with such strength, sweetness, and softness?

"Jess?" Turning, I noticed my twin hurrying near. "It's late. I was coming to get you and . . . who is *she*?"

"Mary. From Magdala. Levi and I call her Maggie." For the first time, I noticed something that resembled true, intense, unbridled emotion in Jude's eyes.

"She's the most beautiful girl I've ever seen," he sighed, staring off in the direction she had taken.

# 53.

In the stark light of the midday sun, I stepped along the footpath that passed by Joseph's workroom. As in Nazareth, he had built a pair of entranceways for this outward extension of the original building. This enabled him to enter his private little realm from inside the main room or from the edge of the wilderness, where I now stood. On such a fine afternoon, Joseph usually left this outer door open so as to enjoy the agreeable breezes and soft sound of rustling leaves in nearby trees.

Grinding noises from the shop indicated that Joseph was hard at work, cutting slabs of limestone and basalt for various projects. Yet this was the Sabbath! How intriguing that my friends and I had, only days earlier, discussed this very subject. I peered in and saw Joseph, without benefit of lamplight, crouched over the machinery, making certain his stone edges were precise.

Hearing me approach, he set the work aside. "Jess. Is that you?"

As always, the room—rough earth serving as its floor, raw materials scattered everywhere, tools haphazardly leaning against limestone walls—played home to airborne dust from his labor.

"I heard you working and was surprised."

Joseph motioned for me to enter and sit on a nearby stool. "Here I am, in my workshop, even though today is the Sabbath. There are those in Nazareth who would stone me for heresy."

"As they once were ready to tear me limb from limb," I recalled. "Do you remember? By the Jordan, when I was five."

A frown passed over Joseph's forehead. I knew that this aging man no longer possessed the impressive powers of memory, which, a few years previous, had allowed him to vividly recall such events. "Refresh me?"

"That was a Sabbath as well," I began.

Absentmindedly, I reached down to discarded shafts of wood that Joseph had dropped on the floor, one piece slightly longer than the other. More out of habit than design, I picked up the longer slat, took hold of a small saw, and set to shaving it down to the same length as its companion.

No reason, really, other than that I liked to keep even the little insignificant things of life in parallel order.

"The good citizens of Nazareth were then engaged in one of their infamous debates concerning the Fourth Commandment."

"Yes!" Joseph recalled, returning to work. "I remember it now. The conservatives wanted to revert to the old ways. Moses long ago had insisted that people who defecated on the Sabbath must die, as that could be constituted as 'work.'"

"While progressives argued that such an approach was, and always had been, madness. For them, the concept of work only referred to what . . . well . . . what *you* are doing right now. Plying one's trade for money."

Joseph laughed good-naturedly. "But that's not the case. I'm making a gift for your mother. Is this then work, or an act of love?"

"Either. Both . . ." I shrugged.

*Nothing is simple. All in life is complex.*

*Even such everyday details as this.*

"Mary and I were always liberal in our interpretations. For instance, that day you speak of? Our family had gone for a stroll along the river to enjoy peace and quiet, basking in the sun on our only day of rest."

"Yet some in the village claimed we were sinners, as walking can be construed as a form of work."

Joseph howled with laughter. "*Our* notion of remembering and keeping the day holy was to enjoy ourselves. If that be sin, let me sin on!"

"It was in springtime. For several days, rainstorms had relentlessly showered the area."

"Joses was with us on that sunny day, wasn't he?"

"Yes. As soon as we reached the Jordan, my twin curled up and took a nap."

Momentarily, Joseph closed his eyes, considering what I had described. "Joses was always Joses, even then," he sighed.

*This may not be the case . . . I know him to be capable of change . . . though now is not the time to bring that up.*

"I played in the mud, running my fingers through the wet dirt for no better reason than that's what children do. For a few precious moments, all seemed blissful. Until—"

"—several priests came running up to Mary and myself. Eyes filled with horror, they led us back to you."

"Ah, your memory *is* returning. Just think: a child, accused of heresy owing to sticking fingers in the mud. 'Work!'"

"Work, Jess, is whatever one defines it as."

*Individual perception! What I most fervently believe in.*

*Thank you, Joseph, for raising me with this rare perspective always foremost.*

"Lately, I'm beginning to believe that about everything. As you told me years ago, 'All in life is relative.'"

"Actually, those meddlers thought you were your brother. They accused Joses of making mischief. Yet it was you, molding clay pigeons out of soft, wet earth."

"They screamed aloud I had broken not one but two of the commandments. First, working on the Sabbath—"

"—second, shaping graven idols."

"To the Greeks, such activity is called 'art.'"

"To us? 'Sin.' You then shocked the priests by revealing yourself as a magician, half a year before you brought that boy back from the dead."

"Likewise, that was attributed to my brother."

"Well, the 'miracle' of Levi's supposed resurrection was preceded by the riverbank incident. When accused of sinfulness, you screamed, fell into one of your fits, and clapped your hands in the air. Then, low and behold, the clay pigeons transformed into birds of flesh and blood, flying off and away on feathered wings."

What actually happened? Considerably more mundane! While digging, I felt something stir. Pushing mud away, I rescued several trapped pigeons, buried alive by the rain, somehow still surviving. I set each aright on the ground. Initially, they were too stunned to move. Hearing the priests' condemnations, I clapped my hands. Off the little creatures flew. Here, to those with positive outlooks, had occurred a miracle. Negativeminded Nazarenes took it as black magic.

"Magic, like miracles, are the words we employ to describe what we perceive but do not comprehend." All at once, Joseph's eyes opened wide. "Oh, Jess! Look. You've done it *again.*"

Confused, I glanced down. Unaware, I'd finished sawing and set the tool by my feet, dropping down the wood. Side by side again, the piece I'd picked up was now the same size as its companion.

"All I did was shave—"

"Jess," Joseph cheered, dancing around on the dirt floor. "I had cut the pieces unevenly, and was planning to throw them away. Such a terrible waste of fine wood that would have been. But you . . . you took the shorter one and, with your wondrous abilities, stretched it to the full length of the other."

Even Joseph, the man who had taught me to closely consider all that happened around us, could fall prey to seeing is believing.

But I knew better. In truth, believing is seeing.

# 54.

"Can we talk?"

"Indeed, we need to," Joses said, yawning himself awake. Once upright, he cast a sly smile in my direction. "Join me."

I sat beside him on his beloved hillock. The shade created a tranquil mood. Chirping in the branches above, multi-colored birds provided a cacophony of nature's music. Sheep grazed nearby, raising their heads occasionally, bleating at the two silly humans a short distance away. Joses reached for his flute. Skilled at making music, he imitated the soft forest sounds, enhancing the profound sense of serenity.

"If only it could stay like this for always," I sighed.

How many times would I repeat that in my life? In how many different situations?

*The truth, as I would learn along the way of my journey: things change. Sometimes for the good, often for the bad.*

*Always, though, they change.*

"More likely," Joses replied, "the calm before the storm."

"That's what I want to speak to you about. Our 'situation' has become terribly complicated."

"You didn't expect that? Come on, Jess. Wise up."

"I guess I did. But I *so* wanted to attend Yeshiva."

"It's only a matter of time before you get caught. Does that pretty girl . . . what did you say her name was—"

"Mary of Magdala. Maggie."

"Mmmmmm. Does she know your little *secret?*"

"No. At least I don't think so."

"I see you're wearing that bauble she gave you."

"It's a religious piece. From what Maggie told me, I'd guess it dates back as much as 1,500 years."

"When our people were in bondage in Egypt?"

I nodded affirmatively. "That's what's so strange. This is Egyptian, meant to symbolize belief in a single god. A most revolutionary idea for that nation, at that moment in time."

"Maybe they picked the concept up from enslaved Hebrews."

"Possibly. Or might we have learned it from them? Anyway, Jude, this girl, Maggie? She's in love with me."

Joses changed positions to better contemplate his sister, facing me now, locking eyes with those of his twin. "You're kidding!"

"I wish that were so. Jude, I'm worried!"

"I can see why you might be," he chuckled.

"It's tricky. I do love her. In a sisterly way, perhaps? In all honesty, I don't know. But Maggie appears interested in marriage."

"What a great surprise," he laughed loudly, "she'd have on her wedding night."

I took hold of the Ankh, lifting the chain up and over my neck. "Not if you were to be me."

At that, Joses leaped up like a surprised frog. "Now I *know* you're crazy—"

"Didn't you say that you find her attractive?"

His eyes went misty. "The most beautiful girl . . ."

"Might you want her for your own?"

"Any man would. But—"

Rising, I dropped the chain down over Joses's head, lowering it around his shoulders. "It could work!"

"You're mad."

"Jude, we're all but identical, other than . . . well, you know . . ."

"Boys will be boys, and girls will be girls."

"Exactly. I'll tell you everything she knows about me."

"What's in it for you?"

I paused briefly at the realization that my twin thought me to be so self-serving. "I get to pay you back for going along with my, as you put it, crazy plan. You'll have your chance with her. Who knows where it could lead?"

Joses nodded, taking this in. "You're right, Jess. It's just crazy enough that it *might* work."

"If it does . . . and it's a big if . . . all three of us would be happy. I'd have helped you, you'd have her for wife, and she'd be . . . another sister to me."

"As to the if?"

I averted my eyes, considering everything and anything nearby, other than Joses. "Well, you know . . ."

"No. I don't. Tell me."

# 55.

An awkward moment of silence followed before I spoke. "She's very bright. And witty! I'm not sure . . . that . . . you—"

"That I'm not smart enough for her? After she's spent time with *you*?"

Joses stepped away, anger pouring off his body like sweat. His face went pale. Aware that something had gone wrong, my eyes wheeled back toward him.

"Jude, her mind is *so* sharp. Forgive me, but—"

"Damn it!" Joses stomped about furiously, then threw down his precious flute. "And damn you for saying that."

"I didn't mean to—"

"You consider me your intellectual inferior?" he hissed, coming close. His rough manner and harsh voice frightened me. "Everyone does. I know it. 'Jess is the brilliant one.' 'She and Joses might look alike but, oh! How different their brains—'"

"You've never expressed any interest in studying Torah, interpreting parables, or our situation under Roman—"

"True. But have you ever wondered *why*?"

"I figured you . . . just didn't care."

"Is *that* what you believe?" His eyes, ordinarily a blue almost as radiant as my own, blazed red with fury. "How do you know I don't secretly care about such things?" He veered away again, perhaps his only means of avoiding a violent outburst. "You don't know me."

"Jude," I gasped, following and taking his hand in mine. "I never guessed—"

"From day one," he sputtered, "it's always been Jess, Jess, *Jess*. What a remarkable girl! Too bad she wasn't born a boy."

"Why didn't you speak up?"

"I did! No one listened. When I offered a comment, everyone reacted as if my words were rough barley. Anytime you opened your mouth, what you said was taken as grains of golden wheat."

"Honestly, Jude? I had no idea."

"And whenever you got in trouble, *I* took the blame."

"This is all so sudden—"

"I'm smarter than you know. Than *any* of you know. Smart enough to have realized early on that while I was the boy-child of Mary and Joseph, you emerged from her womb first. My guess? When they finished praising you, little was left to say about me, beginning on day one."

"You can't know that. Not for certain."

"Maybe not. But I can believe it if I choose to."

*Because, as I myself am coming to realize, ultimately all reality exists in the mind.*

*We think that we share a single world with others. In truth, each of us lives in a world of our own making. Located in the individual human brain.*

"So," I said, spreading my arms outward, "you gave up?"

He pointed down to where the animals mingled, grazing. "Do you really think this is what I want to do with my days? I'd love to be special, as you are, if only for once in my life."

"And I robbed you of that by taking your place at school! Well, from now on, *you* go to Sepphoris while I remain—"

Consumed with self-pity, Joses shook his head. "Too late. I've come to accept my status. I'm Jess's brother. The unspectacular sibling of someone extraordinary."

*I had to find some way to draw him out of this melancholy. He was my brother. I loved him. All at once I had become aware of a depth to Jude I'd failed to notice before.*

"Well, then, here's your chance. You'll speak as you've always wanted to when you woo Mary of Magdala."

"I'm not sure I have the confidence to even try."

"Before, I was only asking. Now? I'm insisting. You've *got* to do this. I'll support you every inch of the way. Please?"

This time, Joses paused while fingering the Ankh. "She *is* very beautiful," he recalled pleasantly.

"You'll win her, Jude. I know you will."

"Well, I guess it can't hurt to try."

We warmly embraced, which we hadn't done in a long time. I felt as if I'd regained a brother whom I had somehow lost along the way.

More importantly, never again would I perceive Jude as a wastrel.

At this moment, he was reborn to me. As a result, I too was, in a manner of speaking, born again.

# 56.

Two days later, heading home from Hebrew School, my mind drifted to Luke. How would I survive until I gazed upon my beautiful Greek once more?

I walked alone now. Levi had taken ill that morning at the halfway point and turned back. Minutes earlier, I'd parted from Barabbas and Judas as they left the main road, taking their westward path home.

Humming to myself, I wondered if Luke would work up the nerve to try and kiss me. Or, if he didn't, might I be brazen enough to kiss him? Once again, I'd slipped deep into my mental world, barely aware of the physical surroundings. So much so that I failed to watch where I was going.

That's when I stumbled directly into Saul of Tarsus. "There's something *queer* about you!" he called out in a hostile voice.

"Oh! You?"

"Yeah, me. Did your sister deliver my message?" I nodded that she had, thankful at least that he hadn't guessed my secret. "Then you know what I think of you," he said with a sneer, stepping closer in a gait that I knew to be menacing.

"I've known for some time." Where I found a hidden source of courage, in the face of this unexpected menace, I don't know. "Would you like to know what I think of *you*?"

Eyes bulging, he continued to narrow the gap between us. Owing to the angle of the sun and where the two of us stood in relationship to one another, Saul's shadow now covered my face. I felt like David facing off with Goliath, though I had no slingshot with which to defend myself.

"I'm listening, you little provincial *nothing*."

"You're a suck-up who only wants to impress Rabbi Annas and be his beloved toady. You're conventional. You repeat tired ideas you've heard a hundred times, without adding a single original thought. You're a phony, who pretends to know more than you do. You're a status seeker, ruling it over the other elites because your father owns half of Tarsus thanks to his tents. Which, I hear, aren't as sturdy as they're made out to be. You're a bully, for you only want to pick fights with those smaller—"

Before I could finish, Saul slowly drew his right fist back behind his ear, then rapidly brought it forward, smashing me in the face. The blow sent me flying backwards. I yelped with pain and, managing to recover several seconds later, ran my fingers across my nose to find out if it was bleeding.

Indeed, it was. Blood flowed everywhere. Meanwhile, Saul started to kick me in the shins. Refusing to lay there and take it, I seized his left leg with both hands, twisting as hard as I could, and bit the exposed flesh above his sandal.

Saul howled. "You fight like a girl!"

He pulled his leg free and began to kick me again, on my legs, my torso, until . . .

"Hold it right there."

The voice—bold, righteous, assertive—roared through the gully where we struggled. Twisting around, I saw that Barabbas had reappeared on the main road. Standing tall, like some great hero of old, back when we Hebrews were a mighty nation led by David: soldier, poet, lover, king.

*A Hebrew Herakles in embryo.*

*For a split second and, despite my still endangered situation, I tried to decide who was the more appealing and attractive: Barabbas or Luke?*

At any rate, the point was here before me was proof such a savior could rise once more. The Israelite warrior of old lived again. His name was Barabbas.

*Or Jesus. We two were connected by that name.*

*And, as I would learn, many other things as well . . .*

As he closed in on us, an aura of absolute confidence rose from Barabbas. Some people, I knew, identify this quality by the term *machismo*.

"What do you want?" Saul's voice sounded different now: anxious, concerned, even a bit threatened by the sight of this unexpected interloper.

"To do to you what you did to him."

Barabbas indicated my mangled body with his left hand as he drew his right into a fist. A sudden wallop into Saul's face occurred so swiftly I couldn't follow the movement with my eyes. That haughty boy dropped to the ground like a bird falling from the sky.

"You've broken my teeth," Saul shrieked.

"That's just the beginning."

Casually, Barabbas approached the dazed Saul, lifted the panic-stricken youth up by his collar, then bashed his own thick forehead against Saul's.

"No more," Saul begged, on the verge of tears.

Barabbas released Saul, allowing him to fall back to the ground. "Fine, so long as you swear to never lay a hand on that boy again." He pointed to me, struggling to rise, wiping blood from my face.

"I swear," Saul pleaded.

Though half a head taller than Barabbas, Saul proved he was precisely what I'd claimed: a bully, terrified of a worthy opponent. Desperate to avoid further abuse, Saul rose and ran away, whimpering as he disappeared around a bend.

# 57.

"Come on," Barabbas encouraged his fallen friend, gently helping me to my feet. "You'll be okay."

"Thank you. I . . . what brought you back?"

"It's strange," he replied, leading me to a rise in the ground. There, he sat me down again, carefully relocating me on a patch of soft, green grass stretching between mounds of dark earth. Barabbas wiped the blood from my lips with his linen shirt.

"As Judas and I walked, I suddenly felt a sense of threat. And, though I don't know why, you came to mind. So I sent him on home and hurriedly returned."

"Thank Yahweh you did." Somehow, I managed a smile.

"What's that?" Inspecting me for injuries, Barabbas noticed the deep scar on my right palm.

"A reminder of something that happened long ago."

"Well, from what I can see, no matter how badly that fool roughed you up, he did no serious damage."

Barabbas considered me with curious eyes, sizing me up, as if trying to figure something out in his mind.

"Is anything wrong?"

"Let's end this masquerade, Jess. Alright?" I froze up, my body tightening into a coil. With a knowing wink, Barabbas eased the shawl off my head, touching my hair with one hand. The other, he ran across my body, smiling with satisfaction. "I knew it! Perhaps from the very first day."

"Knew what?" I desperately replied.

"That you were too pretty to be a boy."

A dozen things flew through my mind; a dozen lies that I contemplated telling. But it was no use. He *knew*. Without warning, I broke down and sobbed. Barabbas held me tight, saying nothing until I regained self-control.

Then, with a wry smile, he gazed deep into my eyes. "Fine. You've had your cry. Now, tell me about it."

For the next fifteen minutes, I did precisely that, starting with my initial idea all the way through to this day's confrontation.

"So I guess that's everything."

Barabbas, who had been staring at me with amazement as I rambled on, offered no immediate response. Instead, he sat stock still, contemplating me, about to break out in laughter one moment or express serious concern the next.

"Jess of Nazareth," he finally said, "you are truly what people call 'a piece of work.'"

"Please don't give me away."

"Of course I won't. Do you even have to ask?"

"Too many people know. No one else must. Not even Judas."

"Maybe you should tell him." Barabbas's eyes expressed serious concern. "Jess, have you ever noticed how he looks at you?"

Embarrassed, I cast my eyes to the ground. "I tried my best to ignore it, hoping it'd go away."

"Things like that *never* go away."

"What, then, do they do?"

"Fester." He paused to consider our friend. "You could solve the problem at once by letting him in on the secret."

"I understand what you're saying. For now? No. My greater fear is that the more people who know increases the chances someone will slip, and I'll be found out."

"Alright then. For the time being, we'll keep this to ourselves. But never forget for a minute he's attracted to you. Or, rather, the boy he believes you to be."

"So is Levi. With the 'real' me, I mean."

"I noticed. At first, I figured he was . . . you know . . . like Judas. Then I realized that wasn't the case."

"So," I said, hoping to sum it all up, "in radically different ways, two boys have fallen in love with me—"

"Make that three," Barabbas interrupted.

# 58.

His statement silenced me. I faced Barabbas again. "Oh no. You—"

"Oh yes. Jess, you are *so* gorgeous—"

"Believe me, it's a curse, not a blessing."

"Ha! No one can accuse you of false humility."

I shrugged. "Well, I do own a mirror." I sensed my face flushing red. "In my own way, I *am* humble. Before the Lord! But I can't pretend . . . I don't notice how men look at me. At least when I'm not disguised in my brother's garb."

He sized me up once more. "At least you're honest about it. Most attractive girls blush, pretend they don't realize how—"

"Oh?" Suddenly, I felt consumed with jealousy. "Then you've been with many girls?"

"No! I'm just repeating what I've heard from . . . friends who—"

Managing a smile, I interrupted, "I have a feeling it's yes."

A pause. Then he smiled, too. "Well, a few, perhaps."

Where I found my nerve, I do not know. "And have you kissed many of them?"

"No way." As I relaxed, Barabbas further raised my ire by adding, "Only the prettiest."

*I wanted to pummel him with my little fists.*

*Or maybe throw myself into his arms once more?*

"I imagine I should be flattered that such an experienced young man of the world would even waste his time with poor little ol' *me*," I teased, easing away.

"Those girls were pretty. As I said, you're gorgeous. There's a difference."

"Thank you," I stated flatly, attempting to conceal how truly flattered I was by his words.

Barabbas's eyes filled with boyish naughtiness. "What if I kissed you right now?"

Flustered, my hands danced in the air as I groped for words. "Well, you'd get blood all over yourself. And I imagine I'll slap you when you're done."

"I can deal with that."

Self-assuredly, Barabbas wrapped his strong arms around me. He tilted his head and gently pressed his lips against mine, my first kiss ever from a boy.

*Not counting my brothers, of course, on the cheek. Once, Levi had kissed me, though also on my cheek, like a brother.*

"I'm ready for my slap," he sighed, pulling away.

"You'll have to wait a long time for that." I realized that I'd closed my eyes while he kissed me. I must have appeared, as I opened them wide again, a fool for love.

I had enjoyed it. Every bit as much as when Mary of Magdala kissed me. Yet I wasn't able to surrender entirely to Barabbas's embrace. An uninvited thought flew through my mind: I wondered if Luke, when and if he kissed me, would do so as delightfully as what I had just experienced?

"Jess, I always knew I'd recognize 'the one' when I met her. I have no hesitation about visiting your parents and asking if they will allow us to become engaged."

*Oh my! Here I go again.*

*Not that I mind the idea, only . . .*

"There *is* one complication," I said, tenderly taking his hand in mine.

"Just so long as it isn't another guy."

I said nothing, guessing that the look in my eyes gave me away. Barabbas, his worst fear realized, froze up.

"Want to hear about it?"

# 59.

For another quarter-hour, I told the story of our trip to Capernaum and my encounter with Luke. Wishing to begin our relationship, whatever turn it might take, with total honesty, I admitted that Luke would soon make the trip down to Nazareth.

"That's all of it," I shrugged.

"That's . . . a whole lot to digest."

*You think that's something? I haven't even mentioned the* girl *who's in love with me.*

"As to this Luke," Barabbas continued, "do you love him?"

"I thought I did."

Confused, Barabbas paused to consider my words. "What's *that* supposed to mean?"

"Until . . . what happened . . . you know, *just now*?"

"Alright then. So you've fallen out of love with him, and in love with me?"

"Mmmmmmmmm . . . yes and no."

"That *really* clears things up."

"I'm sorry. Let's see . . . First? Yes, I've fallen in love with you."

"I *am* deeply relieved to hear that."

"But that doesn't mean I've fallen out of love with him."

"Oh. And Levi?"

"I'm certainly not going to deny that I love my best friend."

"Is there any boy you *aren't* in love with?"

"Sure," I giggled. "Saul of Tarsus."

"Big surprise there."

"Again, I'm just . . . trying to be honest."

"I appreciate that."

"So . . . what do we do now?"

"I don't have a clue."

"Me neither."

"Maybe . . . just play it as it lays?"

"I don't follow you."

"Take it step by step. Deal with each issue as it arises. As you said, you'll be seeing him again soon."

"Maybe when I do, I'll know at once . . . whether that was just a momentary attraction, or—"

"—serious."

"Uh-huh."

"I guess we'll have to leave it at that for now."

I felt terrible. "But that's not fair to you."

"Whoever said life is fair?"

"Well, it should be."

"There are the way things should be, Jess. Then there's the way they are."

The hour grew late. I had to go, as did Barabbas. We rose. I stepped close, hoping he'd know it was permissible to kiss me again. When I realized that he wasn't going to, a wave of disappointment overcame me.

"Barabbas? What's the matter?"

"Not until you've seen him again. And, I imagine, are kissed by him. Only then will you know who . . ."

Barabbas couldn't finish.

"You're right."

We embraced in the manner I always did with Levi. We were, whatever happened, friends. And always would be.

*Though in Barabbas's case, that would become complex beyond belief.*

*Ah! Getting ahead of myself . . .*

As for love? Attraction? Some combination of the two. How was I supposed to know? What I *did* know was that facing such a choice filled me with excitement.

A few months previous, I'd never even felt a romantic attraction to a boy. Now, I was torn between two. For a girl on her way to becoming a woman, in any era and no matter the place, such a problem is a form of bliss.

# 60.

"James, I want to know *everything*."

"Well, little Sister, I don't *know* everything. Why does the sun shine by day and the moon at night? Why do we—"

"That's not what I mean."

James's eyes rolled with impatience. "Jess, if you think I'm able to guess what's going on inside that insatiable brain of yours—"

"Tell me everything you know about my mother and . . . our father."

"Oh."

At noon, with no class scheduled for today, I'd walked to a sprawling farm a quarter of the way to Capernaum where James sometimes found work. Insisting he'd take up a true profession when he came across the right one, my half brother accepted all sorts of odd jobs. He assisted Joseph as stonemason, served as a scribe thanks to his considerable education, and seasonally labored as a simple farm hand.

"Please? I *so* need to *know*."

Sensing my intensity, James set down his rake. His task on this cool, sunny day was to spread barley along the roadside for the poor and infirm. This had been the way of our people from our inception 5,000 years ago. No member of our nation must ever go hungry if any kinsmen owns plentiful food. At every farm, including this imposing place, one-fifth of the year's crops would be made available to the downtrodden, workers leaving such grain along the roadsides.

"Let's talk then. Later, remember: this was your idea."

Not that our generosity knew no bounds. The bran that had been bountifully spread out was barley, to be molded into bread by the poor. Wheat, which fetched a higher price at market, was not so magnanimously distributed. Feeding the homeless was one thing; offering up choice grain another.

James and I sat in the shade of several nearby lemon trees. People in rags hurried up and claimed their fair share. On this autumn night, at least, they would go to sleep with full bellies.

"James, speak to me as you would to a child. A smart one, mind you. Assume my mind is an empty space begging to be filled."

He nodded his understanding, then yanked at his long, wavy hair while trying to decide where to start. "Joseph's first wife, my mother, was named Melcha."

"That, I did know. Not much else."

"She and Joseph met in Bethlehem."

"Both lived there at the time?"

"No, only her. Though born in upper Bethlehem, Joseph had moved the short distance to Nazareth. There he mastered the skills of stonemasonry from a village craftsman. Joseph returned home often to visit his family. On one such visit he met Melcha. In time, they were married. I was born two months later."

There was no stigma attached to this. When a Hebrew couple became engaged, they were required to wait one year and one day before the marriage would be formalized with a wedding party. (No official ceremony, presided over by a rabbi or priest, yet existed in our culture.) In most cases, though, the man and woman would come to 'know' each other shortly after the day of their betrothal. It was not surprising when brides, on the day of marriage, arrived bursting with child.

Just so long, of course, as she had obeyed Yahweh's single all-important rule about sex: the child must without question be the off-spring of her intended. If not, the damaged groom could (and usually would) demand that she be stoned to death.

The exception: Joseph, in the case of my mother, Mary.

"Can you still picture her, James? Melcha?"

"It's difficult." He furrowed his brow and thought before answering. "In my mind's eye, I believe I can. Then again, she died of a flu when I was five. My father often described her to me. Now, I no longer know how much her image in my mind comes from memories or what I imagined while listening."

"Where did they live?"

"Nazareth. Joseph became a full partner in the old cutter's shop, owing to his natural talent and impressive work ethic."

"As to the couple's relationship?"

"I dimly recall us as a merry little family."

"And then she died."

"Joseph was beside himself. Ordinary men weep. Our father? He threw himself on the ground and tore his hair. Still, for several years, we managed on our own."

"That's when Mary entered the picture?"

James breathed in deeply, exhaling even harder. "Jess, are you certain that you want me to continue?"

"I'm not a little girl anymore, James. If I'm ever to truly know myself, I must first know the truth about this."

*Though I tried to keep it from my brother, something was going terribly wrong.*

*Shortly after we sat down, a sudden chill overtook me. Momentarily, I felt faint.*

"You look queasy, Sister. Should I stop?"

"No, no. Continue, please!"

# 61.

However concerned for my well-being, James resumed his tale. "Joseph returned to Bethlehem on occasion. One day, he stopped by a house to request water. The owner's name was Aaron. He had two daughters, the older Elizabeth, the younger Mary. While Joseph had confided to me that it was unlikely he could ever love another after Melcha, there was something about Mary that caught his eye."

"She's still lovely at twenty-seven. I can only imagine how beautiful she must have been then."

"Yes, but that wasn't all of it. Something mischievous about her manner attracted men. Before they were married, Joseph once hinted that there was something unknowable about Mary."

"Were you able to accept her?"

"I didn't have a choice. He announced that she was to be his wife, and I should try to love her as a mother. That was that."

Pains suddenly shot through my lower abdomen, as if some invisible sadist stuck hot needles into my flesh. Meanwhile, a monumental headache forced me to lie down.

"Jess! Let's stop here, and—"

I shook my head no, attempting to conceal my discomfort. James wanted to guide me home, but I insisted that he continue.

"Let's see . . . She came to live in our house, and they were engaged to be married. Earlier that year, it was announced that Herod would reconstruct Sepphoris to the northwest. Men skilled at stonecutting could earn top wages."

"And Joseph responded?"

James nodded, closely observing my physical state. "It was decided that Joseph would go, make a great deal of money. Then, following the wedding, the three of us and later children of their own would settle into the finest home in Nazareth, which Joseph would design and build himself."

"And everyone would live happily ever after."

"That's how it should have been. The way it was? He left, returning for weekends whenever possible. But as the workload increased, Joseph could no longer continue to do so. He necessarily stayed up there in Sepphoris for weeks on end. Mary was always kind and fair to me. Then, as you have heard, the unthinkable happened."

"Mary became pregnant." Following my statement, I gasped out loud. Aches and pains were now accompanied by sharp cramps deep in my stomach and hot flashes in the soft skin directly below my midsection.

"Jess," James said, rising. "We *must* stop."

"Brother? I have the plague!"

Panicky, James touched the back of his hand to my aching forehead and checked me over closely.

"No, little Sister. This is menarche. Do not be afraid. It's completely natural. Your first menstruation."

# 62.

"Jess! What . . . ? Oooooh."

Mary, folding recently washed clothes, heard the two of us stumble in the doorway. She reacted with shock at the sight of James delicately carrying me inside. Momentarily, Mary—being a woman herself—fully understood.

"Your daughter—"

"Yes! Let me help you set her down."

Together, they brought my out-of-control body across the room to where my mat rested, neatly folded on a stool. All of us slept inside again now that early autumn had arrived. My torso felt as if an earthquake had erupted, causing a fire down below.

Somehow, I managed to signal for them to let me be. Mary and James backed away. With difficulty, I nodded my head with appreciation.

"Thank you," I muttered. Once prone, my convulsions eased, the pain diminished, and the alternately hot and cold sweat receded. "Will it always be this bad?" I desperately asked.

"Absolutely not." Mary had rushed to the room's far side, where she seized a clean strip of linen, submerged it in fresh water, then hurried back. Standing beside me, Mary set its cool surface on my forehead. "The first time is always the worst. Though I never saw anyone hit quite so hard as you."

"How can I help?" James wanted to know.

"By going out to bathe immediately."

James nodded and exited, heading directly to those living waters in the *mikveh*. For most nations of the Near Middle East, the stale blood flow of a woman terrified their men, who must at once purify themselves. Though not written down in scripture, our oral tradition insisted this was the punishment meted out by Yahweh for the daughters of Eve owing to her betrayal of man and God. Failing to cleanse immediately could lead to necessity for an exorcism.

*"Thank you, oh wise Yahweh, for sparing me the curse of being born a woman . . ."*

*But what kind of a God would punish innocent people for a foolish mistake made by Eve so long ago?*

"Can you still remember your own first . . . ?"

Mary laughed sharply. "It is not something a woman ever forgets."

"*I* certainly won't forget this."

Mary and I now spoke openly to each other. We had ever since that day in Capernaum. Mary's willingness to let me meet with Luke again had touched me deeply. How could she be so kind when, for the past seven years, I'd been so cold?

147

Not that life was all sweet and happy in the house of Joseph. I didn't imagine it ever would be. At last, though, a gnawing sense of strain had dissipated. If less than perfect, things were better. Which is the most that any of us can hope for.

*That's before I learned the hard way that, when allowed enough time and space, everything turns to shit.*

"When you feel a bit steadier, I'll bring you broth."

I nodded my appreciation and fell into a fitful sleep. The cramps subsided for a while, only to return with a vengeance. One moment I'd be lost in a troubled dream. The next, crying out in agony. After a while, I'd feel my body go weak again. The hot sweat that momentarily consumed me turned cold. Eventually, my headache lessened as insufferable cramps in my lower abdomen worsened. My eyes opened wide with the worst discomfort I had experienced thus far in my lifetime.

*So this is what it's like to be maddened with pain!*

*To actually believe that, if it does not subside, you will truly go crazy.*

"Here's that broth," Mary said. She brought me a clay pot filled with a clear liquid made from boiled onions. No matter how many delicacies I would experience in my life, nothing ever tasted so good.

"That's wonderful. Again, thank you."

I determined to rise up but found that I could not steadily do so alone. With Mary's help, I made my way over to a stool.

"So this is menstruation!" I muttered, again bordering on hysteria.

Mary shrugged. "Welcome to the club."

I glanced around and saw, through a shuttered window, the darkness descending on our little corner of the world. Soon, Joseph and my siblings would appear at the doorway, clamoring for their supper. Well, Jess wouldn't be preparing it tonight.

"No wonder people call it 'the curse.'"

"Today, you left girlhood behind and became a woman."

"I understand."

"However terrible, without this monthly ordeal you could never be a mother. Thinking about that might help."

"Not for me. There's so much I want to do before I even consider marriage."

"In time, you will want a baby. Every woman does."

"Most, maybe. Me? I'm not certain."

Mary's eyes bulged. A smile spread from ear to ear, her face appeared flushed. "Want to know a secret?" Mary's voice resembled that of a giddy child.

"Sure," I replied, with no idea where this could lead, my suffering increased with every single second.

"I'm going to have another! I realized that today."

# 63.

There are times in our lives when we say or do things we had no intention of saying or doing. This holds true for every one of us. Though we might wish to take back our words or actions afterwards, that is not possible. Such a disaster can occur at any time, in any place, and to anyone. Most often, these situations happen when an individual is under intense pressure or pain. At such a vulnerable moment, our hearts like our minds fail to function properly. Then, anything can happen.

As for Jess of Nazareth? Perhaps I, during one of the worst moments of my life, spoke out of my physical misery and the mental torture I'd experienced for years:

*"Momsa! Momsa!"*

*"Tiberon! Tiberon!"*

The echo of those accusations pounded in my brain always. Now, they were combined with the impact of my first mense. However much my response shocked Mary, it did me, too.

"Who's the father this time? Or wouldn't you know?"

Silence had never been, and never again would be, so all-encompassing. Mary's jaw dropped, her mouth remaining open for a long time. We stared at each other intensely for what seemed an eternity. Finally, she emitted a guttural sound, part gasp of disbelief, part muted shriek, part bitter laugh, part heart-felt cry.

Then Mary stepped closer still, slowly drew back her hand, and smacked me across the face as hard as she could.

How I managed to keep from falling off my stool, I can't say. I didn't spill even a drop of the broth. Once I grasped the reality of what had gone down, I laughed out loud. A terrible laugh, from one who has come to see all of life as absurd. A mad laugh.

"So it's time for everything to come out in the open?" Mary hissed. Her tone and demeanor suggested one of those daemons that I'd been told haunt our roadways, leaping out from a hiding place to possess the body of an unwary passerby. "Just so you know, I'm aware of the little game you and Joses have been playing."

Now, it was my turn to gasp. "How long have you—"

"Since the first day."

"And you didn't say a thing—"

"Haven't I always given you freedom to do what you wish?"

I nodded, feeling humble, sorrowful, and guilty. At that moment, Joseph burst in the doorway, simultaneously laughing and crying. "So our little girl is all grown up?"

Half-heartedly, I smiled and nodded as he rushed over to embrace me. Mary said nothing about what had happened, then or ever. She also continued to keep my secret, which only made me feel all the worse.

Not surprisingly, the three-week term of emotional mending that had taken the edge off our difficult relationship abruptly came to an end. From then on, and for the remainder of my stay near Nazareth (which wouldn't be all that much longer), the relationship between us reversed.

Beginning then, whenever I made even the slightest attempt at small talk, or tried to meet her eyes with mine, Mary reacted by behaving as I had previously done: avoiding me yet always remaining, at a bare minimum, polite.

Everything continued on, as usual. Yet nothing again in this house, or this family, would ever again be quite the same.

# 64.

"And so David, son of Jesse, blessed by the Lord, stood by helplessly as his life, and his work, turned to dust. David's son Absalom eventually betrayed him and was executed by the king's guards. Still, David lived to a very old age. In his infinite wisdom, God knew that death would provide David with a release from inner pain. Yaweh wished to put off such merciful oblivion for as long as possible."

I sat in my usual spot between Levi and Barabbas, holding my breath. Feeling ill, my plan was to remain silent. I suffered through Annas's pre-prayer defamation of women, then listened as he rambled on about the importance of maintaining a kosher home before returning to the story of our second king.

That morning, I'd patched the area below my stomach as best I could with thickly knit linens. My hope was to avoid any revelation of my gender through flowing blood. Then I slipped into male attire and, with difficulty, walked (stumbled, more correctly) from Nazareth to Sepphoris.

I shared with Levi details of my situation. And, like the brother he had become, Levi begged me to return home. I, being me, refused. I explained that I didn't want to miss a moment of study. In truth, the primary reason was to see Barabbas again.

For on the following day, Luke would arrive. His most recent note, delivered by a runner, confirmed it.

*Luke was coming!*

*Finally, we'd be face to face again.*

I couldn't gaze into Luke's eyes without once more doing so with Barabbas. What I now must deal with was what I'd often secretly dreamed of: two appealing men, vying for my hand in marriage.

*Naïve? Of course, but also innocent.*

*I'd seen so little of the world and did not yet know its ways.*

Even though (and this perhaps made the melodrama even more amusing) I did not, like most girls, wish to marry. Not yet. Other things must come first. I sensed this owing to a growing belief that Yahweh had set me down on Earth for some higher purpose than to live, breath, eat, urinate, procreate, and, in time, die.

*I was born to fulfill a mission. The tricky part: I had not a clue as to what my calling might be.*

*No matter. That would come. Yahweh would provide a sign.*

"Now!" Annas announced, holding his head high, "as to the story's deeper meaning?"

"As we have often said," Saul ventured, "the point is that we must resist lust, the most dangerous among the deadly sins."

*I'm glad that you didn't say gluttony, the one I'm always consumed by.*

Other aristocratic boys chimed in. Annas smiled and nodded profoundly. As the semester approached its conclusion, he knew that these boys were his. Forever! None would ever again be capable of individual perception.

"I'm not so certain." Barabbas, noticing that I was not well and perhaps couldn't speak today, raised his hand and protested. "How do you arrive at such an interpretation?"

"And how would you, rube of the west, interpret it?" asked one of Saul's small circle of well-to-do friends.

But we had our own coterie as well, not blessed with riches; learning about life not as it is lived in sophisticated cities, rather in the wilderness. Watching goats mate. Observing seeds planted in spring as they sprout in late summer. We heard our parents, sleeping in the same room, groaning together.

As a result, we each of us grasped, without needing to be told, what life is like in the real world. How women and men came together to share pleasure of the senses while fulfilling the necessity of procreation: a natural act, certainly; but, as one ordained by Yahweh, a worthy as well as necessary undertaking.

On farms, I had seen sheep mate. Never had I perceived anything sinful in the act. If Yahweh decided this was how we as well as the animals would mate, how could anyone interpret anything wrong in doing so? I, for one, could not.

*Some claimed that God imposed sexuality on us to test humans. To discover if our race, and individual people, had risen above the level of beasts.*

*Only a cruel god would do such a thing. Not the One True God I deeply believed in.*

# 65.

"If I may?" Levi, growing bolder by the day, supported Barabbas. Familiarity apparently does breed contempt, as our deep fear of Annas, so prevalent that first day of classes, had long since diminished.

"Go ahead."

"You're claiming that Yahweh condemns lustful desire as sinful?"

"Do you have a better explanation?" Saul called out. His bully boys, lined up behind him and mercilessly heckled us.

"I believe so," Barabbas answered. "You mentioned that David had six wives, including Michal, daughter of Saul. Also, eight concubines, none of them Hebrew."

"That is so," Annas admitted, his tone revealing anxiety. Might these provincial yahoos yet trip him up?

"During all those years, Yahweh never turned his wrath on the anointed one. Yet David's sexual desire for all but Michal likely constituted lust, not love."

"Will you make your point already?" Saul howled.

"My point is if Yahweh did not object to David's lust for those women, then lust cannot in and of itself constitute sin."

"When, then, *is* sex a sin?" Annas demanded.

"As the Second Commandment says: coveting a neighbor's wife, as David did Bathsheba," Levi offered, interrupting again.

"Only in breaking God's commandment does lust transform into sin," Barabbas added. "Therefore, logically speaking, sin doesn't equate with sexual desire."

"Yahweh," Levi deduced, "instructed us to go forth and multiply. He never told us that we ought not to enjoy the process."

"Avoid the Lord's single restriction as to sexuality," I dared add, "and sex is separated from sin. Even lustful sex."

That final statement proved too much for Annas. Everything he most deeply believed had just been challenged. The rabbi staggered about, gasping for breath, horrified at such ideas. His eyes slipped back deep in their sockets.

Barabbas rose, purposefully making the situation more difficult by asking, "Wouldn't that hold true for women, as well as men?"

If I hadn't been consumed by pain, I might have joined in again. For Levi and Barabbas had said what I would have, were I up to it, concerning equality for women.

But the best was yet to come. For Judas, drawing on some previously untapped reservoir of courage, dared rise. "Perhaps David believed that since her husband was not a fellow Hebrew, then the rule wouldn't apply. Uriah, though, was loyal to the king. So Bathsheba counts as the wife of a neighbor."

*Judas! You didn't twitch once while speaking. Whatever daemon possessed you in the past has been exorcised.*

*You are free now. Do not again succumb to fear.*

With difficulty, I finally managed to stand. "Even as Adam's sin was not his sexual desire for Eve but biting into the one fruit that Yahweh had forbidden. Sin refers to disobeying the will of God. Not human sexuality."

For a long time, Annas remained stock still. When his face turned crimson red, then a bright purple, I thought the top of his head might explode. At last the rabbi responded: "I curse you, Jess of Nazareth. Do you hear? Yahweh, bring down your wrath on this boy. I beg of you!"

As Annas closed his eyes and angled his head toward the heavens, the pains of budding womanhood gripped me again. First, my head sank, for I no longer had the strength to hold it upright. Then, as the pain intensified, I dropped to my knees. Once on the ground, I was shocked to see fresh blood initially trickling, then pouring out of me, spilling down my legs.

"Look," Saul screamed. "He's possessed by daemons."

"Or perhaps God has sent an angel into Jess's body?" Levi retorted, hoping to cover for me.

Several boys howled in horror. Others rose and ran around in circles, panic stricken. Some threw themselves flat on the ground, calling out incantations, identifying me as a devil in the flesh. A few hailed me as a Chosen One, sent by Yahweh to save all, my own blood surrendered mana-like for their greater good.

"Unclean!" Annas shrieked. "Unclean. Go!"

I pulled myself together and hobbled off, dead silence now overtaking the onlookers. I wasn't certain what this might bode for the future, though one thing was clear: My official education had come to an end.

From this moment on, I would need to learn on my own.

# 66.

Yesterday, I repeated to myself, was the worst day of my life. But as an ancient sage once said, the darkest hour appears just before dawn.

As to this new day, this fresh day? It would be the best ever. I could feel that in my bones. For this day, I would see Luke. Likely hold him close. Perhaps even kiss him. What could be more wonderful than that?

Things would have been even better had my period passed. While that wasn't the case, the sharp pains gradually diminished. Not, though, the aching sensation. Also, the cramps continued. No further spontaneous bleeding had occurred since that devastating incident at Yeshiva.

I couldn't imagine how embarrassed I'd be if that happened in front of Luke. Were Greek men as fearful of a woman at this time of the month as our Hebrew males? Maybe this held true for men everywhere.

*Still, Luke dealt well with my vomiting in Capernaum; the first sign of my 'change,' though I hadn't realized so at the time.*

*And he is, after all, a doctor.*

"Where are you?" I wondered out loud.

I'd washed my body with living water to cleanse the area still haunted by an unpleasant odor. Stale, dried blood had caked on my legs and lower stomach. No matter how hard I scrubbed, the overwhelming scent did not entirely go away.

I'd searched through my scant supply of clothes to find the most attractive item. Finally, I settled on a simple pale-blue sheath that people often admired. But I wished that I could afford something new from Nazareth's marketplace.

I came across several matching ribbons, using them to braid my light-brown hair on either side. Though I knew this to be vanity, I didn't care. However attractive Yahweh had seen fit to make me, I wanted to emphasize these God-given gifts to my best advantage.

I'd heard from Attican travelers—stopping for water while passing by our home—the tales of Calypso and Circe. How the two strange beauties had in turn held the journeyer Odysseus spellbound with their charms. Now I fantasized about Luke arriving at last, seeing me in such a light. I got goosebumps just thinking about it.

Shortly after noon, I'd headed across the pasture to my special place deep within the trees. In a missive I'd sent the previous week, I explained to Luke precisely where to find me. I sat atop a boulder and waited. At one point, I thought I'd scream if he didn't appear soon. Then my mind wandered to Barabbas and how it might be when I met him again after reuniting with Luke.

Even as I found myself absorbed in this thought, there came a stir in the high grass behind me, then a voice. "I'm late. Forgive me?"

With a gasp, I rose, turned, and there he was. Luke, in a bright-white peplum ornamented with black and yellow patterns. Handsomer even than I remembered, if that were possible. The naughty smile, the curly, oiled hair, the twinkling eyes, and the masculine shoulders.

My beautiful Greek! Not as rugged as Barabbas, perhaps. Yet with a casual elegance that Barabbas lacked. And certainly manly enough in every way.

"It doesn't matter. You're here now."

*But which beautiful boy do I prefer?*

*I think maybe I like each the same, though in different ways. Which is no help at all!*

At first, the sensation seemed like a wonderful dream that had suddenly come true. The kind of dream you hope to slip into every night while on the verge of sleep, more likely nightmares arriving instead. We rushed across the stretch of pasture to one another. I felt as if my body were moving slower than usual. I wondered if Luke felt the same sensation: that time and space had lost all meaning owing to our mutual attraction.

"Finally!" Luke exclaimed. I all but collapsed into his arms, my head falling against his strong chest.

"I know, I know," I half laughed, half cried.

"You look lovely."

"I wanted to look lovely. For *you*."

Luke slowly leaned down and kissed me on the forehead, which struck me as most gentlemanly. Then sweetly, softly, on the lips.

*This isn't fair! In my mind, I'm comparing his kiss to Barabbas's.*

*Yet how can a girl caught in such an awkward situation not do so?*

In all truth, Luke's kiss did strike me as more poignant. Perhaps though that was because he was here, with me, now.

*And, for once, I absolutely lived in the moment.*

*Yes! I'm able to do it: seize the day.*

"Three weeks felt like three years."

"For me, too!"

The things we were saying to one another had likely been said by every boy who ever fell in love with a girl. And from her back to him, since humankind first learned to speak.

*I didn't care if our words were common.*

*Only that my turn to feel so deeply was finally here.*

Yes! Even crazy, impetuous, unpredictable, occasionally annoying Jess had found herself in the rapture of romantic love.

"Let me kiss you again." Luke's mouth moved toward mine once more.

"Please do!"

This time, though, the touch of his lips struck me as less delicate. A bit rough, even. Did I imagine he might kiss me as Mary of Magdala had? Sensuously yet sisterly?

How silly of me! So I returned his kiss. He pressed forward again, hard.

At that moment, the sensation ceased to be pleasing.

# 67.

Luke kissed me a third time, rougher still. Less than what I perceived (after my experience with Barabbas) as masculinity in the best sense: firm, strong, and protective. What I currently felt struck me as crude, threatening, insistent.

"Luke, please," I muttered, trying to dislodge myself from his arms, hoping we might speak a while, then perhaps kiss again. "At least let me catch my breath!"

Instead of letting go, Luke held me more tightly still. I felt like a butterfly about to be crushed. While I'd fantasized often about being carried away by my beautiful Greek, the current experience in no way resembled that imagined passion.

"Oh, Jess," Luke muttered in a huskier voice than I'd heard from him previously, "I need you so."

"I need you, too, Luke. Now, let's sit and talk—"

He said nothing more. Arching his strong body hard against me, Luke attempted to force me down onto the ground.

"No," I tried calling out. But his mouth pushed against mine relentlessly. I knew my protest bordered on the inaudible. Still, I tried again: "Luke, stop!"

My knees failed me under his enormous pressure. Panic overtook this slender Israeli girl as I felt both of us fall downwards and backwards. Acting on instinct, I yanked my right arm free and reached up, scratching at his eyes with all the fury I could muster.

"Oooowwwwww! Why did you do that?"

How could he not know the answer? Everything was moving too fast, causing what should have been beautiful to turn ugly. As his male fever rose, and my woman's emotions rebelled, I felt a sudden anguish at how horrible things were turning out. Then I could feel my blood boiling.

"Let . . . me . . . go!" I managed to scream, scratching him again.

"Damn it," he shouted, anger and panic in his voice. "Be still, will you?"

Outraged, Luke half rose, then dropped down on me like a dead weight. Still I struggled, attempting to roll out from beneath him. Every time I shifted my position, so did he.

"Get off!" I desperately screamed.

*Then my temper roared out of control, as it had so many times in the past.*

*My mind ceased to function as absolute anger overtook me.*

By some inspiration, I brought my knee directly up into his groin as sharply as I could. Luke screamed. His body appeared to collapse inward. He rolled off me at last, reaching for his genitals.

Glancing down, I noticed that my blood ran wildly, ruining my lovely blue outfit. The flow poured out in a torrent all over my legs and down to the ground. For some time, I said nothing.

Panting, I wondered what I'd do if he should lunge at me again.

With difficulty, I rose, readying my nails to scratch, my teeth to bite, my knees to kick . . . anything and everything I could to repel this boy who had in a moment transformed from a welcome lover into a despised would-be conqueror.

"Oooooh," Luke moaned, managing to sit, eventually standing.

"Get out of here," I commanded, pointing to the pathway leading back to the main road.

"Forgive me. I guess I . . . came on too strong." Awkwardly shuffling about, he laughed in a silly way, as if this might make everything right.

Tears rolled down my cheeks. "That's putting it mildly!"

Apprehensive now rather than aggressive, Luke once more stepped toward me. I backed away. Comprehending the full extent of my fear, anger, and sense of betrayal, he halted. "Jess, I'm . . . sorry."

"Sorry doesn't fix what you've managed to ruin."

He stood shakily. "It's only that I've thought about nothing but you. All day, all night. Until my body ached. I—"

"You've spoken your peace. Go, now."

# 68.

In a feeble attempt to improve the situation, Luke made matters worse. "It's just that I recalled the flirtatious look in your eyes. And thought you wanted—"

"*What?*" I sprang forward, hitting him with an open hand across his face as hard as I could. His cheek glowed red. "You're blaming *me* for what happened? How dare you!"

It was Luke's turn to cry. And, I guessed, not only owing to the physical pain. He turned away, weeping like a child. At least he seemed sincere in his misery.

"I didn't mean to ruin everything. Honest—"

"What you *meant* doesn't matter. It's what you *did*. Or," I added, with a whiff of triumph, "what you *tried* to do."

His hands furtively wiping away the tears, Luke looked to me as if hoping for pity. "Could it be that on my way from Capernaum a daemon leaped out from hiding and possessed me—"

"I was not assaulted by a daemon but by Luke. A boy I believed cared for me. *Truly* cared! A boy I trusted—"

"Couldn't we sit down now and discuss this?" Fiercely, I shook my head no. "If not now, someday?"

"Not ever."

Luke's mouth opened, but no words followed. A long silence suggested he'd run out of things to say. Then, finally, "Listen, Jess. Despite what I did . . . or tried to do . . . I . . . *love* you."

"I believed you did, once. That we'd experienced . . . what people call 'love at first sight.'"

"Yes!"

"I doubt I'll ever believe in that again."

"But our wonderful time in Capernaum—"

"For hours on end, I doted on them. Now, I only want to banish all such thoughts from my memory."

"All I hoped for was to take the love we experienced and turn it into something we might physically share. In the here and now."

"Whomever I choose to marry, *if* ever I do marry—and I'm less certain about that than ever—I will have been with no other man before my husband on our wedding night."

"Owing to your religion?"

"No. Out of personal respect for my body. And the body of the man I marry."

*And, perhaps, owing to my memories of what nearly twelve years ago had happened to my mother.*

*Though I was not going to mention that now.*

"I want to be that man," Luke begged. He tried his best to sound at once remorseful and assertive.

"What can I tell you? You blew it. Good-bye."

I turned and headed home, sobbing, trying to wipe some of the unclean blood off my body and garment. I did not glance back to see if he remained in the grove. Suddenly I thought of Barabbas, knowing what I would say to him the following morning. If he still wanted me, I would be his wife. Then again, I couldn't tell him when. There was so much for me to see, experience, learn. Most of all, do and accomplish!

Would he still desire me? Furthermore, would he be willing to wait? That had to be his call. I'd completely understand if Barabbas walked away. There was but one way to find out. Tomorrow, I'd head up to where the road to Sepphoris led to that pathway from his village. Put it to him as honestly as I could. Accept whatever he decided, then move on from there.

As horrific as this moment had been, I'd learned something from it. The previous day, I'd believed that lust constituted sin only when it broke the marriage vows. Now, I knew there was another circumstance, even if Yahweh had overlooked it when He delivered the Commandments to Moses.

Forced sex is every bit as sinful. If not to God, then to man. Or, more likely, woman. If I could have added an eleventh commandment, it would be "Thou shalt not impose thyself on another."

*Or in plain English for future readers: Thou shalt not rape.*

Someday, if I ever did become a rabbi, that would be first and foremost among my teachings. If sex, in and of itself, even for reasons having to do with pleasure and not necessarily procreation, is not a sin, then adultery and rape are precisely that.

# 69.

"That's great." Sarcasm mixed with irony wasn't ordinarily Levi's way, so this counted as an exception. "Just *wonderful.* Some men lose at love once. With me, it's happening *again?*"

While walking the now familiar way to Sepphoris, I shared my plan for bringing Joses and Maggie together. However appealing an arrangement for my twin, I knew my best friend would hardly be happy to learn of my intended matchmaking.

"Stop whining."

"I'm not whining," he whined.

I'd devised a plan over the past several days. As I now explained: The following evening, Joses was to meet Maggie in Nazareth, attempting to pass himself off as me . . . or the faux-male version of me I was even now costumed as. Though I would not be attending Yeshiva, all the same I had chosen to dress as a boy. For I would part with Levi when I met Barabbas. Then I must walk the seven miles home alone. How much safer, then, to adorn male garb, if likely for the last time.

*Or so I thought at the time . . .*

"It's awful, but I don't see any other way. Besides, you told me yourself, she's just not that into you."

"Still, I was hoping maybe, as time goes by—"

"Levi, listen. The right girl will come along. She will glance at you with eyes that lock with yours. Both of you will know that what you share is right, and good, and . . . well . . . love."

"You know deep down I want that only with you."

I breathed in deeply. "That's the way you feel now. We're still young. There's a whole world out there to explore—"

"You're saying, then, that what I want can never be?"

"I'm *not* saying that. How do I know? Levi, I haven't yet reached the age of twelve. Like you, I'm trying to learn what 'love' even means."

"You wait, Jess. Someday it *will* happen between us."

"All I can say to that is I hope you're right. You know how dear you are to me."

For a while, neither of us spoke as we continued along our way. We'd left early today. When we joined our friends, I'd signal to Barabbas. Once we slipped back behind the others, I would share with him what I'd decided. And accept whatever his response might be.

But plans have a way of changing, particularly when they crash directly into that obtuse thing called reality. For some, this occurs due to coincidence. For others? The result of destiny.

"Jess! Levi!"

We spotted Judas turning a bend a quarter of a mile ahead and, after passing a line of acacias, rushing forward. He was alone and clearly distraught: eyes wide open, manner frantic, waving wildly.

"What is it?" Levi, shaken by the sight, asked.

"A *terrible* thing has happened." Judas wept. Stunned, we waited till he regained composure, anxious for an explanation.

"Yesterday, Roman guards marched into our village for the first time. No one expected them, as ours is a small, unnamed place, not even on the maps. But there they were, with their black leather boots, plumed helmets, copper breast plates—"

"Herod's personal detachment," Levi concluded. "Everyone insists they're the worst of the lot."

"They went from home to home, searching for some sign of treason. Anything, large or small."

"Did they find weapons, or—"

"Nothing like that. Most men in our village resent the Zealots. We only want to live in peace."

"What then?"

He coughed several times before continuing. "Three of our men had in their trunks packed away old *Tallits*, the ones adorned with a single blue string. In case the law restricting them was ever dropped—"

"They weren't wearing such forbidden *Tallits* at the time?"

"No, Jess. Still, the guards said that failing to destroy forbidden items constituted an act of rebellion."

"Go on," I sighed, fearing the worst.

Judas nodded, then cleared his throat. "They were marched off into a field and crucified."

Levi and I gasped as one. "For such a minor thing?" Levi asked, uncomprehending.

"They hang there still, dead on the crosses. Vultures whirl down and chew at their exposed flesh."

Then, it dawned on me. This might be why Judas had arrived alone. "Where's Barabbas?"

"Some of the villagers attempted to rescue their neighbors before the victims could be nailed on high. Barabbas came rushing out of his family's home and, hearing what had happened, joined the angry men. I witnessed all of this with my own eyes."

I had to sit down on the ground, weakened by concern, now feeling faint. "What happened, Judas? Tell me!"

Levi and Judas kneeled beside me. "Barabbas and the others ran to where the crucifixion was to take place. They begged the guards to reconsider. Herod's men laughed in the Hebrews' faces. That enraged Barabbas, so he attacked them with his bare hands."

*That would be just like him.*

*Me, too, of course, had I been there.*

"Is he . . . dead?"

I breathed a sigh of relief when Judas shook his head no. "Two of the others were killed. Barabbas and several more, re-alizing they'd be overpowered, hurried back. They knew that when the crucifixion was completed, the guards would come for them. Their mothers and sisters wept, tearing at their hair, screaming to Yahweh for help."

"What then?"

"The men hurriedly packed whatever they could, tossing clothes, food, and small containers of wine into sacks. Then ran away."

"Where—"

"Barabbas said, as he rushed by, that I must tell you he was heading off to hide in the hills. He would join the Zealots as he had always guessed someday he would. But he insisted that he would locate us all again, however long it took."

As Judas sobbed again, I considered the remarkable way in which, during the past three days, my life reversed itself.

*Like most people, I rose every morning, assuming things would progress from where they'd left off the day before.*

*All at once, I knew now and forever that this was not true.*

My beautiful Greek had turned into a monster. Barabbas was gone. No matter what he'd said to Judas, likely forever. Forty-eight hours earlier, the future had appeared as ripe as a clear spring day. At this moment, my life resembled the Galilee in winter: grey, drizzly, melancholy.

# 70.

When the sun sets, Nazareth darkens completely. The effect is as if the people living here do not merely slip off to their mats for a night's sleep but cease to exist. Few torches or lamps are present to light one's way through the narrow streets. If the moon should disappear behind clouds, or the stars fail to shine, then to walk through our village after sunset is akin to diving into a pool of pitch and swimming about blindly. As the sky transforms into a midnight canopy, one by one residents blow out their candles. Day is done; night must fall.

The Watch, civil policemen assigned to search for criminals or trespassers, are likely to be found in some abandoned alley. There they squat, guzzling wine and swapping lewd jokes. Knowing how unlikely it is that anyone would enter the village to steal. In a manner of speaking, the Watch is correct. Simply, nothing of material value exists in Nazareth. Here is a crude, quiet place. Its barrenness confounds those who read the prophets.

For scripture insists the next messiah will—*must!*—hail from Nazareth.

As a Jerusalem sophisticate once exclaimed: "When did anything of any value come out of Nazareth?" His response, I understand, elicited nasty laughter from fellow cynics living in that majestic city. Apparently, they were unaware of the true meaning of our village's name: *branch*. Also, they failed to take into account that there are things more valuable than material goods.

*Perhaps they would do well to recall an ancient prophecy, Jeremiah 23: 5-6 . . . "The days are coming, declares the Lord, when I shall raise up for David a righteous branch."*

For most of its years of existence, Nazareth had been an entirely Hebraic village. Recently, a small number of people from other nations, mostly Phoenicians and Samaritans, settled in our easternmost sector. Several Hittites also called this area home. These immigrants, tolerated if hardly welcomed, did not subscribe to the essence of Hebrew life: A new day begins as the great light in the sky recedes.

I noticed that a single wine shop remained open. Inside, men who had drifted here from the west nostalgically celebrated the good old days when Phoenicians were bold seafarers, threatening even the fortified islands of Greece. Now, they bitterly cursed their eventual history of disastrous military losses, foul luck, and economic setbacks. For these forced those "men of the sea" to migrate inland from the Mediterranean.

Joses and I left the main street. We slipped down an alley, the dead of night completely shrouding our movements.

"Best of luck, Brother."

"Put in a good word with Yahweh for me."

An old grotto dominated this sector. By way of a messenger, we had informed Maggie to meet us here. An abundance of trees would cloak our identities should anyone happen by. We were a block and a half away from the village well. There, in daylight hours, citizens bustled about, gathering the requisite liquid for drinking, cooking, and washing. An underground source of water reached this spot from the Jordan. The well had been the reason people built homes on this spot many years earlier. Now the area appeared as desolate as a graveyard.

We reached the appointed place. Joses hurried over to where Maggie sat waiting on a limestone bench. Being out alone was risky for an innocent girl at this hour. She might easily be mistaken for a whore, the only women on the street after dark. But once Joses sat down beside her, I knew Maggie would be safe.

I held back, silent, in a narrow spot where two buildings unevenly joined together, listening. They spoke softly. The conversation suggested that Maggie, at least for the time being, did believe Joses to be me.

"I'm still confused about one thing. You tell me your one God is everywhere and nowhere. How can this be?"

"That is his greatness. I can't explain it. No one can. Contemporary Hebrews believe He can be found in no single place. Yet he exists in the air up above, in the water we sail over, in the clouds. And the moon, the stars, the sun. *Especially* the sun. Some of our people insist that when he descends to Earth, Yahweh lives in the holiest of holy spots within our Jerusalem Temple."

*Very good, Jude. This might actually work!*

Though I could barely make out their shapes, the stone-cold night air allowed me to hear every word. "Explain why you don't make idols," Maggie continued. "That way, you could see an image of your invisible Yahweh whenever you like."

I had coached him on how to speak. We'd sat for hours while Joses studied the precise manner in which my body moved as well as the unique tenor of my voice. He had proven himself an apt student, mastering small details. The question now was whether Joses could follow through with the banter that had begun between Maggie and myself on that first day, which I had conveyed to him in detail.

"My nation believes if one were to see God, then that would mean death—so wonderful and horrifying is He in all His glory. The sight would drive one mad, then to the grave."

It wasn't always that way, I knew. There was a time, more than one thousand and five hundred years ago, when Hebrews did look upon Yahweh. His name had been Adonoi then. The Torah explains that when Moses climbed Mount Sinai to receive the law, our patriarch spotted the lower portions of God's body. From the waist up, Yahweh had been shrouded in pink, white, and blue clouds. Yet God's legs and backside were visible, described by Moses to Aaron as hairy and ill-shapen. Like the rear-end of a goat.

Now? He remains invisible always. Apparently God, *our* God, the God of the Hebrews, is like everything else capable of change. As time goes by, things alter. Even Yahweh.

*If not God, then our current vision of Him.*

*Or as I've asked myself often: why not* Her?

# 71.

"But, Jess! Would a good God allow such a thing to happen?"

"Again, Maggie, you're thinking as a pagan: that there are good and bad gods. Ours is one; *the* one and only. *Everything.*"

"You aren't alone. The Ankh bears witness that other nations believe this, too."

Joses hadn't worn the medallion around the house. Though Joseph and Mary were progressive, there were limits. Such an icon might have been considered heresy. Only the *mezusah,* a stone emblazoned with the first letter of our Hebrew alphabet, could be worn by our men. Some Jewish women chose to wear them as well, proving their equality as well as their own loyalty to God.

*Naturally, I was such a woman.*

*Always my mezusah dangled on a chain over my chest.*

My twin had carefully hidden his Ankh deep in an ash heap behind the furnace, adjacent to the woodpile. Before we two slipped out, he recovered it for our night game and wore it alongside his own *mezusah.*

*Though one is Hebrew, the other Egyptian, there is no sense of opposition here.*

*Merely two ways of expressing the same belief as to a single deity.*

"Fascinating that the metallic circle on top represents the sun. We Jews also have a special reverence for that ball of fire owing to its life-endowing warmth."

"As do the Greeks! I have spoken with them as well . . ."

*You aren't alone there, Maggie. And in my dream, in which you played a key role, so too did the sun. A sun god descended from Helios, steering a golden chariot.*

*Apollo in the Greek tales, Jess of Nazareth in my dream. A Greek and a Hebrew, combined in my creative imagination.*

"I have no problem with any of that. Now, my question for you is this. Do you think that your parents will accept me?"

"I know so! Unlike strict Pharisees, who believe a Jew should only marry another Jew, Joseph and Mary are liberals. They revere the book of Ruth, not born among us."

"I know her story well. Ruth converted. After her husband died, she told her mother-in-law: 'Your people will be my people.' From that moment on, she lived forever as a devout Hebrew."

"And, in time, she became one of our greatest heroines."

How much I had learned about my brother in the last month! Finally, he had matured and begun his *Halakha*: the journey of every individual Hebrew as it runs parallel to the greater "way" of our people. One person and our nation traveling, in time and space, side by side, always in a single direction.

*The individual and the community not in conflict, rather in tandem.*

*But would that prove true for me? Might I ricochet off some stone in my life's journey and veer off on some alternative path?*

"Jess," Maggie continued, "you were so remote before tonight. Now? Intense. As if you are not yourself." At that, Maggie took hold of Joses's right hand, clasping it in her own.

*Jess, of course, was a nickname that could hold true for either a girl named Jessie or a boy named Jesus. We had decided to eliminate that confusion by having me come up with his own special moniker: Judas.*

*Whenever someone in Nazareth, or our humble home to the north, called out "Jess," there was never any question that I was the subject of conversation. However personal "Jude" may have originally been to me, now it signaled "Joses" to all.*

"I am me, Maggie. A favor, from now on? Please call me by my nickname, Judas? Or, as my sister likes to abbreviate it, Jude."

"Why?

"No real reason. Only that this is what I prefer."

"Fine. We'll meet as often as possible," she said. "Talk more, get to truly know each other. Then, perhaps—"

*Maybe some things in life do work out for the best. Only a few, though enough for me to believe that the future may prove brighter than the past.*

*I must wait, watch, and learn if this holds true as my life continues on.*

"Maggie, your uncle. Has he—?"

*Thank you, Jude, for asking that. It's been on my mind since . . .*

"Let's talk about that next time. There is so much to say, and I must hurry back before anyone notices I'm missing."

A moment of silence followed. Likely, they kissed. Might that expose him? Certainly, no two people kiss in quite the same manner. Yet when they were done, Maggie said nothing.

I listened while she returned to the house and quietly slipped inside. Joses, after remaining in place until Maggie shut the door behind her, approached me.

"Everything went well, Brother," I said, stepping out from my hiding place.

"*Very* well. Though one thing struck me as peculiar."

"What, Jude?"

"Maggie held my hand much of the time."

"Nothing wrong with that."

"I know. But she kept fingering my palm. And when she did, a most curious look appeared in her eyes."

# 72.

The rains came. And came again. And again. Then, just when they seemed about to subside, the heaviest rains of the year poured down. This is the way of winter in upper-Israel. People were forced to remain inside for days when the rising waters of the Jordan overflowed. The river gushed so ferociously that a Hebrew might wonder if Yahweh had gone back on His ancient promise. Instead of the fire next time, the Great Flood had seemingly returned.

Whenever the torrents wound down to a drizzle, citizens of Nazareth cautiously returned to the streets. Owing to fear of another sudden downpour, most labor took place inside workshops similar to Joseph's. As for the much-applauded stone-cutter, carpenter, and wizard of repairs, Joseph spent these days plying his trade. When the weather finally cleared, he would journey to some city where his skills at cutting stone would earn large payments.

Occasionally, the skies quieted. Still, they remained a miserable shade of gray, splotched with nastily dark clouds. On such days people hurried up our pathway with requests. Joseph often received orders from those whose lives were nearing an end. Such elderly folk requested that he fashion a stone ossuary. These would be employed for a deceased Hebrew's second burial. Once a body, wrapped carefully in a white sheet, had been placed in a limestone cave and left there for a year and a day, relatives would return to draw forth the bones. These would be reburied in the same spot, the remains now permanently at rest in a solid container.

For carpentry, James supplied the raw materials, chopping down trees in an adjacent valley. Joseph was often asked to create long beams for citizens needing to repair their roofs. After several logs had been laid in rows across the four walls, mud, twigs, grass, leaves, and (for those few who could afford it) mortar would be spread and packed tight to seal off the top.

Sometimes, when the weather permitted, I would accompany James. How I loved the natural world! Still it disturbed and intrigued me that, akin to the pagans, I saw the vast forests, and each tree growing within, not as a nest for daemons but a paradise created by God. Nature not serving as Yahweh's test to learn which among us was evil and could be corrupted into returning to the forest. Rather, His greatest bounty, where perhaps something of God himself might be rediscovered.

*How troubling that on this issue I found myself at odds with my own nation.*

Scrupulously, we cleaned the house daily. Our people were widely known for our devotion, even obsessiveness, in regards to this. Everyone pitched in, from washing walls to removing every single speck of dirt or seed from the floor. "Cleanliness is next to Godliness," Mary would announce. This was one among her many observations that I would recall always, all the days of my life.

*My earthly life, and then my life beyond such limitations.*

Despite endless chores and my daily preparation of meals, I found time to read. Joseph had long ago purchased our own Bible, hand-lettered on yellowed goat-skin scrolls. The lines read from right to left in accordance with our Hebraic belief that movement should follow a westward pattern. This paralleled every Jew's hope, living east of Eden, that someday paradise could in time be regained.

Picking up where I'd left off at school, I discovered that the Bible's tone drastically altered. In Jeremiah and Ezekiel, I came to terms with an idea that I'd heard of but never fully understood: the coming Apocalypse. Naively, I'd assumed it referred to the end of the world and all life on it.

More correctly, the concept as I now came to understand it first-hand referred specifically to the overthrow of our Roman overlords. The awaited miracle would not be celestial but realistic. We would live free again. Following the Apocalypse.

Might that be a prediction of victory for the Zealots? Perhaps, though a violent overthrow of Rome's legions struck me as unlikely. Could there instead be a peaceful resolution? How I hoped that was so . . .

Next I turned to the Book of Daniel. I knew the tale of the lion's den, how the Bible's last great hero had defied his enemies with the help of an angel. Gabriel descended to protect

Daniel, appointed by Yahweh as our latest messiah, the savior for that moment.

For the first time, I read Chapter Seven. As I did, the answer to another riddle from my mysterious dream unexpectedly dawned on me.

The four beasts that had pursued my golden chariot? The winged lion, the mighty bear, four-headed leopard, and multi-horned monster. Daniel described each! Dumbfounded, I realized that these were symbolic creatures, representing four imperialistic nations that had conquered our own: Babylon, Persia, Greece, and our current rulers, the Romans.

A hero, Daniel insisted, must rise to the occasion and win back our independence. This figure would be called the Son of Man. That warrior who paves the way for what the prophets announced as the Kingdom of Heaven. This would someday exist right here, on Earth, in Israel.

How wonderful it was to come upon this good news. My only question: Who among us would be the next Chosen One? And would, according to scripture, that person be born in Bethlehem though raised in Nazareth?

# 73.

One drizzly day, my twin and I kept Joseph company in his workshop. Recently Joses had expressed a desire to learn the trade, likely so that he might afford a home for Maggie and himself if their romance went according to plan.

"Jude? If the weather stays calm, I'll be heading up to Sepphoris tomorrow. Care to come with me and earn a dinar?"

Joseph's invitation took Joses by surprise. My brother had only minutes earlier confided to me that he planned to slip away to Nazareth the next morning and visit Maggie.

"Oh, but *I* want to come," I impulsively said, casting a wink at Jude. "It's been so long since I've seen Sepphoris."

"That's alright with me," Joses shrugged, playing along. "I can go the following day, if that's acceptable."

"Isn't apprenticing a young *man*'s work?" Joseph asked.

"I can do anything a man can do. Right, Jude?" My twin nodded supportively.

"Fine. I did so enjoy speaking at length with you a month ago, Jess. This will allow us another such opportunity."

The next morn, just before daybreak we set out on our trek, carrying sacks of tools as well as wine, cheese, and bread for our midday meal.

"Hasn't the work in Sepphoris stretched on for an extremely long time?"

"Since shortly after your birth. The plan, you see, is not merely to reconstruct the old city but to change its nature."

As Joseph continued, I realized that our task today would not involve repairs on the palace of some affluent citizen. The ambitious undertaking involved rethinking the grid on which Sepphoris stood. Antipas hungered to outdo his own father in every way. The "new" Sepphoris would eliminate any need for residents to ever travel again to Capernaum. An international marketplace would offer clothing, furniture, foodstuffs, and so much more, all imported from distant nations.

*Gradually, Sepphoris would become self-sufficient. After several generations had passed, residents would no longer think of themselves as Hebrews, Romans, nor any other religious or ethnic groups.*

*Rather as Sepphorites in a local sense, and citizens of the vast Roman Empire in a broader one.*

Which was precisely what each of the Caesars had always desired, Tiberius picked up where Augustus had left off. Also the second Arabic king politically ruling over Judea and Galilee: total integration among the populace, leading to ongoing peace while assuring the unhindered flow of tax revenues.

What the centurions had not, with brute strength, been able to achieve might just be created through an ingenious architectural paradigm, a key part of Hellenization: that is, transforming diverse conquered lands into reflections of Rome. And, at the same time, drawing the best from each culture and incorporating it into an emerging order of things, even in Caesar's own great city.

*Is this a good thing, this "integration" concept, bringing us even closer to those Romans living in our land?*

*Or does this threaten our national identity?*

For what appears to be magnanimous might involve an intricate plot, in Israel and elsewhere, bit by bit water down our culture until eventually it ceased to exist.

"So you see, this emergent city will not be the Sepphoris that once was."

During our time at Yeshiva, Levi and I had planned to slip away from the synagogue to see the elaborate construction for ourselves. But our need to arrive early for school, then return home in time for dinner, had squelched that plan.

"I'm anxious to observe such a project as it develops."

I took Joseph's hand in mine. He glanced down in a way that made me feel like a small child again. A bittersweet feeling, simultaneously happy and sad, passed over me. He smiled at my sudden gesture. I smiled back.

During the past half year, my point of view had gradually altered. At this moment, Joseph was indeed my father. Whatever happened a dozen years earlier didn't matter.

*Or so I kept telling myself.*

*For in truth, I was not yet able to use the word father when addressing him.*

"Is such a monumental change for the better?"

"I keep going back and forth on that issue, Jess."

Aqueducts would supply fresh water for all. Cement based roads, patrolled by soldiers, rendered travel easier and safer. No neighboring country would ever again dare to try and invade us for a mighty league of centurions were always on the ready to devastate any such attempt by hostile nations.

Then again, statues of Roman gods were raised everywhere. Such pagan icons could in time be accepted into the evolving mainstream of daily life in Israel.

"The one thing they seldom bother us about is religion."

"Even if we still read Torah, Jess, shortly we will be Jews in name only. Otherwise, appearing, speaking, behaving, perhaps even thinking like those who have quietly conquered us."

As we approached the great gate, it occurred to me that Joseph and I were on our way to help complete a project that might end the way of life which, for the past 5,000 years, defined us.

# 74.

"Is this work proving too much for a girl?" Joseph whispered, careful that nearby male laborers didn't hear. He meant well, so I concealed my deep offense.

"Not *this* girl."

He approached me now from the westerly end of a lavish veranda. When completed, this would extend from a formidable two-story house to a large, circular pool of the style favored by Roman citizens living in our land. Yet this would be the home of a Hebrew family. What most concerned me was not the presence of running water for the purpose of pleasure but that I saw no indication a *mikveh,* for the traditional cleaning process, would also be constructed.

*Would the living waters be the first thing to disappear once our people experienced the delight of Romanesque recreational swimming?*

"Soon, we'll break for the noon-time meal."

"You can, if you like. I want to finish up here first."

In truth, the cutting and fitting of stone turned out to be more strenuous than I'd imagined. But no way was I about to admit this. Joseph had come by to check on me as I labored alongside several young men. A girl at a construction site might raise male ire. So I once again employed my disguise for attending school: borrowing my twin's clothes.

*I had thought that was all over and done with.*

*Apparently, I was wrong.*

"While working," I sighed, "all I could think of was what we discussed earlier."

"In truth, Jess, this has little to do with me," Joseph responded. "I'm over forty. My time is almost passed. It's the young ones like you who must decide."

"I fear a conflict may erupt between members of our nation as they line up on either side. What could be worse than that?"

"Zealots favoring confrontation could perceive those patiently waiting for the Son of Man as enemies," Joseph agreed.

Why "son"?

*Why not "daughter"?*

"I guess we'll have to wait and see," I sighed, finishing up my current task.

"When you complete that corner, Jess, stop for the day."

"Are you done as well?"

Joseph shook his head. "I need to fill out the work forms for my team. While I'm busy with that, why not visit the city? See the shape of things to come."

At Joseph's suggestion, I strolled the avenues, observing a metropolis at its turning-point. Traditionally, Hebraic houses were built apart from one another, such space implying the value we placed on individuality. Here, homes would be built in blocks. The result resembled a bee's nest, middle-class residents all honeycombed together. However fascinated and concerned I was with the evidence of change surrounding me, my mind drifted off to Barabbas. I imagined I saw him everywhere, tailing along behind workers who had finished for the day. Or standing in an alleyway, beckoning me with tempting eyes to join him.

I hadn't heard from him. Barabbas would not have sent missives via runners for fear of discovery by those searching for him. But if all had been silence between he and myself, letters regularly arrived from Luke.

# 75.

The first message to arrive had been apologetic in content and tone. Luke pleaded for forgiveness. He again asserted that a daemon had temporarily possessed him.

I did not reply. Nor did I respond to any of the others, often arriving on a daily basis. Always the messenger, looking more sorrowful with each delivery, asked if he should wait while I prepared an answer. I'd shake my head, and he would turn away, shoulders slumped, ready to begin his return journey to Capernaum.

The second letter had been calmer but no less insistent. Luke attempted to rationalize why we *must* see each other at least once again. We were friends, he wrote. He didn't want to lose that, even if he had ruined any potential for something else.

Surely, I could understand this? If so, let him know. We should meet in some public place as soon as possible. Again, I declined to put my quill to papyrus.

His third I tore into pieces without reading, discarding the bits and pieces of Luke's note, tossing them into the wind. This I did in front of the delivery boy. The youth appeared aghast, perhaps fearful I would transform into a Lilith-like succubus and devour him. I had a laugh at his expense, regretting so later. He meant no harm.

Three days went by without another. I felt relieved, hoping my temperament had been reported and that would be the end of this silly business. Two days later, the runner came again. This time, he was polite but cool, handing me the missive, bowing as if to a superior being. Then he hurried away, not daring to look back.

Momentarily, I thought to rip this one up as well. But my curiosity got the better of me. So I opened and read it. Luke all but wept onto the page. He was hurt, wounded beyond repair. That I would destroy one of his letters without reading it? Didn't he deserve a modicum of respect?

No, I decided. He did not.

Hurt gave way to anger. In the next note he took me to task, insisting I had no right to continue on this way. Yes, he did understand how deeply I'd been disappointed. Hadn't he clearly attempted to make amends?

Outraged, Luke this time *demanded* a reply. I did not respond.

Then commenced a ten-day period in which no letter arrived. I now perceived this roundelay as a game, if a one-sided one, which I had already won. Pathetically, Luke insisted on the right to continue to lose. The next note began: "This is insane." Couldn't we behave like civilized people? Wouldn't I be kind enough to send a note, however terse, agreeing to speak if we might someday chance to meet again?

What a simple request this was. How could I not honor it? Of course I would! He would await my reply.

I did not send an answer and had not heard from him since.

*Yet here is what I cannot resolve: Whenever I spotted the runner on his way toward Nazareth, I wondered if there might be another note for me.*

*And, truth be told, felt a little let down when no more arrived. But back to the present: my stroll through Sepphoris!*

# 76.

A full circle's walk around the half-completed "new Sepphoris" left me impressed by the enormity and intricacy of what workers had achieved. Wild splashes of color provided by wall murals and mosaic patterns along byways added an aura of constant celebration. This was accentuated by contrast with the city's natural backdrop: drab, brown soil, dotted with white stones and black rocks.

Then I smelled it: meat! That rich, succulent scent of fresh shanks grilled over a hot pit filled with blazing coals. The seductive aroma originated at one of the booths arranged at various intersections in a sprawling marketplace.

Against my will, I drifted in that direction. I knew that closer proximity would be torturous as I had no coins in my purse. But for one who enjoyed mealtime as much as I did, the scents proved irresistible. There was no charge to gaze at those enjoying such delicacies. Or to breath in deeply.

I continued on, as if drawn by an invisible chain that linked the food stalls to my adroit sense of smell. People exiting booths swept by me on either side. Each carried a stick skewered through thick chunks of meat. Women, men, and children eagerly devoured their purchases. Grease trickled down their chins.

Amid the others, one particular scent seemed to me as unique and tempting. Initially, I could not identify what meat it might be . . . lamb? Possibly. Chicken? I wasn't sure. Beef?

Then it hit me. *Pork.* I had smelled of it in Capernaum and the precise memory of its scent registered. The flesh of a swine; the forbidden meat, all the more intoxicating owing to its ungodly status. The odor struck me as luscious.

Perhaps, though, this was Yahweh's way of discovering which of his Chosen People were true, as opposed to those who might be led astray.

*Then again, such restrictions were not in his Covenant.*

*Rather, laws added many years later by priests. Not messiahs on the order of Moses. Ordinary men. Passing laws for people living at that precise moment in time.*

*Laws that had been included in our big book, along with every scrap of information about Hebrew history, all packed together—the trivial receiving equal weight with the eternal—in a verbal compendium of who we were and what we had been.*

*The Bible.*

Anyway, I knew one thing: If I lived here, sooner or later I'd lose control and try pork. How could a glutton like myself resist?

Luckily, Nazareth—too small, too remote to be Hellenized, at least yet—kept me far from temptation.

*But what would I have done if, at this juncture, I did have a dinar? Would I glut my stomach and lose my soul?*

*Do I even believe in such an ancient, perhaps outdated, notion?*

Then . . .

"You?"

"You!"

Briefly, I closed my eyes to breathe in the enticing aroma—after all, nowhere was it written that the aroma was forbidden, only the taste—I bumped directly into Rabbi Annas. That much made sense. For here was the hour when classes were dismissed. After, he would head up to his home in the city. What shocked me: like other customers, Annas carried roast pork on a stick, chewing away.

Of all people. The rabbi! And a strict Pharisee at that, or so he had claimed. One who preached the need for absolute compliance with the very letter of the dietary law.

*Thankfully, I had dressed as a boy today!*

"Rabbi," I said, quickly gathering my wits, "It's most . . . interesting . . . to see you again."

"I hoped our paths would nevermore cross, putrid brat who mocks the law—"

"I mock no law, at least none passed down from Yahweh. The Ten—"

"Away!" He waved his free hand in the air, as if hoping that, magician-like, this gesture might make me disappear.

Teasingly, I replied, "Will you not offer me a taste?"

Rage convulsed him. "Arrogant child. *Momsa*, too, I hear."

*Tiberon, a little voice in the back of my mind called out.*

*Not even a fellow Hebrew, but a despised Roman.*

"Better a momsa," I answered, drifting into one of my fits of rage, "than a hypocrite like you!"

"I teach what I mean, and mean what I teach. What did I tell the students? Our way demands each family maintain a kosher home. Do you doubt even for a moment that I do?"

I couldn't believe what I was hearing. Annas, I had no doubt, *did* keep a kosher home. The plates carefully organized to avoid contamination by mixing milk and meat; animals blessed before any lamb was led to the slaughter.

But this public arena? This was not his home. Annas had found a loophole, believing he remained true to the law—the law of man, not God—as circumscribed. True to the letter of the law, clearly stated. If disloyal to its spirit and intent.

*So the whole "pork thing" is merely an elaborate game?*

*Initially dictated at a time when restaurants did not yet exist, now to be bandied about, according to situational ethics?*

"I came to you for inspiration. But your hypocrisy fills me with doubt."

"Doubt that there is a God? Blasphemer!"

"I do not doubt Yahweh. Or his law. Nor could I ever."

"What, then, momsa? Brat? Boy possessed by daemons?"

"The need to obey laws created by men, long ago in power. Their once logical reasoning lost in the mists of time."

# 77.

Close beside the furnace on this cold, nasty day, Simon and the girls played with their new dreidels. These Joseph had crafted as gifts. On this first day of Hanukah, hard rain pounded down on our roof. Yet we remained dry thanks to James, who had thoughtfully relined our thatched roof in late summer. Joses, wrapped in a thick, wool cape, slipped out of the house to check on his precious animals. He returned only when assured they were sheltered, fed, watered, and warm.

Inside, James amused all with music, playing a mandolin he had purchased secondhand. Joses reached for his flute and joined in. They offered lilting tunes from our nation's illustrious past, appropriate for celebrating a joyous holiday. Hanukah was not another occasion for bitter herbs, or fasting, the case with early autumn's Rosh Hashanah, the time of beginning again. And Yom Kippur, a period reserved to repent our transgressions.

Hanukah honored Judah and the Maccabees, those warriors who defeated the invading Seleucids: an illegitimate nation composed of exiled Greeks and outlaw Persians. As the great battle raged on, priests in our ruined temple were amazed when a single day's supply of oil burned for more than a week—an eternal light signifying our continuing faith. Here was a sign, certainly: the Hebrew way would always survive, no matter how threatening our current lot in life might appear.

This event had ever since been symbolically honored with the lighting of a *menorah*. This lamp's eight oil holders, four on either side of a higher centrally located one, recalled those days of heroic combat. The ninth extension held the flame used to ignite each of those eight. An earlier version of the *menorah*, dating back to the time of Moses, had displayed both of Israel's magic numbers, arranged in tandem: two sets of three candleholders, arraigned on either side of, the lighter. Allowing, in their totality, for seven. Today, this prototype was by law restricted from home use, too holy for that and so lit only within the Jerusalem Temple.

A general sense of calm pervaded the house. Gift giving, humble as our presents for one another were, concluded.

"Simon," Mary said, bringing a sop of lighted oil to the delighted eight-year-old, "you are now big enough to handle the *shamash*." In those days before everyone in Israel had acquired candles, a family member would be chosen to employ such a measuring device to ignite the day's measured portion of oil.

"Did you make a wish?" Joseph asked once Simon completed his task. The boy stood tall and proud, not having spilled one drop of the sacred liquid. He admitted that, indeed, he had secretly done so. "And," Joseph chided, "what is it?"

Before the boy could reply, three knocks sounded at the door. "That's probably Levi," I said, rising and crossing the room. "He mentioned he'd stop by if he were able to get away for a while."

As Mary cleared the long, flat table for our coming feast, I opened the door, expecting to see my best friend. Before me, awash in the heavy downfall, stood Luke. Eyes blank, he held a neatly wrapped package.

"Beware the Greek bearing gifts," he said in a joking manner, though not a hint of humor could be detected in his eyes.

"What do you want here?" I asked unkindly once the shock of seeing him here had passed.

"I brought something for Simon."

"I'll take it," I said, rudely accepting the package and making ready to slam the door in his face.

"Jess!" Joseph howled, hurrying over. "Is that any way to treat a visitor? Particularly our friend from Capernaum?"

Unlike Mary, he knew nothing of "the incident." She had deduced what happened from my general moodiness and refusal to mention Luke's name. Even when females barely speak to one another, we notice even the smallest details concerning other women's moods that men almost never pick up on.

"It's Hanukah, and he's not a Hebrew."

With that, I again began to close the door. Now, though, Mary stepped close. She took charge in that unique way the woman of the house tends to do, without any need to raise her voice. "Have you forgotten the ancient laws of hospitality, which must be extended to everyone?"

Mary took Luke's right hand and led him inside, removing his soaked outer garment. This, Mary placed over a chair near the furnace to dry. James reached for a wool blanket and spread it around Luke's drenched shoulders.

"Thank you!" Already, Luke appeared to be recovering from the torrent still raging outside.

"You're very welcome," James replied.

# 78.

"Come, join us," Joseph said to my beautiful Greek. Or, at least, the worthless dung pile I'd once viewed as such. Finally glancing up from his toy, little Simon realized who had arrived. Ecstatic, the child leaped up and rushed to Luke, the two now-curious girls following fast behind.

"Hello, Simon. Remember me? This is for you."

Luke indicated the gift I now held, which I handed to Simon. Excitedly, he tore away the covering. Inside was one of those beautiful boxes fashioned from rare wood, with finely detailed decorations. The sort of treasure chest Simon had so admired in Capernaum's marketplace. I'd forgotten that I had mentioned it to Luke. At the sight of this dream gift, the boy's eyes lit up with surprised delight.

"What about us?" the girls whined in unison.

"Well," Luke told them, speaking as if he were an older brother, "if you promise to be good all year, perhaps I'll bring one for each of you next Hanukah. *If* I'm invited back. Would you like that?"

They smiled and danced about, as if this were the greatest thing ever to happen in the history of the world.

"Meanwhile, here's something I think you'll enjoy."

Salome and Miriam, still a bit wary, edged up to his side. Luke drew a bag of hard candies from his pocket, distributing these evenly to the giddy children.

"That was thoughtful of you," I had to admit. Luke looked over to me, hoping to establish eye contact. I chose not to acknowledge his gaze.

"By all means, be our guest for dinner."

"If you're certain, Joseph, that I'm not intruding."

"Not at all."

Mary, true to her nature, apologized for the little she could offer. "We have no meat today. Cheeses are traditional for this holiday, and the two can never be mixed."

Joseph joined in. "We cook with olive oil, to acknowledge the oil that burned bright in our original temple when despair hovered over our nation, during our calendar's month of Kislev. There are potatoes roasted in the oil, kneaded into crispy treats we call latkes."

"And after that," Salome gleefully added, "sweet donuts for dessert."

"It sounds wonderful," Luke said as he glanced from one family member to the next, attempting to grasp some sense of proper table protocol by observing his hosts. Ritual behavior included lying by the table on a mat rather than sitting or squatting, the case with many nations.

Joseph, who had located an extra wine glass and poured for all of us, raised his own in solemn toast: "*Neis gadol haya sham*!" We lifted our drinks and in unison repeated those words as Luke respectfully listened.

"What does that mean?" he softly asked.

"A great miracle happened here, in our homeland. As a result, our way of life did not vanish from the face of the earth like countless civilizations that have come and gone before and since."

"Because we are the Chosen People!" Simon added.

Luke nodded appreciation for this explanation, then dared look in my direction. This time, he cast me a sweet smile. Before I realized what I was doing, I'd returned the gesture. At once, I regretted it and looked away.

"Now," Joseph sighed, "enjoy!"

During the meal, Luke constantly attempted to reconnect while I kept my eyes low, staring at my plate. As was the custom in our country, Joseph the patriarch related the tale of adventure and faith that inspired this celebration.

"What a wonderful character, this Judah Maccabee!" Luke concluded. "He reminds me of my nation's hero Herakles."

Joseph asked Luke to tell that story, which my family was not familiar with. Eagerly, he agreed, each of us held spellbound by marvelous episodes recounting the many labors assigned to his beloved warrior-king. It did occur to me that we had, if inadvertently, experienced one of those situations that Joseph and I spoke of on the road to Sepphoris: Hebraic and Hellenistic cultures converging in some mid-ground and overlapping . . .

*Perhaps there is only one tale, after all. One enduring, never-ending story, told and retold by every tribe or nation that has ever existed on Earth. Or ever will.*

*Any differences have to do with the manner in which diverse people relate the tale.*

*Always, though, at its center exists the core: A hero must rise to the occasion from out of the wilderness whenever his people are threatened.*

"There is one fundamental difference," I announced, at last looking up. "Judah clearly was as great as a man can be. But he was entirely human."

"Herakles," Luke replied, "was born to a woman, Alcmene, though his father was a god. The greatest god in the pantheon of Atticans, Zeus. Reimagined and renamed Jupiter by our Roman conquerors."

"Herakles sounds a lot like our David," Simon—intrigued by our conversation—piped in.

"Some versions of the story," Joses added, "claim Yahweh played a role in that hero-king's birth."

"Many of our people hope," Mary interjected, "that another such savior will soon arrive and solve our current dilemma."

"He must derive," James added, "from the House of David. As our sacred numbers are three and seven, and multiplication has long been the preferred form of mathematics to the Hebraic mind since God commanded Adam and Eve to go forth and do precisely that, such a messiah would be born twenty-one generations following Israel's second king."

"Our prophets insist he must be a citizen of Nazareth," Joses noted.

"Why this small, out-of-the-way place?"

"When the Romans conquered Israel, our greatest fear was that they would murder all of David's descendants. This would eliminate any potential challenge to Rome's appointed king over the Jews. To avoid assassination, the Davidians left Jerusalem, relocating in the north. To let other Hebrews know of their presence while keeping our secret from the Romans, they named their settlement Nazareth: The Branch. Indicating a final branch on David's family tree. Our next savior must be a leaf from that branch, therefore necessarily raised here."

Fascinated, Luke remained silent as these facts and ideas swirled about in his mind. Eventually, he replied, "Then you, Joseph, by virtue of living here, must be a direct descendant of David."

"That is true."

Luke glanced across the table to Joses. "Perhaps it will be you. Do you ever wonder if you might be the Christos?"

"Christos?" Simon asked. "What does *that* mean?"

"It's the Ionic-Greek term for the Chosen One."

Turning scarlet with embarrassment, Joses replied, "That idea never occurred to me. I'm a humble goatherd."

*Yes. But so was David, and most of our greatest heroes.*

*Still, owing to rumors concerning our birth, you have no way of knowing whether the blood of Joseph, descendant of David, runs through your veins.*

Or, for that matter, mine.

# 79.

"Jess, why don't you walk your friend to the roadway?"

I cast my eyes at Mary, trying to determine whether she intended this as a polite gesture or took pleasure (and a measure of vengeance) in confounding me. Certainly, she appeared aware of my discomfort with Luke.

Perhaps a bit of both?

"Luke can find his way, I'm sure."

"It is our way," Joseph reminded me, "to see someone off on such a long journey."

No doubt Joseph, as always, wished to be agreeable. Not wanting to argue the point, I joined Luke at the door. He slipped into his now dry outer garment, making ready to leave, then smiled graciously and thanked everyone. The girls called out to him, reminding Luke of his promise for the following year.

*Only there would be no future Hanukah feast. At least not for the family of Joseph.*

*Long before then, our little world would shatter forever, if no one could have guessed so at this moment.*

"The rain has let up," I noted as we stepped outside. Luke and I headed up the muddy pathway leading to the Roman road. "You should have a much easier time going than coming."

"I had to see you again, Jess."

"The feeling is not mutual."

"Won't you even—?"

"No."

He halted, hurt—even angry—about my attitude. Luke stared into my eyes, searching for solace. "I was wrong."

"You certainly were."

"Haven't you ever been wrong? About *anything*?"

Those words gave me pause. Some days, I believed that I was wrong about most everything. And nothing compared to my regret over how I'd lashed out at Mary.

"No one is perfect but my God, Yahweh. Or so the Pharisees claim."

"Well, there's where your people differ from us. Greeks believe that our father god Zeus is flawed. Just like people down below on our planet."

"Then why do you hail him as a god?"

"Because he's more powerful than we. And he descended from somewhere in the stars."

*The man at the well, carrying a shofar, said something similar. Only he was talking about the Space Travelers.*

*Then again, he was crazy. Nothing that he told me matters.*

*At least, I don't think so.*

"But not powerful enough to have created the cosmos?"

"No."

"How can you believe in so limited a god?"

"Many don't. A philosopher, Protagorus, has written: 'As to the gods, I don't know whether they exist or not.'"

"They may have died off?"

"Less that, than we created them, in an earlier age. Wise men invented the gods at a point in time when we needed to believe in such grand fables."

"People never outgrow their longing to hear stories. If the old gods are dead to the Greeks now, what will people do?"

"I'm not sure," Luke admitted, shrugging his shoulders. "Create new gods so that there will be new stories, perhaps?"

# 80.

When we reached the spot where our path converged with the road, both of us stopped and turned to face one another.

"Give me another chance, Jess?" Suddenly, Luke's voice sounded desperate. "Just talking like this again means so much to me."

"It isn't that simple, Luke."

"Couldn't we please give it another try?"

*Haven't you ever been wrong? About anything?*

Without meaning to, I cast my eyes to the ground. "I can't answer that right now."

*Who's the father this time? Or wouldn't you know?*

"You're not ruling it out, then?"

*Forgive me, Jess. Let me have a second chance?*

"I'm not ruling anything out. I never do."

*Forgive me, Mary. Please allow me another chance?*

"That's something, isn't it?" I did not respond. "Jess, tell me, on that day when I came down from Capernaum, and disappointed you so. Honestly, now, what were you expecting?"

*After all, Jess. Nobody's perfect.*

"You wouldn't believe it if I told you."

*Not even you.*

"Try me."

I breathed in deeply before beginning. "I wanted what I guess every woman, at least while still a girl, most wishes for, dreams of, perhaps needs: romance. A dream come true of love as it ought to be."

"I'm not sure I understand."

"Remember the statue, greeting visitors to Capernaum on that day we first met?"

"Of course."

"Helios, a sun god, descending from the sky on a chariot pulled by four magnificent white steeds. The driver bedecked in the armor of a hero. Arriving to set everything aright."

"Instead, along came a pathetic, selfish, horny boy."

"I wanted a hero. Herakles, in the temple's final show? The warrior who could conquer a dragon. In my mind, he was doing that to save the woman he loved."

"Iole. His betrothed."

"See? I wanted Helios and Herakles to melt into one another and for the result to be you. I wanted what every naïve girl, whether she'll openly admit it or not, hopes, wishes, perhaps even states outright: 'Someday my prince will come.'"

Luke laughed bitterly. "I was hardly princely."

"You provided a valuable lesson. I wanted a fantasy come true. What I got was a stiff jolt of reality. Perhaps that was the moment I grew up. Or at least began to."

"Then this is it?"

*He means it this time. If I say yes, he'll never return.*

*Confused as I remain as to all that has transpired, I do know one thing: I don't want that.*

*Perhaps I should. But I don't.*

I shrugged. "Well, you did promise the girls you'd return next year with their presents."

"May I come back before that?" he asked desperately.

"Suit yourself."

Luke looked me up and down, as if trying to figure Jess out.

*But how could he?*

*Most of the time, I didn't know what I was doing, or what I hoped for. Not a clue as to why I do and say what I do and say.*

*If I can't understand Jess of Nazareth, how could anyone else?*

Luke hesitantly moved forward, attempting to gently, sweetly kiss me on the cheek. Before he could, I turned and stomped toward the house.

I didn't look back to see if he were still watching. Part of me wanted to. But some deep voice within me refused to let Jess do so.

# 81.

Apparently, Luke had perceived in my smile what he wanted to: the beginning of the end of our dark period. Several days later, notes began arriving once again. These were written under the assumption that our "issue" had been laid to rest during those subdued hours when we ate, drank, and sang together, while rain beat down on the roof like an accompanying drum.

As well as our final moment alone, before he departed.

Clearly, Luke was attempting to control the narrative of our relationship. If we did indeed still have one.

I did not reply. During the following weeks, another such missive arrived each afternoon, written in precisely the same tone. I chose not to answer, at least in part because now I found myself intrigued: how long might this ploy continue?

Then, a day without a letter. The following afternoon, a concerned one, asking if anything serious had gone wrong here.

I didn't reply.

Two more days without a note.

At last, a harried, bitter, angry message. How could I once again ignore him?

My silence remained unbroken. Now his letters stopped, this time permanently.

I harbored one regret: If they had continued, and I in time deigned to answer, I might have asked Luke what he meant when he'd said "beware the Greeks bearing gifts." What an interesting notion!

*How I'd love to know from where that phrase derived!*

"Good-bye, Luke," I whispered to myself while standing beside our house, gazing off in the direction of the road that led to Capernaum. "And good luck."

As winter wore on, I increased my work load in the household. I dared hope that if I assumed most of Mary's chores during her term of pregnancy, she might yet forgive me. Daily routines were becoming more difficult for her to accomplish as the bulge in her belly continually enlarged.

As I learned, though, I was in many ways my mother's child. Even as I refused to budge with Luke, so did Mary with me.

*Could this be punishment from on high?*

*If I were unwilling to offer someone else a second chance, why should I receive one?*

The moment Hanukah had passed from present holiday to a warm memory, Mary refused to make eye contact with me, as I had done so long with her. I wondered if perhaps I continued to shun Luke as compensation for my mother (finally I referred to her as that again) doing so to me.

Essentially, if I'm going to be hurt, then I will hurt back. But if that were true, then I must be a less likable girl than I wish to believe.

*What mixed-up, miserable fools we all are! Most of the time, as I was learning from experience, we create our myriad problems to punish ourselves.*

*What is the perversity in humankind that so often causes us to work against rather than for our own well-being?*

*Might it be that, deep down, none of us truly believes we deserve to be happy?*

When not working, I studied Torah from Joseph's scrolls. He never asked where or how I had learned to read, nor did I offer to explain. After improving my skills. I honed in on *Nevi'im,* the gleanings from our greatest prophets.

And, finally, *Ketuvim,* or The Writings. These included a tale believed by some to have been handed down from the prophet Samuel. Though I vaguely knew the story of Ruth, reading the original impacted on a nagging question: What does it mean to be a Hebrew, a Jew, an Israelite?

Were these different terms to describe the same person, or could the situation be more complex than that?

Also fascinating, here was a scroll named after a woman—a rarity that appealed to me.

The story went this way: Long ago, a terrible famine caused many of our nation to move beyond Palestine, seeking sustenance in neighboring states. Naomi and her husband Emilelek journeyed into Moab. There, he found work. When their son Mahlon grew to manhood, and there were no Jewish women nearby, Mahlon's eyes settled on a Moabite, Ruth.

Though Mahlon's parents would have preferred a female of their bloodlines, reality necessitated that they must deal as best they could with the current situation.

So the two young people were married, in accordance with Hebraic custom. Ruth converted to the way of Yahweh. Everyone agreed this union was sacred. When Mahlon died young, before he and Ruth had conceived their first child, Naomi (long since a widow) made the decision to return to her homeland. She then suggested to Ruth that the still-young and beautiful girl remain behind with her own people.

Ruth surprised Naomi by announcing: "Where you go, I will go. And where you stay, I will stay. Your people will be my people. And your God, my God."

# 82.

When not rereading this text often, to be certain that I comprehended every possible implication, I constantly thought about it while working, eating, or strolling in the forest. Even when lying in bed before falling asleep. Indeed, such mental activity often kept me awake almost until dawn.

The book's immediate impact related to Joses's love for Maggie. If there were any doubts as to the legitimacy of their potential marriage, here—set down in stark words by one of our greatest scribes—the Bible offered a clear corollary.

Naturally, I couldn't wait to share this story with my twin.

Also implied was a justification for the people of Israel leaving the land when necessity demanded. This challenged the current conservative view, in place since our return from Babylon: we must remain within our little corner of the world. But as Ruth's book suggested, there ought to be no stigma attached to a wandering Jew. For me, who and what we were as a nation existed less in regards to geography than an underlying and undying idea. From a progressive perspective, such a person might cease to be an Israelite but remain a devoted Hebrew.

In time, Naomi did return. As should, perhaps must, be the case. Eventually, our prodigals come home.

This had emerged as a significant element of every Jew's life journey.

*And, in the name of equality, what goes for prodigal sons should hold true for prodigal daughters.*

*Remember that, Jess. Someday when you are far away.*

Here, then, was not merely a specific parable but a paradigm for living. If I did travel (how I might manage this, I couldn't yet imagine) someday I too would return.

This must be my way even as it was our way: the individual and the group reflect one another. Two situations collapsing into a great and satisfying oneness.

*An imperfect oneness, perhaps. But offering a sense of unity all the same.*

As to a marriage between a Hebrew male and a gentile woman, the narrative argued that this was not only permissible but required for our nation's history to unfold. In time, Ruth, who traveled to Israel with her mother-in-law, would become the great-grandmother of our most beloved king, David. She, non-Hebrew, had been the progenitor of the precious few original residents of Nazareth.

*We, The Branch Davidians. Joseph among them.*

*And, possibly at least, Joses and myself.*

At this time, James found a new job, which so intrigued my half brother that he knew immediately this was his long searched for life's calling. A new shop opened in Nazareth, owned and run by several well-educated scribes. They offered, for a considerable price, to track anyone's bloodline as far back as possible, even to the beginning: Abraham and the initiation of our people.

I would have guessed that, during times of financial strife, few would partake of such a luxury. In fact, it became all the rage. Everybody apparently desired to know his precise origin so as to better grasp who they were now. James's education qualified him to be hired for the team. He would bring his work home, studying yellowed documents by an oil lamp late into the night.

"When I finish these, I'll do one for *our* family," he confided. The thought disturbed me. What if such a report revealed details I might not be able to face? No such fear for James, clearly his father's son.

Meanwhile, I informed Joses about the Scroll of Ruth and its favorable implication for himself and Maggie. Just so long as she would willingly embrace our faith.

"She embraces our idea of oneness! What fascinates her most? This notion of unity isn't limited to Hebrews. She told me that the ancient Egyptians long ago believed in this."

"Which explains the Ankh she gave you."

"Actually, gave *you*. Which you then turned over to me."

At that moment, Maggie appeared at our doorway. She had seized the opportunity on a mild late-winter's day to visit her beloved. Thankfully, she had not arrived seconds earlier. For then Maggie might have overheard our words and grasped what Jude and I referred to as "the secret switch."

Not that I was convinced she didn't have a hunch. Today, her eyes danced charmingly as she happened upon us, Joses in his rough, woolen goatherd vest, myself in the attire of a proper Hebrew virgin: a blue linen sheath, covering me from the top of my neck to the bottom of my ankles.

"This must be the sister you've told me about!"

Joses and I rose as Maggie ambled close. He played along with the ruse, offering an introduction: "Meet my twin sister, Jess."

"My goodness," she gushed playfully. "You truly are nearly identical!"

Maggie stepped forward to embrace me, as one young Middle Eastern woman would when initially encountering another. Her freshly washed hair smelled delightfully familiar. She took my right hand in her own, held it warmly, and glanced down at my palm as she disengaged.

"Yes," I said. "People often tell us that."

# 83.

Following a brief conversation, I made excuses to leave them alone and headed up to the house. There, waiting for me, stood Levi. He appeared more mature and considerably more certain of himself than the last time we were together.

"Great to see you!" I said.

We embraced as friends. The experience resonated with me. For now (and for the first time) Levi held me in his arms as a woman wishes to be held by a man. Not in the crude, rough way Luke had. Rather recalling the considerate yet muscular embrace of Barabbas.

Could the right man have been here all along and somehow I did not notice until this moment? Might Levi be the golden warrior I'd hoped would someday arrive? Had I failed to spot a budding hero beneath his offering of brotherly love?

"Jess, I've got news," Levi announced after we'd exchanged the warm words of reunited companions. I realized then that a dark shadow hung over him. "The Zealots have made a move. They poured down from the hills and attempted to seize Jodefat."

Levi referred to a medium-sized city located several miles north of Sepphoris. Most of Jodefat's residents were working-class Hebrews. A garrison of Roman foot soldiers were stationed in a barracks on the city's eastern side. Until this incident that Levi now related, there had been little if any tension between the two factions.

"I'm only surprised that this didn't happen earlier."

"The Zealots massacred most of the troops while they slept. A few managed to escape. Survivors hurried to their nearest fortress, to the west, on the borderline with Phoenicia. A fighting force assembled. They marched out the next morning to retaliate."

"Was Barabbas among the Zealots?"

"I don't know. We can only pray he wasn't."

"Why?" For a moment, my mouth felt so parched that I couldn't swallow. "What happened?"

"During the Romans' absence, Zealots pleaded with villagers to join their cause. Together, they could hold the city. Word has it that only a few chose to do so. The others packed up their families and whatever belongings they could grab and hurried off to hide until the oncoming slaughter was over."

"Oh, Levi!" I dropped down on a stretch of rock, sitting there as if my body were an extension of the stone. Levi allowed me a moment of privacy while I sobbed. Once I'd regained control, he sat down beside me. "Of course, he'd be just the type to volunteer," I cried out.

"We'll have to wait and see," he said, extending his right arm around my shoulders, drawing me close for comfort.

"Every day, Levi, I weigh the rights and wrongs of Roman rule. I try so hard to settle my thoughts about this."

"My guess? Everyone in Israel does much the same thing."

"The Romans do protect our borders from possible invaders," I noted.

"Yes," he nodded, adding sarcastically. "On the other hand, they brought us the bountiful gift of leprosy."

That disease, now common throughout Israel, had been virtually unknown in our corner of the world before the arrival of Roman troops. When Pompey conquered us, several legions accompanying him had earlier been stationed in India. While there, many encountered prostitutes. This led to their contracting a disease, for which no cure existed, that decomposed a person's flesh. Once in our homeland, those same soldiers slept with local prostitutes, passing leprosy on to them. They in turn gave it to Hebrew men, who brought it home to their wives . . .

And so the pestilence spread . . .

# 84.

"As terrible, horrible, miserable as our current occupation may be, it's not as extreme as when Judah and the Maccabees revolted against the Seleucids."

*Then our temple had been sacked without provocation. Our women raped. Citizens forced to eat of the pig or die.*

"Granted, Rome allows us freedom of religion. Except of course for the . . . how do I put it? . . . one stickler."

*If only Herod could be made to understand that a large-scale rebellion might be averted if the restriction of our single blue Tallit string would be rescinded!*

*But how to reach him?*

"Are you aware of the new city to be built on our inland sea?" I asked. Levi nodded.

The new metropolis would be called Tiberius. Construction would commence in early spring, once the rains ceased. Already

Joseph had been offered a lucrative contract to oversee the stonemasonry, though he wasn't certain yet if he would accept. Was it worth the money to help bury our culture?

Joseph had expressed his concern several days earlier, as I assisted him in the shop. His initial reaction: "Well, if I don't, someone else will. Why let one of my competitors earn the profits when my silent protest will do nothing to eliminate the problem?"

"Perhaps poverty is superior, in a moral sense, to selling your skills to the enemy?"

"*If* the Romans are our enemy," Joseph had sighed.

"True," I admitted." The Philistines dare not invade. They know the centurions would decimate them. And if those truly threatening hordes were to conquer us again, they immediately would level the Jerusalem Temple, which Herod and the Romans built for us."

"You have a highly logical sensibility, Jess."

This past discussion passed through my mind while, in the present, I sat and spoke with Levi, who then said, "As for me, I've decided. Your advice to me on the way to Sepphoris that first day of school? 'Render unto Caesar that which art Caesar's, and unto God, that which art God's.'"

How amazing that after so many months he could quote the precise words. "You remember *that*?"

"I've thought about it every day since. Jess, I've never told you this, but since learning to read and write, I've begun jotting down the things that you say."

This caused me to smile at last. "You're joking?"

"I know they're only offhand remarks. But they strike me as so profound I want to refer to them from time to time."

Before I realized what I was doing, I'd leaned over and kissed Levi on the lips. He blushed and for a while couldn't form words again. "You were right," he eventually said. "Total freedom would be ideal—"

"Though unfortunately we do not live in a perfect world."

"True! And so long as we have freedom to worship, I for one can live with those other issues. Particularly if the alternative is to die on the cross."

I shuddered, admitting something that I lived in daily denial of. "Levi, I've been having disturbing nightmares in which that is how I meet my end."

"*You,* Jess? Hah! Never in a million years."

PART THREE

# Not of This Earth

# 85.

During the seemingly endless months of Israel's winter, as Galilee suffers the constant deluge so wished for during our scorching summers, snow gathers far to the north on a wide range of mountains. Their high-reaching peaks run diagonally from Syria in the east to Lebanon in the west. Originally known as *Jabal ash-Shraqi*, these spiraling monuments, composed of jagged limestone, appear from a distance to be man-made towers. Tallest and most famous among them is Mount Hermon. Hebrews call this sacred peak *Jabal Harumun*. The nation of Israel, my people's promised land, stretches southward from this natural God-given point of reference. From its flat top, the entire area known as the Near Middle East is, on a clear day, visible in every direction for as far as the human eye can see.

Israelites consider this imposing mount a marker: the northernmost tip of Galilee and furthest extension of our country. Over many centuries pagan tribes, migrating south through Ituraea, reached this wall of rock. Once there, they entrenched themselves on Mount Hermon's northern side. Each group of people laid claim to the peak extending high into the clouds. For generations too numerous to count, warfare ensued.

*I want that! Why? Because it is* there!

*Why else? Because someone other than me covets it.*

Like black and red ants attempting to eliminate each other and occupy a hump of earth, Jews and Syrians continuously met upon the mount to slay one another. But as these were humans, not insects, the conflicts eventually took the form of ritual in their own mental vision of such an ongoing conflict.

*"This place will be mine,"* kings on each side proclaimed.

*"What can we do but follow orders?"* common men from either country wept.

On occasion the Syrians would conquer. Their metal-tipped spears, carried by vast armies that outnumbered those of our smaller nation, aided their warriors in fortifying an area known as The Heights. Positioned here, a lookout could rotate full circle, witnessing the magnitude of the world around him: from the great cosmopolitan cities to stark wilderness dotted with mud and clay huts; from green pastures filled with golden shafts of wheat that grow higher here than anywhere else in the world to the ruthless desert Hebrews avoid, and where only the solitary Arab, profound in his isolation, calls home.

As to the constant warfare, Jewish troops sent sharp stones hurling the Syrians' way. Our own deadly slings dated back long before David, if wielded more famously by that *Mashiach* than any other hero. The deadly hail cut so fiercely into the flesh of our opponents that their enormous reserves of manpower could not effectively assemble themselves for defensive action.

Defeated, at least temporarily, they would desist. We prevailed. For a while, at least. Until the tables turned again. Then men perished and women mourned once more as enemies of Israel proved victorious. In time, the two armies, worn down by decades of combat (each also facing immediate threats on their eastern and western borders) chose to withdraw to boulders, crevices, and thick bushes on either side of Mount Hermon, its coveted crown abandoned. Guards stood at the ready, out of suspicion that the enemy might attack. Envoys regularly met upon this no-man's land to negotiate treaties. But a true peace remained elusive.

To the north of Mount Hermon, the Syrian people went on with their daily lives. As did the Israelis to the south in our farming villages. Most dwellers—simple in their ambitions, hoping only to make it through another day of work—followed life's path of ordinary existence. In time, they (if not their leaders) forgot about the long-disputed, still-unconquered prize: Mount Hermon itself, the subject of many fables, Syrian and Israeli. These related anecdotes about the earliest men to live in this region and how sacred they had considered this specific place.

My guess as to why the nations fought so bitterly was formed while listening to tales told by Joseph as our family crowded close to the furnace on damp mid-winter nights. The wind howled through cracks in the walls and down from small holes in the roof above. The real reason Hebrews and Syrians had always wanted Mount Hermon was to keep the other side from claiming it.

If it were indeed holy, then we, not them, must possess this sacred point.

Whether that was true or not, such a line of thinking became *my* truth. The only truth I needed or perhaps could know. The truth as it existed in my own comprehension of the world, no matter how others perceived things.

Mount Hermon had become more than simply a landmark for our people. It now took on the qualities of an icon. We were not like the Greeks, Egyptians, and other nations allowed to cut pictures into rock or carve figures from wood. Graven images fashioned by humans would anger Yahweh, our one God reflecting the personality and values of the Hebrew people who had defined Him while setting our story down in print for the first time 600 years ago.

Still, we did reserve the right to perceive natural objects as sources of meaning.

Here, then, stood Mount Hermon: the Yahweh-created structure, which, we guessed, stretched as tall as the tower of Babel. With one key difference: this skyscraper had a right to exist. For it derived from God's good work, not the arrogance of men.

# 86.

Towering more than 2,815 meters above sea level, Mount Hermon (actually a cluster of smaller mountains that, from a distance, appear to form a single shaft) would invariably be covered by a blanket of snow from mid-October to early June. Once spring arrived and the melting process began, another pattern of nature resumed. My nation believes this was devised by Yahweh during the creation of planet Earth as part of His master plan. Snow and ice melted into waters: fresh, clean, and pure. As their levels continuously rose, the life-giving liquid poured over Mount Hermon's southern side, emptying into Israel's Golan Heights directly below the peak.

Where the coarse terrain slopes downward southwesterly, this flood of water dissipates into many streams. These trickle lower as the land's contours determine the direction in which all liquid flows. Eventually, the streams reach a juncture where the land consists of innumerable ridges. They force all running waters to re-converge. Here is where those waters come together again and form what, for ages, has been the origination point of the Jordan River.

On this very spot, our existence as a people began: several miles southwest of *Jabal ash-Shraqi*, where the great river appears to mysteriously emerge from out of nowhere. At least for those who do not know the facts I have even now shared with you, but which I remained unaware of when, not yet twelve, I was very young.

*Magic is what people call those ordinary things that they are not yet logically able to comprehend . . .*

*Miracles are those events which primitive people have not yet developed a scientific vocabulary to realistically describe.*

In the year that I was born, Herod the Great had ordered the White Stone Temple built near this place. Over the next twelve years, Antipas continued his late father's plans to construct a grand city to be called Caesarea Philippi, in honor of Augustus. (Philip was one of the many names ascribed to him at various stages in the man's life; some believed that the city's title also referenced Philip, brother of Herod and Tetrarch of territories located to the east.) From a bird's-eye view, the area below Jordan's headwaters form the liquid spine of Israel. Animal, vegetable, and human life sprout along its banks. As Hebrews discovered means of controlling the flow in both eastward and westward directions—either on their own or from The Visitors Gabriel spoke of—our ancestors expanded the geography of Zion.

On its meandering journey from here down to Jerusalem, 150 miles south, the Jordan, considered a living entity capable of thought and emotion, likes to take its time. Picking up speed when the land's surface veers along a diagonal sweep, the bright-blue waters swirl around mighty rocks before pushing on over grey and black stones visible just beneath its surface.

Plentiful beasts and men have mistakenly assumed that the current will remain calm in such enchanting places. But these stretches of white water can be cruel. Living things in the vicinity must always be aware of the river's raw power, for it pays us no mind, carrying away the unwary not out of cruelty but obliviousness.

Eventually, the landscape levels out. As it does, the waters slow once more, snaking around large, solid oaks. So dark brown is their color, and so thick do they stand together, that from a distance the forest appears black.

Small basins collect along the shores, providing a sweet, precious necessity for farmers and herders. In time the Jordan enters the Sea of Galilee, our inland ocean, a great fresh-water lake rich with fish for the netting. Rays from above create the illusion of silver threads on bouncing waves as the wind, ordinarily a calm breeze though fierce when storms arise, whisks over and across the surface. Located along its western bank are centers of commerce: large, small, and every size in-between.

At the Sea of Galilee's southernmost point, the water pours out again, allowing the Jordan to continue in a now direct, even methodical flow toward Jerusalem. On the river's eastern side exists the land known as Decapolis. On our own, a few miles below Galilee, sits a time-worn village called Scythopolis. This serves as the rendezvous point for caravans traveling down the highway and through Samaria to the Dead Sea, where the Jordan abruptly ends.

Adjacent to this salt-laced body of water are to be found the charred remains of Jericho, torched by Joshua after bringing us back to our promised land 1,500 years ago. Here, travelers veer westward, into lower Israel, called Judea. There, pilgrims reach the pearl of our world. Soon I would see Jerusalem for the first time in three years. Economic woes had prevented our family from making the trek three times a year, as our tradition required. The situation was even worse for Galilean families that earned less than we did.

With the increased workload that Joseph had profited from during the past year, his family was among those finally able to afford such a trip once again.

# 87.

Two nights earlier, Elizabeth and John had joined us following their brief hike from northern Bethlehem to Nazareth. According to Hebrew ritual, when relatives are reunited we feast and rejoice. Then together we embarked on our trek toward Scythopolis. For there, all in upper Judea making the pilgrimage would meet for comradeship and protection. However effective the Romans had been at eliminating outlaw bands, some highwaymen still haunted the roadways. Wild boars and lions also posed a threat. So the wise way to travel was with caution and much company.

Several dozen cook fires blazed on hillsides as we arrived at a large campsite south of the city. Jubilation arose as old friends happened upon one another after lengthy periods of separation. Nearby, mercenaries accompanying us circled their own fires. Here was a warrior elite willing to accept the common folks' payment, less comfortable mingling with those that they considered of a lesser order. Owners of camels, donkeys, oxen, and horses held their livestock steady, eager to rent them to those who could afford such luxury. For most, the hundred-mile journey to the Temple Mount would be on foot.

Our family members expressed concern as to Mary's delicate condition. Joseph had suggested perhaps it would be best for her to remain home. Mary would have none of it. He mentioned renting a donkey. She wouldn't even consider that. She was stubborn, even as I am.

*In her position, I would have done the same.*
*Like mother, like daughter.*

All the while, ever more pilgrims arrived. Cliques formed, mostly according to class distinctions: from wealthy landowners to simple farmers and fishermen to the poorer day laborers, everyone drifted as if by instinct to his or her own kind. The journey, however unique in other ways, mirrored everyday life within our rigid social system. And, as always, my family would generally be ignored.

That was alright. We had long since grown accustomed to it.

*"Momsa! Momsa!"*

*That old insult echoed in my mind, though no one shouted this out loud.*

At dawn, a shofar sounded seven times. This rallying call was repeated for a total of three blasts. Our symbolic numbers, so inherent in our nation, were incorporated into our departure, as they were most every aspect of our lives. In unison, people and beasts rose up from where they had knelt or lain, shaking away any lingering shadows of sleep. First, everyone ate, nourishing ourselves for the long journey.

Then we set off. Walking or riding, the people sang in celebration of our national identity. The family of Joseph did not share in this outpouring of community spirit owing to old rumors. All the same, I enjoyed this moment, experiencing a surge of excitement while listening to hymns rich with our common history and heritage.

At last, the moment had arrived. In four days: Jerusalem! This year, Pesach fell on my and Joses's twelfth birthday.

A double celebration! For the community at large and the two of us.

*Coincidence or destiny?*

*Once again, I could only wonder.*

# 88.

"They say," James confided to John, Joses, myself, and Levi, who had somehow managed to locate us amidst the commotion, "that on occasion the salt in the Dead Sea thickens to a point that a person can actually skim along its surface without sinking."

We listened, exhausted after three days of rising early and making camp late. In-between, we walked continuously with only a brief midday break for a cold lunch.

"But how can that be?" I did know something about water. The life of anyone living in Galilee depended entirely on the Jordan's persistent generosity. This intriguing notion fascinated me.

"It's quite remarkable," James began. Then, much like a rabbi, he explained what he'd learned about the lowest, saltiest body of water in the world from people he worked alongside. The Dead Sea lay 417 feet below sea level. Each liter of its liquidity contained an amazing 340 grams of salt that had coagulated here eons before the Jordan first reached this remote point.

Located at the foot of *Ha-He'ekekm* cliff, this inland sea was so heavily salted no living thing could survive in it. Yet in one of those reversals I'd begun to realize were commonplace in our complex existence, the Dead Sea could also give life.

"People travel here from all over, as far as Greece and Rome, to bathe in its waters."

"But why?"

"Owing to the concentration of salt, wise men have long believed that the Dead Sea's waters are able to heal illnesses."

"I can't wait to experience *this*."

In fact, I didn't have long to do so. A mere two miles to the south, we happened upon it: spectacularly stark, as white as chalk, smelling of salt and brine. Here, the Jordan reached its southernmost point, emptying into an immense basin after seventy-five miles of having spread fresh water throughout Galilee as well as Perea and upper Nabataea on its eastern shore. When waters from the north entered into this enormous pool, they were pure. Once here, they quickly absorbed salt from deposits dating back to long before humankind came into existence.

Israel's fertile valleys and rich lands abruptly end at this point. To the south, inhospitable deserts stretch from Judea in the west to Moab in the east. White sands, strangely beautiful in their lack of life, are all a journeyer encounters on the route down to Egypt. Between their nation and our own, a pilgrim arrives at the spot where Moses ordered his people to cross in the wake of our great exodus.

"What's that tower?" I asked James, peering across the shoreline through bright sunlight. In the distance, an oddly shaped construction crowned a high mountain.

"Masada. A vast city rumored to stand so tall that it scrapes the bottom of the clouds."

"No Hebrew would conceive, much less build, such a Babel-like projection."

"Right you are. A pretend-Hebrew, Herod the Great, did so. Forty years ago, I'd guess."

"Why?" John wanted to know. "He owns an ornate palace in Jerusalem, the center of our world."

"And another," Levi added, "in Caesarea Maritima—"

"As the story goes, Herod was beneath his grand cloak of power a sad, threatened, frightened man. Always suffering from nightmares in which enemies took him by surprise. Masada was constructed as his last resort: impregnable. A place where he believed none could pursue and then capture him."

"He never had the chance to find out," Joses snorted.

"Herod's body became cancerous. His stomach filled with worms. He died screaming in pain."

"I wonder if his son, Antipas, is such a person?"

"How would any among us ever learn that?"

A new bit of mischief took root in my mind. I wanted to know. To do that, I'd have to meet this Antipas in person. How I'd achieve that remained, for the moment, elusive. But when I set my mind to something . . .

# 89.

"Let's go!" Levi shouted with anticipation.

We all ran toward the shore, kicking off our sandals. Simon and the girls toddled along behind the rest of us. Off to our immediate right, a group of noble Romans clustered under an enormous tent of many colors. Relaxing in the shade, these aristocrats sipped fine wines and conversed while slaves served them rare delicacies for their midafternoon repast. Regularly, members of their group would rise and swim in the healing waters, which they had journeyed far to partake of, relieving their minor aches and pains.

To our left, a high rectangular fence tightly contained a colony of lepers. Nails and spikes atop each of its sides restricted the sickly inhabitants from attempting to escape. Guards were on hand to escort the inmates to and from the sea, where they could ease their pain by bathing.

*Long ago, I heard the story of a good shepherd here on Earth. For him, it was not enough to save most of his flock.*

*Even the last sheep had to be salvaged. Could these lost souls likewise be saved? And, if so, who would Yahweh anoint to face this challenge?*

"It's true!" I called out moments later. We slushed along on the surface, the waters barely tickling the tops of my toes. Making headway proved difficult. At one point, little Simon sunk to his knees and screeched in fear. We dragged him up and out, assuring the child that it was impossible to go under.

"Watch me now," I announced. All the others turned to see what ever-unpredictable Jess, who must always be the epicenter of everyone's attention, would try next. Once I felt assured that all eyes were focused on me, I threw back my head and laughed. Then I concentrated on a distant rock protruding above the water.

Breathing in deeply, I jogged along, raising my feet so swiftly they didn't have time enough to sink even ankle-deep. Family and friends applauded. Joses, barking with joy, tore off his shirt and hurried alongside me.

The entire caravan had paused so that first-timers could get a good look at this famous landmark. Several pilgrims waved and cheered at the giddy youngsters, joyfully playing in the waters.

We waved back, then circled around to where this gay romp began. Joses reached the shore first, greeted by the masses that had lined up to congratulate us on our escapade.

We gathered our luggage and joined the others. The caravan continued on. Everyone took delight that on the following day we would reach Jerusalem. Some of our fellow travelers occasionally pointed toward Joses or myself and recalled the mirth our shenanigans brought them on this excruciatingly hot day.

"Look!" people would shout. "The boy who walked on water."

With twilight, it was time to set up our final camp of the southward journey. Afterwards our family prepared dinner. We young people ate ravenously following our exercise at the beach. Then my family members dozed off. Only little Simon could not surrender to sleep, likely remembering our gleeful experience from earlier that day as well as the thrill awaiting us tomorrow. He tossed and turned, always holding his grand walking stick close.

At last, Simon ceased rolling about on his mat and, like the others, nodded off. Quietly as I could, I rose and covered my shoulders with a wool cape to protect me against the cold of night. I slipped off in a westerly direction, using the North Star for guidance. In the stark moonlight, I made out the profile of Mount Nebo to the east, as well as rims of the Central Mountain range in the west. Eventually, I spotted my destination; stars, twinkling brightly against a midnight black curtain, illuminated Jericho's ruined walls.

We had arrived at the Dead Sea later than scheduled. This left no time for the caravan to pause so that the pilgrims might explore the remains of one of the oldest cities in the world. But I, being . . . well, *Jess* . . . refused to let this opportunity go unrealized.

The stone's pale surface resulted from thousands of years of rain and erosion. Moonlight sweeping down allowed for the impression of a skeleton city, its meat and bones picked clean by the ravages of time. A shiver of fear passed through me as I gazed at what appeared a ghostly locale. Perhaps such an aura wasn't present in daylight hours, when a sense of reality is created by radiant sunlight.

But this was the hour when things go bump in the night.

*In the daytime, seeing is believing. We notice nothing untoward and are not afraid.*

*In the dark, believing is seeing. For now arrives the hour of the wolf, when shapes and shadows that haunt the recesses of a human mind are projected onto whatever exists out there.*

I felt colder than I had a moment earlier. Nonetheless, I summed up my courage. Stumbling over jagged rocks I moved closer still.

With the full, horrible truth of this silent witness to past events directly before me, I sat on a natural rock bench and, for a while, studied the ruined city. What an honor to be so close to Canaan-land's first metropolis. Also, how impressive it was to view the first gentile stronghold that Joshua, under orders from Yahweh, reduced to near nothingness following my nation's belated return to the Promised Land nearly 1,500 years ago. Thrilled, I felt myself drawn into my nation's history.

# 90.

"Jericho," I called out, raising my arms high.

"Yes. But do you know the derivation of that word?"

"Oh!"

I had thought myself alone, so profound was the stillness surrounding this forlorn place. The voice came from somewhere off to my right. Turning in that direction, I spotted the well in the middle of *Wadi Qelt*, an oasis with high grass, palm trees, and the last fresh water on one's way south.

A tall man hunched over the old well, sipping water from a wooden bucket. He stood far enough away that I couldn't make out his features. "Sorry to frighten you," he called out. "But if this is your first visit to the long-silent citadel—"

"That's alright. And, yes, I'd love to know."

"A young seeker after wisdom then? Yes? Yes! In ancient times, long before the Hebrews arrived and conquered Canaan, a forgotten race of people lived here. They worshipped a deity their priests called *Yraikh*. As they gave way over the millennia to nations that each in turn succeeded them, that god's name became a means to identify this place. Over many generations, this word was modified, gradually evolving into Jericho."

*Yraikh? Not so very different a term from Yahweh.*

*Could some of our Hebraic mindset derive from ancestors of those who would in time be considered our enemies?*

"May I ask what sort of god this *Yraikh* was?"

"In truth, a moon goddess. Some claim that to this very day if you gaze on high from the spot you now occupy and consider the lunar body closely, you may glimpse the outline of her slender form etched into its grey shadings."

Victory was assured as our warriors stormed inside.

To my surprise, the moment I started to relate the story, the unknown fellow squatted on the sand. He drew out a shofar of his own, and set to blowing on it. The soft, lilting music drifted toward me along with the mellow night breeze.

When I finished speaking, he set it down.

"Yes? Yes! Still, a long time ago, while sojourning at a Mesopotamian village, I heard another telling of the tale. In it, Joshua made his way into the wilderness, there to determine how he might conquer this seemingly impregnable city. He gazed up at the sky, hoping for divine intervention. Joshua's eyes were drawn to the seven stars of Orion. Perhaps what occurred next was nothing more than a flight of his imagination. But it appeared that the three largest stars left their positions in the heavens and descended toward Earth. Shortly, they touched down not far away from where he stood."

*Seven stars. Just what I saw on that first day of Yeshiva, before I walked the road to Sepphoris with Levi.*

*Initiating the unique journey that I continue on now.*

"Three short men, or beings resembling people, marched silently toward Joshua. The mighty warrior cowered at the sight. With triangular eyes on either side of their grey, noseless faces, these visitors beamed strange smiles in his direction. Joshua sensed that they meant him and his people no harm."

*It's coming to me now . . . I know who you are . . .*

"Speaking in an unknown tongue, which gradually did become comprehensible, they instructed him to do what you have told me. Joshua vowed to follow their instructions to the very letter. The visitors bowed low, turned, and scurried away, vanishing into the darkness. Soon after, Joshua saw the three lights rise, speeding toward Orion."

*Of course, I know who you are . . . the stranger by the well that day on the road home, Levi walking with me . . .*

"Joshua returned to his camp, told no one of this odd encounter, and fell into a troubled sleep. The following morn, he announced to his officers that Yahweh had spoken to him in a dream, advising them what to do. The ark, they realized that day, was not only a holy icon but a weapon unlike any the world had known."

He had carried a shofar, too, that strange man we had taken for a raving lunatic. And he retold one of our old stories from an alternate point of view . . .

I was dumbfounded. "The way you explain it, the event sounds less like a miracle than as I read it in our Bible."

"A miracle," he said slowly, "is but some everyday event that one's mind is not yet able to rationally comprehend."

*His previous words now echoed in my memory.*

*Things he said here recalled what he told me of Sodom.*

Without warning, wild dogs barked nearby as they raced through the underbrush. Alarmed, I glanced in their direction. When the beasts caught the scent of some small animal in the brush and ran off, I turned back to the storyteller.

Now, though, nobody stood by the well.

Shivering, I rose, ready to leave. As I did, it seemed to me that seven bright lights in the lower sky swiftly ascended north-westerly. Even as they had done that night when I slept on our roof following the initial occurrence of my odd dream.

Perhaps, though, I only saw what I was inclined to see after hearing this sojourner's version of Jericho. Possibly not with my eyes but in my mind's eye.

# 92.

Shit! I just got my period.

The cramps hit me the previous night, creeping into my consciousness. Gradually, an increasingly unpleasant aching sensation woke me from a deep sleep. Trying to convince myself I was only imagining them, I rolled over and drifted back into dreamland. Minutes later, extreme discomfort woke me again.

By then, the soft light of dusk surrounded our camp. In a matter of minutes the high, wide sky above transformed from black to grey, then to the eerie white light that exists for several minutes before the sun rises. Helios (as my lost love referred to it) emerged on the eastern horizon. People and beasts heard the shofar's three-blast call to rise and make ready for the journey's final stretch. Next stop: Jerusalem!

"It's that time!" Joseph called out. I found it charming that, despite his advanced years, our patriarch appeared as excited about what awaited us as Simon. Before we set off again, the two grasped each other's hands and whirled around in merry fashion, age and youth united in mutual innocence and passionate dance.

As for myself, I strained to keep from groaning. Cramps turned to aches, aches to pains, concluding with sharp, stinging sensations. Naively, I had hoped that the second time around might be less terrible than what I'd experienced the previous month. Hah! Had a woman ever gone mad from such discomfort? Or perhaps the mere thought that every thirty or so days this travesty of the flesh would revisit her?

*Think of Job, the most innocent person in the Bible. Yet subjected to such catastrophe he could hardly help falling into a state of despair.*

*What exists behind the incomprehensible strategies of Yahweh? Perhaps the meaning of being human is to search for the answer to that central question.*

Curtly if politely, Mary handed me a plate of prunes and barley. I thanked her and made the mistake of trying to eat. Seconds later, I vomited. Though startled, Elizabeth and Mary understood my situation.

"I'll be alright. Really."

They rushed to my side to determine if I could continue on this day. "We'll walk on either side," the sisters concluded, "in case you falter." This was the first kind thing Mary had said to me since my unforgivable outburst.

Even now, though, she tacitly avoided eye contact.

In minutes, those who owned tents (I wondered how many were purchased from the father and son merchants of Tarsus) folded them. These were packed along with luggage on donkeys or wagons pulled by teams of oxen. We wrapped up our sleeping mats and slung them over our shoulders. Mercenaries, appearing splendid in colorful Persian robes and Roman-style copper helmets, spurred their horses forward. Much merriment arose among the throng, the people again singing of the sort of hymns that had passed through the caravan that first day, when all were fresh and anxious.

Born again, so to speak. That was certainly the mood here today.

"Caravan, ho!" the elected captain shouted, even as the shofar blared three more times. Hundreds of pairs of feet set out on the journey's last lap. Finally, one more blast of the shofar, for a total of seven. I trudged along, refusing to let nature get the best of me. In truth, I felt as if I ought to crawl off, find some private place amid the limestone ridges, and die.

*Could Annas and other like-minded souls be right? Is this a curse, oh Yahweh, reserved for the female of the species?*

Why, in your wisdom, burden an entire gender for one woman's crime?

# 93.

It has been claimed that in the ancient world all roads lead to Rome. True, perhaps. But in the smaller, self-contained world of the Near Middle East, all ways converge in Jerusalem. As the Passover festival approached, thousands of Jews who had meant to visit the temple earlier this year but couldn't owing to money woes were now determined to reach the Holiest of Holies.

We turned a sharp bend as the dusty terrain sloped in a southerly direction. Though five miles away, our destination appeared before us: the thick, high-reaching walls and splendid palaces. Most impressive: the temple dome itself, rich blue and blindingly white in the sun's rays, ornamented with silver and gold.

*What a fascinating combination! The purity of our religion augmented by excesses of mammon. Truly something to think about!*

*Was there indeed a meaning embedded in this building's architectural design?*

A curious moment occurred while our caravan remained some three miles from the city gates. I'd been speaking with

James and John of the many things we hoped to do in Jeru-salem, if only there were enough time. That's when I noticed Joseph, standing apart from the rest of us, on a small hillock. Wistfully, he gazed off into the distance.

To my surprise, I noted what appeared to be, here in Ju-dea, a duplicate of our own home in central Galilee. The simple limestone structure (typical of most houses throughout Israel) looked identical in size and dimension to what Joseph had crafted for us. Also like our own home, this humble building stood alone, apart from a village the size of Nazareth.

An elderly man exited the house, moving in our direction to observe the passing caravan. He spotted Joseph even as Joseph noticed him. The two might have been twins, so closely did they resemble each other. They did not wave or make any gesture of communication across the narrow range. Still, their eyes locked with one another's.

"Alphaeus," James whispered in my ear. I knew that name, had heard it some time ago, though it was not mentioned often in our house. "Joseph's brother."

"I didn't know Joseph had a brother," John said.

"Why don't they meet and greet," I asked, "instead of staring at each other from a distance?"

"There was a terrible rift between them, long ago," James explained. "I don't know the details, only that there remains a great bitterness in each man's heart."

What a shock it is to realize someone you believe that you know, with whom you share a small house and your daily life, speak to constantly about matters great and small, has a whole other side to his life? In my heart, I felt betrayed; how could Joseph have kept this a secret from me for so long?

*And . . . again, that question of questions . . . why?*

"It seems that he lives secluded from his village, as we do back in Nazareth."

James nodded. "That's more or less it, Jess. That little ham-let on the West Bank is named Holon. Alphaeus and his family live near it yet remain outsiders."

"Why?"

James shrugged. "Nobody ever told me. Whenever I asked, my father grew remote, steadfastly refusing to explain."

"I would so like to learn the reason."

"Perhaps, Jess, someday you will."

"In Yahweh's good time," I concluded.

# 94.

When Joseph rejoined us, he said nothing concerning what had occurred. All the same, I noticed a profound sadness in his eyes and manner. Joseph's shoulders slumped more even than usual. He stepped close to Mary, extending an arm around her waist. Initially, I assumed he did this to help his pregnant wife continue on. Then I perceived in this simple gesture a whirl of emotions; as if love, regret, forgiveness, and many other feelings conjoined in the everyday act of a man embracing his wife with whom he has shared a precious few successes and numerous disappointments. Yet somehow, in the end, the two did manage to survive together.

As we approached the mighty gate of Jerusalem's northern wall, our caravan merged with several others. Groups of people, large and small, also pilgrims traveling alone streamed into a large holding area. There, each would be checked for concealed weapons before receiving permission to enter the city.

"The powers that be are terrified that the Zealots might use the holiday as a pretense to create chaos," John whispered.

The differences between Galilean provincials and city dwelling Judeans were obvious. As we poured in from the north, they from the west, our crude hand-made clothes and their tailored fineries revealed social distinctions I hoped might someday disappear. If that were to happen, we could again become a single nation.

And such contrasts existed not only between Israel's separate territories (for Samaria, the waistline of Israel's land-body, cut us off from one another) but within each of them. Everywhere in the nation, there were the rich, the working class, and the poor. Even on a holiday intended to bring all Hebrews together, the status money allows a privileged few became evident everywhere.

"Do you think, John, that the wealthy are happier than we?"

"No. They merely suffer in more luxurious surroundings."

"If they have plenty of money, why then are they unhappy?"

"Jess, the presence of money causes as many problems as does its absence. Most people suffer in their minds not owing to what they possess but what they failed to achieve. And no one ever gets everything they want."

*Cease desiring for perfection on Earth. Find pleasure in what you do have, not what has been denied you.*

*Such thoughts occurred to me before. On this day, they crystalized at last. I can perceive the sense of it now: attitude is everything in life.*

Slowly funneling through the imposing gate, the people of Zion merged as we had done 1,500 years ago to celebrate that passing over from Egypt to Canaan. Any among us faced close inspection if unlucky enough to be singled out by Roman guards. This time-consuming process resulted in an enormous backup.

"This is even worse than the walking," I sighed, ever more uncomfortable.

"Hope and pray some guard does not pull you out of line," John whispered.

Now and again, fierce-looking soldiers would yank those who seemed suspicious off to one side for an extensive search. Herod Antipas's abiding fear, as well as the current Roman governor's primary concern, was violence born of unrest. Indeed, our own aristocracy of temple priests agreed with them completely, at least on this issue. Together, these three factions composed what John had mentioned earlier: the powers that be. A combination of diverse interests with a single thread that tied them together. The establishment of our time, our place.

"Anyone discovered with a concealed Saracen-style blade will be dragged away, subjected to a swift trial, then summarily executed," James explained.

"It would be a double sacrilege," John noted, "for a Jew to commit a murder, even of a Roman, during this holy time."

"From what I hear," Joses joined in, "these Zealots are so fanatical about ridding us of Roman influence they are willing to temporarily set such cherished rules aside."

"Some even launch suicide attacks, murdering Romans yet knowing that they, too, will likely die."

"That's madness," I insisted. Then and always, I believed that all violence, other than in self-defense, was wrong. Even if the motivation behind such an act might be righteous. "You can't violate your most basic beliefs, even for a worthy cause."

My midsection ached. I feared that blood would spill. All the same, I did peek around to see if Barabbas might be lurking somewhere in the crowd. No sight of him, thankfully. Meanwhile, the sun, always intense at this time of year, grew intolerable. I gazed up as the great circular object in the sky transformed in seconds from a rich, mango orange to a ripe-apple red.

I peeked over at Mary, sincerely concerned for her well-being. She, with the help of Joseph on one side and Elizabeth on the other, looked to be holding up surprisingly well. As for me, I felt sick to my stomach.

With deep concentration, I forced my fear of fainting out of my head.

*Mind over matter, Jess!*

*Flesh and blood can always be overruled by the brain, if only you focus.*

"You may pass," an immense, ruddy-faced, high-ranking centurion, clearly in charge of the guards, told an exhausted traveler.

"Watch out for that one," a member of our caravan warned me and my brethren. "They say he's a tough character."

"What's his name?"

"That, Jess, I don't know. But owing to the ferocity of his hatred for transgressors, they call him The Panther."

# 95.

After waiting for three hours, my family finally received permission to pass through the gate. Once inside the high city walls, current arrivals encountered massive crowds. People who made their homes here attempted to navigate to or from work, this everyday activity confounded by unruly hordes of visitors. These included the newcomers like ourselves, also sightseers who had found their lodgings earlier this morning or the previous night.

*What a way to spend my upcoming birthday, as well as Passover!*

*Considering the condition I'm in and the wretched heat.*

Like everyone else, we first had to find a place to stay or necessarily exit again, then search for shelter in some nearby village. We'd heard estimates that more than 300,000 pilgrims would be present for both solemn prayer meetings and festive celebrations, already in full swing. We found our own hunt for quarters thwarted by a momentary inability to move, the crowd now thick as sardines dumped into a barrel of pickling juice in one of Galilee's fishing villages.

Our main concern, other then of course the little ones, was always Mary's well-being. Family members surrounded her to absorb the constant shoving of pilgrims. People massed behind us pushed forward, halting again a few steps further. When those ahead of them were forced to stop, a human barrier resulted. Each of the family members reached for the hands of two others, forming a human chain. We continued on in such a manner for the better part of an hour, inching our way forward.

One ray of hope: I noticed that the further we drifted in a southerly direction, the more these crowds gradually thinned down. Locals turned off to their homes as tourists reached their destinations, easing the situation at least somewhat.

"We're off the main thoroughfare now," Joseph sighed as we opted for a side street. "It should be easy going from here on."

Approaching a street corner, we turned easterly and followed close along the city wall. Dug deep into this formidable structure of rock and stone were man-made caves, carved into softer sections of limestone and basalt. Entrepreneurs who had dug these crude retreats now rented them, and at exorbitant prices during any holiday season, to arriving pilgrims.

Most, as we could clearly see, were already spoken for. Eventually, we happened on a cave not yet taken. A heavyset man wearing a turban, hands on hips, stood proudly before its entrance. By this point, we were so bedraggled that I feared the owner might take us for beggars rather than farmers, and rudely dismiss us. Instead, he waved us over and our patriarch, however spent from the experience of making it this far with his family intact, approached the swarthy fellow.

Joseph haggled with him over the price. This was expected, as all caretakers initially ask for too much. The conversation went from calm to heated, then reached a crescendo of angry confrontation. I feared that at any moment a fistfight might break out. Then, abruptly, each man calmed down. They shook hands and embraced like old friends. A compromise had been negotiated.

*Compromise! Now, as always, a good solution to pretty much any problem.*

*Remember that, Jess. Always!*

The man was paid in shekels, official coin of the temple. Joseph had exchanged Roman dinars for these Hebrew coins while still in Sepphoris rather than deal with the ruthless money changers here. Their booths lined every street. These were shanty operations, thrown together only days before a holy day brought in multitudes.

"Done!" the owner pompously announced with a broad smile. Bowing his head, our suddenly magnanimous host gestured for us to enter, as proud of his cave as if it were a palace. We now were treated like visiting royalty.

"I'll go first," Simon offered, pretending to be a scout for some military force, perhaps the Maccabees. He carried, as always, his walking stick. This could transform into a mighty weapon or magical wand as Simon's latest fantasy took form.

"We'll go with you," Salome and Miriam squealed.

We followed after the children into the surprisingly large cavity. To our delight, the cave proved cool and inviting, particularly following our long ordeal. No one said a word. All of a single mind, and without any need for discussion, we spread out our mats, dropped down, and immediately fell asleep.

# 96.

Eventually, one by one we returned to consciousness. Light filtering in from the cave's entrance assured us that the day had not yet concluded; we could now begin our exploration of the city. None of us had eaten in hours. Mary and Elizabeth, the first to rise, opened one of our packs. They passed around bread, cheese, and watered wine. We hungrily consumed every last morsel.

"Come on," Salome begged, unable to sit still.

"We want to see Jerusalem!" Miriam added.

Mary assured her girls that we would leave soon. But a mother is a mother, so she took time to change their outfits. Her daughters must look lovely for such a significant event. Fashion (at least when we were in public places) mattered to Hebrews, even simple peasants like us.

This held particularly true when it came time to show off the young ones.

"You're certain you can manage this?" Mary whispered, knowing how uncomfortable I must feel. I nodded, hoping to convince both her and myself that this was true.

"I was concerned for you as well," I replied. These were the first civil words we had spoken to each other for some time. Even as I had done, Mary cast me a nod, implying that she could and would handle our initial round of sightseeing. Shortly, we slipped out of our cave and stepped onto the street. We did not fear for the safety of our belongings. Jews do not steal from other Jews, and our "in" (for a week) was located in the heart of the Jewish sector.

Following Joseph, our family excitedly set out on the long-awaited tour.

"Look there," Simon marveled, pointing upward to our first grand sight: an immense overpass, composed of an open walkway toward the Temple Mount and an adjoining aqueduct.

"It's spectacular," Joses sighed.

The aqueduct, Joseph explained, served as the center-piece of a complex system designed to draw fresh water from surrounding springs, distributing the life-giving liquid to every district in the city. Waste was washed away through underground sewers, another innovation of Roman engineering. Or so I believed at the time. In fact, as I would later learn, such devices had existed long before that . . .

 . . . *Back now, Jess, to the present tale.*

*For that is a another story, for another day.*

Only recently had the system been restructured so that this modernization reached all Jerusalem's citizens. Previously, the aqueduct had delivered clear water exclusively to Jerusalem's high-rise area in the southwestern corridor. There, wealthy Hebrews resided in the Upper City, along with several aristocratic Roman families. In time, this luxury (soon to be thought of as a necessity) trickled down to the masses.

"Tomorrow," I sighed, noticing thousands of Hebrews making their way across the bridge-like structure, toward the temple proper with its most cherished destination, the Holiest of Holies, "we'll take that remarkable pilgrimage ourselves."

"Why not now?" Salome whined.

"Too crowded," Joseph explained, "and far too late in the day."

"But we want to," Simon said.

"Patience is a virtue," Mary insisted, speaking once again in the proverbs and platitudes that defined her. Some had been handed down from her own mother, others original. I had no idea which was which.

"High priests, successful merchants, and others of great social standing reside up there," Joseph said, pointing to the lavish three-story buildings. Most were covered in stucco, an expensive application that identified homes of the wealthy.

Secretly, I longed to someday experience the luxury of such a fabulous place. Still, it irked me that so few Hebrews living within the city limits could afford such a gracious lifestyle. Shouldn't all Jews enjoy the same privileges?

*Wouldn't that be a far better way? Yes.* If *we lived in a perfect world.*

*The problem is, we don't. So what to do about that . . . ?*

Our family moved with the human tide, swaying back and forth like waves on the Sea of Galilee when a sudden wind rises, seemingly out of nowhere. At least the multitude was of a single mind: pushing through the clogged street toward that sector everyone referred to as the Old City. This self-contained, expansive area, which long ago had composed the entirety of Jerusalem, imposingly occupied the city's westernmost hill. This sector enshrined the longest-standing buildings, some rumored to have survived the conquest by Babylon 600 years ago.

Reaching the outskirts of a jutting plateau, we could clearly make out the mount's silhouette. Augmented by the great white, blue, and gold façade of the exterior; the forecourts and elevated plazas; also, open areas for strolling in the sun and basking in its warm rays and the glory of God. Finally, the all-important Inner Sanctuary, this the be-all and end-all of Judaism.

*Here, I thought to myself then, is the most wonderful birthday gift any Hebrew could hope for. Being in this place sends chills up and down my spine.*

*Though perhaps such sudden sensations are parcel to my period. No matter. This was worth all the walking and waiting in the deadening heat.*

As to that Holiest of Holies, only Hebrew men were welcome to visit the most remote chamber in this sacred place, accessible by stairs dug deep into the ground. Any gentiles discovered here would be put to death, with Caesar's blessing. To show respect for our religion, Rome allowed us this. After all, the Holy of Holies was the heart and soul of who we were.

Considerably less acceptable to my way of thinking: any woman, Hebrews included, who dared slip inside this hallowed place faced severe punishment, death a possibility.

*That served to not only anger Jess of Nazareth but also intrigue her.*

*Anyone who truly knew me must have understood that nothing was going to deter* this *girl from entering!*

# 97.

"Oh, Joses," I'd whispered conspiratorially to my twin once a plan had taken shape in my mind. We took up the rear during the family's late-afternoon sightseeing.

"I'm not sure what's coming," he said, familiar with my tone of voice, "though I'm certain it won't be pleasant."

"Nonsense! Only, would you please make the switch with me again?"

Joses looked stunned, then concerned, as I explained. "This time," he muttered when I'd concluded, "you are truly, *completely* mad."

"No argument there. So, *will* you?"

Something of the earlier, sly Joses reappeared. "What's in it for me this time?"

Joseph had offered to buy each family member a souvenir. Two for me and Joses, the extra ones our birthday presents. The previous day, I'd noticed Joses eyeing a rainbow colored goblet. As he had no interest in such things, I guessed that my twin contemplated this as one of his choices in order that, on our return, he could present it to Maggie.

I suggested to him that I could ask for this as one of my picks, then turn it over to Joses. That way, he'd have a gift for his dream girl and keep both items that he picked for himself.

"I don't know, Jess." Unable or unwilling to talk further on the subject, he visibly shuddered at my latest variation on the ruse. "This may be taking it way too far."

"If it doesn't bother me, why should it you?"

He agreed to at least consider my plan. So for the time being, we let the matter drop and enjoyed the city's architectural bounties. First, Herod's palace! The magnificent structure went unoccupied most of the year. Antipas, as all knew, preferred to whenever possible remain in Rome, where he had been raised. If responsibilities forced him to reside in what he referred to as "a pathetic place surrounded by a raw wilderness on one side and desert on the other"—Israel—he spent such time in exquisite Caesarea Maritima on the tropical Mediterranean coast.

There, the population was mostly Roman and Greek. Yet as Antipas had inherited the title king of the Jews, he was required to be in Jerusalem once a year for this all-important event.

Antipas's ornate palace dominated an entire square, angled kitty-corner with Antonia Fortress. Here, Roman soldiers and the fearsome centurions were quartered. Nearby, a third palace had been reserved for the latest Roman prefect. They arrived and left in rapid succession, one after another failing to establish order on a high enough level to impress Caesar. But if the men themselves proved mediocre, their residences here in the city left us gazing in awe.

"I've never seen anything like it," little Simon marveled. The adjacent Temple Mount, destroyed by Babylonians 600 years ago, had been entirely reconstructed by Antipas's father. Herod the Great intended this as a tribute to the people he ruled over.

"I know," I replied, hugging him, both of us teary-eyed.

"Do you think anything in the whole world can compare?"

"I don't know, Simon. I haven't seen the whole world. *Yet.*"

*But someday, I will.*

*Just wait and see!*

After observing such grandeur, we visited the marketplace. There, tourists could purchase mezusahs, worn on a silver chain around the neck, announcing a person's Hebraic heritage with a single letter of our ancient alphabet. *Tallits* for sale ranged from simple linen items that anyone above the poverty line could afford to silken variations so expensive even the wealthy considered carefully before purchasing. A variety, at every price in-between, hung on a long rack.

Most visitors could afford to carry a humble remembrance home. Yet as impressive as these choices were, resentment swiftly overcame me. How wrong it struck Jess of Nazareth that such a sacred item had become one more means by which status could be determined and distinguished.

The aforementioned products, along with a wide range of menorahs, only marked the beginning of available merchandise. Souvenir stands, some permanent and others recently assembled for the holiday, beckoned along each avenue. At one of these, operated by an old acquaintance of Joseph, our patriarch purchased for Simon, at a reduced price, a model of the Temple Mount.

The thrilled boy cherished this as much as his walking stick. He played with it whenever we would return to our cave. Miniature menorahs delighted the girls.

Joses chose a set of uniquely shaped flutes, which he'd employ back home to serenade his sheep and goats (as before) and now Maggie, too, as his first gift. (The second was a handsome teak-wood box to keep them in.) For the remainder of our stay, he lulled us to sleep each night, running through his growing repertoire.

As for James and John, Mary and Elizabeth insisted that they would require more time to pick their special gifts. I spotted a splendid goblet for sale at a surprisingly low price. This seemed to me serendipitous, as I didn't want to spend too much of Joseph's money. I glanced over to Joses, my eyes questioning him. Grasping my meaning, and aware that this item would please Maggie, he nodded affirmatively.

"May I have this?" I asked.

We stopped at a wine bar to sip plentifully but not to the point of drunkenness. As a special treat, more in honor of my birthday than the simultaneous holiday, at an adjoining food court Joseph ordered roast chicken with couscous and vegetables to insure that our first meal here would prove memorable.

Soon thereafter, dusk descended. The city lamps were all lit and glowed brightly as the crowds wound down. If only, I heard myself wishing in the privacy of my mind, this magical moment could last forever.

How many times had that thought already passed through my head, on equally wondrous occasions?

And how often would it reoccur in the years to come?

# 98.

More than fifty years ago, after Augustus named Herod the king of the Jews, the new ruler made his first proclamation. He would rebuild Solomon's once-mighty temple, destroyed by the Babylonians more than half a millennia earlier. Joseph, a master storyteller, explained this to the family as we lay on our mats around a fast-fading fire. All listened as he continued, we taking turns sucking on the hookah.

Before each of us one by one dozed off, dreaming of entering that fabled place the next morning, our family patriarch prepared his kinsmen for the many marvels we would experience there.

Herod the Great had been born eighty-five years ago in Idumea, to the south of Judea. His father, a Nabatean Arab and political appointee named Antipater, served as Jordan's prime minister. Herod's mother, an Endomite named Cypros, claimed to be Hebrew though in truth she, too, was Arabic in ethnicity. These parents decided early on that their son's best opportunity to achieve greatness was to rule in Canaan, this land a rich prize of Caesar's conquests. Which explains the lie about her birthright, since Jews expected to be ruled by fellow Jews.

Whatever the bloodline, with this in mind Herod had been raised in Rome as a wealthy Hebrew. Like his parents, he believed this would insure him a greater chance to be appointed king of the Jews by Caesar and, hopefully, acceptance once he returned. As keen a manipulator as his father, young Herod trusted that this could easily be accomplished.

Then something unexpected occurred. As Herod reached the age of twenty, he determined that the splendid Roman lifestyle he had grown accustomed to must be maintained. A gnawing fear of losing such affluence fermented a strange madness in him: subtle at first, then more obvious and, finally, hysterical. Now, Herod's hunger for a political appointment owed less to any ambition to actually rule, more to his daily horror: the grandeur that accompanies such power might yet be lost to him.

*There you go, Jess, providing the ending before you have barely begun this tale.*

*Or, more correctly, Joseph's tale.*

At twenty-four, Herod's ascension commenced. Mostly owing to his father's notoriety, Herod wrangled an appointment from Caesar to be Galilee's prime minister. For most people, that would have been enough. Yet Herod, already scheming to be "The Great" and as such enjoy the finest luxuries life offers, considered this a mere stepping stone in an illustrious career already mapped out in his mind.

Tragically, at least for him, Herod proved to be his own worst enemy. Early on, he vowed to keep the Jews happy. If Israel remained peaceful, an appreciative Rome would promote him. Herod's great concern was that the people might be aware that, whatever lie had been told, his origins were completely Arabic. As such, the Jews might not consider him to be truly Jewish, despite his claim to a purely Hebraic upbringing and loyalty to Yahweh.

While Herod could not alter his biological origins, he hoped there might be other ways to win over our nation.

One strategy would be to marry a Jewish princess. There arose a problem though: he already *was* married to Poras. Herod's Arab bride had born him what every leader most wished for: a son. Nonetheless, Herod self-servingly sent his wife and boy away so as to marry Mariana, a noble Hebrew. Two obsessions motivated him to arrange this union: a genuine desire for the beautiful Mariana and an ambition—now, in truth, an obsession—to rise in power.

Few in Rome or Israel realized that while Herod possessed none of the qualities that make for a successful politician, he had been born an architectural genius. In time, Herod would design Caesarea Maritima on the Mediterranean, fortress Masada near Jerusalem, and Caesarina in Galilee. Initially, though, he set out to restore our Temple Mount. He planned, when the work was completed, to heartily welcome all Jews, with elegant Mariana by his side. Could there be a more effective way to convince the people of Israel that he was one of us, in all ways save blood?

Always, however, there must be a fly in the buttermilk. To his dismay, Mariana despised him. Descended from the beloved Maccabees, she had hoped to marry a Hebrew aristocrat. Forced by Herod into an ongoing depression, she set about making her husband as miserable as possible: withholding sex, falling down on the mosaic floor where she would throw tantrums, drinking herself into a stupor at state dinners.

All the same, he began the work. For many, this was a good thing. Herod hired Hebrews for high-paying work: stone cutters, masons, carpenters, designers, and executives to keep the ever-escalating finances in line as much as was humanly possible. The most educated of our people applied for the latter positions. A larger number of Jews received grunt work as low-paying day laborers.

Impressed by this, Rome raised Herod's rank from prime minister to king of the Jews. Here, though, the torch of outrage burst into flame. For most members of our nation privately referred to him as king *over* the Jews.

Caesar, who still believed Herod to be a Jew, had no idea of what an insult it was for our nation to be lorded over by a man they perceived as Arabic. Descended, that is, not from Isaac, in so many ways the original Hebrew, but his half brother, Ishmael, considered to be the progenitor of those people who inhabited the desert and despised the Hebrews as much as we did them. How could Caesar have been so foolish? With far more important things on his mind, he misconceived Hebrews and Arabs, both Semitic, to be one big, happy family. That, to put it mildly, was anything but the case.

So Jews roared with anger when, to complete the task of rebuilding the temple, Herod raised their taxes. Priests, rabbis, and far-flung local politicians converged on Herod's palatial home, demanding that he halt construction and cut the sums that Jews were required to pay four times annually. Herod—his madness ever increasing to the point where any criticism set him into a fury—threatened to kill them all.

These dignitaries could not have known (perhaps he himself wasn't yet aware) that Herod's body had been overrun by worms. In a great irony, this was likely due to the man who insisted he was a Hebrew having eaten undercooked pork. Constantly, pain tore through his flesh. As to the temple, he was in far too deep to quit. If Herod dared suggest shutting down the costly project, Caesar would consider Herod a cataclysmic failure and replace him. Out the window would fly not only his power base but all the possessions he so adored.

No! Though what had begun as a labor of love had turned into a hateful process, the work must go on. And on.

And on . . .

Inevitably, the temple was completed. A great opening-day ceremony would fete dignitaries from all across Israel, brought to Jerusalem at Herod's personal expense. This king wined and dined them, pampering delegates until the time arrived to reveal his triumph. So the grand tour commenced. Minus Mariana who, complaining of a headache, remained at home. At the conclusion, not one guest hesitated to announce an intense dislike, even contempt, for the new mount.

Too ornate. Too modern. Too large. Too pretentious. Too Hellenistic. Too this. Too that.

"I *hate* the Jews!" Herod the Great shrieked, his voice carrying from the Temple Mount across all of Jerusalem. The full extent of his rage now exploded. Herod declared that his Jewish wife had been plotting to assassinate him. While there was no proof that this was indeed the case, he ordered that Mariana be swiftly executed.

As a result of her death, the Jews despised him more than ever. Yet once she was gone, Herod wandered through the palace corridors late at night, woefully calling out her name.

"But why," Joses wanted to know, "is it that we love and cherish the Temple Mount today?"

Joseph smiled wryly. Once Herod had essentially removed himself from Jerusalem and retreated to Masada, his final bastion of power and last great hope for personal safety from Zealots, our people frequented the construct. In doing so, they discovered how truly remarkable the new temple was.

When Herod died (more or less simultaneous with the birth of Joses and myself), our nation embraced the temple. After all, they had only hated the mount because Herod created it. Now that the complex was no longer inseparable from him, the annual Passover ritual of pilgrimage was revived and once again flourished.

The problem in our current era, Joseph concluded even as I felt myself dozing off, was that his son, Antipas, had inherited his late father's title. Antipas, called this by Hebrews even as we believed him to be "against us," never forgot what our nation had done to his father.

And dreamed day and night of taking a cruel revenge.

# 99.

The following morning we scrupulously cleansed ourselves, as always, this followed by a light meal. Then it was time to set out. This girl's great concern had to do with my physical situation. Vowing not to let the unique nature of Jess's woman-hood ruin this day, I'd risen early with the determination to employ mind over matter, ignoring the lingering cramps.

Thankfully, any aches and pains had receded. While the others made ready, I'd retreated to the most private recess in our cave. There I slipped on several layers of undergarments. With luck, this might sop up any flow of blood.

"Jess? Come on! We're all waiting on you," James called.

"Be there in a moment."

I rejoined the family, everyone impatiently shuffling about. Already I'd begun rolling over a strategy in my mind, having shared the basic plan with Joses. When our party was ready to enter the Inner Sanctuary, he and I would excuse ourselves, hurry to the toilets, and exchange clothing.

Then, amid the ecstatic crowds moving this way and that, I'd slip inside.

It would work. It *had* to! My very life might well be at stake if I failed.

This, I valued enormously!

*Still, once I'd reached a decision—*

First, we crossed the high-raised walkway and approached the northernmost temple wall. From this perspective, I realized that the rebuilt temple had been constructed by Herod the Great as a city within the city. A world apart yet accessible from numerous approaching roads thanks to multiple gates. Clearly, they hadn't called him "The Great" for nothing. How intriguing that Herod designed such grand structures but proved unable to control the ebb and flow of his own life and career.

We peered down at the Tyropoeon Valley below. Then, as part of the mass of singing voices and sweating bodies, my family edged closer to the temple's north wall, featuring its own small gate. Here, the gentiles were permitted to enter. The Chosen People preferred to arrive through the Main Gate, located along the Western Wall. Steadily moving in that direction, we stepped over slabs of purple stone set in place to provide a narrow pathway.

As the space between the edge of this cliff to our right and the wall on our left diminished, we slowed down. For safety's sake, our enormous group cautiously proceeded two at a time, too fearful to even peek into the deep gorge below.

As we rounded one of the wall's corners, the land before us opened up again. Our route meandered in what struck me as an arbitrary pattern, through lush gardens and greenery. Negotiating an abrupt turn, we found ourselves face to face with our destination. Before us stood the Main Gate.

For a terrible moment, though, we held our collective breath at the sight of what had been placed over the Hebrew entrance of choice.

We (the family of Joseph) were not as shocked as some others. For Galileans who had already visited the mount forewarned us of what to expect. An imposing icon had been raised above our entranceway: a golden eagle, its wings outstretched on either side. The visible eye in its horizontally portrayed head focused on us: Hebrews, under the watchful gaze of Caesar's signifier.

Some pilgrims wept. Others stared up at this monstrosity, faces ashen. Many refused to acknowledge it, lowering their heads. For here was the ultimate reminder that imperial Rome did indeed rule over us.

Its symbolic meaning was hardly lost on visitors: Herod Antipas wanted every Jew to remain keenly aware of just how powerless we truly were. As did the current emperor, Tiberius.

The Roman eagle also gave credence to the Zealots' main position: Our nation had been conquered again, necessitating righteous rebellion. If but one in a thousand Hebrews grew so outraged by this glaring offense, the volunteer army gathering in the north would swell. Someday, the pot would boil over.

*If only there were some means to avoid such a conflict.*
*Specifically, if only there were something I might do!*

# 100.

Grumbling, the people trickled into the massive forecourt. Once there, anger over the Roman eagle dissipated. For now the crowd looked in amazement at the glorious white and gold central building high atop the mount. Providing a perfect foil,

Judea's subdued brown and soft-green terrain remained visible in the distance. The natural setting framed this spectacular manmade shrine of majesty with the hues of a land that, according to tradition, would always provide its nation with milk and honey.

"Oh, Jess," Simon sighed. "It's even more beautiful than I imagined."

Sadly, such a happy mood was not to last long. We (the crowd now an organic being with a life of its own and a single mind, too) maneuvered through already existing hordes of pilgrims toward the South Gate. There, seemingly endless rows of ritual baths were diagonally situated across a sloping hillside. Before any visitor could approach the main building, full physical catharsis was required in this elaborate and enormous public *mikveh.*

Living waters, powered by machines hidden in a cavity deep below the incline, continuously flowed over the ridge. Roaring manmade rivers poured down a succession of slides, these twisting right and left as they descended toward the bottom. There, exhilarated bathers found themselves deposited in a sizable pool, the rushing waters diverted to either side of the ramp, where they could then swim.

This process was accomplished by more apparatus, likewise concealed from visitors' eyes. Currents whirled about, creating ripples, bubbles, and foam. Additional underground machinery forced the liquid back up and around again via air pressure created by a series of syphons connected to wheels and wires.

*A miracle! Several members of the crowd gasped.*

*Scientific technology, I thought to myself, recalling the basement of Capernaum's Grecian temple.*

"Look," John said, pointing to the entranceway as if he could not believe his eyes. "They're charging each person to use the baths."

"Three years ago," Joseph sighed, "they were simpler in construction. And free."

*What had Luke said about religion? A business. The bigger the business, the higher the profits.*

*"Not ours!" John had insisted then, to Luke's amusement.*

*If Luke were here now, what might John say to him?*

237

"This is terrible," James added. "What if someone cannot afford the price? Does that mean a Jew would be denied admission?"

"The holy process of bathing should be open to all," John sternly concluded before resigning himself to the addition and unexpected expense. I sensed how deeply this disturbed him. While John would try to set aside his feelings toward this raw commercialization, I grasped that his disdain for the priesthood, which had gone so far as to charge people for the required cleaning, would haunt him always.

As the family joined the long line, I realized how effectively the operation was designed to service the largest number of customers in the shortest amount of time. We proceeded, like sheep to a shearing, up a series of stone steps to the top of a crowning man-made bluff. Once there, people squatted in one of the partitioned slots, then slid all the way down, cool waters shooting up from small nozzles into a rider's face thanks to a succession of spouts arranged along the way.

Even John could not deny, once we'd taken the plunge, that the experience had been pleasurable.

"That was *so-oo-oo* much fun!" Simon squealed. "Can we do it again? Mom? Dad? Please!?"

Other children similarly begged for a second ride. But most were on a limited budget and tight schedule. So parents shook their heads no and set off toward further points of interest, including Joseph and Mary.

# 101.

Next, we climbed an excellent if exhausting stairway to the raised esplanade. Our family moved slowly. In deference to my mother, we allowed eager visitors to whisk by on either side. I also feared such strenuous activity might set me to bleeding. Thankfully, that was not the case.

Once on top, we considered the wide array of diversions. Souvenir stands, wine bars, and stalls selling kosher snacks awaited at irregular intervals. Long tables with accompanying benches, similar to those in Capernaum and Sepphoris, were already packed with people enjoying their midday meal. At one food stand, barrels of pickled carp awaited those in the mood for fish. Lamb on a skewer rated as a popular favorite, judging from the long lines.

Such portable treats could be carried along by those unwilling to waste even a few minutes stopping to rest and eat in the shade of large, blue umbrellas.

I noticed that prices for food items were almost double what a customer would pay on one of the city's busy streets. Once inside the temple walls, visitors had no choice but to fork over excessive sums or go hungry.

"Special discount, just for you," hawkers called out to everyone passing by.

Beyond the food court, seemingly endless stalls situated on and around the great basilica offered items similar to those sold in the city's marketplace down below. Here, though, exorbitant prices were charged for novelties like Simon's toy temple. Only one booth sold any single item. I deduced that vendors paid plenty for their specific monopolies and choice placement among the commercial venues.

To my surprise, people were eager to make purchases. Perhaps the thought of later bragging to friends back home that such an item came directly from the Temple Mount motivated the incessant buying all around us. Products on sale here were stamped: "Official souvenir of the Jerusalem Temple." Supposedly, owing to this distinction these would prove more valuable than those sold on the street.

# 102.

Though I had never been to an Arabian carnival, I'd heard about them from visiting wayfarers and passing merchants. What I experienced here struck me as more like that sort of circus atmosphere than the deeply religious event I'd expected. From the central area, those in search of entertainment could spread out to a variety of attractions, all expensive. Several were designed to enchant children. Circular corrals provided rides on llamas, zebras, and camels.

We couldn't deny Simon, Salome, and Miriam the same enjoyments other children were partaking of. Yet ours were less interested in the nearby petting zoo than boys and girls from large cities. There, caring for lambs, goats, and the like were not necessarily a daily chore. In our wilderness? This did not constitute "fun" but "work." Something else struck me as particularly cynical about this attraction: the owners not only profited through admissions but also charged their customers for packets of feed to be offered to animals, eliminating their own costs to nourish their livestock.

Also, overlooking the balustrade I could clearly see, in every direction, vestiges of Caesar. These varied from Herod's palace to the home of the Roman prefect to Fortress Antonia, where Tiberius's soldiers marched about . . .

*Stop it, Jess! Don't let this ruin the trip for you.*

*Remember why you are here. Don't think. Enjoy!*

We arrived at an elongated counter where people lined up, patiently awaiting their turn to offer sacrifices to Yahweh. Those who brought livestock with them now handed over everything from oxen and sheep to vegetables and grains. The theory behind this: since Yahweh had been kind enough to proffer such bounty on the people, they ought to reserve the very best of their crops and cattle to honor their God by returning to Him the best of the best that He had blessed them with.

Assistants to the priests seized one offering after another. If, long ago, the sacrificial area had been a place where people could demonstrate their faith in a single higher power, the process now seemed to me nothing more than a vast calculated enterprise.

Some assistants rushed to store the farm produce in barrels and vats located west of the rear entrance. Others led animals into a gigantic barn. Once inside, the beasts were slaughtered by butchers while a priest solemnly pronounced the required blessing. At the barn's easterly end, other helpers exited via a rear gate, carrying huge slabs of fresh red meat. These, they tossed on braziers aligned along an adjoining wall. Red-hot coals charred the beef and lamb.

Naturally, an overpowering scent rose and, owing to a breeze, circled the Temple Mount. Like those of countless others, my mouth watered, knowing the feast would be for priests and at-tendant rabbis, any leftovers going to their assistants.

*So how does this in any way prove our love and loyalty to Yahweh?*

*Such sacrifices benefit mortal men. But not all men.*

*Only those in positions of power.*

"It's as Luke told us in Capernaum," John exclaimed.

"Remember, Coz, *you* argued that ours was the exception."

Perhaps once that had been the case, his sad eyes suggest-ed. "I know," John admitted. "I was wrong."

*Remember, future reader, what I initially told you: when al-lowed enough time and space, everything turns to shit.*

# 103.

I noticed a small lamb staring at me with fear-filled eyes. With that sixth sense known to every beast, the kid appeared aware of what awaited him. He mewed, as if having singled me out, those melancholic eyes begging me to save him.

*I sense that you are different from all the others, I imagined it thinking. Do something, please?*

*You, Jess of Nazareth, are my last and only hope.*

I recalled as a small child in Nazareth watching as citizens led a lamb to the slaughter. I screamed for Mary to stop them.

"Should we save this lamb," my mother had whispered, "they would merely pick another and sacrifice it instead. Either way, an innocent creature will die. This is sad, Jess, but true."

I wept, "But shouldn't we at least *try* to do something!"

"There are times when we can make a difference and others when we cannot. As you grow, you'll learn to tell the two apart."

"If that's what growing up is all about, then I don't want to."

"Jess! Everybody must grow up sooner or later."

"Not me. I want to make a difference *always*."

"Sadly, Jess, that is not the way of the world."

*It should be, I'd thought then. I felt the same here and now.*

*Someone ought to rise to the occasion and put an end to ani-mal sacrifice.*

*Even as 5,000 years ago Abraham made the decision that our nation alone would not perform human sacrifice.*

*But who among us possesses the genius of an Abraham? A Moses? A David?*

*A true messiah . . . designated by Yahweh to make the world a little bit better than he found it.*

*He . . . or she?*

As with remorse I accepted that at the moment I could do nothing, the aches and cramps returned within my lower abdomen, leaving me woeful. The shrieks of a hundred animals experiencing sudden death following a quick slit across the neck filled the air. These mingled with the calls of thousands of doves as their delicate necks were snapped. Some journeyers had brought the white birds with them. Most peasants purchased pairs of lovebirds here, to avoid the hassle of transporting them such a great distance.

Doves were the most popular for one reason only: they were the least expensive animals sold for sacrifice.

These were available at stalls offering a variety of other choices as well, from grains and greens to sheep and oxen. I asked Joseph if we might purchase some of the former. Understandingly, he agreed.

*I'm so sorry, little creature. I can't save you today.*

*Maybe someday . . . with Yahweh's help . . .*

Our own sacrifice completed, we followed a bend in the walkway and joined on the end of a long line. The longest of all. For ahead awaited the most exclusive place of worship, the Holiest of Holies. Beyond its wooden gates, a visitor could approach the Inner Sanctuary in all its spiritual glory.

Hebrew females headed off, some to the Court of Women, where they could wait for their men. Others, with children, continued on to nearby rest areas. Here, they might purchase refreshments and keep the little ones occupied.

Incredibly, I realized that the guards positioned at the entranceway not only made certain that no women or gentiles entered but also demanded yet another coin from each man before he was permitted to step inside.

Even here? At the Holiest of Holies! One final payment? Rage consumed me. But, again, what could a provincial girl do to rectify such a hunger for mammon?

*Someday, I will return to Jerusalem. And when I do . . .!*

Elizabeth and Mary, accepting their designated roles as women, drifted off, each holding one of the girls' hands. They settled in a quiet grotto, surrounded by wildflowers. These created a sweet-scented wall around the secluded area.

Incredibly, there was no charge to sit on the benches.

"Oh!" John exclaimed. "I'm fresh out of coins."

"No problem," James said. "Here."

James shared half of his quickly diminishing handful with his cousin. Excitedly, they entered this special place.

"See you later, Jess," each called over his shoulder.

I held back, surrounded on every side by throngs of people, all entranced by the architectural majesty or the base sideshows. Wrestlers locked arm in arm. Acrobats tossed one another into the air. An African wearing a leopard skin threw torches high and, when they returned toward earth, caught them between his teeth, much to the crowd's amusement.

One vendor displayed a baby gorilla. Most of us had never seen such an exotic beast before. The owner sold bananas, which ecstatic pilgrims could feed to the creature. Enjoy yourself, everyone . . . but first . . . pay up! For that is the way of the world.

Perhaps it is. *But it shouldn't be!*

Sighing, I quietly slipped away to the food court to meet Joses.

# 104.

Minutes earlier, Joses had eased away from Joseph, James, John, and Simon, forcing his way through the crowd toward the toilet area. Arriving at the entrance, I learned of a charge (big surprise!) to enter the public restrooms. Once inside, I'd planned to make our switch. Outraged at the almost endless charges for pretty much everything on the site, I nearly surrendered to one of my fits.

This time, though, I refused to lose control.

"I have two shekels. Come on, let's do this as fast as—"

"No!" Joses's tone left little room for argument. He crossed his arms over his chest as if to signify finality. "I'm sorry, Jess. I'm *not* going through with it."

"Jude, you promised."

"I know."

"We had a deal. I gave you the goblet—"

"You can have it back."

"But . . . *why?*"

He reached forward, firmly took hold of my shoulders, and pulled me close. "Because you are my sister. And I *love* you. It's true I always envied the special treatment you received. That means nothing now. *You are my sister.* My flesh and blood. I will not do anything that might lead to your death."

"Alright," I muttered. "That's . . . *that.*"

Releasing me, he sighed with relief. His tense body easing a little, Joses managed a desperate smile. "Come on," he whispered, nodding for me to follow. "Let's head off to find the others—"

"No. I'm going to enter the Inner Sanctuary."

"That's impossible without our changing clothes."

"I'll find another way."

"There *is* no other way."

"There is *always* a way. Some people can discover it, others cannot. I can and will."

"I won't let you."

"You have no say in this now."

I reminded him that there was no rush for me to get this over and done with. Upon arrival in Jerusalem, Joseph had set down the rules for our stay. Never, under any circumstances, could Simon or the girls be left alone. Otherwise, we were free to roam and enjoy, singly or in small groups. Each allowed to seek out his or her own Jerusalem by happenstance.

Wander where you will. Afterwards, we all meet at sunset in the cave.

In less than an hour, the Inner Sanctuary would be the first of the mount's attractions to close. When water clocks announced that four in the afternoon had arrived, guards would admit no further visitors.

Until then, I'd hang about, watching for my opportunity. If none should arise, then it was the will of Yahweh that I do not enter.

That, I would and could accept.

On the other hand, if I saw an opening . . . then my entrance should be considered a part of His master plan.

I'd be doing not only what I wanted to but what Yahweh wanted me to do.

Or, at least, that was the way I understood the situation.

"There's no way of dissuading you?"

I shook my head emphatically. "Go now, Jude. You are free of any guilt as to what might occur."

"I might inform Joseph—"

"You won't."

"What would stop me?"

"Loyalty to your sister. Do not forget it was I who helped you win the love of Mary of Magdala. The two of you will marry and enjoy a wonderful life together. A normal life, of the sort I've come to believe is forever denied me."

"By *who*?"

I shrugged. "Yahweh, perhaps. Destiny. I don't know. Only that this is the way it must be."

For a moment, Joses remained speechless. Chuckling, he concluded, "There is no one like you."

"In all of Israel?"

"In all the world!"

"Maybe that's for the best." I also managed a laugh, if not of the happy variety. "I feel alone always. Not lonely, Jude. I've come to terms with my lot in life, even if I don't understand it. In time, I'll come to know who I am. Until then? I feel my way along like a blind beggar making his way down a strange alley."

We embraced. He turned and stepped away. I knew he would not betray me. Not even to save me.

We had, after many long years, achieved total mutual acceptance.

Which is merely another way of saying unconditional love.

# 105.

The Holy of Holies consisted of a stark, simple, cubicle-shaped building on the mount's highest level. Whereas all other structures present had been cut either from local limestone or imported marble, the solid wall surrounding our place of places had been fashioned from mud, this in keeping with our collective past. After all, long before we became a nation, we Hebrews had been a tribe of wandering goat herders. Yet to acknowledge how far we had come, stucco had been layered over the surface. The Holiest of Holies, then, represented both what we had been and who we were now.

Past and present, collapsed into one another. Which is at the heart of all Hebraic thinking. Then and now.

On the westward horizon, the sun began its descent. Many pilgrims were already leaving, though my family didn't appear to be among them. I inched closer to the doorway. Temple guards stood self-importantly on either side.

Fortunately, people just now ascending from the Inner Sanctuary approached them, inquiring about what they'd experienced below. Also, now that the long line had finally wound down, several stragglers asked about the amount of time remaining to enter and sightsee.

These distractions proved fortuitous for me and my plan.

*No! Luck had nothing to do with it.* Yahweh! *Yahweh and I, actually.*

*Together. We made this happen. What had Mary once said?*

*"God helps those who help themselves."*

I closed my eyes, felt my body stiffen, and begged my Lord to render me invisible so that I might enter unseen. I remained still for several minutes, summing up my reserve of courage. As the first hint of dusk settled in, I sensed that the time was ripe.

As three more Hebrew men exited, seven others approached the Temple guards, also asking questions.

*Our magic numbers, in tandem. I'll take that as a good sign.*

*Alright, Jess. It's now or never.*

Momentarily, the guards' backs were to me. Staring straight ahead and taking a deep breath, I more or less slid toward the entrance and then wriggled inside.

Somehow, no one noticed.

In the semi-darkness, I followed far behind the men as they made their way down a long line of steps, the passage lit by wall torches. The sanctuary had been carved deep within the mount, a recreation of the ark's original chamber in Solomon's First Temple. This provided a final safe haven if the city and temple were besieged, allowing the high priest enough time to save the ark while guards held off the intruders for as long as possible.

This, my nation knew, bought several precious hours when Babylon had besieged Jerusalem, devastating our shrine.

Legends recall that the ark was removed from the building through a hidden passageway. As town and temple burned, the ark, holding its twin clay tablets, was carried off on poles by six servants. The seventh member of this anointed group, a priest, led the way.

Their escape successful, these seven magnificent volunteers spent three months winding their way to the place where the Red Sea meets the Gulf of Aden, through Egypt to a land called Ethiopia in eastern Africa. There, the ark (or as they called it *ngoma)* remained in the hands of the *Lemba,* thought by many to be one of Israel's long-lost tribes.

More specifically, the ark's safety was maintained by their aristocratic cult, the *Byba,* supposedly descended from our priesthood. Even now, they protected the heart and soul of our way of life, Israel awaiting the glorious day for its return.

What had the strange man with his mysterious shofar suggested in the moon glow that night alongside Jericho's crumbled walls? Not only did the spirit of Yahweh reside within the ark, but also a great power that could be employed as a weapon against our enemies. Of course, he was quite mad.

That at least had been my initial reaction when we met at the well between Sepphoris and Nazareth.

*Mad, or perhaps someone who fully grasped the meaning of life on Earth in a way no one else could.*

*Perhaps that, and madness, are one and the same, perceived from different perspectives?*

Not that it mattered. As I'd discovered during the past months, if you believe something to be true, it is true.

If only for you.

# 106.

At the stairway's end, I stumbled into a forecourt. Here, where the torchlights ceased, pitch blackness greeted visitors. Alone and anxious now, I edged forward, eventually reaching an area lit by wall lamps and candles. Once more able to observe my surroundings, I was overcame with relief. Then it occurred to me that these emotions were likely identical to those of every person who entered the sanctuary for the first time. Less mine or anyone's specific emotions, more the result of careful planning. This experience had been as consciously designed as the one awaiting Greeks in their Capernaum temple.

Different as their religion was from my own, the manner in which the masses were manipulated struck me as similar.

Awaiting me: an abundant room in which three colors dominated. The whiteness of the walls symbolized purity. The menorahs and statues of seraphim (child-angels with baby faces and feathered wings), fashioned from gold, here represented our inner faith and the outer world. Each such valuable object had been situated on a fine teak table, its surface covered with a blue cloth.

For here, as always, was the Inner Sanctuary's third color: the hue that defined our people and our worldview. That unique shade embodied our national desire for transcendence from here and now to whatever else might be out there: up above, all around.

A world that existed beyond the reality we daily inhabited.

Behind the mask of our physical world, we were ever more convinced that a metaphysical one existed. Faith insisted that this was so.

Every one of us desired to experience it someday.

I hung back, slipping into the shadows. Those final male visitors wandered about, observing every item, peeking into the side room. In time, they turned and headed back up the stairs. I pondered whether the exiting men, like the guards, had not noticed me because I'd hidden myself well or if Yahweh did indeed render me invisible.

*I didn't know. Or care. I'd succeeded. For here I was.*

*Believing is seeing, I had long since realized. Here was an intriguing and oppositional variation on that theme.*

*If I believed, truly and fully believed, that they could not see me, then this was so.*

*It mattered not whether Yahweh had answered my prayer, rendering me invisible in the most physical sense of that term.*

*Faith, as Mary often told me, can move mountains. Or allow a slender girl to go unseen by those around her.*

*Anyway, now, it was my turn. And, in a more general sense, every woman's turn.*

I observed the seraphim. A year ago I would have accepted them as angels, sent down by Yahweh. Today? Having spoken twice with that mysterious stranger who carried a shofar, another possibility haunted my mind: Star Voyagers.

The Visitors. Watchers. Differing names for a single thing.

Extra-terrestrials.

I noted that seven separate sets of seraphim were arranged at intervals throughout the room, each featuring three cherubs in varied poses. I found myself doing something difficult for me, if easy (natural even) for most people.

I relaxed and enjoyed the wonderful sight before me. I seized the moment.

Yes, Jess of Nazareth basked in their beauty. Marveled at the artistry with which they were sculpted, their wings delicate as feathers thanks to masterful application of the thinnest form of gold. Their eyes suggested eternal innocence. Every feature, fingers and toes even, had been carefully detailed, proportioned, and skillfully carved.

They seemed, then, not to be crafted pieces but actual angels, frozen in time and space. Forever in the middle of what they had been doing at that moment when time suddenly stood still and space, or place, lost its meaning.

*For a brief while, I didn't think. I felt.*

*But, of course, I was me. Jess. Then and always.*

So such a glorious realization could not last long . Even as I reveled in it, the experience gave way to the reality surrounding me.

Try as I might, I couldn't keep consciousness from returning . . .

My inquisitive mind once more took control. Weren't these artistic representations of heavenly creatures?

Well, then . . . if so . . . and as such, how were they any different from the graven images of pagans?

*Were we more like them than we wanted to believe? Did even we Hebrews carry in our flesh and blood—and in our hearts and minds, bodies and souls as well—some trace of our long-forgotten ancestors, and the primitive needs that had caused them to do whatever it was they did in the recesses of dimly-remembered caves?*

*Had we not left the past behind as fully as we might wish? Did some primitive instinct, deep down inside, still beckon us back into primordial darkness?*

*Did the depth of those caves call to us even as did the stars so high above? Ought we to go up for the first time or allow ourselves to be drawn back down?*

*The future or the past?*

*Which should we surrender to in the present?*

*Maybe both . . . if that were possible . . .*

The all-important building in which I stood had been constructed in accordance with our faith in symbolic directions: high on the westernmost extension of the Temple Mount. This particular room stood at the western-most tip of that building. As we all knew, the forecourt by which I had entered measured 2,000 cubits by 2,000 cubits by 2,000 cubits, forming a perfect square. This compound measured 200 cubits by 200 cubits by 200 cubits.

Now, I spied across the way a tiny door leading to the most remote room of the Inner Sanctuary, chiseled deep into the Western Wall.

*The holiest closet in the Holy of Holies.*

*For a Hebrew? The center of the entire universe.*

No one was allowed to venture into this chamber that I now approached. Not even the priesthood. Only the high priest could step inside, and only on Yom Kippur. For here rested a precise replica of our lost Ark of the Covenant.

The once and always *ngoma*. Here stood the tabernacle, in all its glory.

Or, at least, a reasonable facsimile, dutifully crafted following the return from Babylon. At any rate, the rule was well known: look but don't touch!

Nervously, I stepped close. The ark, flanked by a table once employed for sacrifices, remained hidden under a veil of gauzy material; wrapped around the gold-encrusted, wooden box, 20 cubits by 20 cubits by 20 cubits.

In the hazy light, it seemed more a dream than tangible reality.

Whatever you do, do not enter! Here was one rule I for one would never break.

*As the law applied to men as well as women, I had no problem in observing it.*

*Equality is equality, even when it comes to restrictions.*

# 107.

I don't know how long I remained in the middle of the room, summing up the courage to humbly approach this replica. Leaning beside it, I knew, would be a recreation of Aaron's rod, the staff he carried while crossing the desert beside his brother Moses. I thought of my little brother Simon, with his beloved walking stick.

Might he, too, someday become a leader of our people?

Also present: a blue and gold menorah, recalling the Maccabees, last of our great heroes. How deeply I believed that their ordeal and ultimate victory should be included in the big book, already closed at the time of their courageous action.

*Why not reopen the Bible? Add further stories.*

*Someone ought to.*

*But who?*

This, I guessed, would be the one and only time my eyes would ever gaze on the ark's glory. For a girl to enter once might be daring. A second time? Foolish, at least until that rule was changed.

Meanwhile, I had to preserve this moment in my mind so that it would live forever in my memory.

Making ready to tiptoe near, I was shocked to hear voices coming from the most sacred space on our planet.

"Not now, sir. Please? If we were caught—"

"That's not possible. All visitors have long since left. The guards upstairs likely wandered away. We are alone."

"But in this room? Do we dare?"

"Since the day we met, I have fantasized about this. You and I, together, *here*."

"I don't know, sir. Anywhere *but* here—"

"Here! Do you want a recommendation for a high position among the younger assistants to the high priest? Yes? If so, I say: here and now."

They said no more. I recognized those voices. I detected the movement of bodies shuffling about inside the one place even our holy men were forbidden to enter.

Stealthily, I drifted toward the entrance, daring to peek in. Annas stood tall, his head pulled back, eyes closed. He opened his robe even as Saul dropped to his knees and brought his head up close to Annas's torso.

"Ooooooh!"

I didn't mean to gasp. I only hoped to turn and hurry away before they saw me. But the sound slipped out. Shocked, Saul leaped to his feet, eyes red with shame and anger. Annas screeched and yanked his robe back into position, shrouding his partial nakedness.

"You!" Saul cursed, terror-stricken, pointing a shaking finger at me. "Again? *You*—"

"It looks like the brat from school, except—"

"It's his twin sister. I met her once in Capernaum. She's as bad as he. Worse, maybe, being female."

Annas darted from this small sanctuary into the larger forecourt, his scarecrow-like frame out of control. He grabbed me by the hair and spun me about, twisting my arms until the pain became so intense I nearly fainted.

"I'll do to you what I've always dreamed of doing with your despicable sibling, and some day will."

"What are you going to—," Saul asked, stepping near, his voice full of horror.

"It means death for a girl to enter this sacred place."

Annas dragged me, struggling, toward the stairs. Saul scampered along behind like an obedient dog.

# 108.

"You're going to kill her?" Saul gasped. I couldn't speak, as Annas had covered my mouth with one of his clammy paws.

"Stoning would be too swift a way for this troublemaker to die. I want to see her crucified. I'm taking her to the man with the power to command that: Herod Antipas!"

*Crucifixion? I never thought of* that! *As this crime was committed within the temple, I guessed stoning . . .*

*Has my ongoing fear become a self-fulfilling prophecy?*

*Did I myself bring about the very thing I most wanted to avoid?*

Kicking and screaming, I resisted as best I could, which in truth was precious little. Annas yanked me up the stairs by my hair, then outside, the sky now dusky. Next, over and across the causeway. Torches were lit. Lamps and lanterns hung in their places, illuminating the way ahead with an eerie glow. We continued down yet another set of exterior stairs. Finally, I was dragged toward the temple's Main Gate.

When Annas's cruel hand briefly slipped away from my mouth, I screamed out, "I demand a Hebrew trial! It is my birthright."

"A Hebrew trial would be too good for the likes of you."

Once outside, without acknowledging my further protests, Annas proceeded toward Herod's palace. Most infuriating, Annas bellowed that if I dared mention what I'd witnessed below, he would swear I was lying.

My words, he assured me, would be dismissed as a desperate, pathetic attempt to shift guilt from myself to this highly respected man. I knew that he had the power to pull off such a vicious ploy.

Approaching the Westerly Gate, my flailing right arm connected with his head. Momentarily, he paused and staggered about, still holding me tight. Any hope this might allow me an opportunity to escape was in vain. Two temple guards, observing the scuffle from a distance, hurried from their positions to help him. Each took hold of one of my arms, making it impossible for me to twist myself free.

Recovering his wits, Annas with Saul led the way through the gate. The guards followed behind, gripping me tightly. "You can't imagine what's going to happen to you next, *momsa!*" Annas snarled.

As I would later learn, Annas had been reassigned from Galilee, which he despised, to Jerusalem. Always, he had hoped to enjoy an enviable lifestyle as one of the priests. Saul was granted permission by his illustrious father to accept Annas's invitation to accompany him as an apprentice.

"What if she tells Herod what she saw? I'll be ruined."

"No one will take this little daemon seriously. Don't forget, Saul, where we found her."

Crossing the main thoroughfare, we arrived at Antipas's palace. Here the king resided for several weeks during the year, and always on Passover due to political necessity. So it was up another set of steps, Roman rather than Hebraic, composed of solid marble rather than high-quality white stone.

"What's this all about?" a Roman guard stationed at the top of the stairway demanded. He stepped forward to meet us. Three others flanked him, all bedecked in the traditional red linen capes, copper breastplates, and plumed helmets.

"I'm bringing this rebellious brat to Antipas for final judgment," Annas explained. He indicated me with a wave of his chin while I struggled on to loosen myself, without effect.

"Antipas is involved with pressing business today and cannot be disturbed."

"I am Annas of the Temple. He will make an exception."

The guards conferred with one another. However brazenly self-assured they might appear when dealing with everyday Jews, they understood the importance of this particular personage. Nonetheless, such concern had to be balanced against their great fear of Antipas, and the possibility of incurring his wrath by disturbing the current king at the wrong moment.

Trapped in an unexpected vise, they were uncertain what to do. "We'll summon the captain," one guard decided. "You can explain the situation to him."

Annas nodded in agreement. So we waited while this fellow rushed into the building to find the centurion. Half an hour later, he returned with the man.

"Now, what's this all about?" the captain sternly demanded.

As luck or fate would have it, the tall, rough-hewn, broad-shouldered centurion turned out to be none other than the officer we'd been warned about on our day of arrival. A veteran of many violent campaigns, he had proven his worth in battle.

Here stood a man so feared that his own troops, as well as awed citizens, referred to him as The Panther.

# 109.

Moments earlier, I'd bitten one of the temple guards on his right hand. Partially free now, I scratched the other's face. Both cringed as The Panther considered the unfolding scene before him. His eyes filled not with rage, as I expected, but something more akin to bemusement.

"This wretch of a child," Annas shrieked, "dared enter—"

"That much I already know."

"Herod Antipas must be informed—"

"If all the girl did was to enter your Holiest of Holies, wouldn't this fall under *your* jurisdiction?"

Annas scraped and bowed to The Panther. "Indeed. But—"

"You have the authority to order death by stoning. Why bother the king of the Jews with—"

"King *over* the Jews, not *of*," I heard myself correct him.

"Is that so?" I feared The Panther might smash one of his fists into my face. Instead, his eyes twinkled as he roared with laughter. "If you say so, small one."

*Small one? Isn't that a term of endearment?*

*Perhaps this man is not another enemy but my best hope for survival . . .*

"Well?" Annas demanded.

"Alright, then. But leave your guards behind." The Panther turned his eyes from Annas to me. "Girl! Do I have your word you will not try to escape?"

"Yes." My voice turned meek, not ordinarily the case when forced to deal with authority figures. And not out of fear so much as a growing sense of respect.

"Come along, then," he said.

The Panther's eyes mutely ordered that I be unhanded. Annas scowled at this, but knew better than to argue with a high-ranking centurion. He dismissed his employees with a swift hand gesture. Then the three of us, little me between these two tall men, entered the palace.

"Remember what I said about watching your mouth," Annas whispered.

"I'd scream out what I saw if I thought someone might believe me."

The brief exchange between Annas and myself was not lost on The Panther. From his expression, I sensed that our words had registered in his mind.

"Be quiet, now," he whispered to both of us.

We crossed over the colorful floor, composed of intricate frescoes illustrating the city of Rome. Marble statues of their gods, as well as the Caesars, were arranged against the far wall. Tiberius's representation, raised on a dais, depicted him as a demigod, the golden child of some heavenly creature, descended from on-high to impregnate an Earth woman.

*In Hebraic thinking, an angel? Or perhaps, as the strange man with a shofar would suggest, an alien?*

*If indeed there were any difference other than the term of reference chosen by varied observers. Both beings were, after all, extraterrestrials.*

Then it was up, up, up an intimidating set of stairs until we reached the third floor. Guards passed by, marching back and forth in small groups. Scribes and men of minor importance were going and coming as if the specific business each attended to was the most important thing in the world. Their brows were furrowed with worry over whatever specific issues they had been assigned to deal with. One sighed in such a deep, heavy manner as he passed by us that I felt deep sorrow for him.

It was as if all the troubles of the world weighed down on his humble shoulders.

All were in the service of the most powerful man in Israel, excluding only the Roman prefect. And if that important personage wouldn't have wasted his time with someone as inconsequential as me, at moments like this Herod was required to.

"Stay calm, small one," the centurion advised. "None of this is as cataclysmic as it appears."

*Had the notorious Pantera actually deigned to speak to his prisoner?*

*And sympathetically so? This I did not expect.*

Passing through an ornate corridor, I noticed two guards, one on either side of a formidable dark-wood door adorned with black metal embellishments. It wasn't difficult to guess who would be awaiting on the other side. Recognizing The Panther, the guards bowed solemnly. Like living shadows, they swept the door open, closing it tightly after we entered. Inside, we halted at once and waited for instructions.

Far back in the room, in front of a long, horizontal window offering a breathtaking view of Jerusalem, an imposing desk dominated this spacious office. Behind it sat the man who made all decisions concerning the daily lives of my people.

# 110.

Despite the considerable authority entrusted to him, this "great one" did not appear physically powerful. Antipas's tubular body was topped off by a shaven head, heavily greased with oils. An oddly shaped, purple birthmark covered much of this king's face. Only his eyes, which resembled those of a hunting hawk, intimidated me as I stood before him, awaiting judgment.

Ignoring Annas and The Panther, Herod Antipas focused on me. He raised his eyebrows high. His eyes tightened to a narrow squint. It struck me that this king over the Jews had difficulty believing such a little girl had been the cause of so much consternation. "What do you bother me with on this hot, busy day?" he asked, shifting his attention to Annas. Antipas's tone revealed that we had caught him in a most foul mood.

"Of course," Annas began, bowing his head slightly, "I would not bother you were this not of the utmost concern." Angrily, he explained what had happened, omitting only the forbidden tryst between himself and Saul in, of all places, the Holiest of Holies' Innermost Sanctuary.

"And there you have it," Annas concluded. In deference, he lowered his eyes to the floor. Antipas considered all that he had heard. His annoyed eyes shifted from the priest to the centurion, finally returning to me. With a swift nod in the door's direction, Antipas signaled for Annas to leave.

Surprised, Annas nonetheless did as silently commanded.

"So!" Antipas began, rising. His thunderous voice, which set me to shaking, resonated through the room, bouncing off the marble statues in each corner. Behind Antipas were Jupiter and Neptune, lords of the skies and seas. To the sides of The Panther and myself stood Juno and Venus, brains and beauty presented as a duality. "Can you offer me any reason why you committed a crime against your own nation?"

I dared take a step forward, furtively making eye contact. At once, I glanced downward, more in fear than respect. Somehow, I managed to form words. "Perhaps, sir. But if you should decide that I must die, may I beg one favor?"

"You can certainly *ask*," Antipas replied, curious now.

Without meaning to, I found myself advancing. I fell to my knees and, overcome with terror, began to cry. "Please, oh, please. Do not let my death be by crucifixion."

Somehow, I found the courage to glance up again. Antipas's eyes revealed an understanding that my fear was not of death itself but that particular manner of execution, which included immeasurable pain and misery.

He then broke into loud laughter. "Crucifixion is reserved only for those who rebel against Roman power. What you have done may be an insult to your temple, but not to Caesar." He scrutinized me closely, intrigued by this unexpected bit of business. "Unless, that is, you are aligned with those scoundrels known as Zealots?"

I shook my head no, repeating what I'd once said to Levi. "As to taxes: render unto Caesar that which art Caesar's, and unto Yahweh that which art Yahweh's."

Antipas's pock-marked face filled with interest and confusion. He moved closer still, gesturing for me to rise.

"Meaning . . . ?"

"My belief is that, in appreciation of the religious freedom granted us by Rome, we should pay our taxes without protest."

Antipas's demeanor altered. His eyes opened wide, the king obviously impressed. "This is true? You do not lie now to save your worthless life?"

"I only tell you what I believe, which is the advice I share with my friends in Galilee."

Silently, Antipas studied me as if I were some delicate butterfly he'd caught on the fly and now had the power to admire or crush. I must have looked a fright: a slender girl, her simple linen tunic torn and dirty from the recent scuffle. While I could feel The Panther's warm breath on the back of my neck, he said nothing.

"I want more Jews who think like this, not fewer."

Was I to be spared? Don't get your hopes up yet, Jess, I warned myself. After all, they say Antipas is a quicksilver man.

# 111.

"I know the Zealots are a thorn in your side. But I do believe the majority of Hebrews care more about our religion, and its purity, than the occupation."

"How I would love to believe that."

"It's true. You are speaking to the most common of the common. A humble peasant. The child of a stonemason and carpenter."

"Perhaps I can learn more from such a person than some over-educated, over-paid advisor."

"Most Hebrews fear death. Other than a handful of Zealots, we quiver at the thought of crucifixion."

"As Caesar planned. This form of execution was invented to strike terror into the hearts of those who bear witness to the event."

"Well, it certainly works. Most in my nation prefer to quietly go about their daily business."

"Oh?" I feared that his mood might turn ugly. "Then why is it, young . . ."

"Jess. Of Nazareth."

Briefly, The Panther ceased his heavy breathing. Seconds later I could feel the warmth on my neck again.

"Answer this, Jess of Nazareth. Constantly, my spies wander the streets and alleys throughout Israel. Why do they constantly report increases in the Zealots' ranks?"

In a moment of epiphany, I realized that I had not been dragged here by accident. This was part of the great plan! This was what I'd begged Yahweh for. I felt my courage returning, and knew that I must make the most of my time with Antipas.

"When my people returned from Babylon, they were changed. Before, our identity had as much to do with the land as with our faith. Our religion and our history—written down while in Babylon—existed now in a permanent form. If we still adored our land, we knew that it was no longer necessary to be *in* Israel to consider ourselves the children *of* Israel. Some rabbis claimed that if we went into Babylon as Hebrews, we came home as Jews. Anywhere we might wander, our identity went along, too. For now, each of us could carry the big book with him . . . or *her* . . . and read from it daily. The Holy Bible became what the land had once been and, even before that, the ark: the epicenter of our nation."

Antipas remained silent. I feared that something in what I'd said had offended him. At last, he brought his right hand up to his chin, fingering a thick salt-and-pepper beard. "What you're suggesting, if I understand, is that your people have experienced a separation of religion and state?"

It was my turn to hesitate. Eventually, I replied, "I have never used those precise words. But now that *you* do, I would have to say . . . yes. At least, something like that."

"Huh! So a Jew remains a Jew even when separated from Jewry? What a fascinating concept."

"Though I do imagine that all Jews dream of returning to Israel to spend our final days here."

"Why, then, do some of your people relocate so far from their homeland?"

"The world has become a much smaller place during the past century. Faster and safer ships allow business to be conducted on an international scale."

"Yes," he admitted. "No one knows that better than me."

"Pax Romana has turned us all into citizens of the world."

"And you? Not your people. *You,* yourself? What does Jess of Nazareth believe about our Roman conquests?"

"I appreciate traveling on safer roads, knowing sentries will guard me from bandits and wild beasts."

"What else?"

"Freedom of religion. *Absolute* freedom of religion, that is." Here was my chance to engage Antipas precisely as I'd dreamed about during our journey to Jerusalem.

"You believe most Jews feel the same way?"

"I *know* they do. Naturally, we'd like to regain political control over our nation. In truth? Things could be much worse."

"And how does a child, a girl-child at that, speak more eloquently and knowledgeably than most learned rabbis?"

If my courage had been gradually returning, now it reached full bloom. Along with what some considered to be my overblown sense of self. "Other than living in the northern wilderness with other Galileans, I'm not your ordinary Jewish girl-child."

Intending to or not, Antipas once again laughed out loud. Likewise, I could hear Pantera stifle a snicker behind me.

To my bemusement, I found myself laughing, too.

# 112.

"So, Jess, you believe that compromise is for the best?"

"I'm not some idealist who believes it's better to die than meet Caesar halfway."

"Perhaps a realist, who grasps that things change and that your people ought to wait for a fall of Rome's fortunes?"

"'Where there's life,' as my mother says, 'there's hope.' Now, if you want to succeed at your job—"

Another long, loud laugh from Antipas. Followed by: "So a provincial Hebrew child is going to advise me how to run the country?"

"Only if you wish me to."

"Alright, then. I'm listening."

"The majority of my nation agrees with me. But if they will compromise, mark my words, Hebrews will never capitulate."

"I don't understand."

"If we meet Rome halfway, Rome must do the same."

"That's already the case. You pay taxes; we build you a fine temple, excellent roads—"

*This is it, Jess. The moment you've been dreaming about . . . praying to Yahweh for. Your moment has arrived . . .*

"To compare reality to roads, life is a two-way street."

No question Antipas had become fascinated with me, which only bolstered my courage. "If you, and other like-minded Hebrews, were to spread that doctrine, others might refrain from taking up arms."

"I hope so. I believe violence rarely solves anything."

"Yet you do not rule it out?"

"No," I dared admit.

He stepped closer, towering over me. "In your mind, what would justify resorting to violence?"

"Most Hebrews would fight, die, even accept crucifixion to maintain the absolute purity of our religion."

"So, I ask again, why do the Zealots' numbers grow ever stronger?"

*I was not here, before Herod, by accident.*

*Rather because I was meant to be here.*

"Because of your edict on the *Tallit*. Mark my words, Herod Antipas! If you continue to forbid the wearing of a single blue thread, the threat that you so fear will steadily grow. There will be blood in the streets. My nation's blood, and Rome's as well."

"Death, over an insignificant thread?" Antipas gasped.

"A thread, yes. But hardly insignificant. At least to Jews."

Passion overflowed my entire being. I explained what the color blue meant to our nation. This, Antipas already knew. For as Joseph told me, in his youth Antipas had like his father been raised in the Hebraic manner.

"It matters nothing to me personally." To my surprise, he sounded almost humble now. "I couldn't care less—"

"That's wonderful, since *we* care *so* deeply."

"I enacted the law only as it was suggested by the Roman prefect a year ago."

"But hasn't the prefect's seat changed twice since then?"

This apparently made an impression. "That's true. They come and they go." He mulled it over in his mind. "You honestly believe that if I lift this rule, the protests will stop?"

"I cannot lie to you. Those who complain over taxes will continue to do so. Zealots will still plot to drive all Romans away. But for the vast majority of my people . . . my guess? You would remove the thorn from under the saddle that Rome has imposed on us, and which causes Israel to buck and stomp."

Hearing this, Antipas briefly wandered around the room, considering all he had heard. Eventually, he returned to his position behind the great desk, sat again, then brought both fists down with a sudden thud that caused me to jump in place.

"My assignment is to prevent chaos. What matters if the thread be blue or white? Tomorrow morning, the restriction will be lifted. We'll see if this does any good."

"Oh, it will! May I . . . suggest something else?"

"What? There's more?"

"Just one little thing. The Roman eagle atop the Hebrew entrance to the temple? It's a demeaning experience for a Jew to have to step beneath it."

"I have direct orders from Rome to raise the eagle over every important structure in Judea to signify our authority."

My mind worked swiftly. "Are you required to hang it there, specifically?"

"No."

"How about moving it over to the Gate of the Gentiles? That would be an effective compromise, as we spoke of earlier."

Antipas looked deep in thought. "I will think on it."

"That's all I ask."

"Let's wrap this up. As to the personal accusation against you? There's a custom among your people that, each *Pesech*, a criminal is chosen to be pardoned. There are no prisoners in the cells today. That's rare, and providential for you: Jess of Nazareth, I pardon you. Just so long as you promise to never veer from that philosophy spoken here today. And spread the word of compromise wherever you go."

"It is what I have said, and will continue to speak."

He pointed to the door, indicating that our time together was over. I realized with a start that my hearing was completed.

I was free to leave.

# 113.

"So tell me, Jess of Nazareth. What in fact were you doing in the Holiest of Holies?" The Panther asked me this as he and I walked down the stairway, on our way back to the palace gates.

"That's the first time you've addressed me by my name. I'm impressed that you haven't already forgotten it."

"You're a most unique person. My guess? Everyone you meet will remember you."

We exited the building and returned to the street, quiet in the still descending darkness of early evening. The air struck me as fresh and rich, always the case in Israel during early springtime. I was a bit surprised, if happily so, that The Panther chose to escort me out of the palace rather than allow me to leave alone.

What might his motivation be for doing so?

The Panther indicated an empty marble bench alongside a thoroughfare. I sat down. Nearby a wine vender, operating a little stall, served his final customers before closing for the day. The Panther ordered a goblet of wine for himself, and one of water mixed with wine (what Jewish youths preferred) for me.

I nodded my thanks and sipped as he sat beside me.

"When my family and I entered Jerusalem, we were warned to beware the centurion called The Panther."

He laughed heartily at that. "You no longer perceive me as ferocious?"

"Incredibly, no."

"Well, let me tell you a secret," his voice, mellow, even gentle. "Panther is but a nickname given to me by the guards who serve in my command. It's merely a play on my name: Julius Abdes Pantera."

"I understand now."

He nodded. "Do you, Jess? Perhaps we Romans aren't as awful as many Hebrews believe. Those guards back at the palace? They'd like to return home as much as you and your nation wishes them to leave."

I recalled crucifixions carried out along the roads by just such uniformed men. "That may be so. But terrible things have happened. Entire cities leveled—"

"Only when their resistance turned violent."

"And yet it was Roman soldiers—like yourself—who not only killed Jews in combat but hung the survivors on crosses."

"We were simply following orders."

"And you think that justifies what occurred?"

"In all honesty?" He shrugged his shoulders. "I don't know. Despite my years, I'm no philosopher. As you obviously are, green as you may be."

"I must admit, you sound far more sympathetic to my nation than I ever expected from a centurion."

I noticed a heightened sensitivity in his eyes when I spoke those words. In time, he replied, "Maybe that's because I'm a Hebrew myself."

A shiver ran down my spine. Yet as Pantera related his life story, I gradually came to understand. He had been born on Israel's west coast, in a miniscule village situated between Syria and Palestine. Abdes had been his given name. His father, called Panthera, joined a group of Zealots who opposed the invading Romans and were crucified for their effort. The youth was spared and allowed to serve as a slave. Abdes Pantera, the Romans called him, preferring a Greek variation of his last name.

Owing to his strength, he had been presented with the option of becoming a gladiator, which he readily agreed to. So Abdes enjoyed a luxurious life if always aware that each fight might be his last. When he survived for more than two years, The Panther was proclaimed a free man. Now, however, he knew nothing other than the art of killing. When allowed to choose a profession, Abdes requested a position in the legions.

Granted this, he rose through the ranks, eventually becoming a member of the officer class.

"We're sitting here, now, talking because, like Antipas, I believe the solution to the Jewish problem is not attempting to destroy any possible revolution by the sheer weight of brutality. Rather, I would say . . . as you proposed to Antipas . . . a practical if less than perfect compromise."

"If my people are as wise as we are rumored to be, they will greet Antipas's declaration tomorrow with much joy."

"That would be a start, at least."

Barabbas immediately came to mind. "I can think of one friend who will not see it that way."

"If the protestors remain in the minority, then they can only be a thorn in Rome's side. And, as such, no major threat."

"You certainly think with the logic of a Jew."

"No matter what uniform you find me in, I remain what I was born inside. It is my birthright. Nothing can ever change that."

"That's quite a statement. I won't soon forget it."

"I must be going, Jess. Officially, I'm on duty. But do answer my original question?"

"What question?"

"Tell me why you felt the need to slip into the Holiest of Holies when you knew it to be forbidden and punishable even by death."

Without taking time to think, I stated, "First, because it was there. Second, as it was off limits to a girl."

He giggled one final time, then rose. The Panther bid me farewell and good fortune before returning to the palace. I sat there a while, wondering if our paths would ever cross again.

# 114.

The following day was to be our last in Jerusalem. This was true for most Hebrews who had journeyed from the far provinces.

In a final bout of festivity, we danced in the streets, with much joyous singing aimed upward to Yahweh. People passed wine about, sharing with strangers as well as friends and relatives. Happy tears were shed when word spread that the rule regarding the *Tallit* had been summarily dropped.

Everyone wondered why Antipas suddenly relented. Everyone except me. I kept my secret, since to tell the whole story, I'd also have had to admit entering the Holiest of Holies. The crowd might reverse moods and stone me to death. For my transgression truly was considered that serious according to our way.

*Our way for many millennia.*

*Though not necessarily our way forever.*

*Not if I had anything to say about it.*

That night, we all enjoyed our *Pesech Seder* in the recess of the cave, which now felt like a second home. Platters of food were passed back and forth while we relaxed on our mats by the glowing lantern. I fell asleep considering how remarkable these past days had been for all, and especially for me.

The next morning, long before dawn, we packed and rejoined our caravan at an assigned meeting place beyond the city walls. Across the plain, others from diverse territories did the same.

Then, for us, it was off to Galilee.

The return trip would follow the precise route of our original journey only in reverse. That night, we halted and camped at the spot where Jericho, Masada, and the Dead Sea meet. Here, these diverse landmarks form an eerie triangle: a ghostly reminder of our violent past, a spectacular palace of the present, and a body of water that in the Hebraic sensibility exists altogether out of time.

Observed in moonlight flooding down from a stark, starless sky, the area struck me as at once cursed and blessed.

And always under Yahweh's closest scrutiny.

My exhausted family partook of a cold meal and all then immediately fell into deep sleep. Once again, I pretended that I had, too. When I heard Joseph snoring, I wrapped one of Joses's robes around my shoulders to ward off the cool of night and began my secretly planned trek back to Jerusalem.

Hours later, shortly before sunrise, I reached the city's outskirts. As the heavens above turned powder blue, I arrived at

Jerusalem's main gate. Several guards stood on duty. They appeared considerably more relaxed now that the massive crowds were gone and, with them, any major concern of a Zealot uprising. A slender Hebrew boy (or so I seemed in my brother's guise) did not strike anyone as cause for alarm.

"Have you seen it yet?" a fellow Hebrew, eyes aglow, asked as I passed by.

"I don't know what you mean."

"The Roman eagle. It's been relocated from our gate to the entrance reserved for gentiles. This is indeed a great day in the morning!"

With that, he hurried off to tell others, joyfully humming to himself. So I'd won a double victory with Antipas! My breast swelled with pride. Not, though, the false pride of the self-important.

*I had achieved something good for my people. Allowing me to feel good about myself.*

*As with everything else in life, pride takes many forms. Some good, some bad.*

Once inside the city, I hurried to the Temple Mount's northernmost wall. As I'd noticed several days earlier during our initial tour, a small, one-story structure, known as the Hall of Hewn Stones, protruded from the wall outward and onto the city street. Here, a doorway led inside. Joseph had explained this unique recent addition provided a quiet sanctuary for the Sanhedrin, our council of wise men, to meet. I was also aware that on the opposite side, an identical extension jutted into the temple gardens. There, yet another door allowed access to this recluse.

Those rare few people invited here could, then, enter this private place from a commercial Jerusalem avenue on a flower-lined lane within the temple grounds. The room existed halfway between the two, and had been designed with this in mind: the necessities of commerce balanced with the exigencies of policy.

This meeting place had been added a decade after Herod the Great completed the Temple Mount and its surrounding wall. Who had done the stonework and supervised construction? Joseph! Our patriarch had humbly admitted that he served as the project's overseer. How proud we were of him and this great accomplishment.

Always, I would consider this my father's house.

Though I may have been pushing my luck after the previous day's near fiasco, I approached the street-side door and knocked. As always, a motivation lay behind my latest stunt. While we'd journeyed away from Jerusalem, there had been much banter among the pilgrims. One subject in particular caught my attention.

"Did you hear about what may be excised next . . .?"

I continued to pick up bits and pieces of information until I grasped the big picture: No sooner had we left than the Sanhedrin would meet, as they always did, in the hall where mammon and metaphysics comfortably comingled. The men who composed the Sanhedrin came together here annually following the holiday's conclusion. With the feasting, drinking, and worship over, the time had arrived for intense discussions and hard decisions.

Considered the wisest of the wise men from cities, towns, even a few rural villages, they were about to return to an ongoing project: severely editing our Bible.

When learned elders met here during the past several years, certain passages that had long been considered essential now came under close scrutiny. As the essence of what it meant to be a Jew altered over time, our big book was constantly being adjusted for the nation's evolving identity. Once removed, a tale previously accepted as part of our tradition would be dismissed as apocrypha: legends from an old oral tradition, still related now and then by those who found such fables enchanting though never again to be included in the official Bible.

Naturally, I despised this process. I did not want anyone making such choices for me. Particularly an all-male committee responsible for stories that focused on women. So! I'd learned from our caravan's pilgrims that today the Sanhedrin would meet to decide whether the character of Lilith, first wife of Adam, would remain in the sacred text or whether she would be stricken from future renderings.

Likely they would decide on the latter. That would not happen without a protest from me. I knocked several times.

"Who is it?" an annoyed voice called out from inside.

"Jess of Nazareth, sir."

*Purposefully, I slurred the first word so they couldn't tell whether I'd said "Jess" or "Jos."*

"Who?"

"I would like to respectfully address the Sanhedrin before a final decision is made on editing Genesis." All Hebrews (more correctly, all Hebrew *men)* had the right to request such a hearing. But never before, and never again, would such a request come from a twelve-year-old child.

"Enter," the voice gruffly instructed.

# 115.

Moments later, I found myself inside a simple, white, stone room. Counting noses, I observed twenty-three men of diverse ages and varied social classes present. Each participant wore garments distinguishing not only his status but the specific geographical areas of Israel that these wise men called home: wool garments for farmers, linen outfits on fishermen, silk shirts bedecking those who had succeeded in the business world.

The Sanhedrin in attendance stood or sat around a long, oak table. On its surface, scrolls were piled high. Several men held their own copies open. Each studied passages in the text that had been designated for discussion with ink. Hesitantly, I stepped forward. All the elders present turned to consider me.

"I am—"

"We know who you are," their leader interrupted. "You just told us." A haughty, reserved, menacing fellow, he identified himself as Caiaphas, their overseer. His job, as I well knew, was to coordinate this meeting though not participate in the vote. Unless, that is, the twenty-two others divided equally and a deciding ballot must be cast. "Speak quickly so we can proceed."

"I am here to argue that Lilith remain in the Book of Genesis."

My statement was greeted by mild shock. "By what reasoning do you request this?"

Lilith, I explained, waving my hands passionately in the air, ought to be considered essential. Her presence made clear from the outset that God was not perfect, an issue that for some time now had been rolling about in my mind. She represented evil; her creator had to be held accountable for Lilith's existence. Should Lilith be eliminated, Eve's human weakness in accepting the forbidden pomegranate would have no foil for contrast. As the story traditionally played out, Eve could not be thought of as wicked, only foolish and naive. But with Lilith removed, Eve's acquiescence might be misread. Rather than vulnerable, she would hereafter take on Lilith's role in the tale.

This would imply that all women (not only a "mistake" like Lilith) are born bad.

We all knew that it was Lilith inside the snakeskin, tempting Eve, her arms and legs protruding through holes in the disguise. Her menacing eyes peering out of the reptile's fake head. If Lilith were excised, who then was inside?

*So there you have it, gentlemen . . .*

My comments were met by dumbfounded silence. At last, one early middle-aged man, with kindly eyes and a pleasant smile, dared signal Caiaphas for permission to speak.

"Joseph of Arimathea?"

"Personally, I believe this youth makes a most compelling case to leave things as they are." One hand after another rose in response. After the others began speaking in turn, I knew this even-tempered man numbered in the minority.

*He shares his name with our family patriarch.*

*Once more the dualities that haunt my life's journey reassert themselves.*

"Your arguments," an aristocrat with a long, silver beard insisted, "merely serve to justify our alterations."

"Yes," a chubby fellow added. "We are making the change so that Genesis reflects the words now spoken before morning prayer: 'Thank you, Yahweh, for in your gracious judgment not having me be born a worthless woman.'"

"Well, since you've brought that up? I say that it must be eliminated from the ritual. It's unfair, cruel, and worst of all, sweepingly judgmental."

"It's *supposed* to be," Caiaphas declared, temper rising. "The people must be reminded daily of female inferiority."

At that, my inner rage exploded. I heard myself shrieking. Many backed away, up against the far wall, fearing that a mad person or daemon had entered their sacrosanct domain.

"Oh, really? Have you actually read Torah lately? And if so, have you forgotten Rebekah, Rahab, Deborah, Jael? And most memorably Judith of Bethulia, to name only a few of our female heroes?"

While they cowered, apparently fearful that this diminutive "boy" might attack them, I related every great woman's story, reciting the tale exactly as it had been written down in scripture.

"Each came to her country's rescue when our fine men found themselves unable to accomplish anything in the face of overpowering enemies. They are as great as Abraham and all of our male forefathers. Greater still, perhaps, as they had to overcome the ongoing prejudice our otherwise fair-minded nation holds to all our people who are not born without that . . . hideous . . . *thing* . . . between their legs."

"You speak as a woman might," one shouted.

"I speak as any human being should, regardless of gender but born with a sense of fairness."

Men screamed, howled, tore at their hair when I dared say that. Truth be told, I loved every moment of it. When the Sanhedrin calmed down, Caiaphas—almost as out of control as myself—asserted that henceforth the snake would be referred to as, simply, a snake. With no explanation as to who hid beneath its skin, if anyone.

I challenged them: if this were to be the case, and it had not been Lilith inside, how would they explain why snakes today did not have arms and legs, as the snakes in Eden did?

Caiaphas, whom I quickly learned to hate as much as Annas, bellowed forth the new narrative they would henceforth relate: to punish the snake for tempting Adam and Eve, Yahweh cursed this creature by removing its arms and legs. This was why the snake, alone among animals, must crawl across the earth.

That, apparently, settled *that*.

The silver-bearded man of wealth waved a stern finger at me, adding another reason for the change. The Sanhedrin had decided that from now on, Yahweh ought to be portrayed as perfect in all ways. Eliminating God's initial failure in creating a mate for Adam would render the text more consistent with their reinvention of Genesis for our day and age.

"Let me at least see what you have done?"

Joseph of Arimathea handed me his scroll. Thick ink covered entire passages already agreed upon for removal.

# 116.

Some of the increasingly uneasy men remained silent while others grumbled among themselves as I examined their work. "But you have ruined the entire story," I finally exclaimed. "Look here!"

I pointed out that while the name Lilith had been entirely eliminated, they had failed to cut the lines in which Yahweh creates the first female from clay, even as he earlier had Adam. Yet they left in the section detailing Yahweh's fashioning of Eve from one of Adam's ribs.

"I don't see any problem with it," Caiaphas defensively said.

"You maniacs, monsters, and morons!" I screamed, on the verge of falling into one of my fits. "Can't you grasp what you've done? With Lilith gone, yet both of the birth passages remaining, a reader gets the impression that Eve was created *twice*."

"I'm satisfied with our version," another man self-importantly insisted.

"Not me," Joseph of Arimathea countered. "The youth is right, particularly on that point."

Shouting erupted everywhere. Then, the door leading inside from the temple's interior flew open. There stood Annas, eyes bloody red. Beside him was my mother Mary, teary-eyed.

"It's the brother of that horrible girl I found in the Holy of Holies yesterday," Annas howled, pointing toward me. "Get him out of here!"

I guessed at once what had happened. The family woke and discovered Jess gone. Knowing me, they'd have figured I must have returned to Jerusalem for some reason and then hurried back to retrieve me. Later, I learned this had been the case.

Mary left James, John, and Elizabeth in charge of the children. Then, despite her difficulty walking, with Joseph and Joses she headed due south. Once in-city, Joseph had gone to search for me in the cave and Joses set to wandering the streets, hoping to spot me. Mary herself rushed to the temple.

There, the first person she bumped into, and asked for help, happened to be Annas.

"Again, the Nazarene brat causes me consternation," he had replied. None too politely, Annas guided Mary around various sites in search of her wayward child. Eventually, the two arrived here.

"Oh, Jess," Mary gasped, rushing over. She held me so closely I could feel the baby moving within her.

"Hi, Mom."

I was touched; I thought that perhaps my terrible outburst of several months ago had forever ended any love for me on her part. Mary's presence suggested this, apparently, was not the case.

"What are you doing here?" she demanded.

*What was I doing here? Why, this was a room Joseph had built!*

*Wasn't that enough?*

"Where would I be, but in my father's house?"

At that moment, the door leading to the street opened and a centurion stomped inside. "Some sort of trouble here?" The Panther sternly asked of the Sanhedrin.

As they related the details of my intrusion, he glanced across the room. Spotting me in the back, Mary beside me, he grimaced, then chuckled. "No need to explain," Pantera growled, indicating for the two of us to step outside. "We'll leave you now. Return to your business at hand."

# 117.

Shortly, we three stood on the street, the door closed tightly behind us. Even at the ordinarily busy noon hour, the crowd struck me as thin compared to the frenzy on view throughout the city during the recent holiday season.

"Long time no see," The Panther sighed, his tone sarcastic.

"Oh, you must be thinking of my sister, Jess. She—"

As if to confound my purpose, Joses at that very moment came strolling along. Noticing us, he rushed over, relieved to learn that I was safe.

"Your *sister*?" The Panther laughed, kindly keeping his irony to a minimum. With his right hand, he reached for the shawl I'd worn as makeshift camouflage and lowered it to my shoulders, revealing hair considerably longer than was fashionable for an Israeli boy.

"Well, I must admit, it's good to see you again," I shrugged.

"Hello," he softly said to Mary. My mother, I realized, no longer looked concerned but surprised. Shocked, even.

"I sincerely apologize for any commotion my offspring has caused," she mumbled.

"Actually, I'm getting used to it," he snorted. "Things will seem tame around here once your daughter is gone."

"We'll leave Jerusalem as soon as my husband—"

Before Mary could complete that sentence, Joseph came bounding across the cut-stone street, waving with delight that his family was together again, all the while smiling at me.

"It's a wise father," Mary said deliberately, "who knows his own child."

"Well then. I'll be taking my leave of you." The Panther leaned down to address me directly. "Perhaps in the future, Jess, you'll listen to your mother?"

"Yes, sir," I said, embarrassed by my latest fiasco.

"And your father, too. Mind me, now."

Without another word, he drifted off into the crowd, disappearing among the journeymen and women even as Joseph arrived.

"Despite that nickname, The Panther, he isn't so ferocious after all," I said to Mary.

"Giants can be gentle, just as small men are sometimes mean-spirited."

"Here's something interesting! When I met him yesterday, he mentioned that he is a Jew."

"Yes. Not many people in central Galilee knew that when he patrolled our territory more than a decade ago."

Mary's words took me by surprise. "Julius Abdes Pantera served in *our* district?"

"Indeed. Though that was not the name he was identified by then. Shortly before Pantera's service in Nazareth, he'd been freed from slavery by then-future, now-current Emperor Tiberius. To honor that aristocrat's generosity, Abdes assumed a name that paid honor to his benefactor."

"He called himself . . .?"

"Tiberon."

# 118.

On the night we returned home, I fell down on my mat, more exhausted than I could recall having been ever before. Swiftly, I dozed off thinking of the remarkable events that had occurred during the past week. I'd achieved my goals of being the first female to enter the Holiest of Holies and instigating restoration of our *Tallit*. Mary had shown some signs of affection. Perhaps there was a chance this might lead to a reconciliation.

Finally, I'd met the man rumored to be my father. Though a centurion, he was a Jew. And, his ruggedness aside, a kindly person.

While I would have preferred to believe Joseph was my true father, I understood a basic reality: always there exists the way things are as opposed to how one wishes they might be. As I'd said to Antipas, compromise can be a good thing: Joseph or Panther, I now knew that my father was born into my own nation.

Here at least was something to comfort me. This, I fell asleep thinking, had been a good week. Perhaps the beginning of my own golden age?

But as I stated at the outset, when allowed enough time and space, everything turns to shit.

As would my temporary joyous mood.

Such good spirts dimmed early the next day. Not one nor two but three (that mystical number again) crises came crashing down on me.

In the morning Levi stopped by. We continued an intense discussion that we had initiated during our trip home. As we spoke, Joses—like a ball of fire—darted out of the house and rushed past us. Beaming with excitement, he cradled the Jerusalem goblet. (Though he had offered to give me back the souvenir, I would not accept it.)

Heading for the path that led toward Nazareth, he called back over his shoulder that while presenting this to Maggie, he'd sum up his courage and ask for her hand in marriage.

"Give her our best wishes," I shouted. Levi, fixated on the beautiful Phoenician (and, I knew, on me as well), managed to offer a semblance of happiness for Joses.

I wondered, now that I'd matured to some degree owing to passing time and pressing circumstances, also with Barabbas and Luke out of my life, might I seriously consider marrying a boy I loved like a brother? The aura of romance stirred in me for those seductive youths who once caused me to feel girlishly giddy whenever I met either.

When in the presence of each, young Jess felt as if she'd downed too much summer wine far too quickly. In the end, though such attachments left me feeling empty, disenchanted, or abandoned. Might passion be overrated? Perhaps it's best to marry your closest friend and enjoy a long, quiet life . . .

"So, Jess, you were saying?"

Levi would have died if he could guess what I was thinking. No matter. I might bring this up later in the day.

For the time being, we returned to our discussion. Both of us agreed that, with the single infringement on our faith eliminated and the eagle relocated, we stood firmly against the Zealots. The two of us now identified ourselves as realists rather than idealists. We had made progress to forming our joint philosophy.

*Life can't be perfected. But it can be improved.*

*I accomplished that. For me and my people.*

*Was this only a one-time experience, or might I serve my nation again?*

*Something inside, a voice perhaps, caused me to believe that I was just getting started . . .*

"It occurred to me, while in Jerusalem, how many things in our Bible don't seem to . . . well . . . make *sense*."

"You are speaking again about the nature of Yahweh?"

I nodded. "Every day at Hebrew School Rabbi Annas beat the idea into our heads. Do not worship false idols. That is the way of the pagan."

"On that point, at least, I agree with him."

"Me, too. But, Levi, in the Holiest of Holies anyone allowed entrance bows down to an ark that they know to be a recreation rather than the real thing. How is this any different from the metal, clay, and wood representations other nations revere?"

He shrugged. "I never thought about it that way."

"Well, here's your chance. Think about it that way!"

"To question the existence of God is blasphemy."

"I agree. But it's not God that I question."

"What then?"

"Our way of perceiving God."

"Oh, Jess!"

"If the Holiest of Holies truly is Yahweh's favorite place on Earth, then how do we continue to believe our God is every-where and nowhere? For that certainly is *somewhere*."

"Jess, this is all way beyond me—"

"Nonsense. Either our religion is consistent or it isn't. Also, in the old stories, we are told that God lived up on top of a mountain. Isn't that where Moses met him? Well, if that is true, then Yahweh *did* inhabit a specific place."

"Stop. Please!

"Another thing. In Genesis, it says that God created man in his own image. Well, if that's true, Yahweh looks like one of us. But how can He, if He is everywhere and nowhere. Wouldn't that phrase indicate that He is an invisible force?"

We continued talking, me growing passionate as Levi looked ever more threatened. In time, though, our talk ceased as Joses came running up the trail, frantic and sweating, eyes bulging with anxiety. Concerned, we rose to greet him.

"Maggie is gone from Nazareth," he desperately cried out.

# 119.

Joseph, Mary, and the children had left for the River Jordan early that morning. With James at work in Nazareth, we three were alone. While Levi and I momentarily stood stock-still in shock, my twin rushed into the house, grabbed some of his clothes, and haphazardly tossed them into a sack.

"Jude," I asked as Levi and I awkwardly followed along behind. "Tell me what's happening!"

Joses, lost in his own thoughts, failed to respond. Instead he stormed from one end of the building to the other, searching for we knew not what.

"Jude?" Levi echoed. "*Please?*"

At last my brother answered, even as his wild activity continued. "I arrived at the house. Her uncle was there, drunk. He roared for me to leave and slammed the door. I learned from neighbors, friends of Maggie, that the previous night this oaf had completely lost control."

"I did hear rumors that he was a bad sort," Levi sighed.

Joses briefly halted to face us. Less than a year earlier, I wouldn't have thought my twin capable of such deep emotion. This had been a season of growth, certainly; and not only for myself.

"He attempted to have his way with Maggie. She fought and scratched and tore at his eyes, driving him away. Hiding in her room until he fell into a sodden sleep. Then she gathered her belongings and at morning's first light ran away."

"Without leaving any word for you?"

"She did tell the neighbors that, should I want to find her, I should head northwest to the city of Sidon. Her brother lives there with his family. Perhaps they will take her in."

"Well, that's *something*."

"How can we help?" Levi asked, sincere concern ringing in his tone of voice.

"Thank you both. But, no. The Hittites have a wise saying: 'He who travels fastest travels alone.' I can't pause even for a moment."

Exasperated, I stepped closer. "What is it you will do?"

"I'll follow her to Sidon, inquire as to the location of her brother's pub. The Merry Sailors Rest in the harbor area. I should be able to find her there."

"Merry Sailors Rest?" Levi sighed. "That doesn't sound any too savory."

This concerned me, too. Also, the thought of a solitary Maggie passing through such rough country. On foot, her initial journey southwest on the Roman road toward Caesarea Maritima would take a full four days. At least centurions guarded the way. Then, however, she must head north, up the crude coastal highway, for another four days. This rarely traveled route through the wilderness wasn't well-patrolled.

"She's all alone, Jude?"

Joses nodded sadly, his tearful eyes making clear that he was well aware of the risk. "I'll hurry along as fast as I can. Perhaps I may even overtake her before she reaches Caesarea and, if she still wants to go, accompany her the rest of the way."

He paused only to take his beloved Ankh from its hiding place and slip the chain around his neck. Then Joses turned and left. Levi and I once more followed him, this time out the door.

"What will you say if you do find her?" I called after him. Joses, having already reached the footpath, proceeded toward the Roman road.

"I'll beg her, Sister, to marry me."

Suddenly, I found myself filled with dread. "Jude," I shouted. "Will I ever see you again?"

He shrugged. "Only if it is written in the stars, Jess."

My twin stopped, hurried back, and embraced me. Joses kissed my forehead, then turned to Levi and smiled sadly. "Say good-bye to everyone," he said. "I will love them always." Joses turned and walked away. Soon he rounded a bend and was gone. Perhaps forever.

So! Here was the first of three calamities to befall me. The others would follow in rapid succession. Each, if possible, more difficult to bear than the previous.

# 120.

If on the first night back from Jerusalem I slept soundly and woke rested, on the second I slept not at all. In the morning, I rose more tired than when I'd gone to bed. Thoughts great and small danced about in my mind, vying for attention. The theological issues Levi and I had spoken of returned to haunt me. Far more pressing was the situation concerning Joses, which I had explained to my parents upon their return. That ashen, defeated look in the eyes of my twin! He had finally found the girl who could endow his life with meaning.

Now, *this?*

I worried, too, for Maggie: how terrible to think of a young girl, alone on that road. What might happen to her once (if!) she made her way to Sidon's infamous harbor area, with its rough-hewn sailors and other hangers-on from Phoenicia's bygone golden era?

*Worst of all, there was nothing I could do about it.*

*Jess of Nazareth—the doer, the go-getter—rendered passive by circumstances.*

As such, worthless. At least, in my own mind's definition of worth. I achieve good for others; therefore, I exist.

Then there was Mary. My mother, once, now, and always. No matter who my father might actually be. How touched I'd been when, in Capernaum, Mary seemingly forgave me for seven years of slights.

Here was the supportive woman who had nursed me as a babe and then mentored me through my first menses. How horribly I'd treated her, lashing out like the brat that, at my worst, I can be.

Yet in Jerusalem her eyes projected deep, even unconditional love when she defended me from the Sanhedrin.

*I have learned, Yahweh, to understand the stupidity of my selfish, petulant ways.*

*A reconnection with my twin, once begun, had too swiftly been lost owing to chance or fate.*

I would not let that happen with Mary. Or Joseph!

The time had come to set issues of blood aside and fully embrace him. I realized now that Joseph's capacity to forgive Mary for whatever had happened twelve years earlier, as well as his kindly parenting of Joses and myself, qualified him as the father of fathers. The moment seemed ripe to at last tell him so.

Still, the mother-daughter bond weighed most heavily in my head. And my conscience.

"Mary?" Hugging my robe tight about me, I rushed to the spot where she invariably could be found at this hour: in the courtyard just outside the house proper, bathing the children.

"What?" Mary answered abruptly, stepping in through the doorway, considering me with cold eyes.

"I wanted to . . . apologize . . . beg your forgiveness . . . for all the pain I've caused."

"Is that so?" Her voice sounded flat, neutral, distanced.

"Let us be mother and daughter, now and forever, if it is not too late?"

Her eyes condemned me. Her manner turned haughty. She stood frighteningly still, barely breathing.

"Too little," she spat in an unsparing tone, "and far too late."

Mary turned to rejoin the children. Momentarily I remained in place, frozen more by her aloofness than the unforgiving words. But I had to try again. So I followed Mary outside, stepping near to the *mikveh*.

"What I said that day? You remember—"

"'Who's the father?'" she repeated, recalling not only my words but the contemptuous manner in which they'd been spoken. "'Or wouldn't you know?'"

I wept at hearing this repeated. The experience caused more pain than if my mother had slapped my face again. Yet I had no justification to whine in self-pity. This was all my doing.

*If nothing else, I could at least assume full responsibility for my earlier mistake.*

*Here was a value I would try to live by for the rest of my life.*

# 121.

Brushing away tears, I somehow managed to form words, "But in Jerusalem, when you arrived to protect me, you—"

Mary leaned close again, her eyes filled with rage, guilt, betrayal, humiliation, and a dozen or more other emotions, all negative. "You are flesh of my flesh, blood of my blood. You are my daughter. And though long ago you chose to hate me, no matter how I tried to win your love, nothing can change that. When you were in need, and I could be there, I was. That, every mother owes every daughter. If I were in a position to trade my life for yours, I would. And without hesitation. But do not think you can come to me now and take me in your arms; make right what has too long been wrong. The poisonous water that rose out of the deep well of your heart, soul, and mind did not run off under the bridge and away, forgotten. It halted at the dam that is me. And built up, higher and higher, until it broke down all resistance. Then, while rushing over, destroyed any last remaining hint of affection."

"Please, no more—," I begged.

"Never once, since you were old enough to comprehend, did you ask me to explain or I would have. You heard bad things about me and assumed the worst to be true. The years we might have shared are gone. They will not come back. Is it in your best interest to love me now? Too bad. It was in mine to love you then. Now, it is not."

*I couldn't answer. Apparently, any communication between us, other than everyday chatter, was over and done.*

Mary turned, rolling back and forth on her heels owing to the fullness of her pregnancy. Without a backward glance, she stepped away and returned to the living waters outside. I might have screamed, except for one thing . . . one possibility that allowed me to believe all was not lost. For in the next room, Joseph sat, dutifully performing his daily work.

Never questioning his responsibility to provide for us.

*At last, on this day, I can call you by the name I have not used for seven long years: "father!"*

I slipped through the doorway connecting the house to his shop. As I knew he would be, Joseph sat in his seat before a limestone table. He held a saw in one hand, a block of wood in the other.

Who says miracles never occur anymore, or that the Golden Age is over? Not true. Rather, as Luke told me back in Capernaum, speaking of magic: A miracle is not defined by what happens, only the way in which any one of us perceives anything in our world.

Every day, I viewed Joseph sitting here and thought of this as nothing more than routine. Even as I too often took the rising and setting of the sun, or the clear water of the Jordan, for granted.

Now? Things would be different.

"Father?"

Stepping closer, I noticed that the right hand, holding the tool, did not move. His entire body appeared peacefully still, no longer laboring at his craft.

Instinctively, I sensed he was not napping. And that if his current state were to be called sleep, then it was the sleep of death.

# 122.

Halfway between the village and our isolated home, a deep ravine had eons ago been cut into the terrain by earthquakes. Such tearing apart of the land's crust remained with us still in fables, whenever storytellers gathered people together and related our ancient tales. And not only Judaic narrators. Such stories were handed down long before the birth of our faith. As a boy, Abram heard them in the tents of his pagan nation. As a man addressed as Abraham, he reinvented them so that the carnage visited upon Earth was attributed not to the whims of many selfish gods dueling with one another but the moral consciousness of the one true God.

Yahweh.

*Our* God.

And, as the Ankh suggested, potentially the God of other nations as well.

In time, I would discover the concept called science. When I did, I came to understand an alternative view to what early nations, ours included, believed. Long ago, the first creatures that might be called "people" gazed up at the stars and saw the heavens as a celestial reflection of local myths. Or, perhaps, the other way around? Now, a new and still-evolving order of things held that earthquakes, volcanoes, tidal waves, and the like were not the result of metaphysical forces, only natural processes by which the world continues to change.

And will do so as long as our small planet exists.

But as to our own land? Over many millennia, constant rains and occasional floods wore down jutting surface rocks, forming a natural terrace. Owing to its consistently flat surface, early Hebrews who wandered into this territory, blissfully ignorant of scientific rationalism, believed that they had discovered one of Yahweh's most glorious achievements. In choosing to see it that way, the people found a means of drawing the area's appearance into their daily lives.

Once permanent settlements were established, our men had taken up hammers, chisels, and axes. They dug deep into the soft stone. Methodically, our forefathers created a strata of caves that could be employed as tombs. *Kokhim* was the name by which we referred to these shafts, each awaiting some member of the community, withered with age, whose time drew near. Such cavities, covered with heavy stones rolled over the openings, bore silent testament to some Nazarene's life cycle.

Following death, a body would be interred as soon as possible. One year and one day later, the rock would be rolled away, the bones removed. These were placed in an ossuary, then returned to that awaiting *Kokhim.* The rock would then be pushed back over that open wound in the earth.

With this second burial complete, the process ended.

There was no name for our graveyard, at least officially. Most every citizen invented his own to identify what, in time, would be his or her final destination. As for me, I referred to this as the Valley of the Shadow of Death ever since the first time I'd heard King David's twenty-third psalm. To date, the most beautiful poem created by man. Or, as some claimed about David, something greater still: halfway between man and god.

*Isn't that what Luke told me of the Greek Herakles?*

*Did every nation have such a hero? And, if so, were these truly different beings or a single saviour with many and varied names?*

As to the psalm, one of my life's ambitions was to someday write something that hopefully came close to being as sensitive. That remained a long ways off. But as I always like to say, in Yahweh's own good time . . .

Meanwhile, I had announced to my mourning family that I, Jess, planned to recite David's verse even as others placed Joseph's body in his designated slot.

"That's impossible," Mary stated flatly. "Women do not fulfill such functions."

"Women of *your* era, Mother." If her tone had been abrupt, then mine, in reaction, turned caustic. "Things change."

"Yes? But who asked *you* to hasten that along?"

"I asked it of myself. And to myself I replied, 'yes.'"

"How typically arrogant. Precisely what I would expect from you."

For all I knew, sparks might be flying out of our mouths, so heated had our conversation become. "For how long now, Mary? From the day I was born?" I egged Mary on with heightened sarcasm. There were no holds barred now.

"No. From that day you . . . killed a boy."

"Oh, that's low. Really. Even for you."

"Ask in the village. There are those who insist they witnessed it with their own eyes. Then you brought him back to life."

"*If* I did, only with the will and power of God."

A pause. "Some say," she replied, her eyes slowly closing, then swiftly opening again, "you were possessed by a daemon."

I was not about to be bested. "If I do carry a daemon in my flesh, it certainly did not come to me by way of Joseph. Or whoever my flesh-and-blood father may have been."

Mary's eyes revealed defeat. To this insult, there could be no comeback. She turned and swept out of the house, conferring with James as to whether they ought or ought not to bury Joseph with a bronze coin in his mouth.

"You will not do so," I shouted at them, "and if you try, I'll tear it out in front of the mourners."

This concept had in antiquity been practiced by the Greeks. A tradition in their homeland held that the living must always provide money so that the deceased, hoping to cross the River Styx by ferry into the next world, could pay the silent Charon for his services. In the past fifty years, many Hebrews had picked up this habit, one more aspect of Hellenism.

"You busy yourself with practicing your speech," Mary called back over her shoulder. "I will decide *this* issue."

But I would not let this occur. Joseph had been a worker and wage winner all his life. He had nothing against money or the making of it. Still, the thought that an emissary of the afterlife needed to be paid for his services was a form of addition Joseph (like my cousin John) always despised. For such a notion suggested that the poor could not enter the afterlife, even if they had lived decent lives.

No! While some aspects of the foreign culture appealed to me, such worship of mammon would not infect my father's funeral.

*There. I said it! Several times now, in fact.*
*Each time, it becomes easier to do so.*
*Joseph: my father!*

# 123.

"I must speak with you at once."

James entered, carrying seven ancient scrolls. These were research materials for his chosen profession. No nation on Earth had considered the process of tracing people's bloodlines as important as did we Hebrews. We had not invented the concept. Earlier, Egyptians, Babylonians, and several other countries kept close track of lineage for their pharaohs and kings, perceived as demigods. Ordinary flesh-and-blood men (and of course women) were dismissed as too unexceptional for such scrutiny. They were merely chaff; their leaders, golden wheat.

We Jews saw the world, and those who inhabit it, in a new and innovative way. Our great kings, David the prime example, began life not in a palace but on the plain. He tended sheep and goats until the will of Yahweh set David on a pathway to glory.

Born in Bethlehem, raised in rural Nazareth, he became our Chosen One for that place, that time.

*Or, as my nation chooses to put it, a messiah.*

*The Son of Man.*

All Hebrews were wheat, according to our unique vision.

For that reason, each city, town, or village boasted its own scribe. Here was the fundamental reason why Yahweh had, from Mount Sinai, forbidden the coveting of another man's wife. Desire in the sense of sexual hunger was not the main concern, at least in and of itself. If a married man lusted for sexual pleasure that his wife could not provide, he was free to seek out local prostitutes. This remained an accepted if less than respected trade. None of our laws forbade it.

That way, the husband would avoid committing adultery. For if the law of God commanded that men not covet thy neighbors' wives, the law of man decreed that prostitutes could not marry. This arrangement offered a simple solution. Everyone was satisfied. Except perhaps the men's wives.

Then again, our nation did not take women's concerns seriously, not at this point in time. But things change. Sometimes, for the better. However slowly, the status of women in Israel did improve.

I take pride in believing that I may have initiated that process.

*But there you go again, Jess. Once more getting way ahead of the story you are setting down . . .*

"Jess! Did you hear me?"

"James, please. I'm not in the mood just now to share your studies."

With eyebrows raised high and a mouth that transformed in an instant from sweet to stern, James motioned for me to sit by the table. Sensing the depth of his concern, I did. James joined me, dropping the scrolls on the table's crude surface.

"We'll do this quickly."

James spread open three scrolls, allowing me to observe the interconnectedness of their texts. This was not difficult to do, thanks to the letters and numbers he had added. "I was tracing our bloodlines back on Joseph's side as far as I could. I reached twenty-one generations and halted."

"This is all interesting, James. But—"

"Quiet!" I don't believe I'd ever heard James address me in such a shrill tone. "Look, will you? Seek and ye shall find, as the prophets say."

Still distracted by my plans for the funeral, as such eager to get this over with, I did as requested. Then, in one glorious moment, everything changed.

Forever!

Initially disbelieving what I saw, I passed a finger across line after line of notations. A mixed sensation of intimidation, shock, excitement, anguish, joy, and perhaps, most intensely, fear overcame me.

"You are certain of this?"

"Old charts are canonical. They do not lie."

Again, I studied our bloodline. Back past Joseph, to his father Heli.

*Heli! Almost akin to the Greek term, Helios. A visitor to Earth from the sacred sun above.*

*Why didn't that ever occur to me before?*

Then I reached the twenty-first entry from Joseph's past. "King David," I barely managed to whisper.

*Twenty-one. Three times seven makes twenty-one. Our two holy numbers.*

*Combined not through addition, subtraction, or division, but what Yahweh himself commanded us to do in Genesis: multiply.*

"Do you realize what this means, Jess?"

Of course I did. During times of strife for the nation, the case now owing to Roman domination with their dreadful tax burden, our scholars attempted to predict who would be the next *Massach*: a warrior-king, rising from obscurity to organize the tribes into a single entity, Israel. Together, many as one, able to destroy those who had temporarily conquered us through unification.

Our first king, Saul, had begun this process. Every true king, or savior, had taken unification of our surviving tribes a step further.

The next such hero must, the prophets long ago insisted, be born in Bethlehem, even as David had been. Raised in Nazareth: the village of The Branch, where every original settler claimed ancestry from that great king. Our own Hebrew aristocracy, resettled in the most isolated backwater to avoid persecution by pretenders to the throne. Men like Herod and now his son Antipas.

*Hide in plain sight. But far from Jerusalem. In the thick Galilean wilderness.*

*Providing camouflage as well as a shield for the next such Son of Man.*

# 124.

"One of our own family is the Chosen One. Perhaps you, James?"

"Not possible. Earlier prophets insisted that the next messiah must not only live in Nazareth but have been born in David's hometown: Bethlehem!"

"Where Joses and I, alone in this family, were delivered."

"You were born first. And it was you, not Joses, whom our mother named after Jesse, father of David."

"That name altered to its female form. Still, Joses was the first *boy* born."

"Scripture does not state the first-born boy. Only that it will be the first-born. You: Jess of Nazareth."

"James! I've been wondering if Israel might accept a female rabbi. Do you actually believe our nation is ready for a female *messiah*?"

"As you always like to say," James answered, his voice softening again, "there's a first time for everything."

My initial sense of rapture abated as I considered the matter closely. "You're forgetting, though, the questions that surround the legitimacy of my birth. And Joses's as well."

"Personally, I've never believed any of the rumors."

"Because you, James, are a most trusting fellow."

"Maybe you should give Mary more credit than you do."

"She has never told me otherwise."

"Perhaps because you didn't asked?"

The truth of James's words cut me to the quick. I had to change the subject. "Joses might well be—"

"Joses's eyes are a softer blue than yours. The tradition holds that, like David, the Anointed One will have bright-blue eyes. Untypical of our nation, as such so indicative of the one among many."

He sounded convincing. "If I can ever come to believe that Joseph is . . . was . . . my biological father, then . . ." I raised both my hands, exasperated, toward Yahweh.

"If that's the case, Jess, then this should be first and foremost on your mind. Search for the answer to your question."

"Where would I even start?"

"Why not ask Mary directly?"

I only wished that I could. "At this moment," I said softly, "that isn't possible."

"Why?"

"Because we aren't on speaking terms now."

"Then wander the wide world, if you must, until you learn the truth. A great philosopher of the Far East once said that every great journey begins with a single step."

"You're right, of course. But in what direction—"

"No one can tell you that. You must decide."

"I already plan to track down Joses. He may be in Sidon."

"Then your direction parallels the historical one for our people: go west."

We rose simultaneously, taking one another's hands. "As always, I will take everything you say into consideration."

He smiled, knowing at the very least that he'd made his point. James left after mentioning he would see me at the funeral.

Alone, I attempted to recover from my state of confusion. Once more, I read David's most wonderful psalm, silently debating with myself as to how I would speak these words during the bittersweet ceremony.

# 125.

"You prepare a table before me," I recited solemnly, "in the presence of my enemies."

Holding my head high as I spoke David's words, I chose to keep my eyes closed so as to concentrate on what I believed to be the true meaning of what our second king intended. I stood with my back to the open cave in the limestone plateau where Joseph's corpse would shortly be interred. Before me was the sarcophagus in which his body had been temporarily set. Without, I might add, a coin in his mouth

*On that argument I had won.*

Also, on another issue: that a woman would speak at a sacred burial for the first time. Spread out in a semicircle before me a convergence of Nazarenes stood vigil. Seven elders, wearing white robes with blue adornment, dominated the scene. When this brief ceremony had been concluded, and Joseph put to rest (for a year and a day), they would begin the ceremony known as sitting *shiva*: devoutly praying for Joseph over the next three days.

Minutes earlier, the gathered mourners were on the verge of turning into a mob when I dared to step forward. Catcalls, shouts, whistles, and boos were verbally hurled at the sight of a brash girl about to assume what they considered a man's duty.

"Go home!" someone in the crowd shouted. "Cook dinner and clean the house."

At least no one called out "momsa!" Likely, this had been in deference to Joseph, whom all cherished. Yet such harassment ceased the moment I proceeded. For these were the words of David. Whatever anyone thought of me, he—the Anointed One—must be respected always. Even as all our past messiahs: Noah, Abraham, Isaac, Jacob, Moses, and Solomon.

And, of course, the next as well. Whoever that might turn out to be.

"You anoint my head with oil. My cup runneth over."

The words of the young David to Samuel were offered up not to those in attendance but to Yahweh. For I wondered even now whether there might be some truth to what James had said.

"Surely, your goodness, mercy, and love will follow me all the days of my life."

That sentence, in this moment's context, was aimed at anyone who believed I might be a daemon walking the earth in human form.

"And I shall dwell in the house of my Lord, forever."

The final phrase insisted that a single force greater than we can comprehend once created and forever rules the universe.

Arabic people call him Allah; Hebrews, Yahweh.

*When it comes right down to it?*

*Same God, different name.*

"Amen."

"Amen," people chanted.

My family, or what was left of it, held hands. John and Elizabeth were present, hurrying here from Bethlehem after hearing the news. The six arraigned themselves in a line before the open grave, me assuming the central position.

I was the seventh figure, three others on either side.

*Precisely like the candles on an ancient menorah.*

*And every other aspect of Hebraic life.*

The seven males who would sit *shiva* raised the sarcophagus, carefully inserting it through that large gash in the limestone. People embraced one another, kissed, and cried. Mary tore her white and blue garment, an act we call *keriah*: the rip in one's clothing implying a tear in the soul.

Women and men then emerged from out of the crowd to offer material as well as emotional support. Some wanted to know if they might stop by the house with lentil stews. One well-to-do herdsman offered to bring by a fresh-killed lamb, this to be roasted in our courtyard for those who came to comfort us.

Members of other nations may fast after the death of a beloved one. We weep, and then we eat and drink.

This is our way. Life goes on.

"To life!" all would call out, raising cups to Yahweh's solemn promise: Our nation would survive, as it already had from the age of Abraham through the difficult present. Though the future appeared uncertain, we would continue to exist.

In the meantime, for a full week all would mourn the collective loss of Joseph while celebrating his life.

*Though one person would not be there.*

*That person was me.*

# 126.

During the past twenty-four hours, I'd made up my mind. The first step had been packing a bagful of necessities, mostly water, along with wine and food. This package awaited me in the hiding place up near the Roman road where earlier I had stashed it. As the others drifted toward the house of Joseph, I would slip away, pick up my belongings, and set out on what James had proven beyond any doubt must be my life's journey.

"You're *leaving*?"

I turned to face Mary a short distance behind me. No anger could be detected in her eyes, nor any forgiveness either. Badly shaken by the death of her husband and the departure of Joses, my mother appeared spellbound much of the time. Her visage now resembled a mask, revealing nothing.

That, of course, hardly constituted anything new. During our twelve years together, this had been her façade. Her means of coping with the unspoken rumor that whirled around always, if often silent, threatening to smother her.

"Oh? I didn't know we were speaking."

"Of course we're speaking, Jess. Good-bye."

She turned to follow in the direction of the mourners. I couldn't leave it like that. Something more must be said.

*But what?*

"May I ask one favor?"

Surprised, Mary spun around. "Oh? Do I owe you even that?"

"No." My eyes dropped down to the ground, so embarrassed was I by the mess I'd made of everything. "But *I* owe you."

"Don't go all wishy-washy on me now. One of the qualities I've always admired about you is your arrogant indomitability."

"Fine. Then, with full knowledge that you owe me nothing, I ask a favor."

Mary extended her arms invitingly, if with a slight hint of parody. "Go right ahead," she replied smugly.

I became tongue-tied, as Moses of old is said to have done at moments of crisis. But as I had no brother such as Aaron close by to speak for me, I had to find the words myself.

*And, as I have learned in life, when one must, one does.*

"Was Joseph my father?"

Mary paused, took that in, then replied, "Maybe that is one of those things in life you never will know for certain."

Now it was my turn to pause. Finally, I said, "Then, I'll spend my life searching for an answer."

Without hesitation, Mary shot back, "Do that. And when you think you know the truth, come back. Then we'll talk."

That pretty much said it all. Still, one last request fell from my lips. "If we can never truly be friends, Mary, will you allow me but this: that we will never again be enemies?"

For an instant so brief that, when it was over, I could almost believe that what I saw, or thought I had seen, was illusory, Mary's face appeared to glow.

*For once in my life, I had said the right thing to her.*

She offered no reply. Yet something in my mother's demeanor suggested that she had accepted my offer.

# 127.

A phantom moon hung low in the sky. This term my people had borrowed from the Babylonians, during our years in captivity. They earlier acquired it from the Kassite Dynasty, which preceded their own era of domination in that part of the world.

There were some who claimed that the Kassites had taken this term from their own ancient predecessors, the Chaldees. One seemingly invincible nation is replaced by the next, each appearing indestructible until it is gone.

And, in most cases, forgotten.

*Always, though, something remains behind, absorbed into the continuum we call life.*

*For that is the way of the world.*

At the time of our enslavement there, Babylon appeared so powerful that many thought it might go on forever. Until Cyrus the Persian put their city to the sword. Yet the term phantom moon persisted, referring to those days when the milky light of that lunar orb appeared before the red sun finally set on the horizon. Some claimed this only occurred when Yahweh chose to offer a sign up in the sky.

Yahweh certainly did seem to have been directly speaking to me this past year. And always in dualities. Could this be another?

That old devil moon, as a half transparent circle, while the upper half of the life-giving sun remained in sight.

"Jess? Wait!" The beloved voice of Levi wailed behind me.

"Hello, old friend."

"Is it true? You're going away?" He had run here from my home, where he'd gone expecting to find me.

"Yes."

"And we'll . . . never see each other again?"

"Never," I assured him, "is a very long time."

"Oh, Jess," he wept openly. "Where will you go?"

I explained that, for some time now, I'd been secretly planning to set out to discover my inner self by exploring the outer world. Learn its ways, observe people's habits, come to know and hopefully understand how humankind existed beyond our nation's parochial limits.

And, as a result, understand more about humanity—and perhaps the cosmos itself—than I ever could if I remained in Galilee.

"My immediate destination is Sidon on the Mediterranean. The place to which Mary fled, Jude following. God grant that I find them alive and well. Also, I must share with my twin some important facts I learned only yesterday from James."

"That's *such* a long way. Especially without escort. The thought of you, like Maggie, making the trip alone sickens me."

296

Levi's words were well-timed. In the back of my mind, I'd been rolling over the seed of an idea. Now, it sprouted into a bud.

"I agree. Levi, will you accompany me?"

For a moment, silence. "I'm your friend, Jess. You know I always want to be there for you. But . . . to just up and go? Desert everything, from family to—"

"Levi!" I remained as patient as possible. "Do you remember, not that long ago, when we spoke of your jealousy over Barabbas, Luke . . . even Maggie?"

"Of course. But what does that have to—"

"Everything! Hush, now. You asked of me a question that I was not then able to answer."

Levi's eyes clouded with barely held-back tears. "I asked if you might ever come to perceive me as you did them. Not only as a friend, but as a—"

"Lover," I finished for him.

"I've long since given up hoping for that."

"Really? That's ironic. You see, I've finally come to know in my heart that the answer is *yes.*"

He had trouble finding words. "Jess, you're saying—"

"I want to be your wife. I want to have children with you and share our lives in every way. In the workplace during the day and at night when we lie on a single mat. I want to rock and roll upon that mat with you and produce beautiful babies."

"That's . . . exactly . . . what I want. But how, why—"

"Did I come upon this? Truthfully, I fell out of love with romantic love. Love at first sight, that sort of thing. Luke . . . betrayed me. Barabbas left. But not you, Levi. I'm sorry I've caused you the pain of jealousy. I'm a different person than I was a year ago. Experience altered me."

"The very thought of us having babies together!"

"That would be a long time coming. There's so much I must do first. Still, if you're willing to be patient—

"I'd wait forever if I had to. But . . ."

"But what?"

"Jess," Levi admitted. "I'm *afraid.*"

# 128.

I knew precisely what he meant. Not in any way afraid to marry me, however blemished my bloodline. Fearful of leaving this little corner of the world, the only home he had ever known.

Not I.

Jess of Nazareth relished the thought of heading out into the unknown. Moving west. And eventually, walking from Caesarea Maritima up to Sidon, north by northwest.

Following the sun.

But that was me. And Levi was Levi. We cannot, I had learned during the past year, be anything but who we are. However much we might want to.

Still, I had to try one last time.

"I'm not afraid. And I have enough courage for the both of us. Come with me?" I reached out to take his hand. Abruptly, Levi stepped backward, body tense, eyes anxious.

"Stay here, Jess. We can have a wonderful life together."

"You're forgetting how the Nazarenes feel about me?"

"We'll live out on the edge of the wilderness, even as Joseph and Mary did."

"I'm done with retreating from reality. From this moment on, I want to face things head on. And if Yahweh wills it, stand at life's epicenter, not hang out on the sidelines."

"It's not that I don't want to. Only," Levi continued, his voice desperate now, "the world's so *big!* And I, so small."

"Each of us, Levi," I said with all the compassion I could muster, "is as small as we believe ourselves to be. Or as big."

"I know," he admitted, openly weeping. "All the same, that's the way I am."

I'd tried. And, in this instance, failed.

*Or maybe it was Levi who had failed me?*

No matter. Apparently, I would make my journey alone. That was alright, though. I was used to being alone. Though never lonely. That cannot happen when you enjoy and respect your own company.

Privacy is a luxury that few can fathom.

We embraced warmly, then parted ways. As I followed the footpath toward the Roman road, I sensed that Nazareth was not done with me. Not yet.

Patterns now ruled my life.

Recurring patterns.

Members of my family in attendance when I'd delivered my address at the tomb had numbered seven: Mary and James, John and Elizabeth, Salome and Miriam, and Simon.

Simon, carrying his staff, proudly if sadly, to this unexpected event in his young life.

*No pretend magic from your wooden wand, little boy, can bring back Joseph.*

*Lesson to be learned in the real world. The first of many . . .*

My destiny now appeared to be dictated by my bloodline: seven times three. If this were true, then Levi could not have been alone in wanting to speak with Jess of Nazareth before my journey began. There must be two more.

If there were not, then, yes, the figures signified nothing. Life is but random. Chance rules the world. The cosmos, too.

On the other hand . . . if two more people awaited me before I reached the village marker, perhaps destiny does exist. And chart my oncoming journey with choice, not chance.

# 129.

At a point where the village proper ends, a well had been sunk centuries ago. Legend had it that David himself had overseen the digging of this source of water. True or not, this was called David's Well. It wasn't used much by those who lived in Nazareth today. They were fortunate enough to have discovered a more central source for water and did not often venture out this far. Still, it was reassuring to know that a backup existed in case the village well should ever go dry. Specifically since the outlying water supply now measured as considerably more plentiful than anyone previously realized.

Several city councilors had spoken with Herod's messengers about the possibility of creating an aqueduct here, bringing more water to central Galilee. All were aware that more water in any village increased property values. Perhaps this might be a way to lure additional settlers. That had set off a loud debate among those who thrilled at the thought of more people and more money, compared to others, mostly descendants of early settlers. They were horrified that their traditional, long-entrenched way of life might alter, even if for the better.

Perhaps they worried, too, that Nazareth's special meaning–The Branch—would be lost in the process of modernization.

Every afternoon at the wine bars, neighbor argued with neighbor. And later, at home, husbands with their wives.

All the same, what either side believed had nothing to do with me. Not anymore. For the time being, I forsook my identity as a Nazarene to become a citizen of the world.

Yet I could not turn my back on ritual. Whenever a Jew left his home, he stopped at the well to taste of the local waters one last time. This would hold him (or her) until the eventual day of homecoming.

So here was where I had earlier hidden my package of goods, which I must now retrieve before setting out.

As I approached, I noticed a handsomely built man standing under a nearby sycamore's shade, his back to me. All I could see was that he stood tall, wearing a linen sheath stretching from his neck, where an attached shawl hung, to his ankles, abruptly ending just above a pair of glistening sandals.

Strapped over his shoulder on a leather string, a large *shofar* dangled as he partook of water. Hearing someone, he turned, casting a knowing smile.

I had no doubt who this was. I noted, too, that this was, appropriately, the third time I'd encountered him.

Once, I would have thought that to be coincidence. Luck, accident. Not anymore. What happens, as I had learned, does so because it's supposed to.

"That's the *shofar* you played at night near Jericho?"

"Oh yes. My beloved horn," he said, turning to face me.

We sat together on a nearby limestone bench and sipped fresh water from wooden cups. "Always, it seems, we meet by a well."

"I hear wonderful old tales about this particular one. On your nation's return from Babylon, Daniel himself stopped here to drink from David's Well."

"Being a Hebrew, I know the story."

"Do you? Tell me, then, more about this Daniel."

# 130.

So I did. It was a story of the Diaspora. After the forces of Nebuchadnezzar leveled Jerusalem and the First Temple some 600 years ago, then led Hebrew survivors off to the northeast, we were once again slaves. Yet many members of the nation were able to win high positions as scribes, seers, advisors, and teachers to children of Babylon's elite.

In time, the wisest of our nation, Daniel, won admiration and confidence from the king. Feeling fortunate to have such talent in their employ, Nebuchadnezzar (not being a fool) wished to keep this Daniel and his people happy.

When asked what treasure our nation most appreciated other than absolute freedom, Daniel answered: freedom to practice our faith. When we have that, then our souls are in a sense free, even if our bodies are not. The king saw no problem in that. Still, according to one version (and there are many) he wanted to know if Daniel's followers would be willing to pray to his god Baal as well.

Daniel had to wrestle with this problem. Our leader could tell the king "no," though that would likely mean the lash. Or he might say yes and we, the people, would reap many benefits.

But would that constitute capitulation to our enemies, setting us in conflict with our covenant?

So Daniel did what all great Hebraic leaders have always done, down through the millennia: he consulted the Talmud.

To him then, as for me now, the Ten Commandments were the be-all and end-all of Jewish identity. All other laws, including those set down for posterity in Leviticus and Numbers, were merely the laws of men. These were topical and temporary.

The Ten Commandments? Eternal. Our Torah exists for-ever. Everything in it must be closely examined for subtexts of meaning.

Daniel found written: "I am the Lord, your God. You shall have no other gods before me."

Daniel studied that closely. If Yahweh demanded that we worship Him, and Yahweh alone, why in his genius had our Lord not insisted, "You shall have no other gods *other than* me?" But those were not the words.

Set down in stark black ink on a yellowing goat skin, Daniel discovered a phrase that Yahweh had left open to interpretation.

"Yes, we can do that," Daniel told the king.

They must be allowed to worship Yahweh *first,* always. Then, if the king wished, they could say a word or two of praise to Baal, *after*—not before—prayer to our God.

*Absolutism would have proven disastrous. A willingness to compromise saved the day.*

*A truth for me to recall all the days of my own life.*

The king expressed his delight, understanding that only through negotiation can everyone be made relatively happy if less than fully satisfied. Which made sense.

*For to receive complete satisfaction would be to achieve perfection.*

*And perfection cannot exist on an imperfect world.*

Only in that other realm, the alternative world waiting for each of us in that endless abyss, beyond the sea. On the horizon line that separates water from the sky above. Blue on blue.

Eternity awaiting somewhere in-between.

At least for those able to let go of this world and transcend into the next.

For a time, things went as well as they can when a people remains enslaved, which of course is not too well at all. Yet Hebrews weren't whipped, scorned, or executed. They achieved prestigious roles in society. They lived and ate better than most other slaves.

*But with time enough and space, everything turns to . . .*

A Mead named Darius had served as the king's royal advi-sor before Daniel entered the picture and swiftly replaced him.

Desiring to regain his status, Darius grew ever more jealous of the Jew's popularity. To win back his esteem, Darius must eliminate Daniel. He developed a plan: convince the king while drunk to pass a new law. For thirty days, no one must worship any god other than one of Babylon's deities. Once sober, the king—a fool in many ways, but not cruel—grew horror-stricken upon realizing that this violated the pact he and Daniel had made.

Yet the king was loath to change the new law, for fear of appearing weak and wavering in the eyes of his people.

Lesser things have led to political insurrection.

Informed of the new rule, Daniel refused. A saddened king begged him to reconsider, if only for this single month. If not, Daniel must be thrown to the lions. After that, every one of his followers would be executed, should they refuse.

Daniel would not budge. To do so would have been to violate a law of God. And there was no further room in this commandment for interpretation. So a mournful king regretfully had Daniel tossed into the lion's den while the scoundrel Darius danced with joy.

The next morning, when guards pushed the great stone away from the cave where man and beasts had been enclosed, there stood Daniel, safe and sound, smiling as he stepped out.

What happened? The king wanted to know.

Yahweh, Daniel answered, sent down an angel from on-high to keep the lions' jaws closed throughout the night. Stunned to learn how powerful this Yahweh was, the king proclaimed that Darius, along with all his friends and family, would be tossed into the pit.

Which they were.

And it came to be that Daniel served the king until Cyrus of Persia leveled the city nearly a century later, and set the Jews (whom he, too, greatly admired) free.

So it was that our people returned to the land called Palestine, Canaan, and finally, in honor of Jacob, by his alternative name: Israel.

# 131.

"Wonderful! Wonderful story."

"Yes. But, if I'm correct, you're going to tell me yet another version? One you heard in some far-away land?"

"Well," the tall man said, eyes twinkling, "there are only so many stories to go around, and so very many story tellers."

"I'm listening."

"Sometimes visible but more often not, always there are Star People who travel through the heavens in what you might think of as an equivalent to ships at sea. Or a chariot on land. These devices carry the celestial journeyers to far places that they find of interest. The ships cross immense distances in what you on Earth would consider brief moments. For they are able to intersect with your concepts of time, which they bend, and space, which they avoid.

"Some of the planets they visit intrigue them enough that they choose to meddle in the affairs of the beings living there. On your planet, they made such incursions. Many times, in fact. But the people they picked proved disappointing. So they eliminated any trace of such failed experiments through flood, fire, and the like. Finally, they succeeded in creating a new nation far wiser and greater than anything your world had known. The Hebrews. And 5,000 years ago, according to an earthling's misconception of time, there was born a man named Abram. As the offspring of an advanced Earth woman and a Visitor, he had within him potential beyond anyone else in his primitive tribe. With much careful guidance, Abram might venture forth, create a new nation, and lead the way for all those other nations that compose the realm of man.

"They passed over often, these Visitors, just to keep an eye on things. Some 550 years ago, they saw that the Hebrews were about to be demolished. They could not allow this to happen, for then the Star People would have to begin all over again."

"One of these aliens," I said, drawing on his previous statements, "assumed the guise of an earthling and descended for the purpose of intervening in what occurred on this planet."

304

He nodded with enthusiasm at my comprehension of, if not the truth, then at least "his truth." "Earthlings refer to such Visitors as angels. Your term of choice comes closer to the way these Visitors perceive themselves."

We had become joint narrators of this version. "The alien or angel entered the lion's den and called upon powers that might appear miraculous or magical to humans in order to save Daniel."

"Yes, yes. These 'powers' as you call them were but a part of the world that more advanced beings had developed far away. Respectful of Earth's animals, they employed laser weapons to keep the lions at bay without harming them."

*Laser? What does that term even mean?*

*But I'll have to learn that at some time in the future.*

*For now, I don't want to interrupt the flow of this tale.*

"That's difficult for a Hebrew, with our view that Yahweh determines everything, to accept."

"Well, look at it this way, Jess of Nazareth. Call him alien or angel, or something else entirely. As for the gentiles, they chose to refer to such beings as 'gods.' That is a matter of human perception, which is more limited than you can possibly know."

"The point is, something, or someone, that possessed powers in excess of earthlings entered that den and saved the life of Daniel. A being that arrived from on high, descending for this specific purpose."

"Very good! You are the most advanced example of humankind that I have yet encountered in this, your time period."

*I once thought this fellow to be crazy. But what does that term even mean?*

*"Crazy" are the ones who perceive reality in a unique manner from most everyone else. They do not share what we call "common knowledge."*

*And in Jerusalem is known as "the word on the street."*

*But what if, in time, the masses come to see that the person they designated as crazy was also correct?*

*For "crazy" doesn't necessarily imply "wrong."*

*Only "different."*

*And should the world come to see that such a "different" vision was correct . . .*

*. . . then the term "crazy" ought to be replaced by "enlightened," and "far ahead of his time."*

*For when we all come around to such a line of thinking, as
we cannot all of us be crazy, what was once disparaged becomes
the new norm . . .*

"Thank you. As was the case during each of our two previous meetings, I can only wonder whether you are the most
knowledgeable being I've ever come across or stark raving mad."

My companion roared with laughter, then grew solemn. "I
understand, Jess, how deeply touched you are by the loss of
Joseph. A fine man. But let me make you this offer: whenever
in your life you need a father, call on me."

Now, it was my turn to laugh. "Oh? And how precisely should
I go about doing that?"

"Think of me. Feel me within you and around you. Believe in
me, fully and without doubt, and I'll be there at the moment of
your greatest need."

"Believing in a thing makes it true?"

"Absolute belief, yes. But there must be no doubt. Abject
faith alone can work miracles, as you Hebrews call them. The
magical moments to others."

I picked up my baggage, ready to take my leave of this wondrous character. "And by what name shall I summon you?"

"Gabriel," he said, bowing his head low while raising his
horn.


# 132.

During those fretful hours following the death of Joseph and
my reading of the Psalm 23 during the *Kaddish*, I'd fallen asleep
on my floor mat. Once more, I experienced the dream that served
as prologue to what unfolded during the past year. Again, I found
myself transformed into a boy, wearing a breastplate. Holding
tight to the reins of a chariot pulled by four white stallions.

Now, as I reached the point where our path connected to
the Roman road, that phantasmagoria remained potent in my
mind. I arrived at a place where three ways met: the path I
walked upon, the road I would shortly take, and another route

that originated in Scythopolis in the southwest. The Romans had only recently created the latter to provide a direct route up to our village, once the most isolated spot in Galilee. Which was in truth the reason why Davidians had come here following the Roman invasion. The better part of a century ago.

*Things change . . .*

At the point of convergence, I halted, stunned to see the opening image of my self-defining dream actualized as potent reality. Before me, in a cloud of dust, materialized a mirror image of what in the fantasy I'd become: a slender youth, wearing the bright bronze of a Greek warrior, with matching feathered helmet. Slapping at the reins, hurrying on his quartet of horses, each as pure a white as the snowbound crown of Mount Hermon.

*Might I imagine this before me because it remained so vivid in my mind's eye?*

*Did I see because I believed or believe because I saw?*

Moments later, the all-too-real charioteer clicked to his team, skillfully bringing the horses to a halt directly before me. He relaxed his reins, then reached up and pulled off the helmet.

"Hello, Jess," the charioteer awkwardly said, stepping down.

Luke! So *this* was my third encounter. Yes, of course. It made sense, if in a paradoxical sort of way.

"Hello, Luke," I replied in the most neutral voice I could manage. "Fancy meeting you again."

"More fate, I'd guess, than fancy."

Luke stepped closer. Despite my reluctance, I did again see something of the appeal I'd once perceived in him.

*If only things had been different . . .*

"So what brings you here?"

Luke explained that he had long since returned to Caesarea Maritima on the western coast. As a practicing physician, Luke visited the smaller towns to attend to those unable to arrive in the great city. Happening upon Joses, Luke learned of Maggie's disappearance. This caused him to think of me.

Shortly, Luke found himself traveling eastward. Drawing close to Nazareth, he'd stopped at a rest area. While nourishing himself with wine and bread, he listened in on a conversation between several Nazarenes as they discussed the death of Joseph.

After caring for his horses, Luke returned to the road with an even greater sense of urgency. That was several hours ago. As he was about to turn off the main way, onto the coarse trail leading to our village, there I stood.

According to, by what those who believe that life is random and things happen according to chance, blind luck.

To my mind, reflecting on supposed coincidences that had occurred in my life during the past year? Destiny.

"Thank you for your concern," I said emotionlessly. "No need to worry. I'm fine."

Before I could circle past him, Luke stepped sideways, blocking my way. The sun a red ball behind him, I experienced again the intense emotions of that day when my once-beautiful Greek turned into a wild beast. Nervously bringing my eyes up to meet his, I saw none of the violence, hunger, and obsession there.

Only concern. Perhaps even love. At once, any sense of threat dissipated.

"Give me a moment?" he asked, his voice desperate.

"Make it brief," I replied as carelessly as I could. "I'm in a hurry."

"You're *always* in a hurry."

"Yes. 'Hurry' is my middle name. Call me Jesus H—"

"I want a second chance," he said. In those five simple words, Luke's voice opened strong, turned sad, and finally faded into a whimper.

"Luke, I've already told you—"

"I *know* what you've told me. Please listen?"

Crossing my arms over my chest in a studied pose of disinterest, I replied, "Well?"

Luke's shoulders sagged. "I was wrong. Every which way you figure it, I was wrong."

"You said a mouthful there."

"I can't defend what I did. There *is* no defense."

*Congratulations! You've just assumed total responsibility for your own mistake.*

*There are few things I respect more in a person than that.*

"Right. So why are we wasting my time and, not that it matters, yours as well by talking about it?"

"Because I have one question to ask you."

"Fire away."

"Have you ever been wrong? Even once in your life?"

"Never like that—"

"No, because you're you and I'm me. But in your own way, in that unique cosmos that constitutes the world according to Jess, have you ever said or done anything terrible? Has there been even a single moment when out-of-control emotions took over and your mind ceased to properly function?"

*"Who's the father this time? Or wouldn't you know?"* echoed in my head.

"Causing you to hurt someone you loved? Ruining everything? Perhaps forever?"

*Mary? I'm so sorry. Now that I've made such a terrible mess of everything, I'd do anything to make it all right again.*

Without even realizing it, I nodded in agreement. "As my mother used to say, 'let he who is without guilt cast the first stone.'"

"Then try to imagine me, when I came to my senses."

"There are things so brutally unforgivable that they cannot be set aside—"

"Like my own great mistake. But not yours?"

"What do you mean by *that*?"

"Jess! When I asked you that question a minute ago, I could see it in your eyes. You've done or said something that you aren't able to forgive yourself for. Not at least until the person you so terribly hurt finds it in his or her heart to forgive you."

Without warning, I broke down and wept. Partly for myself, but also for Luke. And for all people everywhere who want, need, hope for, dream of, and perhaps—just perhaps, mind you—deserve a second chance.

*What's the proper term for that?*

*Oh! Now I remember: redemption.*

# 133.

"Forgive me, Jess?"

I uncrossed my arms, allowing my hands to dangle by my sides. "Luke, of course I forgive you. But I can't forget—"

"I wouldn't expect you to. And I'm sure that the person you hurt can't forget either. But perhaps that person can forgive? Given world enough and time. Someday? Isn't that what you would do anything to hear from . . . ?"

Answering honestly wasn't easy for me. But I did: "Yes."

"That's all I ask from you."

"I'm an entirely different person standing here today than that girl you met in Capernaum."

"Even as I'm a totally different boy."

*A second chance, Jess? Please?*

*A second chance, Mary? Please?*

As my mind whirled with ideas, it occurred to me that Luke had caused me to face my own great failing in life. Perhaps before one can receive, one must first give. Though I hated to admit so, even to myself, a quality of mercy had always been absent in my relations with others.

How hypocritical, then, to condemn those Nazarenes who could not, would not, forgive Mary for her transgression, real or imagined, when I myself had not been able to do so?

"Yes, Luke," I heard myself mutter, to a degree against my own will. "Yes."

He breathed a sigh of relief. "Jess? I want to marry you."

"Whoooooah! Pull in on those reins, charioteer."

"I know, I know. I'm moving too fast."

"*Way* too fast!"

"I'm telling you what I've thought about every moment of every day since—"

"First, I have no intention of marrying, at least not for the time being. I'm setting off to—"

"—explore the great, wide world. I know."

"In a manner of speaking. More, though, than merely to observe. As my nation refers to it: the getting of wisdom."

"Already, you are the wisest person I know."

"Anyway, first things first. I must track down my brother."

"Allow me to help you?"

There was no question that riding westward with Luke would halve the journey's time. Walking to Caesarea Maritima would take four days. Riding? Two at most.

And if he were to accompany me further, up the coast to Sidon? A far more dangerous trip on poorly tended roads.

"If I do, and note, Luke, I say 'if,' you understand there are no guarantees afterwards?"

"Absolutely."

"Once Joses is located, if I do indeed find him, I am not in any way indebted to you?"

"Accepted."

"Under those conditions, yes."

Luke appeared vastly relieved. "Thank you, Jess."

Impulsively, he reached down, seized my right hand, and brought his mouth close, briefly kissing my palm. Before he let go, Luke once again considered the scar from my childhood.

"Luke, what's the big deal with me? You're handsome, smart, well-born. And, from what I can gather, extremely wealthy."

"That's true."

"I'm a Hebrew peasant. I own nothing. Likely, I never will. To be honest about myself, I can be pretty difficult. I mean, with Jess, nothing is ever easy."

"I grasp that."

"So . . . why *me?*"

Luke remained silent a while, mulling this over before he spoke, clearly determined to find the right words.

"We Greeks have a concept called *kala*: a woman who is all things to one man. One philosopher described such a female as the beautiful, the moral, the right, and the kind. The person a man wants for his lover at night, his friend by day. Mother of his children, sharer of his dreams. A mother to him, when his own mother moves on to the next world. The longer we have been apart, the more I realize you are my *kala*."

"Fine and noble words."

"Let me prove them true?"

"First, a warning. As to the 'kind' part? I can be cruel."

"I know that from experience." (I blushed at that.) "I can take whatever you throw my way."

Wanting to test the truth of that, I stepped closer. Luke may have guessed that I was about to hug him gently. Or perhaps kiss him passionately. Instead, I formed a fist and punched him on the jaw, just as hard as I could. Stunned, he went flying backwards. In his ridiculously ornate costume, I couldn't help but laugh.

The mighty warrior of ancient times, defeated by a single blow from a slender girl.

As Luke struggled to rise, I hurried forward, took his hand, and helped him up. "Now, Luke, we're even." I pointed to the horses, apparently Arabian. "What are you doing in that outfit, and with those outlandish horses for your team?"

Rubbing his swollen cheek Luke said, "To gather the courage to face you again, I tried to get it right this time. Remember, the last time we met—"

"The first night of Hanukah. You came walking out of the rain, looking like a half-drowned puppy."

"Before I left, you told me how, three weeks after we met in Capernaum, you'd dreamed of me coming to see you."

I couldn't help but chuckle. That seemed so long ago now, back when I still clung to romantic illusions. Before reality intruded and taught me the first hard lesson of life every girl must face if she is to grow up as well as grow older.

"So here I am. Herakles," he continued. "And Achilles, Perseus—"

"Luke? I don't believe in heroes anymore."

"Oh, but you must! Ajax, Jason, Odysseus—"

"I don't know any of those names."

"Come with me and I'll teach you. They were among our pantheon, though none could compare to Herakles. Our father-god, Zeus, came down from the sky on a flaming chariot, assuming the form of a swan. He seduced a virginal girl. She, in time, gave birth to a hybrid: neither god nor man. A combination of the two."

"Angel or alien," I said, recalling Gabriel's words. "Or demigod. Different names from diverse nations, employed to describe a single thing."

*If you were here now, Gabriel, would you relate this story again, from the Watchers' point of view?*

Like a gentleman, Luke took my hand and eased me up onto the chariot, then rose alongside me. He drew an arm around me and, revealing considerable skill, clucked to the horses in a knowing manner. Luke guided them in a perfect turnaround, back onto the main road, heading in the direction of Caesarea.

"Will you begin your lessons about the ancient Greeks as we travel westward?"

"I'd be delighted to. What would you like to know first?"

"What does the expression 'beware Greeks bearing gifts' mean?"

Luke laughed. Before slapping the reins and swiftly bringing the stallions to a gallop, he turned to gaze into my eyes. Impulsively, I kissed him. His reaction suggested Luke had just been . . . *well* . . . born again.

"Don't read more into that than I intended."

"Meaning?"

"It may be a *long* time before you receive another."

"I can wait."

"You're going to have to."

"And continue to believe that someday, things will return to the way they once were."

"If that should ever actually occur?"

"Then, we'll live happily ever after."

I laughed sardonically and shook my head. "During the past year, I've come to realize there is no 'happily ever after.'"

"No? What then."

I shrugged. "Just . . . 'ever after.'"

We were off. First, to Caesarea. Then, Sidon.

After that?

I didn't have a clue.

# EPILOGUE

# Once Upon A Time in Palistine, Part Two

Some two miles westward on the road, Luke pulled the horses to a halt at my request. Across the way, on a slight mount, three crosses had been raised. On each hung a crucified Hebrew, all nearly dead. I explained to Luke what Levi and I had once done in a similar situation. And that, as a Hebrew, I now needed to supply tender mercies to these victims of Rome.

So we stepped down again. I ripped a piece of linen from my garment, wrapped it around the tip of a stick I found lying on the ground, and poured watered wine from my goat-skin sack onto its surface. Then I approached the suffering souls in turn, extending this humble balm up to their parched lips. With difficulty, every man managed to touch his mouth to the fabric. Momentarily relieved, each cast me a look of humble appreciation.

At least Barabbas was not among them. My lost friend, whose mother had, like my Mary, named her child after the father of David: Jessie. So the never-ending story of our people would come full cycle. A savior must appear once more at a time of need. With that thought came another, more frightening still.

There but for the grace of God goes not only Barabbas, but me!

Recall now my old prayer, begging Yahweh to be merciful, allowing me to die when my time came in any manner but this. Please, God of Gods, King of Kings. Spare me only this?

*What if that were not possible? What if this might prove to be my unavoidable destiny?*

*Don't even think on it, Jess. For that way lies madness.*

It is not the way of the Hebrew to allow a kinsman to die alone. We waited in silence until each passed, then slowly made our way, hand in hand, back to the chariot.

"Look, Jess," Luke remarked, pointing up into the sky, behind those crucified brethren. I brought my right hand up to shade eyes and better see, despite the setting sun's blinding rays.

Rising from some place behind the crosses, I spotted seven white lights. They rose swiftly up into the sky, moving in the direction of Orion, now becoming visible. They resembled a succession of phantom moons as the sun sunk out of sight.

Up they went, seven moving in the precise pattern I had seen twice before and now viewed for the third time.

Three of them, the brightest, led the way for the others. Higher and higher.

Until, as Luke clicked to his horses and we began our journey west, they disappeared into the blue.

The story of Jess of Nazareth will resume in Book Two
# PLANET JESUS: BODY AND SOUL

# ABOUT THE AUTHORS

DOUGLAS BRODE is a novelist, graphic novelist, playwright, screenwriter, cinema historian, and multi-award winning journalist. Also a multi-award winning educator, Brode created the Film Classics program for the Newhouse School of Public Communications at Syracuse University. He has over the years been employed as a movie and theatre critic, a radio announcer, TV talk show host, and museum lecturer.

SHAUN L. BRODE received his undergraduate degree at the University of Central Florida and his master's from Syracuse University. He has been involved as part of production teams for numerous movie and TV films in the Los Angeles area. This marks his first literary collaboration with his father.

For More Information:
**www.planetjesustrilogy.com**

*Douglas hangin' with John Lennon and Yoko Ono at their suite in midtown Manhattan; Fall, 1971. Conversations between the three included music, movies, and in particular the manner in which both mediums could be collapsed into one another in order to create art on a metaphysical level. (Courtesy Richard Brown.)*